THE TRAFFICKING CONSORTIUM

Be careful with whom you share your personal information

Consortium Book 1

Second Edition

RICHARD VERRY

Copyright 2017-2021 © Richard Verry
All Rights Reserved

ALSO BY RICHARD VERRY

Consortium
The Trafficking Consortium (Book #1)
Perfect Prey (Book #2)
UnderCurrents (Book #3)
Infiltration (Book #4)

Mona Bendarova Adventures
The Taste of Honey (Book #1)
Broken Steele (Book #2)
Lucky Bitch (Book #3)
Angry Bitch (Book #4)

Her Client Trilogy
Her Client (Book #1)
Her Overseer (Book #2)
Her Essentia (Book #3)
Her Client Trilogy (Boos 1, 2, & 3)

Novellas and Short Stories
The Breakup
A Mermaid's Irresistible Curiosity

THE
TRAFFICKING CONSORTIUM

Be careful with whom you share your personal information

Consortium Book 1

Richard Verry

Copyright 2017-2021 © Richard Verry
All Rights Reserved

No part of this book may be reproduced, scanned, stored in a retrieval system, transmitted in any printed or electronic form or means including electronic, mechanical, photocopying, recording, or otherwise, except for brief quotations embodied in reviews, without the express written permission of the author.

This is a work of fiction. Names, characters, places, and events depicted are products of the author's imagination. Any similarities to persons or places are merely coincidental.

This book is intended for mature adult audiences only.
Suitable for all readers 18+

Published by Richard Verry
Rochester NY

Copyright 2017-2021 © Richard Verry
All Rights Reserved

RichardVerry.com

THE TRAFFICKING CONSORTIUM

Be careful with whom you share your personal information

Consortium Book 1

Second Edition

RICHARD VERRY

Copyright 2017-2021 © Richard Verry
All Rights Reserved

Prologue

Spread out in every major city in every country worldwide, a secret thousand-year-old organization operates a network of operatives seeking qualified talent suitable for their needs. The group pays well for the leads submitted.

They work in innocuous jobs and stay in the background as they go about their talent search. They work as secretaries, receptionists, and non-professional clerical positions, these operative's live paycheck to paycheck. They often struggle with how to pay their rent or put food on the table. The bonus money they receive from their submissions gives them a welcome relief from these worries.

Their jobs give them full access to the public, patronizing their establishments. These businesses include high-class bars and restaurants patronized by millennials, rich and poor alike, and professional offices such as law firms, medical centers, and political offices. Spas, salons, brokerage houses, real estate agencies, and hotels host the agents' rest.

Despite working for two masters, the operatives act in good faith, although some knew that their activities are illegal. However, the risk is minimal, and the money is excellent. As recruiters, they believe they are finding talented and exceptionally gorgeous young men and women to consider for posts in exotic locations worldwide.

Well-paid operatives welcome a finder's fee for each candidate they submit, followed by a significant bonus for each accepted candidate. Encouraged only to submit candidates that are likely for selection, they know that they will lose their source of easy money if they present too many non-qualified candidates.

These contract operatives are not officially members of this secret agency; they do not know each other and never interact. They also have no idea what the real purpose of the organization is.

It would horrify the contract operatives to find out that they were fronting for an organized human trafficking agency operating globally. Their paid bonuses helped send unsuspecting men and women into bondage and eventual death.

This secret organization's roots trace back to the Roman Empire's withdrawal in Europe during the first millennium. As

Christianity arose in Eurasia, filling the vacuum left behind the withdrawing horde, the papacy banned fellow enslaving Europeans. However, it encouraged the practice among local and foreign pagans from all over the world. Unforeseen consequences of the ban resulted in a small group of wealthy individuals assembling to share and enjoy their debauchery's common expression.

As the second millennium progressed, their influence stretched to all parts of the known world. So did their access to larger pools of unsuspecting men and women caught in their web. By the start of the third millennium, their global reach extended to every continent. With their extensive reach and influence, who would miss so few men and women culled from the billions living worldwide, fulfilling their vicious desires?

Membership in this organization was expensive, extraordinarily private, and most members could trace their ancestral membership for several centuries.

Members of this organization called themselves the…

'Consortium'

Chapter One

"Damn, this day is dragging on, and I have another meeting to attend." Avril lamented. The day had been a very long one, and she was glad it was almost over. It was a couple of hours past lunch, and the afternoon's lag was making her a bit sleepy. Leaning back in her chair, she tilted her head back and rubbed her eyes.

"Avril, are you coming?" A co-worker asked as she walked past her office. "The client's here."

"Oh, sorry, I'm coming." Avril jumped up, picked up a portfolio, her coffee cup, and sped off towards the conference room. Arriving on her co-worker's heels, she took a seat just as her boss said, "Let's get started."

Ninety minutes later, Avril dragged herself back to her office, dumped her portfolio, and breathed a sigh of relief. Done for the day, she packed up her desk and was more than ready to go home.

"Good night," she bid adieu to the department secretary, who responded, "Good night Avril. See you bright and early tomorrow."

"Sorry, hun, I have a doctor's appointment first thing. I should be in around ten or ten-thirty."

"Okay, sweetie, see you then. Good luck!"

"Oh, it's just my annual physical, nothing special."

"Ah, alright, good luck anyway." The secretary offered as Avril moved off towards the exit door.

Taking the elevator down to the lobby, she exhaled after taking a deep, cleansing breath. The elevator had several other riders already in the car, but thankfully, she didn't know any of them. She wasn't in the mood to take part in any light-handed conversation. As the elevator doors opened on the ground level, Avril made her way to the street and walked to the corner to hail a cab. Settling into the back seat, Avril closed her eyes as the cabby started the meter and drove off. Avril tried to ignore the insanely obnoxious monitor placed right in front of her, advertising things of little interest to her. The annoying ads didn't care whether or not she watched. They just droned on, one after another. They were all the same, day after day, and they annoyed her. Closing her eyes, she wished she could jail the people who thought to put the advertising monitors in cabs was a good idea. Oh, right? It was her agency. They did it. Now she wished they hadn't. They were annoying.

Avril worked for a prestigious advertising agency on Madison Avenue in New York City. She was an Account Executive and managed several clients. Fortunately, she only had one major account while the rest were smaller companies situated around the state, in towns she otherwise wouldn't have known. She also worked with a group that watched over several enterprises across the country. Frankly, she didn't know much about the country outside the surrounding counties. To her, they didn't exist. Her world revolved solely within the city. As for the rest of the country, well, it didn't matter much to her.

As the cab navigated the rush hour traffic, she stared out the window and watched the tens of thousands of people rushing towards the bus stops or MTA stations, which were eager to get home like her. Although her apartment was only ten blocks from her work, it took nearly forty minutes in stop-and-go traffic to get there. If she weren't in her work clothes, she could have walked the distance faster. As it was, her agency required her to dress professionally but with a sexy flair. So, walking the ten blocks in a dress and high-heels wasn't very practical. Usually, she took along a pair of sneakers but had forgone them this morning, preferring to ride to work today.

Paying the cab fare, Avril crawled out, trying hard not to give pedestrians a show. She was a lady, after all. Unlocking the door to her apartment, she tossed her keys onto the entryway table, dropped her handbag, and kicked off her shoes. Making her way to her bedroom, she abandoned various clothing items along the way, looking forward to getting comfortable and heading out for a run. Twenty minutes later, she was jogging on the running path in Central Park, only a block away from her apartment. Ordinarily, she liked to run around the pond, which she elected to do today. There was etiquette to running on the path, and she respected it. Nothing annoyed her more than a runner going in the wrong direction. Their disrespect disrupted the flow of other runners running in tandem.

After developing a nice sweat, she made for home an hour and a half later, running the entire way. Jogging in place at the light, she waited for the signal to change before moving into the street. A taxicab trying to jump the light screeched to halt an inch shy of her knees. Glaring at the driver, Avril kept going and arrived at her building minutes later.

After a nice, long hot shower, she made a small dinner, enjoying it with a glass of red wine. Around ten o'clock, she put on a sexy dress with deep cleavage and took a cab to her favorite pickup bar. She ordered a vodka martini with a twist and began scoping out the talent sitting down at the bar. It didn't take long before someone came by and offered to buy her a drink. An hour later, she made her selection, and not paying for a single drink, she took him home. An hour after that, she closed the door behind him as he left and leaned against the closed door. A quick fuck always made her feel better. Tossing his number in the toilet and flushing, she went back to bed.

Groaning at the obnoxious ringing from the alarm on her cell phone, Avril rolled over and draped an arm over her eyes. Slamming her hand down on the phone, she slowly crawled out of bed and made her way to the bathroom. After dressing, applying her makeup, and skipping breakfast, she left her apartment and headed out to her doctor's appointment.

Grabbing a cab, she gave the driver the address and sat back. Staring out the window, she watched the world go by without actually seeing it. When the cab stopped in front of her doctor's office, she retrieved her purse, paid the fare, and went into the building. Standing in line, waiting for the receptionist to recognize her, she caught sight of the sign that read:

> *Wait here until called for*

Shrugging at the obvious, she just stood there and waited.

When the receptionist looked up at her and motioned for her to approach, she checked in. "Avril Gillios. I have a nine o'clock."

Checking her out, the receptionist nearly stripped her naked with his eyes before looking at the schedule and checked her in. "You're all set, Ms. Gillios. Please have a seat. Someone will come for you shortly."

"Thank you," she answered.

Undisturbed by the leering inspection by the receptionist, she sat down to wait. Picking up a two-month-old magazine and crossing her legs, she shook her heeled dangling foot in a slow, relaxed sort of way as she flipped away at the pages. A few minutes later, she heard her name and followed a nurse to an examination room.

The nurse took her vitals and asked several preliminary questions. "Your B.P. is 116/60 and pulse 45. Both are excellent." She reported.

"I'm going to take your temperature. I'm just going to slide this across your forehead and behind your ear." She warned her, indicating an instrument she now held in her hand.

"Good, temp is 97.9 degrees. Have you ever felt at risk of falling or being hit?"

"No," Avril answered.

"Do you smoke, or are you taking any illegal drugs?"

"No."

"Any changes in your medications?"

"No, again. Just what you have on record." Avril answered again.

"Are you sexually active?"

"Yes, I am."

"Are you monogamous?"

"No, I'm not."

"Two or three, or several, and how often?"

"Several and maybe about ten times or so a month," Avril answered, watching the nurse for her response.

"All with different partners?"

"Usually," Avril answered.

"You are careful, right?" the nurse asked, concerned.

"Oh, yes, I insist on condoms that I supply every time."

"Good. Do you have any questions regarding sex with multiple partners?"

"No, I know the dangers of not being vigilant. I am very picky with whom I go to bed."

"When was the last time you had sex?"

"Last night," Avril answered, smiling at the memory.

The nurse looked up at her and smiled. "I should be so lucky," the nurse longingly admitted, suggesting that she had a bit of humanity within her.

"Yes, well, it was okay. Honestly, though, I need to find a real man who can turn my world upside down. I need one who can take command in bed and make me feel like a genuine woman. A man that I want to take control and make me feel like there is no one else in the world but the two of us."

"Sounds nice. Let me know when you find one," the nurse wistfully ventured before she went back to being all business.

The nurse finished her pre-examination interview with a couple more questions and jotted the responses on the chart. Before leaving, she locked down the computer and told her, "The doctor will be in shortly."

"Thank you," Avril told the nurse and sat back to wait.

A couple of minutes later, and after looking at her watch, Avril picked up her phone and began scrolling her social media messages. Tweeting, she wrote, "I'm stuck, waiting forever for the doctor. When will he ever get here?"

Just as she pressed the 'Send' button, transmitting the message into the ether, she heard a knock on the door, and the doctor walked in.

"Sorry to keep you waiting. My rounds went long."

Doctor, my appointment was to be the first of the day. I didn't want to be kept waiting."

"Yes. I understand. Sorry. I try to keep to my schedule, but these things happen. Shall we get started?"

"Yes, please. I don't want to be any later for work than I already am." Avril replied, mentally calming her annoying attitude.

An hour later, after a thorough examination, including an extensive internal exam, Avril retrieved her purse and made her way to checkout. After handing her paperwork to the checkout medical clerk, she waited.

"Your copay is $20.00," the clerk said as Avril passed him her credit card. He ran it through and handed the card back. "We'll see you again in a year. Do you want to make your appointment now or wait?"

"I'll wait," she said as she signed the charge slip.

"We recommend scheduling at least six months in advance," he reminded her.

"I'll remember. Thank you. Have a good day. Bill? Isn't it?" Avril asked.

"Yes, it is. Thank you. You have a good day as well!" the clerk replied before putting her paperwork off to one side.

"Thank you, Bill," Avril replied.

As Avril left, she didn't notice that Bill put her records off to one side, away from the other patients' files. After reviewing Avril's medical records as the doctor examined her, Bill figured he would get a big fat bonus for submitting her. Besides, they were sure to offer her a fantastic job in an exotic location. It would be a win-win for both of them.

Later, alone, and without patients coming up to his counter, Bill inserted a flash drive into his computer's USB port. Immediately, a single text field discreetly appeared on his screen. He typed Avril's patient number from her file and pressed 'Enter.' The text field vanished, and seconds later, a small icon in the system tray appeared, asking him to remove the flash drive. He pocketed it, knowing that he had just copied Avril's personal and medical history to the thumb drive, committing a clear violation of the 'U.S. HIPAA Laws.'

Breaking the law didn't concern Bill. He had done this many times before, and no one had caught on after all the years. Bill never understood how the flash drive worked. All he knew was that the flash drive copied the medical history of the keyed patient I.D. to a hidden encrypted area on the flash drive and removed all traces of the intrusion on his computer. Even if he lost the flash drive or had it confiscated, all anyone would find was a blank flash drive.

Bill knew that it was highly unlikely that anyone would catch him, and they paid him well. Besides, he was getting behind in his rent, and if he didn't suggest someone soon, he would be in a real bind. He knew that in submitting Ms. Gillios to his contact, she would also benefit from the opportunity. If they liked what they saw and offered her a position, they would pay him a hefty finder's fee. Bill figured Avril was guaranteed to get the job. Not only was she young and beautiful, but she also had the intelligence and wherewithal to succeed at whatever she wanted.

Bill was already thinking of how to spend the bonus. "Perhaps I'll get a new seventy-inch, 3D high-definition flat-screen television. Oh, wouldn't that be sweet?" he thought as he picked up the telephone and dialed a number from memory.

When the phone on the other end answered, he didn't speak into it. Instead, he typed a code on the keypad, as if he were responding to an auto-attendant, and hung up. Smiling at his good fortune, he sipped his cup of coffee and with a far-away look in his eyes. "Yep, a new flat-screen T.V. was just the thing."

That evening, he met up with his contact, exchanged the thumbnail drive for a new one, and pocketed an envelope filled with five one-hundred-dollar bills. Now he had enough to pay the rent and even buy that new video game he had been eyeing.

Bill did not know that he started a chain of events that changed

Avril Gillios's life forever. His handler forwarded the flash drive deep into the organization for examination. A favorable evaluation of Avril's file motivated the assessment unit to assign a team to study, photograph, and investigate every nook and cranny of Avril Gillios's life within a week. It would take months to uncover all the details they were interested in, but they were not in a hurry. They wanted to be sure that she would satisfy their needs without unmitigated exposure. Their scrutiny would continue until they got the answers that they wanted.

If she didn't measure up, they would discard her file, forgetting that she ever existed. If she did, then the fun would begin in earnest.

"Good morning Avril. Mr. Curlebba is waiting for you in his office." The receptionist told her as she walked into the reception area after her doctor's appointment.

"Alright, thank you. How was your evening?"

"Good, quiet, just a glass of wine and the television, nothing special."

"Did he say what it was all about?"

"Mr. Curlebba? No, but I guess it had something to do with the client meeting yesterday. Don't worry; he's not angry or anything. He's just his usual, boneheaded self. I believe he wants you to pull his nuts out of the fire again. I think he promised something he doesn't know how to deliver."

"What else is new? All right, if he asks, I'm on my way. I want to drop my stuff off at my desk and pick up a cup of coffee. I'm starved. I wasn't allowed to eat or drink anything until after my doctor's appointment."

"Oh, how did that go?"

"The usual. The doctor kept me waiting and then poked and prodded me to no end. I just tolerated it all and got the hell out of there as soon as I could."

"Doctors, you can't live with them and can't live without them."

"Ain't that the truth? Alright, let me go find out what Mr. Bonehead wants."

Five hours later, tired and wiped out, she had a plan to pull Mr.

Bonehead's ass out of the fire once again. Avril disappeared into her office and made a few phone calls to get things rolling. After calling together her team and giving them her instructions, she packed up her desk, grabbed her purse, and left.

"Good night, Avril," the receptionist said in farewell.

"Good night. See you tomorrow," she replied.

Over the next few weeks, it was more of the same. Wake up, dress, and go to work. Most days were simple, nothing special, just more of the same. Once or twice a week, Avril would go out and get laid. She never once had to pay for anything; the guys were more than willing to buy her drinks. She accepted every one of them, eventually settling on a guy and taking him home, fucked him silly, and sent him on his way. Many times, she didn't even know their names, but she didn't care. She didn't want to get involved with any of them. They were just a means to an end, and walking them to the door ended it for both of them.

Avril needed to preempt various problems that threatened to affect her clients and her boss every so often. Most times, Mr. Curlebba either ignored or didn't recognize the building problems that faced them. Avril felt it was one of her jobs to make her boss look good, so she often saw opportunities to resolve issues before becoming genuine problems.

After work, she usually ran around Central Park. The days were getting shorter, and she was determined to do well in the upcoming New York City Marathon set to take place in November. Needing to maintain her qualifying times for the event, she strove to keep her time under three hours. While she qualified for the race, she wanted to use the race as a stepping-stone to the Boston Marathon, arguably the premier race on the east coast. While she had already registered for the competition scheduled to occur next April, she needed to use the NYC Marathon to guarantee her a good starting position in the race.

It was going to be challenging, but it would be well worth it. Running gave her a personal goal and a kind of euphoric contentment that was, at times, better than sex. Therefore, on weekends, she ran the equivalent of a marathon, and on weekdays, she ran until dark was setting in. Never in her wildest dreams would she continue running after dark. That was asking for trouble. With the New York City Marathon only a couple of months away, she redoubled her efforts to be ready for the race.

Come November; she thought she had done well after running the NYC marathon. She finished in the top twenty with a time of two hours, forty-nine minutes. For Avril, though, it was not good enough. She kept running, though not in Central Park. Since the weather had turned, she ran on a treadmill she purchased to avoid the exorbitant gym membership fees. Except for weekends, the days were just too short to run outdoors. Besides, she could use the treadmill at any time, even if it was only for a half-hour or so.

Buying the treadmill was the best investment she ever made. It was easy, and she found a great deal on it at a reputable store across the river in New Jersey. From the first day when the delivery people brought in and set it up in her apartment, they took their time, showing her how to use it. She enjoyed running the miles on the moving platform as she looked out at the Manhattan skyline while mornings crept across the city or watching the sunset, painting the town with a vast array of colors. Plugging her iPhone into her audio docking station and setting it to play her favorite playlist, Avril disappeared inside herself as her feet ran mile after mile on the treadmill.

As the holidays rolled around, she shared a pleasant Christmas dinner with a girlfriend. They weren't close, but each was committedly single and without family to speak of sharing the holiday. Avril and her girlfriend talked about everything over several glasses of wine after a delicious surf and turf holiday dinner. They spoke about her NYC Marathon finish, the men they dated, which ones they slept with, comparing their sexual encounters, both good and not so good. They talked about a hundred other topics that two millennials were likely to discuss. Both of them laughed and giggled well into the night before calling it a night.

If Avril had any regret in her life, she couldn't celebrate the holiday with her family. Avril was the only daughter of a pair of career-minded parents. The two of them had done well for themselves, working together for an investment firm in the Wall Street area. They had died in a car crash driving back from a party in the Hamptons in 2008. The police reported that the accident involved no other vehicles. The car just ran off the road at high speed and dived into the Great South Bay marshes, bordering large portions of the south side of Long Island. They pulled their bodies from the water after their car sank to the bottom. EMTs pronounced them dead at the scene. An autopsy later revealed that they were intoxicated, and neither should have been driving. Their blood alcohol levels registered several times the legal limit. Authorities ruled their deaths an accident and closed the investigation. After the will's reading, Avril moved into their apartment, an apartment she couldn't afford on her income alone.

Avril celebrated New Year by accepting an invitation to a party from a guy she knew. He was all right though he wasn't the marrying kind. That was okay with her as she also wasn't ready to commit to a monogamous relationship either. Still, he was good in bed, and as a friend with benefits, they both knew that after watching the ball drop over Times Square, they would celebrate the New Year in bed. The following morning, eminently satiated and just wearing a loosely buttoned shirt, she made breakfast for the two of them before kissing him goodbye at the door. Turning and leaning against the door as it closed, warm thoughts of the exuberant sex from the previous evening flooded her mind. Much of it was a blur, but she relished the contented feelings she revisited while absent-mindedly caressing her lower region.

Walking back into her living room and not wanting to shower off the comforting scent of their time together, she collapsed alone on the sofa with a cup of coffee. She watched the Rose Parade just getting underway in Pasadena, California. She quietly slipped off to sleep, only to wake well after the parade was over. After a light dinner and a glass of wine, she went back to bed.

Returning to work after the holidays, Mr. Curlebba called Avril into his office and gave her a modest bonus. The money would come in handy in paying for some of the bills she had incurred buying her staff presents. She wished he had let her charge her department's budget for the gifts, but Mr. Bonehead wouldn't sign off on them. Instead, he gave her the meaningless bonus, which would appear on her taxes as additional income, charging her a higher withholding tax. It sucked, but it was better than nothing.

As the winter rolled by, she continued to run on her treadmill on weekdays and, weather permitting, around Central Park on the weekends. While she held timings on the treadmill well under three hours, she knew that running outdoors in the streets was an entirely different matter than running on a treadmill. She pressed herself more and more, sometimes finishing in two-and-a-half hours. Conceivably, those times would help in the actual race.

In April, with the Boston Marathon just days away, her dickhead of a boss tried to get her to pass up the race, asking her to stay in New York and work on one of his client's issues. Putting her foot down, she declined his demand and went to Boston in time to take part in the pre-race festivities.

On the morning of the run, she woke very early, too excited to sleep and eager to get to the starting line. Determined to do well, she arrived at the check-in table before dawn. Fired up, both from her annoyance at her boss and the crowd's excitement, she pinned her racing number to her shirt. She was ready.

She wasn't even worried about disruptions to the race, as had happened a couple of years earlier when a couple of pressure cooker bombs detonated in the middle of the event. She believed that since she couldn't do anything about it, she would not worry. She just wanted to run the race of a lifetime.

After the race, she met up with a girlfriend who came with her to Boston to cheer her on. They were celebrating her top ten finish with a time of two hours, forty-one minutes. The time guaranteed her an automatic qualifier for next year's race. Taking time off from training, she drank up a storm and partied just as much. By the wee hours of the night, she found herself in bed with someone whose name she couldn't remember. He left before dawn, and she rolled over and went back to sleep. By the time she woke up, she was saddle sore but eminently satisfied. She slept in until housekeeping knocked on her door, wanting to clean the room.

Packing quickly, she checked out, met up with her girlfriend, and headed to the airport for a relaxed flight to NYC and home.

She never noticed the people following her, documenting her every move, and learning everything about the girl named Avril Gillios.

Chapter Two

Unbeknownst to Avril, the Consortium scrutinized her as if under a microscope over the next year. They looked into her background, behaviors, and everyday life. They checked out her birth records, documenting her childhood right up to the present day. They discovered the death of her parents dying in 2008 was probably a good thing. They were weeks away from being charged with insider trading by the Securities and Exchange Commission. Avril never learned her parents were subjects of a criminal investigation, suspected of bilking their clients of millions of dollars. They saved their daughter from learning about their illegal activities. Where the money went was a mystery and presumably lost in the crash later that year. Still, the SEC recovered as much as they could before they quietly closed the case.

The Consortium delved into her finances, pulling her credit report and credit score. They knew to the penny what her bank and investment accounts were worth. They even discovered a secret bank account in the Cayman Islands set up by her parents in her name. Assuming she checked out as they suspected, she would never need to access those funds. Unknown to her, they inserted hooks into every one of her accounts to transfer the balances to their hidden offshore accounts at the appropriate time.

They knew about her passion for running, working towards a spot in the NYC and Boston Marathon. They had people watching every mile of the two races, watching to see how she would finish. During her hours of training, they had runners following her around Central Park, and they had even used their people to deliver her new treadmill. The delivery allowed them to duplicate the key to her home and access it whenever they wished. Within a week, they wired the place for high-definition sound and video. They put cameras everywhere, including in the bathroom and shower. They watched her wash and shower, eat and drink, sleep, and fornicate. They observed and cataloged everything she did. They watched and photographed every inch of her and everything she did. Privacy, as she understood it, didn't exist.

They investigated her medical history, everything from the records they received from their operative in the office. They looked into her ancestry, her fitness, and her life expectancy. From her blood work, they knew she was of northern European descent, probably Scottish. Her red hair almost guaranteed that she came from the British Isles. She was free of any disease or gene patterns that indicated that she was unlikely to suffer any chronic diseases that often arrived as one got older. All indications implied that she would live a very long life short of an accident or catastrophic event.

They knew how often she had her hair colored, cut, and styled. They followed her to her manicures and pedicure and knew what colors she preferred. They even had their operative book her appointments to learn as much as possible. If Avril had any idea how much her hairdressers liked to talk about her personal life, she would have terminated them immediately and found new ones.

Her gynecological exam confirmed that she was fertile, and her hip structure implied that she could carry many offspring. They knew, to the day, her monthly menstrual cycle. Factoring in her sex life, it surprised them that she hadn't caught accidentally. During their investigation, they learned that she was fastidious in making sure her partners used condoms that she supplied.

They even investigated her psychological background. Though she had a stressful job with little reward, she maintained a composed demeanor in her life. Little seemed to upset her or stress her out. As the summer progressed into winter, they tossed various tests her way to see how she would handle herself. Some of these tests involved her job, creating fictional situations with her clients or her boss's clients to see how she dealt with problems.

They would create problems for her in her personal life, such as unexpected closures of her favorite running paths. They even got their people to pick her up and take her home for a night of sexual pleasure. The following morning, they reported every detail about their encounters, relating every little detail that she liked and did not like in and out of bed.

They knew everything about her. They knew what she liked to eat, whom she slept with, her sexual preferences, and whether or not she masturbated. She did almost every morning, especially the mornings after a night of good sex. They knew she used masturbation as more of a daily routine than a satisfying release.

Overall, she was a healthy woman. When her file came up for a vote, she garnered a unanimous vote. She was in; they wanted her, and they would have her. Now, they would wait until they found more like her. They had all the time in the world. It was better to find the right candidates than fill in slots with defectives. When ready, Avril would be in splendid company. They were tracking and investigating several dozen individuals like her.

"Target is exiting her office building. I detect no deviations in routine. All indications imply that she is going directly home." Said a man into a small microphone hanging from his ear, casually standing across the street from where Avril worked.

Falling behind at a strategic distance, a man kept a close eye on the subject. He stayed back about half a block, and in this crowd, it was unlikely she would detect him. After all, they had been following her for months now; not once had she noticed them.

Following her had become routine, but he didn't mind. She was stunning. Watching her ass sway to-and-fro on those sexy heels kept his mind focused on the target. If there were any distractions, they usually emanated from the subject. Overall, he enjoyed this assignment.

For a moment, the target stopped, as if deciding to walk or take a cab. Choosing to walk, Avril resumed the trek home. On the way, she briefly stopped at a pharmacy and bought a package of condoms. The man following her smirked, knowing that she would never get to use them.

Despite the heels, she made excellent time walking the ten blocks to her apartment building. The heels never once impeded her ability to walk at any speed. However, as she got closer to her building, she seemed to slow her pace, fatigue clear in her gait. The fatigue would help make things easier all-around.

Listening to the steady stream of conversations in his earpiece, he knew that everything was ready. Their mini-van, painted out to look like a cab, was moving into position. It would stand by a block away from the target's building. He heard a readiness check in his ear as the team checked-in. "Three, ready, a half-block behind and closing," he reported.

Three was the designated number assigned to the man following the Avril. "Three, close to four meters," he heard in his earpiece.

"Three, roger that. Closing to four meters," When the agent reached his position, he reported, "Three, in position."

"Final check," he heard in his earpiece.

"One, go. The sidewalk is clear. Traffic is clear."

"Two, go. 'Transportation' is ready."

"Three, go. 'Takedown' is ready."

"Four, 'Bird' is ready, go."

"This is Leader. The Op is a go. I say three times. Go. Go. Go."

"Roger," 'Three' acknowledged, recognizing their mini-van stopped at the curb just ahead. He picked up his pace just as the side door of the cab opened. 'One' stepped out in front of the target, forcing her to stop to avoid the sudden obstruction.

In one swift motion, 'Three' stepped up behind the target and pushed her into the cab's open door, right into the waiting arms of 'Two,' who clamped a chloroform-soaked cloth over her face.

Jumping into the van, 'Three' slammed the side door closed and turned to assist 'Two,' landing on Avril and holding her down. There was little need to help. The target was already succumbing to the anesthesia effects of the chloroform. A moment later, she was out like a light. By this time, the van had already driven off, turned right at the corner, and got lost in the crowd of yellow cabs making their way uptown.

They stopped and transferred the target to a white, windowless panel van seven blocks up. After switching vehicles, the van made its way across town, through Lincoln Tunnel, and headed towards Newark Airport. By the time the van entered an enclosed hangar, they had stripped and bound the target, and an IV inserted in her arm, pumping a heavy sedative into her bloodstream.

The target would be out for hours, giving the team ample opportunity to transfer her to the waiting plane and watch the aircraft take off. Ninety minutes later, the plane landed a thousand miles away, and another team unloaded her, sans the IV, and deposited her into a clear acrylic chamber, and welded it shut. Once done, they carried the container over to the side and placed it among several other receptacles filled with more captured occupants. Before leaving, they attached a pair of fresh air hoses to supply fresh air to the new arrival to the stacks of clear acrylic containers lying around.

High fiving each other, the team turned and went back to their coffee and conversation as they waited for the last plane to arrive. With only one more to go, the team with their prey needn't wait too long.

Leaving work exhausted, Avril decided on a quiet night at home. She wasn't due back to work for a couple of days and postponed going out until the next evening. Tonight, she just wanted to relax at home and soothe her exhaustion.

Fatigue apparent in her body language, Avril ignored her environment, relaxing her guard as she walked past the subway station. Walking down the street towards her building, she stared at the sidewalk, working hard to ensure that one footstep landed firmly in front of the other.

She failed to notice the yellow cab pulling up at the curb and a man stepping out of the passenger door right in front of her with only a block to go. Since he wasn't looking in her direction, he forced her to stop to avoid bumping into him. Avril scowled in annoyance. As she did so, she didn't notice a second man step up right behind her.

In the blink of an eye, the two men pushed her into the cab's waiting door. A second later, the door closed, and the cab leisurely pulled away from the curb and drove down the street.

Inside the cab, startled at her sudden onslaught, "What the hell? Let go of me…" she yelled.

"Humph!" interrupted her complaint as a man fell on top of her, pushing her into someone else's waiting arms.

A pair of arms wrapped themselves around her, trapping her underneath the man's weighty body as a foul-smelling cloth clamped over her mouth and nose, stifling her screams.

Struggling, trying to get away, she scratched desperately at her assailants, trying to break their grip on her. She flailed as her resistance slowed, and her eyes clouded over as she slipped from consciousness. Before she knew it, the cab's interior and her assailants vanished into uneasy darkness.

Chapter Three

Slowly returning to consciousness, Avril tried to open her eyes and sit up. Unable to move much, she tried to assess her situation. A massive, raging headache induced her to groan, adding to a stiff achiness all over her body. She was miserable, and she knew she was in trouble.

Looking through blurry eyes, she figured out that she was no longer in the cab. A nagging ache in her jaw, wrists, and ankles revealed she was bound and gagged. She was also naked, her clothing mysteriously missing. As panic set in, she vainly struggled to remove her bindings.

"What the fuck?" she thought to yell, wiggling her fingers and failing to reach her bindings. "And who are they?"

Apparent she would not free herself anytime soon; she worked on calming herself. Avril knew enough that panicking would not help in this situation. It would probably make things worse.

Looking around, she decided she was in a kind of box, but it was no ordinary box. Tapping the sides, she determined it was a clear, thick acrylic plastic. It is rigid, and she couldn't seem to find any seams anywhere. The box appeared molded in one piece, with her inside it.

"Where am I? Who did this to me? What do they want?" were just some of the many questions flashing through her mind. "And what is this thing in my mouth?" She thought as bile began rising from her stomach.

"First things first," Avril thought as she tried to push the gag from her mouth. As hard as she ached to work it out, the gag sat firmly behind her teeth, depressing her tongue. Without wiggle room, the gag forced her jaw wide open. It also had an appendage wedging itself into the back of her throat. It took all of her willpower to keep from gagging on the damn thing and spitting up her stomach contents.

"I'm going to die," she thought, fighting hard to keep from drowning for her saliva and bile.

Squeezing her bound hands up and over her head, she found that the gag was part of a harness placed over her head and locked in place. A padlock hung from a hasp on the side of her neck. Unless she could remove the lock and release the straps, she would remain gagged for the interim.

"Help! Can anyone hear me? Help! I need help!" she screamed, her cries barely escaping beyond her lips. What she heard was a dull, muffled grunt, which drew no one to her aide.

Other than the gag and her bound wrists and ankles, she is otherwise unencumbered. She could freely move about her container. The walls of her box, cell, coffin, or whatever it was, barely left her room to wiggle. Rolling over onto her side or sitting up was impossible. All she could do was lie on her back and wait.

"Wait for what?" she wondered. "What do they want from me?"

"Who the hell attacked me and why?" she continued to ask herself as the hours ticked by and unable to figure out her predicament.

"Are they going to ransom me? If so, they're in for a big surprise. There's no one she knew who would pay a ransom." She thought. "How sad is that? I have no one who cares enough about me to pay a ransom." She realized. "SHIT!"

"Fuck that! Okay. I'm on my own. It's up to me to figure out how to get out of this." She decided.

Determined, cold, and covered in goosebumps, Avril looked around to discover that she was not alone. The tiny box she was in was just one of many stacked around a large, open room, each containing young men and women. As best as Avril could tell, no one was older than their late twenties, and some might have been even younger than that. Each occupant, men and women alike, were exceptionally attractive. Each was bound, gagged, and naked just as she was. Further, the men had their hands shackled to their penis and scrotum in such a way, as they couldn't move their hands much without enduring significant discomfort. Most of them were trying to escape from the shackles with no success.

Concerning her was the vast number of acrylic boxes she could see. Counting them all was impossible. Except for one, each box contained a living, breathing person, many of whom were struggling to find an escape from their confinement. The sole empty acrylic box was presumably waiting for a new arrival.

"Shit!" Avril mouthed to herself. "This is no random kidnapping," she continued in her mind. "This is a well-planned and organized snatch and grab. Damn it all. I'm in deep shit! What the hell are they going to do with all of us? Whatever it is, it won't be good."

Despite her failures to free herself, she struggled to search in vain to free herself. Studying the nearby boxes, she determined that they were all similar in design to holding her. None of them appeared to have a seam or lid to open them. Unable to see behind her, where the top of her head met the box's edge, she studied her companion's boxes.

That is when she noticed a pair of hoses running from each box's ends and disappearing off in the distance. Thinking about their function, she realized that they conditioned the air, keeping her alive.

Looking over at her next-door-neighbor, she mouthed the words as best as she could with the ball gag firmly seated in her mouth, "What's going on?" The neighbor merely shook her head in resignation, "I don't know."

After what seemed like hours, for she had no way of telling time, two men came in, carrying an unconscious, bound, and naked blonde young woman. The woman appeared to be about eighteen years old and exceptionally pretty. Dumping her in the last acrylic box, they used a heat gun to weld the acrylic box shut.

"Well, that answers that question," she thought to herself. Now she knew why there did not appear to have any seams in any of the boxes.

Maybe a half-hour or so later, the new woman stirred and woke up. Panicking, she pounded and thrashed at the walls of her box, screaming and crying at the same time. After a while, exhausted, she seemed to calm down and inspected her environment.

Avril watched her with compassion, unable to help her or herself. Lying back, she closed her eyes and waited. Just as she drifted off, she realized that her air supply now included a sedative.

"What now?" she thought as she slipped into unconsciousness.

Suddenly awakened by loud noises and jostling all around her, Avril awoke with a start. Opening her eyes, she discovered that her acrylic box was no longer lying in the room it once sat. Instead, the containers were stacked in a vehicle, perhaps a truck. She didn't know what kind it was. All she could tell was that they were moving.

There were boxes filled with people all around her. Above her and to the sides, she could see the backs and profiles of other people. They were all stacked like freight, transported to some unknown destination.

Looking up, she was staring right at the back, shoulders, and ass of another woman. Looking to her side, she could see the slow rise and fall of other people's breathing chests in the same situation as she was. The women on either side of her, naked and afraid, were frantically looking around just as she was.

All Avril could do was think, "Oh, shit! We're all in some deep shit!"

Eventually, Avril realized that they were in the cargo hold of an airplane. She had flown enough to recognize the up and down shaking that went with flying. She was merely cargo in transit.

"In transit to where?" she wondered.

As the plane's movement bounced her around, Avril decided she was probably in a private plane. Because of her limited vision field, she couldn't tell how many of the kidnapped there were. It had to be quite a few, though. Twisting her head around, she could almost make out several acrylic boxes like hers beneath her, and more stacked behind her head and beyond her feet. Between what she saw when she first woke up and now, there had to be several dozens of us in the cargo hold of the airplane.

"Us?" she realized as she understood the depth of her predicament.

It was plain to her that the plane had a full cargo load of an untold number of naked men and women of all ages and races. Looking around as best as she could, she noted most were in their late teens or early twenties. For some unknown reason, intuition perhaps, she felt that she might be one of the oldest of the cargo. She wondered if any of them would live to see their next birthday.

"Will I even see tomorrow?" she considered.

As she pondered her situation, her dead parents flashed in front of her, and tears flowed down her cheek. Unable to stem the tide, she broke down, unable to curtail the tears of despair.

"Please, God, help me? Help all of us. Please?"

After what seemed like hours, she felt the plane descend before touching down on a runway. She felt the reverse thrust of the engines slide her down what little room she had so that her feet firmly came to rest against the box's end wall. As the plane slowed, she felt it turn to the left and taxi a bit before coming to a stop and shutting down its engines.

Wondering what was going to happen next, dreading her fate, she wished someone would rescue her. However, she didn't believe that liberation would come anytime soon. Still, the authorities might catch her kidnappers and save them. However, slight that possibility was, it was still possible. Crossing her fingers, she waited.

After a time, she heard a door open, and light flooded into the cargo hold.

"Ugh," Avril thought. The woman in the box above her could not contain her bowels. She streaked the bottom with brown stains as dirty water sloshed around her entire body.

"Thank God for the A/C unit," was all she could think of, compassionate for her neighbor before realizing that she too would soon need to relieve herself.

"Let's load them up, everyone," Avril heard from the doorway.

A moment later, several men began disconnecting their air hoses and unloading their human cargo. One by one, they carried the acrylic boxes off to destinations unknown.

"Aw, shit. Look at what this bitch did to herself," Avril heard as the men lifted the box containing the woman above her.

"Don't worry about it. They'll clean her up, right soon enough," someone said.

Eventually, they grabbed Avril's box, disconnected her air hoses, and slid her towards the cargo door. Two other men picked it up and carried it out into the blinding, bright light. Avril realized that the light in the cargo hold had been dim during her stay inside the plane. Now, the light suddenly flooded that her, assaulting her eyes. Closing her eyes as tight as she could, she feebly tried to cover them with her hands to shut out the painful light.

Uncaring, the men carrying her bounced her back and forth against the sides of the box. Disoriented, all she could do was grin and bear it. They carried her over to a flatbed truck and dumped her roughly on top of the other captives.

Since she was now on the top of the stack, she had no shade to protect her from the bright, scorching sun blazing down and blinding her. Turning her head and forcibly squinting her eyes closed, she prayed that this would all end soon. A piece of logic in the back of her mind told her that it wouldn't and that she was in real trouble. Avril tried not to dwell on just how dire her situation was. She knew if she did, she'd fall apart.

Eventually, they placed a tarp over the entire cargo load, providing relief to her tortured retinas, and the truck drove off. The ride wasn't smooth at all, as she bounced against the walls of her box.

"At least it's not a coffin," Avril jested, trying in vain to ease her fear.

On at least two occasions, the truck must have hit a pothole. She bounced straight up and hit her head on the top of her box. One time, she smacked her nose hard, eliciting several painful expletives to feel better. Fortunately, it wasn't hard enough to give her a nosebleed.

Without the A/C hoses, the air in the box grew stale. It was also getting hot, lying here in a terrarium under a blistering sun beating on the tarp-covered coffin. It didn't take long before perspiration pooled beneath her, and she surfed on her sweat swelling beneath her. Still, it could be worse. She could be like that other woman, swimming in her piss and shit.

On and on, hour after hour, the truck drove for miles as specks of the bright light leaked between the tarp's threads. She resolved to keep her eyes closed and tilted her head to one side as much as possible to alleviate the stabbing to her retinas. Eventually, the truck slowed and came to a stop. A tap of the horn ushered the sound of a large door opening, and the truck drove inside a large building, shutting out the blinding sun, providing blessed darkness. She could just make out the sound of the men getting out of the cab and doors slamming before untying the tarp and uncovering the truck's load of human cargo.

One by one, they moved the boxes from the truck and roughly deposited them on a flatbed cart. With the cart fully loaded, they pushed it towards a freight elevator, and everyone descended into the depths of hell.

Arriving at her destination, men cut the top of the boxes with a grinding wheel and lifted each person from their prison one by one and in succession. Eventually, it was her turn, and over the sharp noise of the grinding wheel, they removed the lid and crudely dragged her to the shower area along with the rest of the captives.

Depositing her in a shower room, they attached a chain to her ball gag harness and shackled her to the showerhead. It also forced her to stand, not that she cared too much. Her body welcomed the upright position after being compelled to remain flat for far too long.

The men spoke not a word as they went about their work. Looking around, Avril found it interesting that neither sex nor race had factored into whom they brought to the shower room. They chained men and women of every color and creed to the various showerheads. After they had brought in the last captive and shackled her in place, a man dressed in a dark gray suit with highly polished shoes stepped into the room.

"Hello, everyone. Thank you for joining us today," he said amidst the gagged groans of the surrounding people. Watching him closely, she concentrated on what he had to say, searching for the remotest chance to escape and return home.

Almost as if he read her mind, he said. "Now, now. There's no need for any of that. The lives you used to have is no longer a concern. You will never return to them. It would be best if you concentrated on the here and now."

Among the growing tears, he continued. "As of today, you are now mine. I own you. I went to a lot of trouble to acquire you, and I mean to make up for my expenses. After cleaning up, you will join others who, like you, are awaiting their destiny. Over the next two weeks, we will instruct you on the behavior we expect you to follow. Exhibit good behavior, and we will allow you to live to another day. As for bad behavior, well, let's say you will learn just how painful your lives will become. Training will be minimal, as your new owners will take on the responsibility of any additional training you may need. That's correct. You heard me correctly. Right now, I own you, and by the end of your training, I will auction you off to the highest bidder."

"Let me say this. I have a significant investment in each of you. I expect to receive top dollar. I anticipate making a substantial profit on every one of you. Pray that someone bids for you with the minimum bid. Minimum bids barely earn me a profit. The higher the bid, the more likely you will find a decent life down the road. Those that do not garner top dollar will reimburse me in other ways. Ways that I guarantee you will not appreciate nor enjoy."

"Right now, all I expect of you is to shower and clean yourself up. Take care of any business you need right here. The water will wash away any dirt and fluids. Use the soap and shampoo provided. No exceptions. Anyone who does not properly clean himself or herself up will remain here while my associates properly wash you. A word to the wise. They will use rough scrub brushes and enjoy cleaning you inside and out."

"After that, get some rest. Tomorrow, your training begins in earnest."

"Turn on the water, boys," he commanded as he turned and walked out of sight.

Immediately, hot water sprayed out from the showerheads, drenching them as they stood chained. Taking the opportunity, she released her bladder, adding to the volume of water racing towards the drain. As her bladder emptied, her bowels urgently communicated their need to evacuate. Thinking about it for a moment, she decided cleaning her insides herself was preferable to letting the lechers watching them do it for her. Squatting down and relaxing, she emptied her bowels onto the floor, careful to make sure that as the water rained down on her, it washed away the dirt from around her feet.

Feeling better, she stood up and finished watching the last of her dirt disappear down the drain. Looking around, she thought most of them did the same. Streams of dirty, brown water raced to the drain from all directions.

She noticed one woman, the last one to join them in the clear, acrylic boxes, just standing there. Crying from under the water, she wrapped her arms tightly around her chest, futilely trying to cover up. Almost comatose, she just stood there crying, her knees touching, and her feet pigeon-toed. Shaking her head, Avril couldn't help but pity the woman who had a lot to learn. So far, she was on target to enduring the guards violating her. A fate she did not wish to suffer.

Turning towards the soap, she picked up the bar and began thoroughly washing. Feeling her skin tingle with cleanliness, she took the shampoo and washed her hair. As she massaged the shampoo into her scalp, she couldn't help but notice the stupefied eighteen-year-old, still immobile, doing nothing to wash.

Shaking her head, she tried to get the woman's attention standing alongside her to get her to help the woman. She received a shaking of the head. Avril couldn't blame her. They were all on their own, and it would take all of her wits to survive the ordeal. All she could do was to finish washing.

Despite the gag in her mouth, the harness around her head, and a strap over the top of her hair, she felt she did a decent job shampooing her hair.

It took a while and several trips to the shampoo bottle, but eventually, she felt she had done the best she could under the circumstances. Standing upright, she welcomed the steaming water cascading over her body, superficially cleansing away her fears. By this time, most of the rest of them also finished washing, all but one.

The eighteen-year-old woman remained steadfast in her immobility. If it weren't for her crying and shaking in fear, one would have thought she was a statue.

Despite the leering looks of their guards, the eighteen-year-old refused to wash. With everyone else finished, four naked guards with cocks in full attention approached her. She tried to resist, of course, but it wasn't very reasonable to think that they would have mercy on her. She screamed and wailed, trying to avoid their assaults with little success. In full view of the rest of them, they forced her to pee and moved her bowels.

Next, they cleaned her, alternately stuffing their erections into her ass and pussy while the two others took soapy scrub brushes and washed her. After the first two men had their fill and shot their load, they switched places and repeated the violation. By the time they finished with her, they had violated her repeatedly, leaving her skin raw and crudely washed hair. Shampoo remained stitched between the strands of her hair.

She wasn't the panicking, immobile statue anymore. She was a rubbery mess, barely capable of standing. The guards withdrew with wicked smiles on their faces, leaving the quivering girl whimpering under the falling water. Only the chain shackling her to the showerhead kept her from slipping to the floor.

Avril stood under the hot shower, numb to what she witnessed. She immediately felt chilled as goosebumps again bespeckled her body after they shut off the hot water.

Returning, the guards unlocked them one by one, led them away, and placed each of them in a holding cell. The holding cells were the expected kind, with metal bars and a lock on the door. A single steel toilet and sink hung on the wall in one corner, and a bunk against the opposite wall.

The only thing else in the room was a single thin towel and a pair of high-heel shoes.

A note rested upon the towel and shoes, which read.

"Dry off and place the wet towel outside the cell. After you dry off, put the shoes on and stand up straight in the room's center with your hands clasped behind your back. You have ten minutes to comply. Failure to adhere to the time limit will result in severe punishment."

Glancing at her other cellmates within view, she could see that some had already dried off and were putting on the shoes. Picking up the towel, she quickly dried off her body and dried her hair as best as possible. Since the room temperature was warm, she felt it wouldn't take long for her hair to dry completely as well.

Picking up the shoes, she sat down on the bunk and began strapping them to her feet. The highly polished high-heels had an ankle strap and four-inch stilettos. While she had worn this kind many times, she knew that she would need to acclimate to wearing such a high heel for any length of time. Typically, she only wore two-inch heels or less. She would need to get used to the higher, four-inch ones.

As she studied the shoes, she heard a man yell out, "One minute."

Hurrying, she had just barely finished buckling the second ankle strap and stood up as instructed when a guard walked by to check her progress. With a bit of dejection in his face, he bent over, retrieved the towel, and moved on.

Several cells down the aisle, she heard him sharply speak to another woman, "Time's up," he announced, as he unlocked the door and stepped into her cell. A moment later, she heard a loud slap followed by a woman crying from shock and pain.

"Do you want some more? You had better put those shoes on and be right quick about it."

From the sound of her cries, she could tell that the woman was the young eighteen-year-old. Avril figured that the woman was finally putting on the heels.

As soon as the woman finished, he shoved her up against her cell for everyone to see. Her breasts bisected by a bar as he roughly fucked her. He took great pleasure in making sure the others could see how he treated her. Avril knew, without a doubt, that they were all nothing more than a piece of meat.

Done with her, he left her up against the bars and spoke sharply to everyone else, his erect wet cock dripping.

"I'm still ready to go. Who else hasn't put their shoes on?"

By this time, they were all wearing their heels and standing in the center of their cells.

After relocking the eighteen-year-old's cell door, one guard retrieved the damp towels while others inspected the other cells' occupants. As soon as the guards left, she could hear several of the other women's whimper, all on the verge of tears. It had taken a long time before the violated young woman stopped crying, too exhausted to cry any further.

Sitting on her bunk, she surveyed her cell. Barely four feet wide and seven feet long, was it scarcely big enough to stand up and pace back and forth? Beyond that, there was nothing. There were no pictures on the walls, a window to look out, a piece of clothing to wear, or a blanket on the bunk to cover their nakedness. Only a single light source recessed in the ceiling of her cell illuminated her surroundings.

Lying on the bunk with its thin but thankfully clean mattress, she contemplated her fate, suppressing her fear as best as she could. They had yet to remove her gag. Sleep came slowly to her.

Before falling off to sleep, her final thought was, "To hell with them. No way am I going to give them the satisfaction."

On the following day, in order, they retrieved each of them from their cells, complete in heels and mouth gag. They took her to what she guessed was the training area. First things first, though. With one guard clenching her arms behind her back and forcing her chest out, another guard approached her and clamped a pair of slotted forceps over her left nipple.

"Ow!" Avril tried to scream through the gag. The guard just smiled and went back to his work.

Once he pinched her nipple between the forceps, he picked up what appeared to be a long, thick needle and shoved it unceremoniously through her nipple. Surprising Avril, it didn't hurt as much as she suspected it would. Pinching her nipple with the forceps hurt much worse. A thick ring, about three-quarters of an inch around, followed the needle through the hole.

A minute later, a second ring pierced her right nipple, joining the left one. Taking a deep breath, she hoped they had finished mutilating her body. She was wrong. Cringing when they approached her with a small but white-hot welding torch, they welded the two ends of each ring together.

The heat from the bright blue flame radiated immediately from the ring, fire searing her tender nipples.

"Yeow!" She screeched as loudly as she could through her gag.

The screams seemed noisy and intense, but the guards just laughed as they finished welding the rings closed to her. Once welded, they placed a wet cloth over her breasts, hastening the cooling metal.

As the rings cooled to a bearable level, they removed the ball gag, damp cloth. Gratefully, they gave her a small amount of food and water. She hadn't realized just how hungry she was, and within minutes, the food vanished.

Expecting them to replace the gag and harness, they surprised her when they left her mouth unencumbered. Escorting her to the showers, she had thirty minutes to wash, shampoo her hair, and dry off before putting her heels back on. Once finished, they took her back to her cell, warning her to keep the piercings clean, washing them with soap and warm water several times a day.

Over the next several days, except for her shower time, she always wore those damn high-heel shoes, even to the point of sleeping in them. Twice a day, they took her from her cell, naked, walking on the stilts attached to her feet. At each training session, they coached her on what they expected of her. They forced her to walk around with her shoulders back, her hands cuffed behind her back. They wanted her to thrust out her chest and embellish her walk with hip thrusts. They wanted her to walk like some damn runway supermodel.

"What kind of shit was that?" she complained to herself, knowing full well that they would beat her or worse by speaking her mind. As it was, she had to suffer the occasional sting of a crop on her backside when she didn't do something exactly as they wanted. She quickly learned to do as they said.

Initially, she found it difficult to walk that way, with her hands forcibly held behind her back and tiptoeing on her feet. In time, she got better at it. They kept her at it until she got it right. The training was tiresome, especially to her thighs, calves, and back. By the end of the day, she looked forward to getting off her feet and lying down on her bunk. By the end of the week, she could walk a perfect runway walk, pirouetting after several dozen steps, throwing her hips as she walked, before turning around and returning to her starting point.

Once a day, they took her to the shower room. She looked for the freedom of a shoeless thirty minutes to herself in the showers and took advantage of every second. Like the first day, they repeated training them and making sure everyone had adequately washed. Thankfully, no one needed to defecate in the showers. From what she could tell, the young eighteen-year-old was barely coping with her new reality, requiring discipline several times a day. Being brutally fucked in the ass was no longer adequate punishment. Eventually, three or more of them would descend upon her and simultaneously invade her as they beat her and had their way with her. All the rest of them could do was try to shut out her screams as they ravaged her body.

Chapter Four

"Are they ready?"

"They're getting close. Most are ready, though a couple still needs work. One, in particular, is not playing ball at all. She refuses to learn to walk and just stands there, crying."

"Is that the eighteen-year-old petite blonde, the one that refused to shower that first day?"

"Yes, Sir. That's the one. I get the sense that she'll never move past the wailing."

"Can we salvage anything so that she'll make it to the auction?"

"I don't think so. Except for her incessant crying, she's practically comatose. Even as the guards discipline her, she just wails and cries. She doesn't even put up a fight, which might attract some buyers. If she fought back, then we could easily find a buyer who enjoys that sort of thing. As it stands now, I don't think anyone will bid upon her."

"That's too bad. She's quite the looker. Small, petite frame, easy to toss around, and a nice pair of tits to go with it."

"Yes, Sir. I thought the same thing as well."

"Have you had a go at her?"

"I did. She has a nice tight pussy that grips you firmly. We're still breaking in her ass, so right now, it's nice and tight. I'm a bit surprised by that, seeing how many times the guards have punished her. They have been brutal with her. She doesn't seem to get it. Perform, and you'll live. Resist, and you die."

"Is she resisting? That could be useful."

"She's not resisting in the typical sense. It's almost as if she's comatose. As if her brain disconnected from her body. She stands there as they beat, fuck, and brutalize her. Of course, the guards know enough not to damage the goods too much. They recognize that you would not be happy if her bruises were so bad that she could not participate in the auction on schedule. That doesn't stop them from having fun with her in other ways."

"Hm, that is too bad. I had hoped for a good profit on that one. Tell you what. I want to taste the goods for myself before I decide."

"So, you're thinking of making her the example to the rest?"

"Yes, I am. Set it up for first thing tomorrow morning, right after breakfast. In the meantime, bring her to me tonight. If she has any redeeming qualities, I'll substitute her for tomorrow's demonstration."

That evening, the guards brought the sniveling eighteen-year-old to a room and chained her ankle to the floor. Smirks were evident on each of the guards' faces, as they knew what would happen to the girl. They were a bit jealous, even though they each had already had their way with her.

After they had left, the woman remained standing where they deposited her. Knees touching and her heels splayed out, she appeared pigeon-toed. She grasped her hands together over her breasts, ineffectively trying to shield them from prying eyes. She continued whimpering, an endless river of tears dripping down her cheeks onto her dampening chest.

"So, you're the one giving us so much trouble." He said as he entered the room and viciously backhanded her across the face. The woman immediately dropped to the floor in shock, pain, and surprise. Taking a hand, she began rubbing her cheek.

"Stand up," he commanded her.

Failing to do as he commanded, he stepped up and viciously backhanded her again on the other side of her face.

"I said, stand up."

The woman took a moment and stared at him, maybe a bit of life in her eyes after all. Decision made, she first moved to all fours and then slowly, cautiously stood up on her heels.

"That's better. Do as you're told," he told the girl.

She stood mute. Her eyes unfocused, she retreated into the back recesses of her mind.

"Put your hands behind your back," he commanded.

Slow to comply, her arms moved hesitantly but eventually wound their way behind her back. He slapped her hard on one of her tits with an open palm, immediately revealing an angry handprint on her breast.

"Yeow," she screamed and tried to cover up her breasts with her arms.

"I said, put your hands behind your back. Do not make me repeat myself."

Robotically, but with great hesitation, her arms slowly dropped as her hands made their way behind her back.

"That's better," he said as he painfully slapped her other tit, eliciting another painful wail from the young girl.

"They tell me you are not cooperating. Why is that? You know the rules, and you know what I expect of you. Why won't you cooperate and practice your lessons?"

The woman stood mute, frozen in fear, and lost in the back of her mind.

"It's just a simple thing. Just learn to walk as we wish you to walk. It's not hard. Everyone else in your class has learned the lesson. Why don't you?"

The woman didn't answer. He wasn't sure whether she wouldn't or couldn't answer. Oh, sure. He knew that she could. Physically, she could speak all she wanted. Their examination of her background proved that. What concerned him was that as thorough as their investigation was, her file did not anticipate this kind of reaction to them taking her.

They had figured her to be the perfect, kept woman, capable and willing to perform anything a client might wish for in and out of bed. In her old life, she had been promiscuous to the degree that even they found surprising. She had slept with teachers, professionals, classmates, and strangers. They gave her anything she wanted, and then she discarded them as casually as one would dispose of a dirty tissue. Now, however, she behaved, unlike the sexual animal her file implied.

Stepping closer to her, he gave her an imposing stance as if he were ready to pounce. He tried to garner a reaction from her. Instead, she continued to stand unmoving and comatose.

Turning away, he took a step before striking. He backhanded the girl across the cheekbone in a wide, fast arc that might have broken it. However, he had already decided. Her only usefulness to him now was as an example to the others.

After she fell to the floor, he loosened his tie and removed his suit. Over the next couple of hours, he ravaged her. Between his beating and his brutal invasion of her private parts, he had his way with her.

When he finished his assault on her body, now used up, he redressed, thinking to himself, "Yes, she was useless to him at the auction. She wouldn't fetch a single Euro."

As he closed the door behind him, he took one last look at the spent but breathing prostrate body; he muttered. "What a shame."

By the middle of what Avril guessed was the second week, a day of reckoning arrived, and the suited man from the first day reappeared again.

"Good morning, ladies and gentlemen," he began. "I am rather proud of most of you. Your progress in your training is going very well. All but one," he said as he glanced around the cells. Everyone knew to whom he was referring. "I am about to rectify that situation. Everyone, move forward, face the bars, and stick your arms out."

Everyone complied, some more sheepishly than others did, but they all complied. With a guard following, the suit took handcuffs from the guard and snapped them around their wrists. Cuffed, they could not pull away from the bars and turn their backs.

As he did so, he spoke soothingly.

"What you are about to witness could happen to any of you, without warning, assuming you do not follow the rules. I require you to face forward at all times. Do not turn your heads, nor avert your eyes. You will be under observation at all times. If you cannot follow my instructions, I assure you that we will punish you, like you are about to witness. There will be no warnings, no second chances. Do I make myself clear?"

No one spoke up. Avril acquiesced, looking dispassionately straight at him, minimizing the fear raging throughout her body as best as she could.

After he had finished shackling everyone, he turned to the front of the block and said with a commanding tone.

"Bring it in."

Moments later, a pair of guards wheeled in a sturdy platform that sat a tall and substantial post into the room's center. Draped over the top of the post sat a sturdy rope. It stretched over the top and down to a reel and handle attached to the post about waist height.

Looking at the other end of the rope, Avril noticed to her horror that they had tied a noose. She almost looked away in dread but caught herself at the last moment and continued to look at the platform.

Looking at the gentleman, she noted a sly smile appear on his face, almost as if he looked forward to anyone turning his or her heads away.

Turning to his inventory once more, he spoke again.

"Do you see this? I presume you know what this is. The rest of you need to know that unless you do everything required of you, what you are about to witness will happen to you without pause or delay."

"Not may, but will. Of that, I assure you." After allowing his words to sink in, he spoke up once again. "Bring her."

The suit stepped up onto the platform and waited with his hands behind his back.

The guards approached the eighteen-year-old's cell, who was only now realizing just who they had their sights on. She tried to back away, kicking and screaming. Crying loudly, she tried in vain to avoid the guards. After entering the girl's cell, two guards grabbed her from behind while a third removed the handcuffs.

Yanking her arms hard, they cuffed her wrists behind her back. Then, using a short length of cord, they tied her elbows tight together to touch each other behind her back. She yowled at the rough treatment. Resisting, she tried to stab at them with her spiked heels, to no effect. Her petite frame was no match for the three burly guards wearing heavy work boots. One of them picked her up and casually threw her over his shoulder, carrying her out to the cell block center and depositing her onto the platform.

Dropping her in front of the post, they forced her to step backward until she had nowhere to go. Pleading and tears raining down her cheeks, she stood there, on her high-heel shoes with her back firmly up against the post.

She took a moment, looked upwards, and saw the noose above her head. Collapsing in a heap, she fervently tried remaining immobile. Smirking, a guard bent over and calmly stood her up once again against the post. This time, he held her there against the post, two hands firmly holding her in place by her tits.

"Thanks for the quickie feel, bitch," he sneered. "I hope you like it. It'll be the last time anyone ever touches those cute little titties of yours."

"No, please, no. I don't want to die. Please, I'll be better. I promise. PLEASE!" The eighteen-year-old begged as tears streamed down her cheeks.

She continued to beg for forgiveness and mercy. Somehow, like the rest of them, she knew it was all in vain. Ultimately, her begging slowed, replaced with a quiet whimpering that sounded a lot like praying for God's forgiveness.

The suit spoke so that everyone would hear him while facing the unfortunate girl.

"You did this to yourself. You disobeyed the rules. I warned you that violating the rules would result in severe punishment. You will suffer your punishment so that the others learn from your mistakes and don't repeat them."

"Please, Sir, I don't want to die. Please, I promise I'll be good."

"Sorry, girl, you had your chance. Many, in fact, and now you are out of chances."

He told her as he lowered the loop of the noose over her head and around her neck. She continued to whimper as he tightened the noose, placing the knot just behind her head.

Walking to her side, he took the handle of the spool and engaged the ratchet. Turning the handle slowly, one slow click after another echoed around the space. Captives and guards alike watched as the noose dragged her ever so slowly upwards. He stopped cranking when she was standing on tiptoes, her heels suspended above the platform.

The woman could hardly breathe. It was apparent to everyone that it was a struggle to remain upright, maintain her balance, and draw breath. Every so often, Avril could hear the condemned woman cough and choke as she tried to suck precious air into her lungs. Sounds of her struggles permeated throughout the space, permanently etching the sounds into Avril's psyche.

The suit walked around to face her, stroking her body and breasts before groping her pussy. Avril couldn't tell whether his fingers intruded inside her, but did it matter? The woman was about to die.

"It's a shame, really. You have such a fine body." He said, withdrawing his fingers and putting them up towards his nose, inhaling her essence. "You would have sold for much. You might have even garnered the highest bid of the day." He said, shaking his head. "Alas, you will soon become meat and feed my table."

As the last words rebounded in the young girl's head, she finally realized just what he meant and bellowed a piercing scream. Avril couldn't figure out just how she could do it, scream as she did with a noose around her neck, slowly choking her to death. Somehow, she managed it. Avril's ears and teeth ached from the screeching sound.

Once again, she almost turned away from the gruesome scene. Catching herself once again, she forced her attention back to the room's center before anyone noticed.

As she watched the scene unfold in front of her, she saw the suit stick his hand out behind him, palm up. Immediately, one guard placed a three to four-foot whip into his hands.

Then stepping back, he unwound the whip and snapped it in front of the helpless woman supported by the noose. The whip looked mean and deadly from where Avril stood.

The eighteen-year-old girl's eyes widened further in fear, and her screams ceased when she saw the villainous whip in his hands.

With the whip swishing back and force, the suit made a show of snapping the whip tip. The condemned woman tried to back away and move out of the whip's reach, only to struggle with the tightening noose forcing her back.

"Just so you know," the suit began, "I enjoy this part, though I rather doubt you will." He said as he snapped the whip hard, connecting right on the center of her stomach just below her belly button.

She screamed, a large red welt immediately forming on her gut. The suit swung again, this time connecting just above her belly button. He snapped the whip eight more times, leaving her belly crisscrossed with the large, angry welts.

The unfortunate woman twisted this way and that, trying to turn and present her back to the suit.

Her efforts were for naught. The noose kept pulling her back against the post as she tried to remain up on her toes and breathe. On the tenth stroke, the suit paused, allowing her to feel the pain of the whipping spread throughout her body.

A couple of minutes later, he resumed his whipping. At first, he targeted the girl's breasts and nipples. The woman screamed out in pain with each strike. Avril unconsciously cupped her breasts, protecting them from an imagined assault.

As the suit whipped the struggling girl, Avril realized the suit wanted the poor woman to suffer before killing her. After several brief respites, giving the young woman time to recover between whipping sessions, he moved on to her belly, thighs before finally landing several strokes to the unfortunate girl's privates. Avril cringed, knowing just how painful each touch of the whip must be to the girl's most sensitive region.

Holding up his whip and circling the girl, he addressed the captives.

"See this stupid girl? See what happens when you break the rules and don't do as we tell you. I trust you are learning how to avoid this fate. Break my rules, and I guarantee you, this will be your destiny."

"Live by my rules, and you will survive to see another day. Perhaps one day, you will enjoy your new lives. Perhaps not, but either way, I don't care. We've sealed your fate, and only you can determine the course of the rest of your lives."

As the suit spoke his last words, he lashed out with the whip and snapped it right on the girl's genitalia. She screamed like a banshee as he delivered painful stroke after stroke. Avril lost count of the strokes, each one landing perfectly right in the center of her clitoral region.

By the time he finished, she was a mess, blood dripping to the platform. Avril rather doubted she would ever again be able to use her body to attract a man and give birth to a child should the unfortunate woman survive the ordeal.

She wanted to close her eyes to the horror. Still, the guards' eyes continued to concentrate on all of them, eager to find an opportunity to add yet another victim to the ranks of those awaiting punishment.

The suit stepped down from the platform. For the next thirty minutes, the well-dressed suit silently circled the cellblock, alternately looking at each of the women still in their cells and then towards the unfortunate woman on the platform, slowly strangling in pain and anguish.

Eventually, the suit returned to the platform and stood in front of the condemned girl. Looking into her eyes, it seemed to Avril that he might pity her. Was that a look of eager anticipation? Avril wondered.

The woman looked back, her eyes telegraphing her conviction that she knew that she was about to die. The suit took hold of the handle and started turning it.

'Click, click, click,' echoed as each tooth of the ratchet settled into another notch, breaking the silence throughout the room. With each click, the noose lifted the girl, bit by bit, up into the air. Her feet lost touch of the platform, her toes stretching for the floor. He stopped turning the handle when she dangled about a foot off the floor.

Her legs and feet thrashed about violently, trying in vain to find something to stand on and relieve the tightening rope around her neck. Her eyes seemed to squint as her eyebrows took on that indescribable look of pain and anguish. Ridges appeared to extend from the bridge of her nose and up her forehead. Her eyebrows slanted downward towards the side edges of her eyes, taking on that look of fear and alarm. Her mouth hung open, her jaw flapping ever so slightly as her tongue stuck out past her bottom lip, trying in vain to open her airways and catch a breath of fresh air.

It was not to be.

Looking downward at her killer, now standing in the middle of her view, her face turned a dark blue as the noose continued to cut deeply into her neck.

She struggled for what seemed like many minutes, though, in reality, it could have been just seconds. Her eyes popped out of their sockets, turning red in the process. In time, her struggling slowed, and her legs and arms relaxed to a mild twitching.

A long moment later, her eyes glazed over, and she became still. Her body wholly slack and her limbs hanging limply, her bladder relaxed, and piss ran down her legs and onto the platform, a sure sign that the woman was dead.

The suit turned and walked out of the cellblock with a joyful look of satisfaction.

In leaving, he added one last comment, "Do not stop watching her until the guards release you. Afterward, get some rest. This weekend will be busy. I expect all of you to pass your final exams."

With that, he disappeared and down the hallway and out of sight. The guards all turned and looked at them, each with a wicked, devious smile painted on their faces. Avril was confident that they had enjoyed the show. Avril, on the other hand, did not.

Shaking her head, Avril could only imagine what was in store for them tomorrow. The guards left them standing there, shackled to the bars for over an hour, the dead girl draped in front of them. She hung there for the rest of the day, a reminder of the consequences of breaking the rules. In the meantime, Avril resolved to stand straight and avoid looking at the horrific scene before her. It was a bit of defiance she could get away with. In the meantime, she continued to look for an opportunity to escape, as slim as it seemed.

Chapter Five

Three mornings later, she woke up later than usual. Avril had not gotten much rest over the past couple of weeks. Sleeping naked and without cover guaranteed that she got up the next morning feeling cold and unrested. She usually slept curled up on her side, facing the wall in a fetal position.

Her bladder demanded attention, and after taking care of that, she washed up. The small sink didn't offer much, but it was better than nothing at all. She hoped they would allow her to shower. Hot showers always warmed her after a chilly night.

"This was the day, but the day for what?" She muttered under her breath.

Her final exam for sure, that's what the suit had said the other day. "But what does that mean?" she asked herself.

She washed up but did not feel clean because her teeth went unbrushed. She sat back down on her bunk, her hands under her thighs. She tried to envision what was ahead of her. Breaking her out of her reverie, a guard delivered a light breakfast of buttered toast, a poached egg, and a melon slice. Even trying to eat slowly and savoring every morsel, the meal disappeared in short order, and she sat wondering what was next.

A little while later, a guard retrieved the empty food plate and threw a toothbrush and a small tube of paste onto her bunk.

"Hurry up with that. I want it back in five minutes," the guard said and moved on to the next cell.

Moving quickly, she brushed her teeth. Her mouth finally felt clean and refreshed; she tossed the toothbrush and toothpaste out of the cell onto the floor. Sitting back down, she awaited her calling.

The morning dragged on, and noon came and went. The cells around Avril slowly emptied. Their occupants never returned. It was hard to tell what time it was. Avril still didn't have access to a window or door. What she thought was mid-afternoon might very well be well into the night or breaking dawn for all she knew. There was just no way to tell.

They took them in groups of three, leading them out, hands cuffed behind their backs as was customary. Eventually, they came for her, near the end of women's queue, systematically disappearing beyond the doorway. She left with her head held high and her back straight, walking to her fate.

The guards led her along a labyrinth of hallways and intersections. She quickly got lost in the meandering path their course took her. Her heels tapping on the floor, she arrived at their destination.

Walking into the large room with her companions, they led her onto a stage. She saw a large electronic sign with several rows lit up off to one side, indicating starting bid and current bid. Above was a sign indicating she was the next item up for auction.

She figured out what her final exam was. "How much am I going to sell for at the auction?"

One by one, they shackled them to the back wall of the stage.

Beyond the bright lights illuminating the human products on display, she could tell it was a full room. Rows and rows of all sorts of people sat in the dim light, staring up at the three new arrivals. The vast numbers intending to bid on her surprised her.

Beyond the glare, she could see they were well-to-do people. The men were dressed in the finest suits and tuxedos, while the women were all wearing designer evening gowns and expensive jewels.

"Yup, I'm about to become someone's bauble to abuse and display?" She thought to herself. "How long will it be before they finish and discard me?"

Her reverie broke when someone at a podium off to the side started speaking. She had not noticed him before. He was the suit that brutally executed the young woman earlier in the week. He was probably the Master of Ceremonies.

"Ladies and Gentlemen, we shall begin." The suit began.

"We move into the next phase of the event tonight. Unlike previous lots, the final two groups are not being sold as a lot but individually. From here on out, we are offering them to you individually."

"As in the previous sets, we certify to be in perfect health and superb condition. These final ones are the best of all the offerings presented today. Each earned high marks in their evaluations throughout their investigation and training. I expect that the lucky bidder for each of these fine young women will exceed your expectations as they give you months of superb service."

Pausing for a moment, he continued.

"Before we get started, we will allow you to inspect the merchandise. However, I remind you, there is no touching or questioning the stock. You may look, but that is it. I give you five minutes to perform your inspections, and then we will begin."

With that, about a dozen people, mostly women dressed in their finest, walked onto the stage. In those excruciating long five minutes, they walked back and forth in front of her, inspecting her, studying her, scrutinizing her. They looked at every part of her body, even squatting down in front of her to examine her genitalia. As embarrassed as she was, she felt even more indignant by the scum parading around in front of her. Keeping her mouth shut, she waited out the inspection.

"Times up, everyone. Please return to your seats so we can get started," the suit announced.

As the stage cleared, she couldn't help but notice one woman giving her a hungry glance in her direction, licking her lips as she did so. Despite the hot, bright lights, a chill ran through her, and she shuddered in response.

After a few minutes, the room quieted down, and the suit once again spoke up.

"Ladies and gentlemen, I present to you our auctioneer for the rest of the evening."

Stepping aside and lightly bowing, the suit stuck out his left arm, pointing to a new person approaching the podium. When the auctioneer arrived, he looked down at the forms in front of him and began speaking.

"Ladies and gentlemen, I am pleased to offer you the next-to-last group. I watched them throughout their training. I assure you each will more than live up to your demands and expectations."

"They're all high-quality gems. There is not a single flawed stone in the bunch. They are among the finest for tonight's offering."

"This group comes from America. We select each for their unique and selective attributes, which you find documented in your tablets. I assure you, whoever acquires these specimens will not be disappointed."

"For the final two groups, we are raising the minimum bid. Bidding now starts at €200,000, and minimum bidding increments are €10,000."

"Shall we get started?"

Standing naked and shackled against the wall, a guard came up to the first one and unlocked her. Poking her in the back, he had her walk to the front of the stage.

At first, she just stood there, her hands still cuffed behind her back, frozen in fear. After a bit of prodding, the woman walked the runway as they had practiced over the last two weeks. Swaying her hips, placing one high-heeled foot in front of the other, she walked the runway's length before stopping at the end.

To Avril, the girl's confidence was overrated. She knew that they frightened the woman to no end, just as they frightened her. Standing there, like some high-class model with one foot in front of the other, the woman pirouetted until she faced forward again, stood there for a moment, and then pivoted and walked back to the stage.

The guard directed her under the bidding sign, and she resumed her pose, one foot in front of the other, hands still cuffed behind her back.

"This first one comes from Southern California. She has blonde hair, stands 175 cm tall, and weighs 50 kg. That's 5'9" tall and 110 pounds for those of you still using imperial measurements."

Avril stopped listening at this point, not interested in the barbaric proceedings. Her mind wandered, hoping that this wasn't happening to her. Yes, they were going to sell her to the highest bidder, and after that, who knows what would happen. It didn't look good for her; of that, she was sure.

"Sold for €375,000," the auctioneer announced. A guard led the blonde off to the side of the stage and out of sight. Another guard approached the second woman and unshackled her. They made her repeat the runway walk, just as the first woman had done.

"Next up for bid is a brown-haired, Southern Belle from the Southeastern United States. Trust me when I tell you, she has an accent that will tickle your fancy and excite your mind."

He noted her vital statistics, and once again, Avril stopped listening. Fear and panic grew in her belly. Her legs became weak, and she started sliding down the wall. A sharp look from a guard made her stand up straight.

"Bidding will start at €200,000. As before, bidding will be in increments of €10,000. Shall we start?"

"Do I have my first bid? Yes, #122. Thank you. Do I hear 210? Thank you, Sir. #315 bids 210. Do I hear 220? I have 250 from #122. Thank you, Ma'am. Do I hear 260?" and so the bidding continued for several more minutes.

She stopped paying attention to the bidders when she realized that the bidding climbed higher and higher, surpassing what Southern California blonde had garnered.

"What did that mean, anyway?" She wondered to herself.

"Sold for €450,000 to bidder #122. Thank you, Sir."

"For the final offering in this lot, I present to you a fiery redhead from the Northeastern United States for your consideration. Hailing from New York City, as an Account Executive for a major marketing firm, she handled millions of dollars for her clients and earned significant bonuses along the way."

"Uh, oh, that's me," she thought to herself.

Unshackled from the wall, her guard poked her in the back, indicating that she must walk the runway. Eyes focused straight ahead; Avril walked as they trained her to do.

Half listening to the auctioneer, she threw her hips back and forth with each step, slowly moving to the runway's end. Reaching the end of the runway, she stopped and looked yearningly at the exit door staring at her square in her face at the back of the room. Instead, the audience gawked at her nakedness, uncaring about her previous life and ogling her body.

Finishing her pirouette, she returned to the stage and stood under the bidding board, when she returned to listening to the auctioneer in earnest.

"This beautiful specimen, if you ask me, she is the crème de la crème of all of our offerings tonight."

"She stands 172 cm tall and weighs 48.5 kg. Her measurements are 86-53-89. That's 5'8" tall and 107 pounds, and measures 34- 21-35 for some of you. As you can see for yourself, she's long-legged, high-waisted, and possesses lovely wide hips. We feel that makes her ideal for carrying spawn to term, should you wish to use her as an incubator."

"She typically runs six to ten kilometers a day. A word to the wise, make sure you keep this one on a short leash. She is a runner, doing this distance in well under an hour. She's fast, very fast. She's competed in the Boston Marathon, finishing sixth in her age group and tenth in the women's overall. She has a BMI of 18, which is a bit low for a fertile female in her age group. I suppose that being an athlete accounts for her low rating."

"Keep a close eye on her, or she'll leave you in the distance should you let her slip away. Something I'm sure of you would never let happen." The auctioneer finished with a grin.

"Huh? What the fuck? How can they know I like to run and how fast I can run? How is that possible? How do they know all this stuff about me?" She wondered to herself.

"As I mentioned earlier, before joining us, she was an account executive for a prestigious advertising agency. She was privy to conversations of the upper echelon in her job. Not that we care about such things as advertising."

This last comment elicited a ripple of laughter from the crowd.

"She is well-versed sexually, affording the lucky buyer hours of pleasure should you care to use her that way. Besides, virgins are for marrying, and no one here intends to marry any of these items, do we?"

He teased, which the crowd responded to another round of laughter.

"She has a fiery personality, as clear by her fiery red hair. Throughout her stay with us, she maintained her composure throughout her ordeals. She scored among the highest on her tests." The auctioneer went on.

"While composed, she hides a fierce desire to escape her fate of servitude. She's strong, so I suspect she can hurt even the strongest of you if you get sloppy. She will patiently wait until you are at your weakest before striking. We do not doubt if, given the opportunity, she will strike before she escapes. Shall we begin?"

Seeing the nods around the room, he continued.

"Good. Bidding will start at €200,000, and this time, because of the overall exceptional rating of this item, bids will be in increments of €25,000."

May I have the first bid, please? I have 200. Do I hear 225? Yes, thank you, Madam. Do I hear 250? ..."

And so, it went. The bids climbed higher and higher. Try as she might, Avril tried to figure out who was bidding on her. She also could not figure out how they knew all this information about her. They didn't talk about friends and family. Well, why should they? These people did not care much about that. They only cared about what she could do for them and what pleasures she could give them. She had resigned herself that she was about to become someone's personal property.

"Shit, but what kind?"

She figured whoever bought her would use her as a subjugated sex worker, banging clients for money she would never see. Or was it to be something else? She contemplated.

She had no idea, but she hoped it would not be too bad. Sure, she would bide her time, satisfying these pricks until she found her opportunity. The auctioneer was right. She would attack before escaping. The trick was to stay alive until that happened.

Damn it all, being kept naked prevented her from finding and hiding any weapons.

They knew that.

"I have 550, do I hear 575?"

"Huh? Wow, I am going for top dollar," Avril realized.

Seeing the digital board hanging from the ceiling above her, she imagined the numbers quickly rising.

"I have 575, thank you, Madam. Do I hear 600? Thank you, Sir. I have a bid for 600. Do I hear 625?"

After a long pause, he repeated. "Ah, come on now. Look at her. She's well worth the investment."

"Madam, will you give me 625?" Avril looked out, trying to see the woman who had been bidding for her. "No? Alright," the auctioneer said.

"Are there any more bids? I have 600 going once… 600 going twice… sold for €600,000 to bidder #10. I congratulate you on your fine purchase, and to be fair, I may be just a bit jealous. Congratulations, Sir." He chuckled.

"Ladies and gentlemen, please take a look at the last lot's descriptions as we bring them up onto the stage. As soon as they are all set, we will start the last round."

"Yes, you heard me. This is the last lot up for bid this evening. These are the last three. If you haven't yet purchased your choice, now is your last chance for today. Please stay in your seats. We will begin momentarily."

While the auctioneer spoke, a guard came up to her and escorted her away from the stage. The lights in the audience came up a bit, allowing her to see the bidders briefly. She tried to find bidder #10, but unfortunately, she could not tell who had bought her.

As she searched, the guards pushed her towards the stage wing. With two guards on either side, they escorted her to what appeared to be a holding cell. Locking her inside the small cage, the guards placed a placard with the number ten on it and left. From her position, she had a full view of the stage.

Leaning back against the bars of her tiny cell, she contemplated her fate. Looking around, she saw similar holding cells, all but three occupied by the captives with whom she had spent the last weeks.

She hadn't found out anything about them, except that everyone was nothing more than a commodity, bought and sold. Before long, she detected activity from the stage where they brought in the last lot for auction.

After a spirited round of bidding, they led the last of the group to the empty cages. Avril noted that none sold for more than she did, making her the highest earner. She didn't know what that might mean to her in the long run. She almost didn't want to know.

"How about that?" she realized with a feeling of wonder and awe.

After the auction, the group locked in their cells looked nervously around, many looking like deer frozen in the headlights. Shortly after that, they rolled out a large platform onto the stage with a flurry of activity. On the platform sat a couple of long benches.

"Hm, I wonder what they are doing?"

Vaguely interested, she watched them perform their work. Next, they rolled out a box on wheels and deposited it behind the platform. Opening it, one guard reached in and withdrew a coil of rope. The guard tossed it to another guard, who uncoiled it, tossed it up into the air, and over a long wooden beam suspended above the stage. He loosely tied it off the rope's dangling end to a cleat to which she had recently shackled her during the auction. Then they repeated the set up two more times. When they had finished, a collection of three horrifying nooses hung from the beam, just above the front bench.

Avril wondered why she hadn't noticed the beam before. "Had they just lowered it, as they do with stage props during a play?"

Avril looked on in extreme fear of what was undoubtedly about to happen, staring wide-eyed and frozen in place. Looking around, she noticed that all the other prisoners were watching with the same look of horror she felt. Many were shaking and crying, knowing that soon, like the eighteen-year-old woman from the other day, three were about to die, hung by the neck for the audience's entertainment.

Whoever they were, the people in charge let everyone stare at the nooses dangling above the center of the stage. Half the audience waited in anticipation for the last event while the other half applauded.

After about a half-hour, several guards came in and approached a cage containing three women sold earlier in the day. Unlocking the cell and undeterred by the struggling women, they attached a tag, numbered one to three, to each of their left nipple rings.

The guards dragged the whimpering and crying women towards the stage. With looks of fear and panic on their faces, they forced the girls to stand behind the first bench. Tears rolled down their cheeks, painting lines of black mascara in their wake. Furled eyebrows and creases in their foreheads displayed their extreme terror and sorrow.

She felt sorry for them but was glad that she was not among them.

"Ladies and gentlemen, may I have your attention, please." The suit started saying after he walked up to the podium.

"Tonight, the winner of lot three graciously donated this group for this evening's entertainment. We are now taking bets on which one will out-survive the others. The last one alive will determine the winner as judged by our celebrity auctioneer."

"As an added incentive to the contestants, ensuring that they will do their best to outlast the others, we will offer the winner her immediate freedom."

"Please enter your bets now on your tablets. We set the odds of survival for each contestant, but please remember, we used unscientific methods to calculate odds. I admit it. The odds are entirely subjective, based upon the opinions of the leadership of the consortium."

"The contest will begin after entering the wagers. Good luck to all."

Avril could hear the flurry of tapping fingers on the tablets from her position in the stage's wings. She figured that the audience was furiously placing their bets. As the wagering continued, the guards helped each woman stand on top of the bench, one woman under each rope. After dropping a noose over the heads and around each girl's necks, the guards adjusted the ropes, removing all slack, and securely tied them off on the cleats behind them.

The suit spoke into the microphone, briefly interrupting the betting.

"Ladies and gentlemen, may I have your attention, please? We are going to offer an additional category of wagers. We are inserting identical butt plugs and dildos into each of our contestants. The butt plugs place extra pressure against the dildos, making it harder for the competitors to push out their dildos. Moreover, they just look good, don't you agree?"

"We are also offering a trifecta bet. The descending order will determine the winner. Who will drop their dildo first, second, and third? The one who drops their dildo last will determine the first-place winner. Those that wager the exact order will win the trifecta. We've sent the betting sheets to your tablets, along with odds determined by the consortium. Again, good luck to everyone."

"Oh, my God," Avril mouthed in disgust and horror. "Not only are they taking bets on who lives the longest, but they're also wagering on a stupid game as they die."

Meanwhile, the guards shoved large butt plugs and matching dildos into each woman standing on the bench. One woman was so wet with fear that the dildo slipped in effortlessly, while with another girl, the guard needed a second guard's assistance to hold her open as he forcefully coerced the dildo into her crotch. The butt plugs' dry insertion helped ensure they would remain in place throughout the competition, not to mention the guards' pleasure observing any discomfort the unfortunate women experienced during their installation.

Before long, all three weeping women were standing still, precariously perched on the rickety wooden bench. They each pleaded for mercy from the crowd, terrified of the nooses wrapped around their necks.

From the audience's perspective, the entertainment was already underway. To Avril, the last act in the horrific spectacle was still to come.

Saying a silent prayer, she asked God to welcome the women into his care. They did not deserve to die like this. Meanwhile, the suspense was riveting to the crowd and excruciating to those still locked in their cells. Job over, the guards removed the second bench and walked off the stage and down the side aisles to watch the spectacle.

"Time is running short on our competitors. Please finish up your wagers so we can get started." The suit asked the crowd. A few moments later, he announced, "Betting is now closed. Are you ready to find out which of your wagers will win? Well, I am, so let the show begin."

The suit stepped up onto the platform and walked behind the

women, verifying the guards tied each noose correctly and securely seated dildo and butt plug in their appropriate orifices. Satisfied, he moved to the center of the platform and took a position behind the women.

Eagerly anticipating what was to come, Avril could sense the audience sitting on the seats' edge, waiting for the contest's start.

A showman to the end, the suit made the audience wait until they were champing at the bit. When he sensed that they could wait no longer, he put his foot up against the bench's edge and looked out at the audience.

The entire room held their breath as he rested his foot on the bench. Teasing the audience, tormenting the condemned further, he waited for a pregnant pause. A collective gasp arose from the spectators. Avril held her breath, horrified at what she knew was about to happen. Keeping everyone's attention, and after a quick feint, he kicked out his leg.

Ever so slowly, almost as if in slow motion video, the bench tilted forward as the women in unison scrambled to remain standing on its surface.

It was not to be.

The bench fell forward, leaving nothing for the women to stand on. Their high-heeled feet found nothing below them as the three dropped. Their legs flailed about, trying in vain to find something to stand on, and their bodies slowly twisting under their weight.

Cheers erupted from the audience as the women dropped, their fall halted only by the ropes cutting deeply into their necks and silencing their pleas for mercy. Each swung out before swinging back when they reached the end of their arcs. They seemed to twirl around as they swayed back and forth, each time slowing as they dangled by their necks from above.

Watching in dread, Avril observed the three women flail their legs about in all directions. Fluctuating between them, each of the women spread their feet wide or pedaled their legs as if they were riding a bicycle. All of them were trying hard to find something to stand on. Although their hands handcuffed behind their backs, that didn't stop them from trying to reach up and grasp the noose wrapped around their necks, trying hard to find relief from the rope cutting off their airways.

Mesmerized in horror and unable to avert her eyes, Avril watched as her companions slowly strangled to death in front of her. Unlike the spectacle earlier in the week where the eighteen-year-old woman was already half dead before being hung, these animated women were very much alive.

The women didn't stop shaking and twisting about, trying to undo the damage to their throats and airways. Twisting about with legs whipping back and forth, it wasn't long before the first of them dropped their dildo.

From her angle, she couldn't tell which woman lost it, but the crowd sure did. Cheers erupted from the crowd while dejected gasps echoed around the room from those that bet wrong.

"What the fuck is wrong with these people," she muttered under her breath.

As the women strangled to death, she noticed that each of their heads turned blue and flashed purple. Each of them had their jaws wide open, gasping uselessly for air, while their eyes seemed to look down at the floor below them.

The platform might have been inches or miles away. They still could not reach it, and that knowledge reflected in their expressions. As they hung there, their bodies slowly spinning as their flailing limbs relaxed. They seemed to rotate on the end of their ropes as if they were marionettes manipulated by some unknown person from above.

As their faces darkened and turned purple, cheers erupted when another dildo dropped, hitting the platform. The trifecta determined; the winners congratulated each other, high-hand slapping their excitement before turning back to the show.

All that was left was to see was which of the women outlasted the others. The crowd focused their concentration, trying to pick out which of the three would survive her companions.

To her, watching from the stage wing and her cell's deceptive security, she thought it was taking a very long time for them to die. Unable to gauge time, it felt like it had been hours since the suit knocked the bench over. Time ran ever so slowly, and still, the women clung to life.

Little by little, their thrashing legs slowed, and a general limpness took over their bodies. Eventually, one of them stopped twitching all together. Her body seemed to grow an inch or more as it relaxed in death.

It was odd, she noted to herself. After the woman first dropped on her noose, her feet were about half a foot above the floor. Now her toes swung an inch barely above the platform. An inch or a mile, it didn't matter. She was still dead.

Now, it was up to the final two to determine which of them would be the winner. As Avril stood vigil, she couldn't help wonder what she would do if she were up there, hanging by a noose. Would she try to die quickly or outlast the rest so that she could earn her freedom? Avril honestly didn't know. Somehow, she didn't trust these bastards. She might survive the ordeal only to gain her freedom by being killed outright. Avril knew one thing. Unless she found an opportunity to escape, these bastards would kill her one day, and she would never return home.

'Bang,' she heard the third and final dildo's sound bouncing off the floor, forcing her to return her attention to the swinging women. Both were still twitching, but one woman seemed to squirm just slightly more than the other one. With sadness in her eyes, Avril watched them as their twitching slowed and finally stopped.

All three women were now… dead.

"Well, folks, hang on a moment, no pun intended, but let's see if there's still life in one of them." The celebrity auctioneer spoke up, joking as he walked up to one of them. After jabbing behind her kneecap with a hatpin, he failed to get a reaction.

"Well, this one is deader than a doornail. Let's see about the other one."

Jabbing the hatpin behind the other girl's kneecap, her foot magically and without reason, jerked.

"We have a winner. Number two is still alive," he shouted as he turned to the crowd.

The suit turned to the assemblage and spoke up. "It's official. We judge number two is still alive, paying off the wagers for the winners immediately. Check your tablets. Disbursements to your accounts are underway as I speak."

"Hey! What about the winner? Shouldn't someone give the winner her freedom?" Someone shouted from the crowd.

"Huh? Oh, that. Hang on a sec. Who donated this lot? Would you like the honor?" He asked of the congregation.

The donor immediately stood up and jumped up to the stage. Walking up to the unfortunate girl, after fondling her tits and flicking a finger into her crotch, he wrapped his arms around her waist and jumped up into the air. Falling, he maintained his grip on the girl. As they came down together, Avril heard the sharp snap of a breaking neck assaulting her ears. Breaking the girl's neck ensured her demise.

"I just love that," the donor said with a smile as he stepped in front of his property and admired the three lifeless bodies slowly spinning by their ropes.

"She won, and I gave the winner her freedom. Let's wish her a fond farewell," the donor added before returning to his seat to the crowd's applause.

"I was right," Avril thought to herself as she turned away from the scene and slowly sat down on the bottom of her cell. "I guess that will be my fate before too long."

"Ladies and gentlemen, that concludes the auction and tonight's entertainment. You may collect your purchases as soon as you settle your tabs. Thank you, and have a good evening." The suit added as he turned and walked off the stage to mingle with the crowd.

Left to her anguish, Avril crossed her arms over her knees and rested her head on them. Expecting the worst, she felt like crying.

"Damn it. I won't give the bastards the satisfaction of seeing me cry. The hell with them," she muttered to herself.

Wiping away the moisture that had built up in her eyes, she returned her head to its resting place as she sat there and waited for someone to collect her.

"That went well, Mr. Chairman."

"Yes, it did. What did you think of the crop this time?"

"Oh, I think the foragers did exceptionally well this time. From what I could determine, the product substantially exceeded the standard."

"Except for that one executed earlier in the week."

"Sir, as you know, we typically do execute a sacrificial lamb to teach the others we do mean business."

"Yes, but this time, that one wasn't the lamb we intended."

"No, Sir. You're right about that. However, we included the lamb in the group used for tonight's entertainment."

"Just as long as we don't accidentally sell off the lamb and upset the membership. We select the lambs as we don't expect them to please the clientele. We were lucky this time. I intend to bring this up at the next board meeting. The selection committee must do a more thorough job checking our product's backgrounds, behaviors, and likes. If that one had slipped through, I would have hated to recompense the buyer. What are you going to do to identify the bad blood sooner?"

"Sir, I thought we did well in the identification of this one before the auction."

"I want better. You identified this one barely a day before the auction. I want them classified within the first week."

"Yes, Sir. I'll see to it."

"Be sure that you do. Onto other matters, the payments for your staff are over there on the table. Make sure they remain happy and silent."

"Thank you, Sir. I will do that."

"After they finish cleaning the room, and processing the bodies, make sure they clean and disinfect the cells. I don't want any DNA left behind in any of them. As usual, I will make a thorough inspection of their work. When I approve, they can have two weeks off. We scheduled the next group to arrive in six weeks. I want them back preparing for their arrival."

"Yes, Sir. I'll see that everything is as you wish."

"How are the deliveries coming along?"

"Many of the buyers took their purchases with them as they left. The rest will ship out within twelve hours."

"What about my purchase?"

"Your private transport is being readied as we speak. She'll be in the air by morning, along with the rest of your purchases. They will arrive at your compound two days hence."

"Good, that'll give me time to finish up my business here and be there upon arrival. I'm looking forward to breaking in this one. There's something special about this one. That fiery red hair may have something to do with that." The chairman said with a smile on his face.

"Sir, may I ask you a personal question?"

"Within reason…"

"Sir, you buy several items at each auction, and yet, with this one, you took a special interest. You paid much more for that one than you normally would have. If I'm right, you paid over twice what we estimated she was worth. What is it about this one that caught your eye?"

Well, you're right. I paid more than I expected, but so what. I don't mind. What's money without being able to use it? Besides, I had fun outbidding that bitch who just wanted to cook her for dinner."

"That would have been a real shame. She's a real beauty, and to roast her, would be a real shame."

"Yes, indeed, there's something about her that intrigues me. She made me curious, and I want to see how that develops." The chairman reflected. "Tell me, did you buy something for yourself?"

"Yes, Sir. Thank you for the substantial discount."

"Think nothing of it. You perform a valuable service to the Consortium. The discount is small compensation for the work you do for us. Have fun, and enjoy yourself." The chairman remarked before turning his attention to his receipt ledger. Without looking up, he said. "Will there be anything else?"

"No, Sir. I was just leaving."

"Thank you. Just be sure to have the crew clean up the area before everyone leaves." The chairman said as his underling turned and left him alone.

Looking down at the ledgers, he opened his computer and began typing. By the time he had finished, he had transferred the assets of his purchases to his private accounts, less the Consortium's fifty percent cut. Even with the discount, he had made a tidy profit, most especially on the redhead. The hidden Cayman account had several million Euros in it, which he had just transferred into his private accounts.

Sitting back in his chair, he smiled at the thought that the fiery redheaded woman had just used her own money to sell herself into bondage.

The irony of the situation amused him.

Chapter Six

Twelve hours later, Avril found herself in a padded wooden box lying flat on her back. She could hardly move as the box barely the size of a coffin. Or maybe it was a coffin.

When they collected her at the auction house, they removed the handcuffs. They bound her hands together behind her back and escorted her to what appeared to be a warehouse.

Still naked and in her high-heels, they dropped her into the coffin. After tying her feet together with more cording and placing a breathing mask over her mouth and nose, they sealed it tight with what sounded like heavy metal latches. As the lid closed, she could hear and feel the whoosh of air as the lid's airtight seals isolated her from the rest of the world. Thankfully, her breathing mask supplied fresh air to breathe, and the cushioned coffin made it a somewhat comfortable resting place, even with her arms bound underneath her. However, after shutting her inside, it was so dark that she couldn't see a damned thing. She couldn't even sense the lid just inches from her nose.

After what seemed like forever, she felt them pick her up, coffin and all, and deposit her into what she presumed was a truck. After the faint sounds of the loading of more containers like hers, she heard the telltale sound of a freight door closing, and a moment later, the truck drove off.

An indeterminate time later, the truck came to rest, and they transferred her to an airplane. As soon as they finished loading, the plane took off to God knows where. Where she was going now was anyone's guess.

Falling asleep, the jolting of the airplane's wheels touching down awoke her with a start. They transferred her to a truck, which drove off when they finished unloading the plane. She fell asleep again. This cycle of sleep and awake continued for some time. She had given up trying to figure out what was happening out there. All she knew was that sometimes the truck would stop, unload, and continue its journey.

When they finally opened the lid to her coffin, she could hardly see a thing. After being in the dark for so long, bright light assaulted her eyes when they opened the coffin lid. All she wanted to do was shield her eyes. It was impossible, of course, with her hands still tied behind her back. All she could do was squeeze her eyelids shut.

As she dealt with the blinding light, she felt them cut away her feet bindings, as two sets of hands lifted her from the coffin. Walking between her escorts, they led her down a flight of stone steps and a stretching hallway.

With the subdued light, she carefully opened her eyes and looked around. Two burly men were escorting her down a long stone hallway with heavy wooden doors spaced about thirty feet apart on either side of the aisle. She figured there had to be at least twenty of these doorways and an unknown number behind her. They stopped in front of one door, about halfway down on the left. A guard took out a key, unlocked the door, and opened it.

After untying her hands and prodding her in the back, she stepped into what she presumed was her new cell. Before she could turn back towards the men, they locked the door behind her.

Turning to face the room and rubbing her wrists, she surveyed the cell. She expected that it would be a typical windowless small cold cell made of stone or block.

Astonishing Avril, the cell wasn't a cell at all, not in the usual sense of the word. Instead, she saw a well-appointed room found in any high-end resort. It was an elegant room with furnishings and draperies, enhancing its charm. The decor of the space used warm colors, comprising various reds, oranges, and gold. If she hadn't known better, she would have believed she was in a high-scale luxurious New York City hotel room worth thousands of dollars a day. Perhaps even sitting atop the Ritz-Carlton or The Plaza Hotel.

Continuing her inspection, she noted, sticking out to one side of the room, a king-size bed, with dual bedside tables anchoring it to the wall. On the mattress were sheets, a bedspread, and several throw pillows. The bedspread appeared to have gold threading stitched throughout the fabric. The sheets were to die for; to her critical eye, she figured they were 1000 count fine Egyptian cotton sheets.

Around the windowless room, silky crepe drapes hung from the walls' tops and cascaded onto the floor, implying an elegant living space rather than a prison cell. There was a sitting area of an upholstered feminine loveseat, a masculine looking wingback chair, a rectangular coffee table, and a small area rug. A small desk, complete with a chair, sat next to the loveseat. Missing was any sign of media or electronic devices of any kind. There wasn't a television, radio, media player, clock, or computer anywhere in sight.

The prominent coffee table concerned her, as it seemed out of place and stood out from the rest of the delicate furnishings. It was approximately three by five feet and had a thick top sitting on short, sturdy legs. It had a heft to it that contrasted with the finer furnishings in the room.

On the far side of the room were two doors. Upon investigation, they revealed a decent-sized walk-in closet and a luxurious en-suite. Investigating the closet first, Avril discovered a full-sized room filled with several evening gowns, jewelry, and erotic lingerie. All the clothing was in all sorts of coordinating colors and fabrics. She did not find regular underwear, shirts, slacks, tops, socks, and shoes such as sneakers, which, in one way, did not surprise her. It meant the clothing was for show rather than for comfortable, everyday wear. Avril shook her head in disappointment.

Inspecting the en-suite, she found a large curbless open shower with multiple heads, a toilet, a bidet, and a scrumptious bathtub built for two. The tub had lights and water jets galore, and she imagined that she would spend quite some time in it. On the vanity, she found an assortment of designer body washes, shampoos, and conditioners. Some were brands she fancied, while others were of a superior brand she could ill afford. In one of the vanity drawers, she found a vast assortment of makeup, including many of her favorites. Of the rest, she would need a makeup artist to learn how to apply them.

Shaking her head in disbelief, she muttered. "Man, they really do know a lot about me." Returning to the center room, she noticed a note sitting on the top of the bed. Picking it up, Avril started reading.

'Welcome to your new home. I hope you will find your stay here comfortable and relaxing.'

Avril snorted, "Yeah, right, it's still a prison."

'Unless otherwise directed, you will remain naked and wear only the high-heel shoes given to you at the training center at all times, including when you sleep at night.'

"What? Wear the heels to bed?" she squawked.

'In the desk drawer, you will find a book outlining the rules. You will obey them at all times. Failure to follow the rules will earn you severe disciplinary action. I sincerely hope you will avoid punishment, as I assure you, punishments are excruciating. I will undoubtedly enjoy disciplining you should you violate even a single rule.'

"No doubt, seeing what I've observed over the past couple of weeks," she conceded.

'The clothing and things in the closet will remain untouched until I give you specific instructions to wear them.'

Avril just nodded, having already expected this turn of events, taking a brief look at the closet door. Returning to the note, it continued.

'Meals and drink will be delivered to your room through an access panel in the en-suite. Assuming you follow the rules, you will be well nourished. Failure to follow the rules may result in missed meals. You will keep the room clean and straightened up at all times. You will make the bed immediately after you wake and unless otherwise directed, it will remain made throughout the day.'

The note finished with one further command.

'You have one hour to shower and clean yourself up. Shave your legs, underarms, and pubis. I expect you hairless from the neck down at all times during your stay. In time, you will receive laser hair removal treatments, thereby making shaving obsolete.'

'Put your heels back on immediately after your shower and await me, kneeling in the designated spot. See rule number fifty in the rulebook for my exact expectations. In the meantime, study the rulebook while you wait. How long or short your stay here is up to you. It should come as no surprise to you. This is the last home you will ever have.'

Dropping the note on the bed, Avril leaned back, supporting herself on her hands, and looked around. With a sigh, she leaned down, removed her heels, and walked to the shower.

Exactly one hour later, nude, showered, shaved, and wearing her heels, Avril sat down on the loveseat with the rulebook, flipping through the many pages. The book was approximately nine by twelve inches in size with an embossed leather cover and, unsurprisingly, contained a whopping two hundred and forty-nine rules and regulations.

As she read, she realized it would take her months to know entirely and understand the rules. She also realized that she would not have the months necessary to memorize them all. She was destined for punishment when and not if she broke them. She had placed the note inside the back cover of the rulebook, and after dropping it on the desk, she closed her eyes. After everything she had gone through, it bewildered her by the events of the last two weeks.

"Was it just two weeks ago, where she had a normal life, going to work, running, and going out at night? What the hell happened anyway?" She asked herself.

The rulebook dealt with dress, cleanliness, behaviors, and similar manners of behavior. As Avril studied it, it was apparent to Avril that her captor expected her to entertain male and female visitors, satisfying their deviant needs, presumably sexual, on a whim.

Eyes still closed, reflecting upon her situation, Avril almost missed the turning lock on her door. When it finally registered, she looked up in a panic and tried to kneel in the floor's designated spot. Just as she got into position, the door opened, and a man dressed in a dark charcoal gray suit, light gray shirt, and a silver-gray tie walked in. Knowing that there was no alternative, she finished kneeling on the required spot, clasped her hands behind her back, and stared at the floor.

"Slow, all too slow," he said to her. "Next time, I expect you to follow directions and kneel exactly when told."

"Yes, Sir," Avril answered.

"Stand up," he commanded her.

Avril stood up as gracefully as she could manage without assistance.

"Practice that. I expect improvement the next time." He scolded her as he walked around, inspecting, and evaluating her. She hoped he would tell her how pleased he was with her effort in preparing for him. She did not get it.

"Tomorrow, someone will be by to wax you, then every few days as needed. Be warned, nicking yourself while shaving will not do, and you will incur my wrath."

She stood there, mute.

"What's rule number one from the book?" He asked her.

"Never, under any circumstances, lie to you or anyone in this house."

"Good. Never forget it. Should you lie, I will know about it. Lying will gain you the severest of punishments. So, you know, you are destined for punishment, and I will enjoy giving it to you."

"I look forward to you earning your first punishment. What's rule number two?" he asked.

"Always refer to you as Sir, especially in all responses to your commands." She answered immediately.

"Did you?" He pressed.

Uncertainty immediately displayed on her face.

"Well? Answer me! Did you?" he demanded.

"Ah… yes, Sir. At least I think so," she replied.

"Yes or no, I will not tolerate a qualifying answer. Yes or no, I will not ask again."

"Ummm, no Sir," she guessed, believing that she would still fail his query and incur his discipline either way.

"Hm, you surprised me. I thought you were going to lie to me by saying yes. When you answered my question about rule number one, you failed to add Sir to the answer. What's rule number three?"

"Never apologize for my behavior, Sir."

"Why?"

"Because Sir, I won't mean it. As your property, it presumes that I will always resent you and would never apologize to you unless I can gain an advantage over you. Therefore, it is meaningless and a waste of breath."

"Hm, an intelligent answer, you continue to surprise me. Was that written anywhere in the rulebook?"

"No, Sir. Not that I have discovered so far," Avril responded.

"It's not. How did you come to that conclusion?"

"Sir, it's obvious. Rule three states never to apologize under any circumstances. The reason seemed clear to me."

"Well said. I ask you, should I include your reason in the next edition of the rulebook?"

Thinking carefully before responding, Avril said. "If it will please you, Sir, unless you have a reason for keeping it out."

"Hm, a well-crafted answer, yes, I do believe that you are as intelligent as they said you were."

Since he had not asked a direct question, Avril kept her mouth shut and did not respond.

"Turn to the bed and bend over. Keep your legs locked with your knees in contact with the side of the bed and place your head face down on the mattress." He commanded her.

She did as he ordered her.

"Spread your legs shoulder-width apart," he added.

She moved her feet apart, anticipating that he would fuck her, sticking his filthy dick inside her and getting his rocks off. Well, he could do it, but she wouldn't give him the satisfaction of enjoying it.

A moment later, she heard him undo his belt and slide it out of his trousers' belt loops. Assuming he was about to drop his pants, she suddenly felt a sharp, excruciating pain on her bare buttocks. Before she knew it, he had taken his belt to her. She yelped in agony as a burning sensation scorched across her bottom.

Gripping much of the bedspread with her fingers and holding on for dear life, she felt a second strike of the belt against her buttocks, adding fire to the already scorching sensation.

Screaming out, she couldn't help but express her pain and anger, mixing with her tears. As she was getting control over her body, he struck her again, eliciting more shrieking cries. Another one landed on her already burning flesh, adding to her misery.

Sucking air while processing the heated agony radiating from her buttocks, she bit down on the bedspread and bore down.

Just as she waited for another strike, he spoke to her once more.

"From now on, you will count out the strokes as they occur. No exceptions. Failure to count will cause additional strikes. You will find this in the rule book. Follow it. Repeat to me what I just told you?"

Between her tears and sucking air, she spat out the bedspread and croaked out.

"Count... out... as you... punish... me.... Missing... a count will... add more... strokes... Sir."

"Good. You're learning. Do you know why you earned your punishment?"

"Um... yes, Sir, at least I think so," she stammered between her tears, "for failing to... take my kneeling position immediately... after I showered... and when I failed to address you as... 'Sir'... when you asked me the question... about rule number one."

"And how many strokes did you earn for each of those infractions?"

It took her a moment to add up in her mind how many strokes he beat her with his belt. When she came up with four, she answered. "Ah... two, Sir."

"Is that a question or a statement?"

"A statement... Sir, two."

"Two. That is correct. The next infraction will incur five strokes. Do you understand?"

"Yes, Sir. Five strokes… for the next infraction."

"The following one after that will incur ten strokes for each violation of the rules. Look up rule number fourteen. I will grant you a pass on missing that one, but your pass expires the moment I leave the room." He said to her, with a commanding attitude in her tone.

"Clean yourself up and put on the emerald-green silk evening gown. You have one hour before I collect you for dinner." He finished.

"Yes, Sir, I'll be ready."

"Good, you may stand up. Wait for me to leave before you go wash up."

Avril stood up, faced him, dropped her eyes, and clasped her hands behind her back as the book instructed her to do. The heat radiating from her behind warmed her hands.

"Sir, if it permitted, may I ask a question?"

"Go on."

"Do you have a name?"

"Yes, I do, but for now, to you, my only name is 'Sir.'"

"Yes, Sir," she answered, grateful that he hadn't punished her for asking a question. "Oh, shit! Is there a rule in the book about asking questions?" she thought to herself, her expression telegraphing her sudden dread.

"Ah, I see you just realized that yes, there is a rule about asking questions. Find it and when I return, report to me its number and its full language. I will also want your interpretation of the rule."

With that, he walked out of the room, closing and locking the door behind him.

Rubbing her hands on her aching backside, Avril considered that she might not be able to sit at dinner tonight.

Hm, she was confident that it was going to be an uncomfortable dinner for sure.

"Right now, I need to find that rule. I can memorize it while I clean up." She muttered to herself as she made for the en-suite.

Chapter Seven

She had found the rule, number one hundred and thirty-seven to be exact.

It stated,

'Never ask a question until you are given permission beforehand.'

Using the facilities, she repeated the rule in her head. She continued to recite it out loud as she showered. Avril resisted the urge to inspect her ravaged bottom. As she finished with her hair and makeup, her resistance wavered, and she spun her head around so that she could see her backside in the mirror.

As expected, her ass exhibited four bright red swaths across both buttocks. They looked angry, as if they blamed her for their very existence. Well, they were right. If she hadn't failed, they would not exist. By tomorrow, they would look even angrier.

The more she thought about the marks, the more confident she was that he would have kept at her until she failed at something, anything. She now knew he intended to give her a beating even before he stepped into her room.

"Bastard," she muttered under her breath.

The emerald green silk dress he told her to wear was exquisite. The silk slid easily over her body, hugging every one of her curves in all the right places. Even though she wasn't wearing panties and the dress left a breast completely exposed, it felt good to wear something again.

High quality, high-density fabric in a solid shimmery fuck-me emerald green color dress had no additional adornments woven into the material. White piping sewn into the left shoulder strap, bisecting her breasts, left her right breast entirely exposed, and carried around her back before returning to her shoulder. The hemline mimicked the shoulder strap's asymmetrical cut, starting high on her left hip, ended at just above the right knee, before returning to her hip, slicing over the left ass's cheek. The angry red welts from the beating glared beyond the hemline, drawing attention to her punishments to any casual observer.

Still, after being nude for the past two weeks, having something to wear made her feel more like a woman again. After smoothing out the dress, she couldn't help wonder how perfectly it fit. How did they know her exact measurements? She didn't know how her abductors had managed it. Just how they knew so much about her private life was beyond her.

Since there was nothing to gauge time with, she didn't want to risk another beating. She tried to get into position well before he returned. Before moving to kneel, she reread the book's rule to make sure she got it right. She replaced the rulebook on the desk with a cleansing breath, satisfied she knew the regulation. Kneeling in the specified spot, she took the required pose and was ready and waiting for him to come for her.

As she knelt, keeping her very sore bottom from resting on the back of her heels, she reflected how much her life had changed in the past two weeks. She wondered just how long it would take to sit comfortably again and whether she could ever get used to kneeling for this bastard. She was not one to surrender control quickly, but by God, she would do it until an opportunity to escape this nightmare presented itself. Until then, she would grin and bear it, determined to escape. She had just thought about her family and coworkers when she heard the lock turn. Kneeling up in attention, as required by the book, her hands once more clasped behind her back, and eyes focused on the floor, she was ready for him to see her in compliance with his demands.

The door opened, and he barely crossed the threshold of the room. He said, "Attend me," before turning his back, facing down the hallway.

She had hoped he would ask her to recite the rule he instructed her to find. Alas, it was almost as if he didn't care whether or not she knew it. Upon reflection, she recognized that he already knew she found it and had obeyed his instruction. Getting up as quickly as she could, almost tripping over the hem of her dress, she slid in alongside him.

"Take my arm," he told her, and so she did. Together, they walked down the hallway and up the stone steps to the main level.

The view that greeted her amazed her. She had envisioned a very different space from what she saw. Instead of the elegant fabrics and elaborate turnings and woodwork, she discovered an ultra-modern room, decorated in cobalt blues and vibrant whites with black accents. A silver crystal chandelier adorned the foyer with matching silver crystal sconces lining the room. They had exited the 'basement' from a stairway at the rear of the entrance hallway. A grand double door faced them.

On either side of the door stood two naked women wearing silver chokers tight to their necks and thigh-high stockings with little bows affixed to their tops. Each stood on highly polished stilettos. One woman was wearing white stockings and heels while the other wore black ones. The woman wearing white was darkly tanned, while the woman in black had pasty white skin. It looked to Avril as if she hadn't seen sunlight in a year, which might very well be true. The hair on their heads cascaded down like a lazy river rippling over rocks in the stream. However, their carefully arranged hair avoided covering their exquisite breasts. Both sported a crystal dangling from their nipple rings and the tops of their vulva. Like herself, they were without a trace of hair from the neck down.

"One day, like them, you may earn the honor of presenting my guests. For now, you will serve us as we drink and dine. Stand over there by the bar. As my guests arrive, you will serve them drinks. The bartender will know what each guest prefers. You will not speak to any of my guests or the other servants. You will not spill a single drink. Serve them as you would attend me and then stand in the corner until needed again. Pay attention to any guest with an empty glass and have a replacement ready before asking for one. Do I make myself clear?"

"Yes, Sir. Serve drinks to your guests and make sure they always have a fresh one on hand."

"Very good. When we sit down for dinner, it will be your job to pour the wine for each guest and keep their glasses filled. Go now and attend to your duties."

"Yes, Sir," Avril answered and turned towards the bar. So far, none of his guests had arrived, but the bartender seemed ready to pour as they made their appearance. The bartender was a minimally dressed, full-chested woman, just like every servant.

"Wow," Avril realized, "she was a servant just like them." She had voluminous breasts that completely dominated her frame. They looked heavy, and Avril was glad that her breasts were of a more manageable size.

The bartender wore what looked like a tuxedo collar and bow tie over a silver choker around her neck, but without the customary blouse. On top of her dark brown hair, she wore a featured black hat, tilted to one side and adorned with various beads and sequins. She wore a short frilly skirt around her waist that seemed to sway back and forth as she walked on black high-heel stilts. The fabric did nothing to cover her nakedness underneath.

Facing the bartender, she gave her a questioning look, who turned her eyes over to the corner where she was to stand. Moving to the side, she took up her station, her back to the wall, her hands clasped behind her back, and waited.

The front doorbell rang just as a far-off grandfather clock chimed eight bells. Sir opened the door and greeted a man and a woman. Together they made for an elegant couple. As soon as the bartender saw who it was, she immediately turned and began preparing two drinks, a glass of white wine and a scotch on the rocks. As soon as the drinks were ready, she placed them on a serving tray and stepped back.

"That must be my cue," Avril thought to herself.

Picking up the tray, she approached the new arrivals and offered them their drinks. After they had retrieved their glasses from her tray, Avril turned and walked back to the bar. "Okay, white wine for the lady and scotch on the rocks for the gentleman," she repeated in her mind.

She had no sooner gotten back to her assigned corner when the bartender placed two more cocktails on her tray and pointed to a new couple entering the room. Jumping to action, Avril raced over and delivered the refreshments. Over the next fifteen minutes, three more couples arrived. She found it hard-pressed to keep up with the demand. Finally, another couple appeared, this time, two women. Avril got the drinks to them without issue. However, she realized that the first couple's glasses were nearly empty. Turning to the bartender, she pointed them out to the bartender with the query on her face requesting fresh drinks. Avril noticed a new set of glasses already resting on a serving tray when the bartender pointed down.

Nodding her acknowledgment, she put her empty tray down and picked up the fresh one. Navigating around to her intended targets, a different person picked one of the new drinks from her tray and replaced it with an empty one. Horrified, she turned on her heels and retrieved a fresh drink from the bar. This time, she successfully met up with her targets and exchanged empty glasses with full ones. Without missing a beat, she avoided the original transgressor and returned to the bar. With a willful sigh, six more drinks were waiting for her. Picking up the serving tray, she returned to the crowd. Panic rose in her throat as she forgot to whom to deliver the glasses.

This time, she mingled and allowed his guests to replace their empty glass with a fresh one. As she walked about, she got the sense that the group was intentionally trying to screw with her. She was sure that the lady with the white wine had changed to a mixed cocktail, and another selected a red wine over the white she had been drinking. The gentlemen were a bit kinder, preferring their drink of choice rather than mixing it up on her. Returning to the bar, Avril couldn't help shake the distinct feeling that all eyes were upon her, searching for an opportunity to force her to make a mistake. Well, two can play that game, she thought to herself, resolving to perform flawlessly.

After about an hour, Sir and his guests migrated to the expansive dining room. She was astounded to see a naked woman laid out on the dining table's center. The woman had various finger foods and fruits resting all across and around her body and face. As the diners sat down, they waited for their host to select the first morsel. Sir picked a strawberry from the girl's pubis and, smiling, popped it into his mouth. In the meantime, Avril scanned the glasses in front of all the diners. Seeing empty wine glasses on the table, she turned and noticed several bottles of white wine.

Reaching for the corkscrew, she was about to pull the cork from a bottle when she heard, "Shall we start with a toast of champagne?"

Noting empty champagne glasses and several bottles on the serving buffet, she recovered and picked up the first of the champagne bottles. Popping the cork, holding it in her hand to prevent it from flying off, she poured champagne in each of the glasses and delivered them around the table. Returning to her post alongside the buffet, she stood back and waited.

As dinner proceeded, Avril was feeling good about herself. While she felt as though her situation wasn't of her choosing, she was determined to remain alive until she could make her escape. She did as she was told and strived to stay out of trouble, making the best of things.

"Your new acquisition is intriguing. May I examine her?" She suddenly heard from one of the woman guests at the table.

"Certainly. Just understand, I haven't yet availed myself of my privilege," Sir responded.

Smiling, the woman pushed back her chair and walked around the table, stopping in front of Avril. Gulping ever so slightly, Avril cast her eyes downward while maintaining her attentive posture. Feeling the eyes of the woman grazing up and down her body, Avril waited.

"She's fabulous, perfect in every detail. I love the dress. I suspect she would look even better without it. I see you haven't put her training collar on yet. Why not?" She asked Sir without removing her inspection of Avril.

"In time, my dear. The bitch only just arrived a few hours ago. I'm seeing just how she behaves on her first night here."

"Oh, that's a first. Don't you usually cage and beat them into submission before putting them on display?"

"Normally, yes, but I thought I would try a different tack with this one. I sense something in her that excites me. I want to see if I can root it out."

"Hm, well, good luck with that. I see she's holding back, even now."

"You have a keen eye, my dear," Sir confirmed. As he spoke, the woman began stroking her body, first starting with her bare neck, shoulders, and arms before moving on to her breast. Cupping it in her hand, she played with her nipple, feeling it harden. Avril sucked in a cleansing breath, as her nipple was still extremely sensitive after the piercing two weeks earlier.

Rubbing the ball of her thumb across the nipple, the woman felt its texture and hardness grow under her touch. As part of her fondling, she cradled it between her thumb and forefinger and pinched it hard. The nipple turned white, and Avril sucked in a soft cleansing breath, holding back her discomfort. Clenching her jaw tight, she stifled her discomfort as the woman dug a fingernail into her tender flesh. Avril struggled to maintain her composure until the woman released her grip. Exhaling, she felt a sigh of relief mixed with pain as blood returned to the abused nipple.

After a time, the woman continued the caressing inspection of Avril's body, slowly drawing her hand down her side, over her hips and thigh. Avril tried to ignore the touch, but just then, the woman suddenly reached under the dress, and forcibly grabbed her pussy, and stuffed a finger inside her. Startled, Avril involuntarily shrieked and looked the woman right in the eyes. The woman smiled as she continued swirling the finger inside her. Stroking in and out while twisting the finger, the woman explored every nook and cranny of her interior.

Thankfully, she finally extracted the finger from her vagina and, placing it in her mouth, tasted Avril's wetness. "Delicious," she said with a gleeful grin before turning away and returning to her seat. "I can tell you this much. She's got a tasty cunt. Too bad it's going to waste."

The others around the table chuckled, knowing something Avril didn't.

"I would like to book an appointment," she said to Sir.

"I'll arrange it, just not tonight. As I mentioned before, I have not yet taken my privilege." "Oh, no rush," she replied. "When she's ready, put me down for a session."

At that, the other guests also made requests for an appointment. Sir just replied, "You're all in the book. I'll let you know when."

Just like that, the dinner party broke up. Since she didn't have any new instructions, Avril remained standing next to the wine buffet while he escorted his guests from the room.

A long time later, Sir came back and ordered her. "Come with me."

Falling in behind him, she followed him to the stairwell leading to her room. Gingerly walking down the stone steps to avoid losing her balance, she followed him, expecting him to lock her in her cell. However, immediately after entering her room, he said. "Take that off."

Nervous, she slid the silk gown off and let it fall to her feet. Stepping out of it, she bent over to pick it up. "Leave it," Sir commanded, followed by "Come," he said in a defined, forceful tone.

Walking out of the room, he turned away from the stairwell. Following behind, Avril tried to stay with him. However, he was walking so quickly that she almost had to run to keep up with him. Stopping at the end of the hallway, he turned to a door on the right and opened it. She followed him inside.

"You embarrassed me," Sir reported, "and now you will pay for your insubordination."

He grabbed her by the wrist and dragged her over to the wall. Hanging high on the wall was a pair of shackles. Pulling her wrist roughly over her head, he locked it around her wrist. Grabbing her other wrist, he secured her to the second shackle and stepped back.

As she hung from the restraints, her feet barely touched the floor, and the sharp edge of the shackles dug into the flesh around her hands. Despite how high her shoes were, the heels seemed to float just above the floor. She could not plant her feet without painfully stretching and pinching her wrists.

"No dinner for you tonight, and I haven't yet decided how long to keep you there. I may keep you there for several days. That's how egregious I consider your behavior was."

Stepping back, he studied her for a time, finally settling on the look of "What did I do wrong?' plainly written on her face.

"Do you know how you embarrassed me?"

"Ah, no, Sir, I don't. I honestly thought that I had done well with the assignment." Avril answered him.

"You screeched when she touched you. You should have allowed her without the theatrics."

"She stuck her finger inside me, roughly I might add, and... um, um...' she yelled, trying to explain herself. Her defense fell upon deaf ears. Realizing that, Avril tied another tactic.

"I'm sorry, Sir. She just caught me by surprise. I apologize for embarrassing you."

"What's rule number three?"

"Um... never apologize for my behavior... Sir," she answered, almost forgetting to add the word Sir to her reply. "Yes, I broke that rule as well."

"You did indeed."

"Yes, Sir," she added.

"As an added incentive to reflect upon your abysmal behavior, you're going to wear this." He said as he picked up a ball gag from a nearby table. Stuffing the ball into her mouth, he pushed her head downwards so that he could buckle it in place behind her head. Satisfied it was nice and tight, with the ball pulled back deeply into her mouth, he stepped back to review her image.

"I'll leave you to reflect upon your behavior. I hope you will learn from this experience and rectify your atrocious behavior," Sir said, stepping out of the room and closing the door behind him.

A moment later, she heard him lock the door, and an eerie silence settled in. With the door closed, Avril found herself in complete darkness. Not even a sliver of light peeked through the doorframe. Sighing a deep breath, she wiggled the chains of the shackles in frustration. Minutes later, she was yelling through her gag in frustration and rage, roughly yanking on her chains. Her intelligence was telling her that she was going to be there for a while. It also said that she didn't deserve the treatment he forced upon her.

It was going to be a long night and perhaps many long days.

"Shit!" she uttered in complete frustration, mixed with a bit of defeat.

Chapter Eight

The sound of the door unlocking and opening did little to stir Avril. The sound registered in her brain, but she was too weak, too hungry, and too thirsty to acknowledge it. Avril sensed Sir coming in and unshackling her. Throwing her over his shoulders like a sack of potatoes, he carried her back to her room. Dropping her on the bed, he left, closing and locking the door behind him. Curling up into a fetal position and ignoring the gag still securely seated in her mouth and fastened around her head, she fell asleep.

Later, she stirred from a restless, terror-filled dream state and opened her eyes. Slowly, they focused, and the blurry image of her room resolved into clarity. Shivering with cold, she managed, with some difficulty, to pull back the covers and slide underneath them. It took a while to get comfortable. Between the choking ball gag in her mouth, the severe achiness in her wrists, and the fucking spikes of her heels snagging on the sheets, she struggled to get comfortable. Eventually, fatigue won out, and she fell peacefully asleep.

Many hours later, she stirred again. Groaning, it took a while to recall just where she was. In a flash, Avril remembered. She was a prisoner, or rather, she was more than that. She was a peon, sold to some bastard that had bought her at auction. Grumbling, resting her arm over her eyes, she laid there contemplating her situation. She was in a bad way, that was for sure. Thankfully, the gag was gone, though she couldn't remember when he removed it. She flexed her jaw subconsciously, soothing her stretched jaw muscles. Her bladder aching for attention, she gave in and threw the covers back and dropped her feet to the floor. Just as she was about to stand up, startled, she saw Sir sitting there on the wingback chair, watching her.

"Ah, I'm sorr... um, good morning, Sir."

"Good morning, sleepyhead. Go take care of yourself. Clean yourself up and leave the door open. After you thoroughly wash and get ready for the day, and not a moment before, come back out and join me."

"Yes, Sir."

Shit, how long was he sitting there? She asked herself silently. How long was I hanging there on the wall, and how long was I sleeping in bed? Fuck! These thoughts and more raced through her mind as she made her way to the en-suite and sat down on the toilet. She tried hard to suppress the sound of her peeing, but it echoed loudly throughout the space. A sudden passing of gas added to the reverberating echo inside the bowl. Resigned to taking care of the need rather than being ladylike, she finished her business and flushed.

Turning on the shower to warm it, she brushed her teeth before removing her heels and stepped under the hot water. She let it run hot this time, turning her skin pink. However, the bruises on her ass forced her to adjust the taps to a tolerable temperature. While the hot water felt grand everywhere else, it was a pure, burning fiery pain on her ass. She almost shrieked when the scorching water first touched her bruised buttocks. As the water cascaded down her body, she inspected her wrists. The ligature marks were a bit raw. Overall, they weren't too bad. She estimated that it would take only a day or so for the marks to fade.

She took her time in the shower, ensuring that she was clean, inside and out. She even made sure her ass was immaculate before doing the same to her fingernails. Finally satisfied, she shampooed and conditioned her hair. Feeling better overall, she stepped out and toweled off before using the hairdryer to complete the routine. She didn't know how long it took her to do as he asked, but she didn't care at this point. He told her to clean herself up, so that is what she did.

After putting on the cursed heels and applying a minimal amount of makeup, she walked out of the en-suite, naked as usual, prepared for an inspection. Instead, she found him sitting at a small round table with breakfast laid out. Standing, he went up to her, briefly held her by her shoulders, and kissed her on the cheek. Just as quickly, he held out a chair for her at the table. Hesitation abruptly passed through her thoughts before she accepted his offer of a seat. Sitting down on her bruised bottom, as ladylike as could manage, she waited for him to sit.

"I thought you would like breakfast. You must be hungry."

"Yes, Sir. I am. Thank you, Sir."

"You've been asleep in that bed for almost two entire days."

Now that was a surprise. "Really, Sir? I had no idea."

"Really."

"Sir, I have a question if you will permit me." Nodding his permission, she continued. "Sir, about my punishment after the dinner party, how long was I there?"

"Until mid-afternoon the next day, about twelve hours, I think."

Nodding to herself, she maintained her silence, reflecting upon what he told her. Since he had only given her permission to ask a single question, the rest would have to wait.

"Do you remember why you earned the punishment?"

"If I recall correctly, you said I embarrassed you, though I did not mean to, Sir."

"Is that an excuse?"

"No, Sir. I just wanted you to know that there was no intent involved in my behavior. I was just startled when your guest grabbed me and stuck her finger inside me that way."

"I suggest you get used to it. I expect that and much more of you. However, enough of that now, please eat. You will need all your strength."

Staring at her fork, Avril contemplated for a moment about shoving it into his eye before she came to her senses and cast her gaze to the bounty. A bounty of food, including fresh fruit, bacon, scrambled eggs, toast, home fries, oatmeal, and juices, lay across the table."

"Would you like some coffee?" he asked.

"Thank you. I would, Sir."

He poured a cup and passed it to her. She found it interesting that it was a blend almost precisely as she would have made at home. As she sipped the hot coffee, she came to believe that it was, in fact, her favorite brand and blend. This realization reaffirmed that he and the kidnappers knew everything about her. They knew right down to the coffee she liked to drink.

After placing the cloth napkin on her lap, she selected a small bowl and filled it with fresh fruit. After she had finished that, she scooped hearty portions of the bacon and eggs onto her plate. She also dished up a bowl of oatmeal, garnished with a tablespoon of brown sugar. Shit, he even knew how she liked to eat her oatmeal.

Picking up the fork, she tried to eat slowly, relishing every morsel. Not knowing how many meals she skipped, her hunger took over, and she found it impossible to eat slowly. Together, they ate in silence. It wasn't long before she had finished a second helping and put down her fork, and wiped her mouth on the napkin.

Leaning back, she drank more of the coffee and studied her captor, now her owner.

"Good?" he asked her.

"Yes, Sir. Thank you, Sir."

"You're welcome. The rest of the day is yours. I will leave you in peace. Eat, sleep, and study the rulebook, whatever you want to do. I shall not return until tomorrow when your training starts in earnest."

Just like that, he left, leaving her alone, and locked in her room. Looking around, she sighed and drank more of her coffee. Just what the fuck was up with him. He was controlling and cruel for sure, but he could also be gentle and compassionate.

She had never met anyone like him before.

The following morning, a ceiling light came on in her room, presumably an artificial indicator of the next morning. Stirring from her slumber, she groaned and rolled out of bed. Gingerly making her way to the en-suite, she used the facilities and showered. As hot water cascaded down around her, she realized that her ass didn't hurt as much as it did yesterday.

"That's a relief," she mumbled to herself.

As she washed, she reflected upon what happened yesterday. After drying her hair and putting her heels back on, she made the bed and cleaned the room.

She spent a significant amount of time reading the rulebook. She practiced imagining hearing the key entering the lock. She repeatedly practiced jumping up and kneeling in the prescribed spot before the door opened, and he came in. Mostly, the timing was tight. She felt she had moved fast enough to be in position before he entered the room. However, the proof was in reality, which would only happen when he came for her.

She quickly ate the breakfast she found in the food slot and returned the dirty dishes to the alcove. She stayed close to the designated spot, moving the desk chair nearby to ensure a quick response. She had just sat down when she heard the key's scratching in the lock.

Jumping down to her knees, she shoved the chair over to the desk and settled into her kneeling pose. She was more than ready when the door opened, and Sir stepped in.

"Perfect. From now on, as soon as you finish breakfast, you will assume that pose until I come to get you. No sitting down and jumping into position just before I arrive. You will kneel there for as long as it takes until I come for you. It may be as little as a couple of minutes to several hours. Failure to maintain the pose will result in disciplinary action. Do you understand?"

"Yes, Sir."

"How the hell did he know what I was doing?" Avril wondered, keeping the question to herself.

"Restate my request in your own words." Sir directed.

"Yes, Sir. As soon as I finish with my morning routine of washing, making up the room, and eating breakfast, I am to kneel in this spot, just as I am now. I am to stay in position and wait until you release me personally, no matter how long it takes."

"That is correct. Remember it. Now, do you know why you are here?"

"Ah, no, Sir, that is, I know that you bought me at auction, and that is how I ended up here. However, I do not know why they took me in the first place, nor why I came to be your possession."

"The simple answer to my question is. You're here to please me. That is why you are here; to please me."

Maintaining her posture, she waited for him to continue.

"What do you think about that?"

"Honestly, Sir, I don't like it. I was taken without my consent, against my will, and sold into bondage. I did not choose this life, and I don't want to be here. However, notwithstanding, I am here, and I intend to make the best of it."

"A real honest answer, I like that. However, I understand that there is more to your response than you shared. You intend to make the best of it until you can escape. Is that not correct?"

Avril nodded at his answer, as what could she do? He was right. At the first chance she got, she intended to escape this horror.

After Avril nodded, Sir continued. "To be clear, I don't care whether or not you want to be here. You are here. I have you, and I intend to keep you. I own you, and you are my property. You will stay for as long as I wish it, and for as long as you please me. There is no escape, no returning to your old life. Even if you escape, you can never return to your old life. I will hunt you down, recapture, and return you to here. Your old life is over. You might as well accept that. You will remain here for the rest of your life, for as long or as short as it may last, or until I pass you to someone less benevolent than I am."

As he finished, Avril noticed that he reached into his jacket pocket and withdrew what appeared to be a silver hoop, about a half-inch thick and maybe a half-foot in diameter. She had no idea what he intended to do with it, but one thing was sure. He intended it for her, and she would not like it. As he walked past her, he continued his monolog.

"As you saw at the dinner party the other night, you are not the first to come into my possession, and you will certainly not be the last. How much you come to accept your stay here and how much you enjoy it is entirely up to you. You can have a somewhat comfortable life here. This room is a testament to that. However, I could just as easily move you to another room similar to the one you spent the other night in and make it your permanent quarters. I guarantee that your stay in that room will not be pleasant. The amenities in this room, the ones I grant, and you enjoy, will end. It's up to you. I suggest you do make the best of it. In that regard, you are in complete control of your destiny here."

Sir paused, allowing her a moment to reflect upon his comments, before proceeding.

"Therefore, the answer to my question is simple. You will earn your keep, you will entertain my guests, you will attend to me, as one of my many possessions, and you will please me."

As he said this, he took the hoop and placed it around her neck. After snapping it in place using an odd tool, he secured it snug around her neck. It was, oh, so tight that at first, she could barely take a breath. As her fear diminished, her breathing became more comfortable.

"This is a training collar. It designates that you are my property. Anyone who sees you wearing it will know that you are mine. No one will touch you without my permission. Nod if you understand."

Avril nodded ever so slowly, swallowing her fear at its meaning.

"You cannot remove the collar. It isn't locked in place in the usual sense. It uses a unique seal of custom design that only I can unlock. The collar has a locator chip, allowing me to know where you are at all times, anywhere in the world. The chip will also activate my security system should you approach any forbidden areas, incapacitating you. In time, you will learn where these areas are. I'm sure you already know the important places, such as any door or window that leads to the outside. If you approach a forbidden area, you will feel a warning buzz at the back of your neck."

"Backing away will automatically stop the buzzing. Ignoring it will deliver excruciating pain, pain as you have never felt before. It will incapacitate you as you scream inside your head until I turn it off. By itself, the collar should not harm you, but I make no promises. Excessive, prolonged activation can cause paralysis or brain injury. I also can't say the same when you fall to the ground after activation."

"At least one of my girls died from hitting their head, unable to control their fall after testing the collar's strength. Theoretically, you can last hours or even days thrashing in pain and anguish to where you will wish you were dead. However, to date, no one has tested that feature for more than an hour or so. You are free to try it. I'd welcome watching you writhe in agony."

"Oh, one last thing. Don't remove or cut it off. Embedded in the collar is a circuit that maintains the integrity of a lethal charge. Any attempt to remove or cut the collar off will disrupt the circuit and instantly separate your head from your body. I suggest you don't test its limits. Do you have any questions?"

"Sir, how long must I wear it?" she asked hesitantly.

"Oh, I thought that you would know the answer to that question. You will wear it for the rest of your life. I may swap it out for another from time to time. Some are more obvious than others. You saw some of those the other night at the dinner party. Yours informs the household and my guests of your standing within the house. That is, you are at the bottom and still in training. You have nowhere to go but up. They may tell you to do something. Unless I give explicit instructions to the contrary, you will do what they say, as if it were I who commands you. Life may be difficult for you during these early months, but I feel confident that you will successfully navigate the issues and learn to behave as I expect."

"Thank you, Sir, for my collar. I will remember your lesson." Avril answered cautiously, remembering rule fourteen in the book.

"Good, now stand up and approach the bed and bend over."

Gulping, fearing that she was about to receive another beating, Avril gently rubbed her still recovering bottom as she stood up and walked over to the bed. Bending over, she planted her face into the covers. Gritting her teeth and taking a substantial amount of the bedspread in her mouth, she waited for the first wallop. It never came. Instead, she felt his cock press up against her vulva and drive inside her. With long, firm strokes, he invaded her.

His stamina was incredible and seemed to last a day and a night. Even without a clock for reference, he carried on for a long time. He even breached her ass, using her slick juices as the only lubricant for her sphincter. He felt big. At first, she didn't know if she could accommodate his length and girth in her virginal anal opening. Perhaps that is why he fucked her pussy so much, presuming her wetness would flow, and ease his penetration into her rectum. Whatever it was, she found that he was an experienced lover.

Despite herself, her desire for relief grew and grew. Only he never let her cum. Instead, just as she seemed to tip over the edge, he would change their position and force her to restart her rise to relief.

During these shifts, she found that he demanded more and more from her. One time, in particular, he forced himself into her mouth and down her throat. Sure, she had blown guys before, but she was in control of the act. Now, he determined how fast and how deep he penetrated her. All she could do was to hold as he fucked her mouth. She gagged on his penetrations several times and discharged her stomach contents, coating both of them with bile and slime. He didn't seem to mind. After barely allowing her to recover, he would stuff his cock back down her throat until there was nothing more to retch up.

Back and forth he went, moving from hole to hole, thrusting his cock on what seemed to be a whim. After a while, Avril was sore. Her jaw ached, her pussy dried up, and her ass, well, it just felt like it was on fire. Hour after hour, it seemed as he took her. He came several times, shooting his cum into all of her places, and still, he maintained his erection and continued to take her. She couldn't fathom just how he did it.

Towards the end, she was lying flat on her stomach. Lying on top of her, pounding his cock in her ass, he grabbed her hair and pulled her head sharply back, and stuck his fingers down her throat. She coughed and gagged, dry retching. After that, he flipped her over on her back, wrapped his hands around her throat, choking her half to death. Her eyes rolled into the back of her head. Her lungs burned as he drove his cock relentlessly into her, begging for relief. It rarely came.

He never allowed her to climax, and when he finally rolled off her, she felt like a jellyfish, washed up on the shore, and unable to move at all. There was nothing left in her, nothing more she could give. Exhausted, she didn't have the energy to move even a finger. She felt spent and used up.

Getting up, he dressed and told her on his way out. "Now, you are mine. Never forget that. Clean yourself up. You will find clean sheets in the en-suite. Put them on and throw the dirty ones down the laundry chute. Tomorrow, we begin again."

Groaning, not caring whether or not he heard it, she buried her head in the pillow and wept.

Chapter Nine

For Avril, the routine was the same for days and maybe weeks on end. She had lost count of the number of days she had been there. Every day was the same. She woke up, washed and made up the room, and then ate breakfast. Sometimes she ate with him and sometimes not. Kneeling in her appointed spot each morning was at first hard. Sometimes, he made her wait for hours before he came to her. He ravaged her for hours each day. She thought she was going to die each time he violated her. Always, by the time he left, she was limp, sore, and unsatisfied. Her body confused her. She knew that he would not give her the satisfaction it craved, but her body didn't care. It responded to him as if he was going to bring her to climax. Denying her climaxes frustrated her terribly.

During these same weeks, Avril earned herself several punishments, most for the tiniest of infractions. She didn't understand his decisions when she appeared to break a rule and when she didn't. It didn't matter, as every few days, she found herself beaten with his belt. The last few times, he used a thin bamboo cane. She didn't know which was worse, the belt or the cane. Both hurt a lot, but eventually, she came to admit that the cane was worse. The only difference that she could tell was that while the belt burned, the cane stung with a sharp, biting agony that left behind long, narrow, lingering stripes. Caning her did more severe damage to her bottom and took longer to heal. After a while, she gave up trying to figure out his punishments and grew to expect them.

Once a week, after he finished taking her, one of his servants would come in, dragging a machine behind her. Sitting in his chair, Sir watched as the servant stripped the hair on her body from her body with laser treatments. As the weeks went by, the girl treated her legs, arms, pubis, underarms, and any area with even a hint of body hair. It took many weeks to ensure that all traces of hair below her neck vanished forever. The tingling felt odd as the laser slowly moved across her skin, the whiff of burnt hair occasionally floating past her nostrils. Initially, it bothered her to have the girl there with the smell of sex still permeating the air after her session with him. Sir sat in his chair observing the proceedings, occasionally interjecting comments to the girl to ensure she got it perfect. After a few sessions, Avril almost forgot that he sat there, watching her and the girl performing the laser treatments. Between treatment days, Avril noticed that the need for shaving slackened. Eventually, the need for shaving became a thing of the past.

The only good thing about the experience was that she got better at accommodating his cock more easily. From the moment he stepped into the room, her femininity instantly became wet. By the time he pushed inside her, she was dripping and didn't need any additional lubrication. She no longer spit-up when he shoved his cock down her throat, holding it there until her lungs burned for air. She even learned how to relax her sphincter, making it easier to penetrate her ass, his cock sliding into her more comfortable than the last time. Her body still begged for a climax, but he had not yet granted her this simple pleasure.

What hadn't changed was his endurance. His ability to maintain his erection after climaxing several times was beyond her experience. She had never met a man who was that multi-orgasmic. Usually, they needed at least fifteen or twenty minutes to recover before getting it back up, and never more than twice. Not this bastard. He maintained his erection even after shooting his cum, and by God, did he ever. By the time he left her, his cum had coated her face, chest, pussy, and ass. She had to wash gobs of it from her hair. He even made her learn how to keep her eyes open as he covered her face with the gooey stuff, landing it right into her open eye. Sometimes, that stung a little, but often, it didn't.

She understood nothing about this man and his sexual desires. However, he reminded her often enough. She didn't have to understand them. All she had to do was accept and obey him.

Little by little, she was less sore, less spent, after each session. Her jaw became accustomed to being held open so wide. After maybe a month, though it could have been more, Avril realized that she didn't feel so much like jelly as he was leaving. Even after choking her nearly to death while ruthlessly thrusting into her, she found her body welcomed the experience, despite the fear projected in her eyes and her mind rejecting the strangulation.

"Was it possible that my body approved and cherished his visitations?" Avril suddenly wondered.

It was the act of walking him to the door that this revelation hit her. She felt as if she slammed into a brick wall. Reaching down, rubbing her lower abdomen, she sat down on the bed and took stock of her new awareness. Pondering the ramifications, she welcomed the stamina she now felt despite the ordeal. It was like the runner's high she used to feel. Endorphins were flooding her bloodstream, giving her a feeling of euphoria. It was almost like existing outside her body. Now, instead of feeling that way as she ran, she could feel that same kind of high with sex.

"God, I miss running. Well, if he would not let me cum, then by God, I'm going to enjoy the sex." Avril decided.

With a renewed step in her gait, she got up and stripped the bed, remaking it with fresh linens. Drawing a bath, she decided to take her time and enjoy the brief respite from the heels. The hot water soothed her sore muscles and body. She still didn't understand why she had to wear the heels, day in and day out, even as she slept in the bed. The spikes on the heels invariably snagged on the sheets, disturbing her sleep. However, her feet no longer hurt wearing them, even after standing on them hour after hour. He made her do that as well, usually in the evening, standing in her appointed spot where she met him kneeling in the morning.

"Why the evening, for God's sake, when I am tired to most?" She asked herself frequently.

By then, she was at her worst, worn out by submitting to his demands. He required her to keep the room clean and made up. Since she hadn't been out of the room all this time, it was an easy chore and gave her something to do. Besides, the only reading material she had was that damn rulebook. By now, she had read it several times over and felt she had a good understanding of what he expected of her. She was well on her way to memorizing it.

One morning, after taking her body as he had done each morning, they shared lunch, sitting around her small round table. During lunch, she found a way to ask for something to do during the day. He suggested a sketchbook and some pencils. It surprised her when he granted her this small accommodation. Not only did he give her several sketchbooks and pencils, but he also supplied her with a full set of drawing pencils of various hardness, including blending stubs, a pencil sharpener, and a gray eraser. After that day, her routine included spending the time sitting at the desk and sketching. It gave her a way to pass the time and to exercise her creativity.

One morning, after she had showered and dried her hair, she walked into her room, ready to receive him. About to kneel, she noticed a piece of paper lying on the floor near the door. Fearing that she had missed this little bit of housekeeping, she bent over to pick it up and dispose of it. Curious, she looked at it. It turned out to be a note from Sir.

She started reading.

'Enjoy the rest of the day and the next several days. I will not come by for our regular training session. Rest and catch up on your sleep. I expect you to be well-rested when I return.'

Her spirits lifted. Regardless that she was starting to enjoy these sessions, she continued.

'Even though you will not see me for a few days, I still require you to spend the mornings kneeling in your customary pose. Once you take your position, you may only get up when you hear the lunch tray delivered to your room.'

Sighing, she resumed reading the note.

'Now, for a bit of more good news. Please remove your training heels and drop them down the laundry chute. You will no longer need them. In the closet, you will find a new pair. Put on the cobalt blue similar in style to the ones you are wearing. On the heel, you will note a single crystal, denoting a promotion. Wear them just as you wore your old ones. It is time for you to learn to wear an even higher heel than you are used to.'

Groaning, she continued to read.

'I expect you to keep them clean and polished at all times. The rules regarding them remain the same. Day and night, awake or asleep, you will wear them at all times. The only exception is that you may remove them to shower or bathe. Otherwise, they are to remain on your feet at all times.'

"Really? This is becoming tedious," she thought to herself. Shaking her head, she continued to read.

'When I return, there will be a dinner party at the house. I require you to resume your role as a barmaid, ensuring everyone maintains a full glass. You know just what that entails. You will also entertain my guests after dinner. I expect you to be on your best behavior and do everything asked of you. I don't need to remind you not to embarrass me in the least. Make me proud, and I will reward you. Disappoint me will earn you a punishment. I will come by early afternoon to greet you, after which you will have two hours to get ready. I will tell you what to wear at that time.'

Sitting down on the desk chair, she hurriedly removed the hated training heels she received at her capture and tossed them down the laundry chute.

"Good riddance," saying goodbye to them as they disappeared into the darkness. Going to the closet, Avril noticed her new ones for the first time.

"Huh? How did these get here?" she asked herself. "They weren't here yesterday. I would have noticed. Shit, he must have put them there while I slept or showered."

Avril picked the shoes off the shelf and examined the cobalt blue peek-a-boo toe pumps with a tall five-inch stiletto heel and an ankle strap. Sure enough, a single clear crystal lived on each spike's back, just below where it attached to the shoe. Clearly new, they were beautiful and expensive. There was no designer label on the shoes, but she realized they must have cost well over a thousand dollars. Carrying them into her room, she sat down and slipped them on, buckling the strap around her ankles. A perfect fit, and even though they had a higher heel, they were extremely comfortable. Walking around the room, she couldn't help but look at her feet, admiring the leather's quality and the look they presented at the end of her legs. Walking up to the full-length mirror, she stood there looking at her reflection. She looked gorgeous, even in her nudity.

"Oops, I had completely forgotten that I'm naked. Wow, when did that happen?" She pondered the question. "It feels almost normal for me to be naked all day long. Wow, how about that?"

Testing the shoes, she hopped up and down and even walked as fast as she could across the room. They were 'the' most comfortable shoes she had ever worn. Returning to the mirror, she stood in front to gaze at her reflection. Then a new revelation hit her. Yes, she was gorgeous, but not just because of the shoes. She almost didn't recognize the person she saw in the mirror. She realized that she had a perfect hourglass figure despite the food and lack of running. She looked like a real woman, a sexual woman. Delighted, she smiled.

Studying the woman's body in the mirror, she knew that while running had kept the weight off, it had never given her a body that looked like the one she was now seeing. Her breasts appeared fuller yet quite firm. They almost looked like the ones she had when she was an eighteen-year-old girl, only fuller and more voluptuous. Even her nipples seemed somehow darker and puffier to her, though she didn't know how that might be possible. All these years later, she was a mature woman, with the curves and hips to match. Her pubis maintained their hairless look because of her weekly laser hair removal treatments. Her vulva peeked up from between her legs, capping off an open triangle between her thighs, allowing her to see right through between her legs. Her legs, still powerful in the thighs, gave way to gentler curves that accentuated her calves. Her ankles looked svelte, gracefully transitioning to feet wrapped in the blue elegance of the heels. The shoes gave her the impression that she was wearing a wrapped gift.

"Well, there is some truth to that," she realized.

Twisting around, she looked over her shoulders at her back and buttocks. She hadn't realized it before. Though she had a slightly fuller ass, it was somehow prettier, more feminine. Turning again to study her front, she realized that she genuinely wore the body of a healthy, sexual woman. Her long legs seemed longer than ever, and her hips rode up her torso before narrowing at her waist just below her ribs. She always knew she was high-waisted, but now, she really was. Studying her chest, she noticed that she was carrying her breasts higher than before. There wasn't a hint of sag in them at all. Just looking at them, they seemed to appreciate her inspection as her nipples instantly hardened, poking back at her, as if to say, 'thank you.' Even her nipple rings seemed more polished than ever. Checking out her arms and shoulders, they also seemed different somehow, just as strong as ever, only softer. She didn't know how to explain it.

"How was that possible?" She asked herself. "Was it all that sex I'm having?"

"Wow" was all she could think to say in answer to the question.

In the old days, she knew she was a woman. Now, she was a WOMAN. She was a desirable, sensual woman to cherish and fuck. She suddenly wished Sir would return so that she could show him her appreciation.

"Is everything ready?"

"Yes, Sir. The latest batch is ready, and the guards are setting up the stage now."

"Good, did you have any problems with the product?" the chairman asked his first underling.

"No, Mr. Chairman. Like the last batch, they all broke down, becoming compliant in the first couple of days. After that, they appreciated the significance of their situation and are taking to their lessons."

"And the sacrificial lamb?"

"Oh, that one was spectacular. Including the execution. The guards had quite the time showing off to the others what would happen if the others didn't come around and accept their fates."

"How was she put down?"

"In the usual way, I whipped her first at the post as I ordinarily do and then hung her."

"In the center of the cell block, for all to watch, I presume?"

"Yes, Sir."

"So, what made this one spectacular?"

"Well, first off, the guards made an example of her right there on the post. They took turns fucking her incessantly, despite her begging for mercy. I think it was her begging that goaded them on. Then, after I hung her, she took a very long time to die. She hung on the end of that rope for the better part of an hour before finally giving it up. It was her violent struggles and her facial expressions that sunk in with the others. One of her eyes nearly shot out of her skull during the last minutes. Despite the number of times I've done this, I've never seen that before."

"Sounded like fun. Sorry, I missed it."

"Believe me, it was. The final straw was that as she died, her body pissed what must have been several liters all over the place. It stunk up the cell block for hours."

"Too bad I didn't get to watch. I would have liked to have seen that."

"I'm sure you would have, Sir. I rather enjoyed the spectacle myself."

"Then we're ready for the auction. You don't anticipate any problems, do you?"

"No, Sir. The culling amassed a dozen men and five times that many women, mostly from the Western Hemisphere. Most are from the U.S., with the rest from Canada, Brazil, Chile, Argentina, and various Central American countries. A few are from Western Europe and the British Isles."

"How about the two we've been monitoring from Hawaii?"

"They were not in this group. I presumed that the committee had not yet voted on them as yet."

"Hm, that's strange. We voted to include them. I wonder what kept them from being picked up?"

"I don't know, Sir. Shall I make inquiries?"

"No, I'll handle that. You just make sure tomorrow's auction comes off without a problem."

"Yes, Sir. Is there anyone in the new group that you have a specific interest in?"

"I've got my eye on a couple. I haven't decided whether or not to pursue them. I may just replenish my stock to account for my losses."

"Shall I prepare a private viewing?"

"No, I don't think so. However, thank you for asking."

"Yes, Sir. Is there is anything else?"

"No, thank you."

"Then I'll leave you to it, Sir."

As the door closed behind him, the chairman opened the new group's file on his computer. Filtering the results to young women only marginally trimmed the result set. Since he wasn't interested in the barely legal ones, he further restricted the result set. That left a manageable list. He started reviewing the remainders. So far, he saw nothing that particularly stood out or caught his eye. He would sometimes click on an entry in the list, opening the detailed file on the woman. Mostly, he closed them within moments when nothing seemed to stand out or intrigue him.

After doing an initial scan of the available women, he leaned back and thought about his options. That redhead he bought a couple of auctions ago was taking up all of his time and interest. She intrigued him. He still couldn't pinpoint just what it was about her. He had a list of the qualities that a candidate had to have. He had a short 'must-have' list and a longer 'would like' list. She appeared to have all the qualities on both lists. It remained whether she would fulfill every one of the 'must-haves.'

In the meantime, he still needed to replenish his losses through attrition. That was one benefit of being the chairman. He had advanced information on the offerings in each lot, including their financials. Besides himself, only the senior selection committee members had that information. The rest of the members knew only what he made available to them. No one knew whether any of their purchases had any assets to refill their private accounts.

That was the thing about the redhead. Her dead parents had established a nice nest egg for her in the Caymans. He presumed they would tell her about it someday, but fate stepped in, and they died long before that happened. After he had cleaned out her accounts, he had made a tidy profit on the deal, given his expenses. His financial investment in the woman was insignificant.

His real investment was more in his time to train her. She was coming along, but she still had a long way to go. She still hadn't broken, but he felt confident that would soon happen. He was pushing her hard, intending to break her. Until that happened, nothing would happen.

He needed to break her and soon.

In the meantime, he needed to get ready for the auction. Regardless of what he wanted, the auctioneers and the members needed to know something about the products. It was up to him to trim the data on each unit into something the membership could use in making their selections. Besides, he needed to sell out the entire group. Those that didn't sell didn't contribute to recovering their investment expenses. Of course, there was their value for the evening's entertainment, but that was insignificant compared to the Consortium's investment.

As the chairman, essentially, he was the Consortium.

Chapter Ten

Days later and a couple of hours after the lunch, Avril was kneeling in her designated spot as she waited for Sir to come for her. She had so much wanted to show him her appreciation. Notwithstanding her captivity, which still made her angry and resentful, she had learned to appreciate the euphoria she felt anticipating his cock inside her.

"It was strange," she thought. "How can I resent my captor and my captivity, resent his presence, and still want him to fuck me hard at the same time?"

Her mind in turmoil; she could not figure out how to balance the two sides of her emotions. All she could do was wait and let them play out. Being locked in this room, though bigger and nicer than a prison cell, it was still a cell. Confined and not in control, she both loved and hated the place. She wanted to see the sky and feel the wind on her face. When she could feel fresh air again, warm or cold, she had no idea.

She suddenly heard a key in the lock on her door. Straightening up and perfecting her pose, she waited for him to enter. A moment later, he stepped in and stopped just inside the door.

Untold moments or minutes later, she finally heard him breathe a single word. "Wow."

She couldn't resist a smile at the compliment. She knew she looked good, but to hear Sir affirm it, well, it was just precious.

"Stand up," he directed.

Rising gracefully, she took her pose, one foot slightly in front and crossed over the other. Hands clasped behind her back, head up, eyes down, shoulders back and chest out; she awaited his scrutiny.

"Knock me down with a feather. You are dazzling."

"Thank you, Sir. I trust you are pleased."

"I am. Perhaps I should stay away more often. The return is ever so more delightful."

"If it pleases you, Sir, however, if I may, I would like to show you my appreciation for the new shoes."

"They do look perfect on you. I gather you like them."

"I do, Sir, thank you. I very much would like to show you just how much?"

"Go ahead, show me."

Avril stepped forward, stopping just in front of him with barely an inch between his chest and her breasts. She leaned in, took his head in her hands, and kissed him deeply on the mouth. Shocking him in the process, she showed him just how much she appreciated the gift. In all this time, never once had they passionately kissed on the mouth. However, she felt compelled to do so. Though in the back of her mind, a part of her cringed at kissing him. Locking her lips to his, she kissed him as two lovers kiss, probing his mouth with her tongue, putting all the hot, passionate feeling she could turn into an expression of gratitude. Stepping back when she finished, he exhaled and looked at her square in the eyes.

Reaching for her waist with both hands, he pulled her tight against him and kissed her back. For many minutes, the two shared their fiery passion, as neither had ever experienced before. Their hands roamed the other's body, straining to connect on a deeper level. As they kissed, Avril loosened his tie and dropped it to the floor. Then she unbuttoned his shirt and freed it from his trousers, all the time, maintaining a lip lock on each other. Slipping the shirt from his shoulders, it dropped to the floor and reached for his belt. Pulling it from around his waist, she presented it to him and squatted down, her face staring straight at his groin. She pulled down his trousers and shorts, freed his already erect cock, and pressed it against her closed but moist lips. Sir let out an impatient sigh as she brushed his cock head back and forth across her mouth.

Teasing him, she occasionally flicked her tongue on the sensitive underside before resuming painting its head with her lips. Exploring further, sliding her flared lips along its length, Avril could feel heat building within his cock and spread to her mouth. Gazing up at him, her eyes wide open, she watched him enjoy his pleasure, as a similar pleasure built inside her. Estimating just the right moment, she stared at the monster right in the eye and fully engulfed him in one fluid motion. He reacted instantly, throwing his head back as her lips ground themselves against his groin, his cockhead firmly planted in the back of her throat. He elicited a growl she had never heard before. It was a moan of sheer pleasure from his gut. Listening to it drove her excitement up to another level of happiness.

For as long as she could, she held him there before her body demanded a fresh gulp of air. Her lungs satisfied, she thrust her head back onto him, driving his cock into the furthest reaches of the back of her mouth. Feeling his soft belly hair on the tip of her nose and with her lips wrapped around his girth, she started sliding her tongue along the underside of his cock and tasted his balls. She felt him build towards an explosion as the heat in his balls grew and tightened. Extracting him so that she could take in another cleansing breath of fresh air, she engulfed him once more, forcing him in as far as she could. As she did so, his cock grew, and he seemed to swell immeasurably. A moment later, his balls contracted. He rammed himself into her throat's deepest recesses. At the apex of his thrust, he exploded his cum down her throat.

Buried as deep as he was, she couldn't taste the hot cum spurting directly down and into her gullet. However, she could feel it. The heat and slickness of his cum driving down her throat gave her a reaction she didn't expect. She tried to suppress it, as this was all about him. She failed, and she exploded with an orgasm denied for so long. Her body racked in delight, and she no longer felt the need to breathe again. All she wanted was the pleasure flooding her mind and radiating throughout her body.

As soon as he finished, he picked her up and threw her on the bed. Stepping out of his shoes and trousers, he attacked her, driving into her. He fucked her with a passion she hadn't felt before. It was as if he couldn't get enough of her. He jack-hammered her repeatedly, shooting his cum deep inside her or splattered on her belly and chest. Throwing her heeled feet over his shoulders, he took her ass, pile driving his cock until he came again. Back and forth, he took her, fucking both her holes. Reaching for her breasts, he grabbed them firmly and squeezed them hard. She felt his painful grip but didn't care. His knuckles white with the intensity of his grasp, he dug his fingers deep into the tender flesh as he pounded away inside her.

When he finished and pulled off her, Avril wasn't the quivering mass of jelly she used to feel. Instead, if he was so inclined, she was ready for more. This revelation surprised her. Earlier, she finally got to taste his cum when he withdrew from her mouth. That taste still lived with her, and for some unknown reason, she wanted more, much more.

Panting, lying on her back with her knees up in the air and spread wide, she could feel his cum dripping onto the bed. Eager to have him back inside her, she rocked her hips, enticing him to give her what she craved.

He didn't. Instead, he admonished. "You didn't ask permission to cum."

"Uh?" she thought. "What?"

Unfortunately, she was at a loss to figure out just what he meant. He saw the hesitation in her expression.

"Did you cum when I was in your mouth?" He asked her.

"Uh, oh," she thought to herself. Rule number one hundred, never cum without first asking for and getting permission. She broke one of his rules. "Oh, shit. I did," she realized.

"Oh Sir, I'm sorr… um, Sir, it wasn't intentional. It just happened, and I… I couldn't stop it. Please, Sir. I… I didn't mean to."

"Intent is not the issue here. You came without asking for or getting my permission. For that, you earned yourself a punishment. Turn over and put your feet over the edge of the bed."

Gulping, she did as commanded and awaited his discipline.

"It doesn't matter that you were trying to do right by me, show me your appreciation and all that. The pleasure you gave me was incredible. I grant you that. That doesn't change the fact you broke a rule. Now, I will take even greater pleasure in punishing you. What is the penalty for breaking this rule?"

"Ah, ten strokes, Sir."

"Yes, ten strokes for each infraction. You broke two rules. First, you did not ask permission, infraction number one. Then you came without permission. That makes two infractions. How many strokes did you earn?"

"Um, twenty, Sir?"

"Are you asking me, or tell me?"

"Um, twenty Sir, ten for each infraction," she told him, careful not to use a questioning inflection.

"Excellent. Prepare yourself. It will be easier if you relax and accept it. If you tense up, it'll go worse for you."

Try as she might, relaxing and accepting the blows didn't seem right to her, and she found it impossible to relax. Instead, she tried to take it, thinking, "It is what it is."

Just as that thought crossed her mind, she heard him wind up and begin his swing. Unable to stop herself, she tensed. Her sphincter tightened up, and her ass cheeks clenched. At that same moment, the first stroke landed across her buttocks.

She screamed, a burning pain erupting from her bottom. He struck her again, and a new fire erupted across her cheeks, adding to the previous one. She screamed louder, tears forming in her eyes and spilling onto the bed.

"You're not counting."

"I'm... not... what... Sir?"

"You're not counting the strokes. Let's begin again."

After an all too short respite, he landed a new stroke on her ass.

"Um... one, Sir," she screamed, biting down on the sheets between her teeth.

A half a second later and barely after uttering the count, he landed another stroke."

"... two... Sir," and she screamed again.

He continued landing stroke after stroke on her ravaged bottom. Avril stayed with the count, but she found it impossible to relax. At every strike, she tensed. According to him, tensing up allowed the blow to feel worse. Tensing up slowed down the dissipation of the energy in each stroke. She couldn't accept it. On and on it went. The excruciating pain burning her bottom continued as she counted aloud. When she reached nineteen, she sucked in a deep breath, glad that the beating was almost over. On the next stroke, she said the count, twenty. What was strange was that just before the final stroke, she forgot to tense up. Instead, she was focusing hard that it was the last one and forgot to tense up. She discovered that the final stroke didn't hurt as she expected.

Finished, Sir dressed and walked out of the room. Before closing the door behind him, he said. "Go draw a cold-water bath and sit in it. Though cold, it will help you feel better sooner and help you heal faster. I excuse you from the dinner party tonight, and I'll see you again in the morning.

Still crying profusely, she sobbed. "Thank you, Sir."

Stopping in his tracks, he turned back to her and asked. "What are you thanking me for?"

With a stuttered response mixed with her tears, she croaked out. "Thank you for my well-deserved punishment, Sir."

Smiling, he turned and left, locking the door behind him.

After a time, she got up and gingerly walked to the en-suite and drew the cold-water bath. Taking off her beautiful blue heels, she slowly and carefully lowered her body into the chilly water. It felt icy at first, but after a few minutes, she felt better. Grabbing a nearby towel, she draped it over her shoulders to slow her shivering and allowed her mind to go blank.

Later, much later, she got up, drenched a towel in cold water, and made her way back to the bed. Unable to sit, she somehow put the heels back on and then lay down. Facedown and on her stomach, she carefully placed the wet towel over her abused bottom, thankful for the slight relief. Carefully, she pulled the covers over her body, and a few minutes later, sleep took her.

The following morning, she woke up, still on her belly. She rolled out of bed and onto her knees, endeavoring to prevent her bruised ass from touching anything. Using her arms for support, she slowly stood up. Walking to the full-length mirror, she inspected the damage. Shaking her head, the once beautiful ass she had so admired yesterday, was this morning, a mass of black and blue, with bright red angry welts crisscrossing across both cheeks.

Carefully walking to the en-suite, she tried relieving herself by squatting over the toilet rather than sitting on it. It was hard, but she got most of it into the bowl. Cleaning up the spillage, she started another cold-water bath and repeated the experience from the day before, sitting in the cold water with a towel around her shoulders. A half-hour later, she took a tepid shower, washing her body and her hair. Too tired to condition the hair, she toweled and lightly dried it with the hairdryer. Her hair still slightly damp, she leaned against the vanity, careful to avoid putting any pressure on her buttocks. Sighing, she put on her heels. Walking into the main room, she found him sitting in his wingback chair.

"Go finish drying your hair and make sure you style it."

"Yes, Sir," she said, resigned to do as he commanded.

Fifteen minutes later, with her hair dry and styled and a minimal amount of makeup, she returned to the room and stripped the bed. After dumping the soiled sheets down the laundry chute, she remade the bed with fresh linens. When she finished, she moved to her designated spot, knelt, and waited.

It was a long time before he spoke. "You missed a fun party."

She didn't give a flying fat rat's ass about missing the party. It was the furthest thing on her mind. Instead of replying, she kept her mouth shut. Inside, Avril was seething. The anger and fury buried for months raged to the surface. Pent-up emotions consuming her, she gritted her teeth and softly muttered, "I hate you."

Not meaning to say it aloud, she discovered that he heard her when he asked. "What was that?"

Finally, free to express herself, she yelled, "I HATE YOU! I HATE YOU! I HATE YOU! You're despicable. I despise you. I hate you!"

On and on, she ranted, the resentment she felt all this time finally spewing out her mouth. The damn cracked, at last, split wide open and washed away everything in the valley below. Her rage unchecked, and her resentment erupting, her tirade continued for many minutes.

Getting up from her kneeling position, she stormed up to him and began beating on his chest as the venomous words continued spewing from her mouth. Time seemed to stop. It took a long time for her emotions to disgorge her pent-up fury, leaving behind an empty shell and a spent body.

After waiting for an appreciable time, confident that she finished, he said. "Okay. Now we can begin in earnest."

Choosing to ignore him, Avril collapsed and curled up in a fetal position on the floor at his feet, sobbing. Knowing he sat there, seemingly uncaring, did nothing to resolve the despair and anger she felt. In a disconnected sort of way, she was just thankful that he didn't stop her need to cry.

Later, empty tear ducts leaving behind only dry hacking, he squatted down beside her.

"The training house informed me that you had yet to break down. You've been bottling up your rage for a long time now. I had hoped it wouldn't take this long to let it out."

Avril barely heard him, but somewhere in the back of her mind, she knew just what he was saying. The funny thing was, she agreed with him.

"You are strong-willed and intelligent. That's one reason why I chose you. You're very organized and perceptive. You systematically plan everything. However, you need to realize. You cannot solve with logical thinking. Sometimes, all you can do is accept what life has thrown you and deal with it."

He paused a moment, tactility her shoulder.

"I know that you don't care to listen to me right now. That's all right. I know that you are hearing me and that you agree with what I have to say. I had hoped you wouldn't have waited this long to express yourself and your true inner emotions. Now that you have, we can begin anew and build you up into a stronger, better person."

Standing up, he moved away from her, presumably towards the door.

"Now, when I return, I trust I will not find you lying there, blubbering like a child. I require you to clean yourself up and be ready to renew your training. Whether you do is up to you. I told you on your first day, the direction of the rest of your life is up to you. If you do not live up to my expectations, I will not allow you to live here much longer. I told you then, and I tell you now. You will never return to your old life. You will either thrive or die. The choice you make is solely up to you. After lunch, we will begin again. You know what you must do between now and then. You know how I expect to find you. I trust you will not disappoint me."

A moment later, she heard the door close, and the loud sound of the door locking followed immediately afterward.

Avril laid there on the floor, exhausted from her emotional release. Eventually, she sat up and wrapped her arms around her knees. Sucking her legs closer to her chest, she renewed her sobbing. After a while, her mind processing the morning events, Avril considered her options. She didn't know how long it was before they delivered lunch. Frankly, she didn't care. She wasn't hungry. Lunch was just a milestone before he would return.

But what am I to do? Take back her life or surrender to death? To be blunt, she almost wished for death, but that was not like her. She was a fighter, and damn it. She wanted her life. Resigned, she slowly extended her feet and rolled up onto her knees. A moment later, she stood up and walked to the en-suite.

Chapter Eleven

After lunch and kneeling in her designated spot, Avril waited for his return. Cleaning herself took a bit longer than she expected. Her face was a mess, with mascara running everywhere, blackening her face. She was exhausted, and her hair knotted and gnarly. Still, she found the energy to shower, style her hair, and reapply the small amount of makeup he required. When lunch arrived, she played with it but ate little. After returning the tray to the food alcove, she took her position on the floor, kneeling with her hands clasped behind her back, and waited.

She waited and waited. Hour after hour, she knelt immobile. She held her face focused on the door while her eyes studied the pattern in the carpet on the floor. Not for the first time, he kept her waiting.

"Damn, where, the fuck, was he?" she muttered to herself, anxious to get up from this position. Maybe an hour later, as the thought crossed her mind for the hundredth time, she heard the key in the lock, and the door opened.

"Good. I see you decided to take the high road rather than wallow in despair." Sir said as he walked into the room. Taking a seat on his wingback chair, he crossed his leg over the other and sat back. Feeling his concentration on her, she maintained her pose and did not look over in his direction.

"You may not believe this, but I am glad, grateful even, that you experienced your tantrum. You sounded like a spoiled child. However, it was a long time coming. I thought you would never let yourself go, but I'm pleased that it finally happened. Would you like to say anything? I permit you to say anything you want, ask any question you care to ask, without recrimination. After that, we will begin your training anew. Is there anything you wish to say?"

"Sir, I don't understand all this. Why?"

"Why did you throw a tantrum? Why are you here? Why did I buy you? Why did were you taken and sold?"

"Well, Sir, all of that, maybe more. Why?"

"The easiest question to answer is why you're here. I have already answered that, but I don't mind repeating it this time. You're here because I wish you to be here. I selected you so that you could take care of my guests and attend to my needs. Above all that, you're here to please me."

"But why me? What is so special about me that interests you? I'm just like any other woman, but why choose me? Why not choose someone else?"

"Believe it or not, I think you are special. It's that special uniqueness that identified you to the Consortium and ultimately brought you to me."

"Sir, I'm sorry, but I don't feel special or unique."

"Nonetheless, you are. If you don't believe it, just know that I intend to help you find it and feel it."

"Even if I don't wish it?"

"Especially since you don't wish it. You will accept and believe who you are and what makes you special. If not, you will die despite it."

"I still don't understand. Who are we? Who is this Consortium? Why do they snatch women, I mean, people off the street and sell them into bondage? What did we ever do to deserve such treatment?"

"Hm, a lot of questions. I'll answer the last one first, what did you do to deserve such treatment. Again, a straightforward question. You did nothing. You came to our attention, and we liked what we saw. We decided a long time ago to take you. Plain and simple."

"But why?"

"Because we wanted you. I wanted you."

"So, you just took me?"

"To put it plainly, yes."

"And you are a member of this Consortium?"

"Yes, I am. I am one of the ranking members, and I exert a lot of influence over the Consortium."

"So, when you found out about me, you decided that I was to become yours."

"Yes. It is in my nature to take what I want."

"Without regard to the feelings of the people you take?"

"Yes."

"I see. So, tell me more about this Consortium of yours."

"The Consortium? That could take a while, so I'll give you the abstract. The Consortium came into existence nearly a thousand years ago with the express purpose to satisfy the needs, wants, and desires of its members. Members express their wishes, and the Consortium works hard to meet those needs as best as we can."

"By stealing people off the streets and subjugating them?"

"In part, that is one of our more important activities. Finding men and women to satisfy the membership's needs is just one aspect of what the Consortium does for its members. They also secure meat for the table, hard-to-find organs for transplant, or offer mere entertainment. You saw that at your auction. The Consortium hung those three women for entertainment only. It did not care that they were people. They care little for the human lives they take and kill. You also witnessed an execution a couple of days before the auction. That was both a punishment and a message to the rest of you. A teaching moment, you could call it."

"And you brought me here to take care of you sexually?"

"Yes, in part. When you are ready, you will attend me in other ways, and at times, with my guests."

"I don't think I will appreciate being a sex toy."

"Oh, but you are already starting to believe that. Remember the day I promoted you and gave you your new heels. How did you feel for those few days?"

"Well, perhaps, but I reserve the right to change my mind."

"A woman's prerogative. Still, I believe you will one day relish your new status in life and grow in leaps and bounds as a result."

"Even if I don't wish to grow in that way."

"Correct."

"Wait a minute. Earlier, you said the Consortium secures meat to satisfy peculiar dietary needs. Do I understand you correctly, your members eat us?"

"Yes, indeed, some of us do. You understand correctly. Rest assured, I am not considering serving you on my dinner table, though there have been times I had to serve a woman in that way. Most of the friends in my circle do not indulge in human meat, but I have done it, for the sake of my guests."

"That's abhorrent."

"On that, we agree. However, I understand their needs, and frankly, human flesh can be quite tasty."

Avril shuddered at the thought.

"You should know that you could just as easily have been roasted for your meat and served at the dinner table. I paid the price I did for you to keep you from suffering such a fate. I was bidding against someone who wanted to roast you alive and serve you at her table. So, in one respect, you might say, I saved your life."

"Well, you didn't do me any favors, did you?"

"Perhaps, however, I see a future in you that otherwise would have been snuffed out."

"And you're okay with people eating other people?"

"No, but what someone else does or believes is not for me to judge."

"Except for me…"

"Well, yes. There are exceptions. You are my property. With you and all those I bring here, it is up to me to say what you will do or not."

"So, you are not okay with eating people, but you do it. Why?"

"When necessary, I respect the feelings of my guests or if I am a guest in their house. The bidder seemed to desire you above all else, almost without regard to her finances. Do you realize? Others see something special about you. Several of the members noticed you, but only she and I could bid on you."

"She? Do you mean to say that the bidder you were competing against was a woman? Women are members of your Consortium?"

"Oh, yes. Nearly half of our memberships are women."

"That's incredible."

"Not really. Remember, the Consortium has existed for a thousand years. It's only natural that the membership would match the general population."

"So, you're telling me that this woman wanted to buy me, kill me, roast my body, and then serve me for dinner."

"Well, not exactly. She wanted to roast you all right. However, she wanted to roast you while you were still alive. She planned to run a spit through your body and roast you alive on a rotisserie, spinning over a bed of hot coals."

"What? You mean she wanted to shove a skewer through my body and roast me like a suckling pig. Would I still be alive after the spitting, spinning as I cooked? That's barbaric."

"Yes. I suspect you would have survived the spitting and placed above the coals alive. This woman is very skilled at spitting people alive. Most of her acquisitions survive the spitting process. I have little doubt you would have been alive through all of that, at least until you succumbed to your roasting. Barbaric, maybe, but that would have been your fate if I had not intervened. If I hadn't thought you could serve and please me, she would have certainly served you for dinner. Let me ask you, do you remember the membership inspecting the three of you before the auctioning began?"

"Yes, I remember."

"Do you remember the woman who studied you, and just as she was leaving the stage, looked back at you, smiled, and wiped her lips with her tongue?"

"Yes, Sir. Was that her?"

"Yes, it was. She was disappointed she lost to me. I knew exactly how much she had available to pay for you. I could have bid on you with an amount that would have immediately taken you out of her reach. I didn't, as the auction is as much about the bidding as it is in the winning. I wanted to beat her, and I wanted her to suffer along the way."

"So, what did she do?"

"She bought a woman from the last batch. She served her at a dinner party I attended a few weeks ago."

"Are you telling me that a woman I spent those two weeks at the training facility was spitted alive and roasted over an open fire?"

"Yes, that is just what happened."

Shuddering, Avril said. "I hope I never get the chance to meet this woman. She must be horrible."

"Oh, you already have met her. Do you remember your first night here; you were acting as my barmaid?"

Gulping, she nodded.

"Do you remember the woman who came up to you, touched you, and then grabbed your pussy, sticking her finger inside you?"

"How could I forget? Wait, that was… was that her?"

"Yes."

"And you allowed her access to me?"

"Yes. I wanted to taunt her with what she missed at the auction. She was angry, but she's over it now. I satisfied our honor by offering her one of those women you saw standing by the front door in compensation. Do you remember the ones dressed in white and black?"

"I remember. I… ah, Sir. I… don't want to know."

"Fair enough, you see, neither of them measured up to my expectations. Neither one is still a member of my house. Most of the ones I buy do not last long. As a result, I don't care about them or their futures. They ultimately fail me, and I replace them as needed."

"Do you mean that since I have come here, you have purchased more women through the Consortium?"

"Yes, of course! I'm surprised you asked that. No one individual can meet every one of my expectations. I spread my expectations around as I need to. As I said earlier, you are special. I will put a lot of effort into your training. I suspect you will satisfy me in ways that no one else has ever done before."

"And what do you expect of me in the long term?"

"Don't worry about that right now. You just need to deal with the here and now. In time, you will know."

"Sir, I'd like to change topics. I have questions about the rule book."

"And you're telling me this, why? The rules are plain enough. I see no reason to ask questions about them."

"Nonetheless, Sir. I have them. I have difficulty with them that ends up in a Catch-22."

"Hm, how interesting. I'd like to hear more about this quandary."

"Thank you, Sir. My question has to do with asking permission to cum. The rule states that I must ask permission from you before I cum."

"That's correct. What about it?" Sir interrupted.

"Sir, if I may continue. Asking permission to cum is a question, something the rule book specifically states I may not do without your permission. How then can I ask permission to cum, especially in the moment's heat, when I may not ask the question?"

"Ah, what an interesting question. See, I knew you were unique. No one has ever asked me that before. It's quite insightful and a wonderful dilemma. If you ask my permission to cum, you break a rule. If you don't and cum anyway, you break another rule. You're damned if you do and damned if you don't."

"Yes, Sir. That is my difficulty."

"I'm sure you can figure it out."

"Sir, that's not fair."

Interrupting, Sir said as a matter-of-factly as he possible, "Who said anything I require of you is fair. Life is not fair. You being here is not fair, at least from your perspective. Get over it. You're smart enough. Figure it out. Do you have any more questions on this topic?"

Fuming, Avril retorted, "No, Sir. I think the one said it all."

"You don't like my answer, do you?"

"No, Sir. I don't."

"Too bad. Get over it. I don't care if you don't like the rules, whether the rules aren't fair, or whether what I tell you to do isn't fair. You are my property. I own you, and you will do whatever it takes to make me happy, including suffering my punishments when you break the rules. You know how much I enjoy hearing you suffer under my torment. I hope you never get used to them and stop screaming for me."

Thoughtfully, Avril retreated to her thoughts and considered what he had told her. She had forgotten all about kneeling in pose and remained that way during their entire conversation.

She knew she still had questions. However, none came to mind. The sheer audacity of what he said overwhelmed her. Then, suddenly, a question arose from the quagmire of her mind.

"Sir, what is your name, your actual name?"

"Sorry, that will have to wait. You have already asked that question. Do not ask me again. You may learn it in good time, after much more training. You must earn the privilege to know my name. Do you have any more questions or something else to say?"

"Sir, only this, I resent being taken off the street, sold at auction like a piece of meat, beaten, assaulted, and forced to follow your silly rules. However, until I can do something about it, I will continue to remember your lessons and abide by your rules. That's all I have to say."

"Understandable, and if I were in your position, I would say the same thing."

After a pregnant pause, he continued. "As of this moment, I rescind my permission for you to speak your mind, ask questions, and talk freely. I expect you to follow decorum and behaviors as outlined in the rulebook. Do I make myself clear?"

"Yes, Sir. I am not to speak unless spoken to. I shall not question you. I will do as you ask, and I will behave according to your expectations."

"Good. Stand up."

Though her derriere still pained her, Avril tried to stand up as gracefully as possible. Standing at attention, with her shoulders back and her chest out, she clasped her hands behind her back and waited.

Getting up from his chair, he walked around her, circling her, studying her, inspecting her. Eventually, she felt him stop and examined her derriere, finally touching her lightly as if to feel the darkening bruises.

"Good, cool to the touch. I will arrange for you to have chemical ice packs brought to you, as well as a healing cream. Do you know what they are?" He asked.

"Yes, Sir. When I crush the chemical pack, they turn icy cold, and I can place them on my bruises to help speed my healing. The cream, well, its name is evident."

"That's correct. You will consistently use the ice packs twenty minutes on and twenty minutes off until I say you can stop. Use the cream as directed on the package."

"Sir, I don't have a watch or a clock. I won't know how long twenty minutes will be, and I fear I will fail you."

"The chemical ice pack will stay cold for about twenty minutes. Once it warms, you will know how long twenty minutes is. Use that as your measure of how long to wait before starting a new ice pack. Deposit used ice packs down the laundry chute after each use. New ones will arrive with your meals. Does that answer your question?"

"Yes, Sir."

"Okay, I give you the rest of the afternoon to yourself. Tonight, I will take you to dinner. Wear the cobalt blue dress you will find in your closet. As usual, you will not wear underwear or any of the lingerie in your possession. The dress matches the color of your heels. You will also find a pair of crystal earrings and a matching necklace in your closet.

Put them on and await me. Dinner will be at eight."

"Yes, Sir. Thank you, Sir. I will be ready."

As he walked to the door, he stopped and turned back towards her. She felt his eyes surveying her, and just before she heard him leave, she thought she heard him mutter, "Beautiful, just beautiful."

When she heard the door close and lock, she relaxed. Smiling, she looked down at her body, and over her naked breasts, she agreed.

She was beautiful, and she knew it to her core.

Chapter Twelve

That evening, Avril was ready for him. Her ass felt so much better after all the icing. Earlier, she feared sitting would be extraordinarily uncomfortable, but after testing her limits a short time ago, she figured she had healed enough to manage a sit-down dinner.

She found the dress and jewelry in the closet. Again, she had no idea how it got there. She briefly surveyed her lingerie she found but did not put on any of it. Instead, she just fingered the delicate fabric, yearning for the opportunity to wear something under the dress. Like the lingerie, the dress was superb. Made of the finest quality materials, the clothing he gave her to wear continued to astonish her. She couldn't afford to buy even one piece she found with her limited income. Her closet was full of expensive clothing and jewelry. Seeing what was in there, she still didn't fathom what he wanted from her.

Sure, to please him, that she knew. The trick was what it took to satisfy him. Confident she could please him sexually. If she had to entertain his guests sexually, she could do that as well. However, he hinted at much more. What more? She had no idea. All she could do was wait to find out.

After bathing one more time, she slipped the dress over her head. Like the emerald green gown, it was exquisite and fit her perfectly. White crystals similar in style to the ones affixed to her heels adorned the dress. The dress was short, barely covering her pubis while standing up. Sitting down, it rode up her body and fully exposed her genitalia and ass to the seat beneath her. It was a sleek dress, carefully following the lines of her frame.

What most excited her was that the dress covered both of her breasts, revealing impressive cleavage she didn't know she had. Standing in front of the mirror, she realized that the dress, as elegant as it was, covered her and yet didn't. It was almost as if she weren't wearing anything. Her pierced nipples poking at the dress's fabric, and darts in the bodice defined the fullness of her breasts. It was almost as if the dress was showing off her body. Well, she figured it was. It was gorgeous, but it was not a dress to wear to the office. No, this was a dress designed to let a man intending on fucking you appreciate her. Well, so be it. Fucking was so much better than taking a beating, even if she could not enjoy the climax.

In time, she resumed her kneeling position and waited for her designated spot. Barely five minutes later, he unlocked the door and entered.

He just stood there on the threshold of the door. Avril felt his eyes appraise the entire length of her. She sensed him scan up and down. Eventually, he moved slightly to one side and repeated his appraisal, this time from a partially offset position. Finally, he said.

"Beautiful. You are stunning."

"Thank you, Sir."

"You may stand up. I want to take a closer look at you."

"Yes, Sir," she replied, complying as gracefully as she could.

Circling her as before, he appraised her from every side. Returning to face her, he said. "You please me greatly. I appreciate the effort you took in preparing yourself for me."

"Thank you, Sir," she replied appreciatively.

"I never expected you to look as good as you do now. I even like how you did your hair. You pulled it up, and yet, it still flows long around your shoulders. I don't know how you did it, but I do like it."

"I had hoped you would like it, Sir."

"I do. Now, are you hungry? You must be. It's been over a day since you last ate." He asked, not expecting an answer. Instead, he gave her his elbow, and together, he escorted her out of the room.

Taken aback by his behavior, she felt stunned. The last time she had walked this hallway with him, she followed a half step behind him. Now, she was side-by-side with him, arm-in-arm. As they arrived at the main level, he led her to a small, intimate dining room, already laid out with two place settings of similarly elegant china and crystal stemware. A pair of candles burned in the center of the table, and soft, romantic music filled the space. Escorting her to the table, he pulled out a chair for her. Gulping, she looked down, fearful that sitting on it would hurt. A comfortable cushion on it, suitable for sitting on a sore bottom, invited her. Nodding to him and his gentlemanly behavior, she sat down, testing her seat as she did so. It was as comfortable as it looked, and she looked at him with appreciation. After tucking her chair up against the table, he moved to the other side and sat down.

"I thought this would a more comfortable setting for you rather than that enormous dining hall you saw last."

"Yes, Sir. It is. Thank you."

"Would you like a cocktail? Anything you wish, I can offer you. It is my understanding that you like Margaritas without salt over the rocks."

"Thank you, Sir. If it pleases you, I would be happy to share a cocktail with you. I would welcome a Margarita."

Snapping his fingers, a young woman entered the room. Like her normal wear, the woman was naked except for a pair of black training heels and a collar.

After giving her their order, Sir turned back to Avril and said.

"For the balance of the dinner, I release you from speaking out of turn to and not asking questions unless I have given you a directive that you may. I hope that we can sit down over dinner and talk about whatever comes to mind. I have only one restriction. You are not to bring up the Consortium nor how you came to be here."

"I understand. Thank you, Sir."

When their drinks appeared, the barmaid first gave Avril's cocktail before turning to provide Sir with his. As she left, the door closing behind her, Avril spoke up on her own.

"Is she one of your new acquisitions?"

"Yes, she is. It's her second week here, and she is taking to her training quite nicely."

"I assume that you don't expect a lot from her."

"Perceptive, as always, you are correct. I don't. I suspect she won't last long. However, I will give her opportunities to succeed in her new life. Unfortunately, she doesn't seem to excite me very much, especially when compared to you."

"Well, please don't judge her by your standards for me. You've told me often enough that I am unique. Being unfair to her would devastate me. I suspect, using those measures, she will never meet your expectations."

"I agree, and yes, I promise you, I won't."

"Can I ask you a personal question?"

"You may."

"Have you fucked her?"

Smiling, he looked over at her and took a sip from his cocktail before answering,

"Straightforward as always. Yes, I have, and before you ask, I fuck all the women in my stable. Frequently, in fact. You do not differ from them in that regard. I can tell you this. I suspect that one day, your sexual talents will surpass those of everyone else in my experience. The other day attested to your potential."

"But that is not all you are looking for from me?"

"True. I have much bigger plans for you."

"Care to share?" she queried.

"All in good time."

"Very well then, what can I do for you now?"

"Please, sit and enjoy the meal with me. I like your companionship. That is enough for now."

Thoughtfully, Avril considered what she should say next, but before she could, he piped up. "Tell me about running. I understand that you like to run. You even ran in the New York and Boston Marathon. I understand that you did very well in Boston."

And so, the dinner continued, focusing on the light conversation of her life before and after her capture. Sometimes, it was hard for Avril to answer his questions. They allowed sad memories and unpleasant feelings to surface. During dinner, she feasted on a delicious filet mignon, cooked rare as she preferred, a baked potato with butter and sour cream, and grilled asparagus. The salad course included a red leaf salad drizzled with a balsamic vinaigrette dressing and Italian lemon sorbet for dessert. The meal was delicious, and in any other circumstances, she would have welcomed the attention her companion gave her. Instead, her spirits remained dampened and buried deep down inside her. She still hated him.

As dinner concluded, he took her hand and escorted her to what she could only describe as a library or study. He poured her a glass of red wine and a brandy for himself. Showing her a seat nearby, she sat down and cradled her wine in her hands.

"You must know. I am not sorry about your circumstances. I intended to have you, and now I do."

"Yes, Sir. I know."

"Knowing is not the same as accepting. Would you agree?"

Sensing a trap coming, Avril answer cautiously, "Um, yes, Sir. I agree."

"One day, I am confident that you will not only accept your place here, but you will embrace it."

"May I speak honestly, Sir?"

"Always, it's in the rulebook."

"Sir, I did not forget. I wanted to be sure that now it was okay. Why is it important for you to buy and sell people? Not just me, but anyone."

"You know, I don't rightly know. I guess it's my upbringing. I come from a lineage going back dozens of generations. We have always taken what we desired, and I presume we always will."

"And you're not sorry about taking innocent people, abusing and torturing them before you kill them? You don't consider what you are doing is wrong?"

"No, I don't. There will always be those who take and those taken. That is the way of life. Even in the animal world, predators do not consider the needs of their prey. They take what they need and never look back. They are not sorry, nor believe that it is wrong. I don't think that it is any different from what I do."

"And you don't think it immoral?"

"Morality is a joke. Sorry to be so blunt, but morality is a sentence imposed by an unjust system. A system meant to subjugate the collective for its agenda. The moral society is being dishonest with the general population. On the other hand, I am honest, not only to you but also to myself. Honesty, believe it or not, is important to me."

"Honesty is just as important to me, as well."

"Then let me ask you, would you lie to your best friend to protect her feelings?"

"Of course, not…"

"Really?" Sir interrupted. "What if you found out her husband was cheating on her or hiding that he was gay, hiding his true self? What if he had been lying to her for years while hiding the truth from her?"

"I suppose it would depend upon the circumstances."

"Yes, of course, it would. You would agree that there might be some circumstances whereby you would not tell your best friend the truth to keep from hurting her?"

"Put that way, and I suppose I might hide the truth from her."

"And isn't hiding the truth the same as lying?"

"Yes, I suppose it is."

"Then, by extrapolation, you could lie to your best friend to keep from hurting her."

"Yes, I guess I might."

"And there lies the difference between you and me. I will always tell you the truth, even if it should hurt you."

"Then tell me your name."

"My name is not important. It does not matter whether or not I tell you my name. My decision to withhold my name is not a matter of truth or lie, but a conscious decision to withhold it from you. However, I am honest by telling you that I will not tell you my name, rather than lie and tell you a false name. Further, please do not make me remind you that I will tell you my name only when you earn it. Not before. This is the third time you've asked me. I suggest that you check the rulebook about asking the same question multiple times."

"Yes, Sir. You're right. I shall not ask you again. Thank you for your indulgence."

After refilling their glasses several more times, Avril and Sir talked well into the night. Eventually, he noticed her stifling a series of yawns. Standing up, he said to her. "Let's call it a night and walk you home."

Putting her wineglass down, she stood up and accepted his arm once more. As he led her to her room, she thought about the evening and their discussion. Opening the door to her room, he stepped back and kissed her goodnight on the cheek. Startled, figuring he had intended to bed her, she stepped back and gestured that he was welcome to come in.

"Tomorrow, maybe, after we resume your training. Rest up and get a good night's sleep. You're going to need it. You don't need the reminder, but the standing rules go back into effect when this door closes. Deposit your dress down the laundry chute. It will be cleaned and returned to the closet. Tomorrow, we begin again. Be ready."

With that, he closed the door and locked it.

Dumbfounded, Avril stared at the closed door. She slipped the dress off, letting it fall to the floor, and stepped out of it. After removing her jewelry, returning the pieces to their proper place, she dropped the dress down the laundry chute. Washing up and a bit drunk, she made her way to the bed. Pulling back the covers and she climbed in, naked but for her heels. The moment her head hit the pillow, alcohol and fatigue took her, and she fell fast asleep.

Chapter Thirteen

"Wake up, lazybones. You've missed breakfast." Avril heard, startled into consciousness. Opening her eyes and focusing on her surroundings, she saw him standing there at the side of her bed.

"Oh, shit!" realizing she had overslept. Jumping up, she almost apologized but, at the last moment, held her tongue.

"Go clean up. I expect you showered, shaved, teeth brushed, and the bed made in thirty minutes. Do not keep me waiting a minute longer."

"Yes, Sir. I'll be ready."

"Be sure that you do. We are already off to a late start, and there is so much to do today."

"Yes, Sir. I understand."

As she responded, he sat down in the wingback chair. Seemingly disinterested in her routine, he just sat there while she showered, washed, and dried her hair. After stripping the bed, she remade it with fresh sheets and knelt in her designated position, wearing just her high-heels with barely a second to spare.

After a minute, looking at his watch in confirmation, he stood up and said. "Follow me."

Getting up, she followed him as he walked in the direction opposite from the stairwell. Gulping, she realized that he was walking towards the very room where he had chained her the first night of her arrival. Nervously following him, she wished and prayed that he would not open that door.

Confirming her worst fears, he stopped at that very door and opened it. Stepping back, she stared at the open door, fearful of what she was going to find in there. Frozen in fear and uncertainty, she found she could not move her feet.

"Inside, go," he commanded her.

Trying to will her feet to move, they steadfastly refused even to take a tentative step.

"I won't tell you again. Failure to obey me will earn you a punishment."

Gulping, she took a tentative step forward and then another one.

Taking her initial steps allowed her to follow them up with additional, tentative steps.

"Stand in the center of the circle of light," he told her.

Scanning, she quickly found the circle of light he mentioned. It took all her willpower to walk over to it, fear trying to make her turn around, and run from the room. Slowly, hesitantly, shallow step by shallow step, she arrived at the edge of the circle of light. Looking down, it looked to her as if the light came from the floor itself, rather than from overhead. Though she was already on the edge of the circle, she could see shadows start to play across her body from the light source below. Two tentative steps later, and she was standing in the center of the circle.

After taking a deep, cleansing breath, she took her standard standing pose. Content with her posture, she finally found the courage to look around. What she saw didn't make her feel comfortable, but at least the fear of the unknown seemed to dissipate.

"Alright, today, we move on to the next stage of your training. I see that you are nervous. Please relax. I will not punish you. Do you understand?"

"Um... I think so, Sir."

"Listen to me. I will not punish you," he repeated with a commanding tone.

"Yes, Sir."

"Alright, we are going to begin the next phase of your training. First off, you are going to learn a new pose. Anytime you are in this room and need to take a pose, you will take the one I am about to show you. It is okay to ask questions for now. You must get this right. It would be best if you didn't learn a bad habit because you didn't ask. Nod if you understand. "

Avril nodded.

"Put your hands behind your head and interlock the fingers." He waited for her to comply. "Good, now square up your shoulders and make sure your forearms are parallel to the floor."

After adjusting her arms, he told her. "Good, but you need to push your elbows up towards the ceiling a bit more... better... a bit more please... perfect. Now, I push your elbows back so that they are in line with the back of your head. I want you to think of a meter stick. If I place it behind your head, the tips of your elbows should touch the stick, and the lines of your arms should follow the meter stick exactly."

Avril thought she had her arms in the correct position, at least until he came up behind her and yanked her arms further back.

"There, that's better," he confirmed.

As she tried to maintain the pose, she thought to herself, "Hm, this is hard. I don't know if I can do this, Sir."

"I know that this may seem hard at first. That's okay. When you get back to your room, you will practice this pose by standing with your back against the wall. If your elbows can touch the wall, you comply. It would also benefit you to stand to see yourself in the full-length mirror in your room. That will allow you to make sure your arms remain square to the floor. Alright?"

"Yes, Sir. I will practice this pose back in my room, and I will practice it until I get it right."

"Good, now, one more thing. Move your feet a little more than shoulder-width apart. Each foot should line up outside of your shoulders. That's good—but a little wider. There, that's better. You're doing well. Comfortable?"

"Frankly, Sir, no, not really."

"That's alright. It will become second nature to you before long. Just keep practicing in your room. Hmm, one more adjustment, I think. Curve your spine just a bit more. To understand what I mean, you should be able to slide the rulebook behind you, just above your hips, as you stand against the wall. It should slide freely, almost on the verge of sliding out to either side but not down, past your ass. Do you understand?"

"Yes, Sir. I do. Is this better?"

"Yes, it is. The corresponding kneeling pose is like this, and it may even be an easier pose to maintain. With this pose, keep your knees wide apart, well beyond shoulder-width apart. I want your legs to be perpendicular to each other at your groin when you are correctly in position. Do you know what I mean by perpendicular?"

"Yes, Sir. My thighs should be at ninety degrees to each other."

"Yes, that is exactly right. You are not used to having your knees that far apart, so I want you to practice it until you can get it right and can hold it indefinitely."

"Indefinitely, Sir?"

"Yes, that is what I said. Indefinitely."

"I will try, Sir."

"Maybe I didn't make myself clear. There is no trying, you will practice it, and you will do it. There is no reason why you can't. The physiology of a woman's body makes that pose possible. It's all in teaching your muscles to behave. There is no time limit on how long it takes to learn to hold that pose. All I require is a concerted effort to practice it every day, intending to meet the goal. Am I clear with the expectations?"

"Crystal, Sir."

"Good." Then, after a pause, he continued. "I am about to talk to you at length. I want you to maintain this pose throughout our conversation. However, if you fall out of the pose, I will not punish you. Just resume it as quickly as you can. Alright?"

Avril nodded.

"Excellent. First off, I want to tell you that you are doing very well in your training. In many ways, you are exceeding it, despite the punishments you earned. Most of the women in my care suffer much worse. You should be proud of yourself."

"Thank you, Sir."

"Now, I want to talk about you and why I think you are doing so well. Your first series of lessons were all about exploring your sexuality. I know you were sexual in the past. However, our assessment indicated that you didn't feel like a sexual woman, a real woman. Together, we explored that. You may have thought that I was getting my rocks off, and maybe I was. I enjoyed myself, but I have many women for that. However, with you, there is a plan."

That plan was to free yourself from inhibitions implanted in you during your upbringing that carried across into your adulthood. It took a while, but your success in your sexual growth allowed you to graduate and receive your first crystal on the heel of your shoe. There will be more successes and added crystals as you progress. I will tell you, even though we are moving on to another stage of your training, we will still exercise your sexuality. There will not be any letting up or regression of mastered lessons just because I introduce new ones."

Sir allowed her to consider his words before continuing.

"Next, we will explore another side of your body and incorporate your mind in the process. You will resist. You may even fight it.

However, I am asking you to trust me. Yes, I know that you don't right now, but I ask that you do so. I have your best interests at heart, and I believe in what we can do together."

After another brief pause, he continued. "But before we get into that, I want to talk about you. In your previous life, the one lived before you came to me, you worked as an executive assistant to an officer of a major marketing firm in New York City."

Nodding, she waited to hear where this was going.

"You were very successful in your position and, as a result, made a decent income, not a great one, but enough to live decently in the city. In reviewing your file, you were living from paycheck to paycheck. Is this not correct?"

"Yes, Sir. I was."

"Wasn't that difficult?"

"Yes, Sir. Some weeks were harder than others, but usually, it all worked out."

"Were you able to save money?"

"Ah, no, Sir, at least not much."

"As I understand it, you borrowed money from a friend or loved one to make rent."

"Yes, Sir. I did, on two occasions."

"Did you ever pay them back?"

"I did it with my friend. She needed the money as much as I did. However, I borrowed money from an uncle. He and I aren't that close, so I didn't want to ask him for the money, but I was desperate at the time. So far, I haven't paid him back. Honestly, I don't know how or when I can. I think of the debt from time to time. When I do, I push it to the back of my mind and try to ignore it. However, it bothers me that I owe him the money I can't repay. Besides, I don't think he cares if I pay it back or not. He told me at the time that he had a debt to my parents, and this was a way of paying it back."

"Well, you won't have to worry about it anymore. I paid off all your debts in their entirety."

"Sir, that's over well over ten thousand dollars!"

"Don't worry about it. It's a small amount compared to what I have already invested in you."

"But what about my family? They don't know what happened to me."

"You're not to worry about that right now. We'll talk about your family later. Now is not the time, but I promise you, we will talk about them." Avril nodded. "For now, I want to talk about your job. Let me ask you an important question. Could you have done the job of your immediate supervisor?"

"No, Sir, I don't believe I could have. His job entailed responsibilities that I was not privy to."

"I want to tell you something. You were crucial to his success as an officer of the company. You made him look good, and you fixed many issues before they became issues."

"Sir, isn't that what an executive assistant should do?"

"Yes and no. You did more than what a typical assistant does. You met with clients, you handled their issues, and you made them feel warm and welcome. In return, they gave your company their business, knowing all the while that you were there to take care of them."

"I am proud to announce that in your absence, your company made many changes. A month after your disappearance, they put your supervisor on probation because of his accounts' poor management. His customers filed a series of complaints. After another month, they terminated him for those same reasons. Everyone at the firm, except him and you, knew of his failings. They also knew that you were there to fix things when things went bad."

"Sir, you mean they fired him?"

"Yes, they did. My sources tell me that if you had shown just a bit more initiative in those areas of responsibility, I mentioned a moment ago, they might have promoted you. Most of the executive staff recognized your competence and competed to transfer you to their department. Your supervisor knew he had a good thing going and spent much of his time blocking their efforts to get a hold of you."

"There's something else you should know regarding your supervisor. Months before we took you, we interviewed your supervisor regarding you. Our operative pretended to be a headhunter for a recruiting firm. We interviewed him to see whether we should approach you with an opportunity. During that interview, he spoke highly enough to clarify that he wanted you to stay. However, he also disparaged you and your reputation, telling our operative that your work was mediocre and your attention to detail was lacking. In the report, your supervisor did everything he could to dissuade the headhunter from pursuing you any further."

Shocked, Avril almost broke her pose to turn towards him.

"A good supervisor does everything they can to help a subordinate grow and succeed. He did everything but help you. He held you back. You may feel you are an unwilling captive now, but you were just as much a prisoner back then. A prisoner with a leash around your neck and held by an incompetent fool. The difference now is, with me, you know where you stand. You didn't then."

"Sir, I don't know what to say."

"Say nothing right now. I have more to tell you. Let me ask you, do you believe you could run the entire company?"

"You mean as the President or CEO?"

"Yes, that is just what I mean."

"No, Sir, absolutely not. I'm not qualified to run that company, nor any company. I don't think I could even compete with them at even a small, independent firm."

"So, what do you think qualifies your CEO to hold the job?"

"Education, experience, the backing of the board, and I suppose a lot more."

"Let's put that aside for a moment and get back to you. You hold a B.A. in Merchandizing and an M.S. in Marketing. You also earned your M.B.A. Quite an accomplishment for an executive assistant. Did you know that executive assistants ordinarily possess just a B.A. in Liberal Arts? Don't answer that. The question was rhetorical. The point is, regarding your education, you are more than qualified. As for the experience, don't you think seven years dealing with high-value and important clients, their issues, and successes, qualifies you?"

"I don't know, Sir, perhaps, maybe."

"Then let me tell you that yes, it does. So, how does one get the backing of the board? One is money, not how much the CEO makes but how much value, called ROI or return on investment, the holder of the title CEO brings in to the company. In your case, while you were there, your department was one of the top earners in the company and had the single highest paying, long-term client. That client was Richardson Investments."

"Well, yes, Sir. How did you know that?"

"How I know is not important. Careful there. Your pose is slipping. Good, you have it back. Elbows back just a bit more, please. Good."

"Now about Richardson Investments. Your company fired your supervisor because Richardson pulled their account. The reason? He fucked up the account royally and failed to solve a crucial issue. As a result, the client lost a lot of money and pulled their business. All because you were not there to fix it and make him look good."

"Wow, I had no idea."

"Nor should you. He was an ass, and while everyone but you and he knew it. Management let it go because you were always there to cover up any issues that arose. With your leaving, his issues became theirs, so they cut the cord and let him go."

"So, you believe I could do his job?"

"Yes, absolutely, but enough about him. Let's talk about the CEO. Do you know what his educational background is?"

"Ah, no, Sir, I don't."

"Well, apparently, the board doesn't either. I have it on good authority he forged his resume. Only no one did a background check. They just assumed his resume was factual. I don't plan to correct their assumptions. Their business is not my concern. If they don't care to find out the truth, why should I tell them? What they don't know is that he only has a B.A. in Applied Arts. You're more educated than he is by far. He has that you don't, experience at the highest levels, and the ability to think outside the box. Do you know what I mean by thinking outside the box?"

"Sir, as I understand it, it's thinking beyond the expected."

"Well, that's as good an answer as any, but it is incomplete. Your training will help you learn to think and behave creatively and dare to innovate. I know you like your nice neat little world, and as a result, you always know where you stand. I challenge you to consider that your little world holds you back, starving you in both opportunity and experience. We are going to work on that, even if you kick and scream throughout."

After a brief break, he continued. "I submit you would make an excellent CEO for that or most companies. As their CEO, I bet you will double the company's value within the first five years. Ah, straighten those elbows. You're starting to slip… good, that's better."

"Yes, Sir. Sir, I find it hard to believe that I could run that company."

"I understand, but I believe it. However, I doubt you would ever become CEO of that firm because, to be honest, I have higher expectations for you. That company is full of old traditional farts. They would not appreciate you or your talents."

"I don't know what to say, Sir."

"Say nothing. It's unnecessary. I know you don't believe it now, but when you finish your training, you will. I have confidence in you. Now, let's get started with the next phase of your training. Are you ready?"

"No, Sir, but I suppose I had better be quick."

"That's my girl, and for Pete's sake, straighten your elbows. When you get back to your room, you will practice that pose for a half-hour, every hour for the rest of the day. Tomorrow, you will extend that to a full hour, every other hour for the next five days. On the sixth day, you will extend that to two hours every four hours. I require you to work towards maintaining your stand-up pose for six hours a day, every day, for a fortnight. You may work on your kneeling pose after that, as you are able. Your standing pose is the most important, as it will allow you to get the placement of your arms and elbows perfect. The kneeling pose can wait until you master keeping your arms and elbows perfectly aligned."

"Yes, Sir, but what is a fortnight?"

"Ah, yes, they don't use that word anymore in America. A fortnight is two weeks."

"Thank you, Sir. You're right. We don't use it anymore, though I should have remembered."

"That's alright. Now, do you understand what I want from you?"

"Sir, I am to make sure I get the standing pose perfect with my arms square to the floor and my elbows touching the wall at all times before I am to work on the rest of the poses. You will measure success when I can maintain a perfect pose for six hours a day for fourteen straight days. However, once again, I am uncertain how to time my practice since I don't have a way of measuring time."

"For this exercise, I will grant you a simple countdown timer, which you can set for any increments up to twelve hours. It's like an oven timer. Spin the dial to whatever duration you want, and a bell will ring when the timer reaches zero. You will take it with you as you leave here.

I have it sitting there by the door. One word of caution, I don't want you watching it during your practice settings. It will make it seem time passes slowly. Rather, focus on your pose and reflect upon our conversations and training sessions. Alright?"

"Yes, Sir."

"Then let's get started."

Chapter Fourteen

Standing in this room, in her new pose, Avril was getting tired. The strain on her arms, her shoulders, and her back were getting the best of her. Frankly, she doubted she could hold the pose much longer. Trying as she might, she felt her body begin to fail her.

As she struggled, Sir stepped up in front of her and pulled something from a pocket in his trousers. Showing them up to her, she saw that he held two little silver bells on a short silvery thread. Leaning in, he tied one to each of her nipple rings and let them dangle. Looking down, she noted that the bells, small versions of what she thought of as cat bells or Christmas bells, hung about an inch below her nipples. As she looked from one to the other, he flicked them, causing them to ring a beautiful, sensual tone. The music they made surprised her, and to be honest, they weighed almost nothing. If they didn't sing as she moved about, she could easily forget that they were even there.

Smiling, he said to her. "This way, I can hear you coming and going. Seriously, though, they do have a purpose other than they sound like music to my ears as you walk. When you are in pose, I want you to make sure they do not ring. Any movement will cause them to ring, meaning that your pose is wavering, and you are failing to maintain the pose. As you practice your poses, work to make sure they stay silent. Okay?"

"Okay, Sir. I got it."

"They will measure your success in holding your pose. If you can keep the bells from ringing for six hours a day for a fortnight, then you have successfully mastered the pose. However, I will not accept your mastery until you prove to me that you accomplished your assignment. If they jingle, you will restart the count of days from zero. I am not giving you a time limit to master the pose. Understand this. I do not anticipate that it will take you more than a couple of months to succeed. You have it within you to accomplish this minor achievement. I expect you to take ownership of the task and master it in short order."

"Yes, Sir. I understand what you require from me."

"I'm sure you do. Put your arms down and follow me."

Dropping her arms to her side, she took a moment to stretch the aching muscles, even swinging her arms around like a propeller to help relax them and get the blood flowing again.

"It will get easier with time," he reassured her. Nodding, she completed her flexing and stretching as they roamed about the room. As they walked, her new bells made the most curious music she had ever heard. It was strange. Even though they were only two bells, they seemed to ring in distinct tones. She didn't understand how this was possible, but she liked what she heard.

Breaking her from her reverie, Sir spoke on. "I want you to know. I never intended to use this room for punishment when dealing with your disobedience. Your conduct your first night forced me to react without forethought. I erred, and now I have to deal with your fear regarding this room. I'm confident we can get past that. I tell you now. I will never again use this room to punish you. You can believe me or not. I hope you will believe the former rather than the latter, as I have already promised you, I will never lie to you."

"I understand that you say that, Sir. However, you are right. If I am perfectly honest with you, I don't know if I believe you right now. For me, only time will tell."

"Fair enough," he responded before continuing. "However, let me also be clear and forthright. While I will never punish you in this room, I will punish you elsewhere. I expect you will earn many in the months and years to come. Is that understood?"

Absentmindedly, she rubbed her bruised derriere as she replied, "I understand, Sir."

"Good. Now, let me add, and please note, I did not say you would never feel pain in this room. On the contrary, you will. Sometimes it will be mild and other times severe. We will get to the specifics of that shortly. I only promised that I would not punish you for disobedience in this room."

Gulping, Avril nodded as her fear returned, causing her to yearn for the door. "Don't worry," he reassured her, "it is not as bad as it sounds. We'll get to that soon enough. In the meantime, I want to show you around."

For the next hour, he showed her all sorts of equipment and devices. He told her that he considered this a space to come and play. A Playspace, he called it. Seeing the furniture, appliances, and equipment within her view, she had difficulty thinking of it as a playroom. There were dozens of pieces of equipment. Some looked like simple furniture while others looked... well, frightening.

After circling the room, Sir stopped alongside a sofa, stuck out his hand, and offered her a seat. Avril took it gratefully. She needed to sit down. Flopping down on the comfy cushion, she crossed one leg over the other, giving him a good long look at her toned legs capped off with the beautiful high-heels. Once settled, he sat, angling his body towards her, and draped an arm across the back of the sofa. Looking around, Avril realized she had a perfect view of the entire play space and most of the equipment.

Giving her time to get her bearings, Sir asked. "Do you know what BDSM is?"

While Avril understood some of the equipment, she had never explored the concept of BDSM. Answering cautiously, she responded. "Sir, it's that kinky stuff that people do to hurt each other while having sex."

"Hm, let's for a moment, take your response and break it down. Word by word, you are correct. Overall, you could not be more wrong."

Sir's response elicited a close questioning look on her face as it scrunched up in disbelief of what he said.

"BDSM is so much more than that," he continued. "BDSM is an anachronism for something much more, and something incredibly intimate. Do you know what the letters stand for?"

"Ah, no, Sir."

"They stand for 'Bondage, Discipline, Dominance, Submission, Sadism, and Masochism.' It's a mouthful, right? There's a lot of meaning in those four little letters. What they stand for only scratches the surface of what we consider BDSM. What I am about to say applies especially to me. It is 'the' most intimate act that two or more people can share and experience together. It is more personal than sex, kissing a lover, taking part in a wedding, or mourning a loved one's passing. With the right attitude and partners, BDSM raises the intimacy between the participants to stratospheric heights. They bond in ways that are stronger and more enduring than marriage and sex. Bonds created in the realm of BDSM usually cannot break, even if the parties part ways and never see each other again. These bonds can permeate every cell of one's body and take residence in one's soul."

"And is that what you hope and intend to happen between us? Sir?"

"And who said you lacked skills. Oh, right, your ex-supervisor. Did you know they found him dead weeks after they fired him from an apparent suicide?"

"I suppose it should surprise me, even make me upset. Strangely, I'm not. Did you or the Consortium have something to do with that?"

"Let's just say, my lack of an answer to that question is affirmative. He was a pig and a disgrace to humanity. But let's get back to you."

"Did he suffer?"

"Same answer as before. Let my lack of a reply be your answer."

"Good." Avril surprised herself, hoping that he suffered in excruciating anguish for a long time.

"About BDSM and how it relates to the two of us. Here is how I see things. One, like me, you portray dominance, but you've never considered yourself to be dominant. Your behavior for most of your life was anything but dominant. I intend to bring that out in you. But before I can do that, you will need to learn the other side of dominance, that is, submission."

"Please understand, I don't think you will quickly take to submission, but you have it in your power to do so. You already demonstrate that you can submit. However, I am not referring to what you have always thought of as submission. Nor what you did in your previous life. The behavior you exhibit here to date proves that. I just feel submission does not come naturally to you. You embrace it because that is what your upbringing taught you to do from birth. You completely suppress your dominant side. Together, we will explore this aspect of you, using the other terms involved with the definition of BDSM. I am first going to show you what true submission is, and then, when you are ready and have mastered submission, I will expose to you what it means to be dominant, all within the realm of BDSM."

Avril was grateful that Sir paused a moment to allow her to gather her thoughts and think about what he just said. It seemed like a lot to take in, and she knew that she had to understand what he was saying before she could accept his instruction. She didn't know what to make of it, but she was glad he paused. It gave her time to reflect. As she pondered submission and dominance, he continued, interrupting her train of thought.

"There is one other aspect to BDSM that I haven't touched on, and it's important. Parties engaging in the art do so willingly. There is no force or pressure from one on the other. It is a willful exchange of power by each party to the other. By rights, a dominant should never expect a submissive to take part solely because the dominant demands it. Each must willingly enter the relationship before one can think of it as BDSM. Otherwise, it is more abuse of power than a power exchange. It's the willingness to feel it and exchange power with each other that raises one's intimacy to the extraordinary heights I mentioned earlier."

After a momentary pause, he continued.

"In the everyday world, millions of people engage in BDSM activities and relationships all around the globe. They do so willingly, and each side surrenders power to the other. I will go into this later, but first, you need an introduction to the experience. One session cannot address to anyone's satisfaction just what that means. It will take many sessions before a novice to BDSM can begin to recognize the significance of the experience. I plan on taking you through the experience, step by step."

"Sir, I don't understand something. If both parties must accept a part in the experience, how can I freely agree if I am your captive property who does not have a choice? Mustn't I be free to choose or not?"

"That is an excellent question. You're right, of course. For you and me to experience the stratospheric intimacy that I described, you must freely agree to what I am offering. We must exchange the power dynamic, including my surrendering something to you as you surrender something to me. You must also be free to say no, thank you. I also grant that you have little say in what I do with you or to you as my property. For now, we will go through the motions of what I am describing, but I have no expectations that either of us will achieve the intimacy I crave. At this point, I hope that one day, you will accept what I offer and will, on your own, give yourself freely to me so that together, we can achieve the state of intimacy I hope to realize one day with you."

Stopping, he allowed her to reflect upon his words. "When you return to your room, I want you to review our conversation in your mind and consider its ramifications. Study it, reflect upon it, and analyze my comments. You will undoubtedly have questions. At the appropriate time, I will give you leave to ask them, and I will answer them as best as I can to your satisfaction. In the meantime, we will begin slow and cautiously for the rest of the week. Alright?"

Avril nodded her acceptance. Only this time, he spoke up. "I need to hear it in words from your mouth."

"Alright, Sir. I will see where this goes." She answered him, frankly doubting that she would ever willingly submit to him.

"Then, please come with me."

He led her to what appeared to be a church kneeling bench. Only this bench had a waist-high shelf that tilted down and away from the kneeler. It also had multiple straps hanging from it. "This is a spanking bench. Don't worry. I will not spank you today, though I will sometimes, not as punishment but as part of the BDSM experience. This bench has many uses besides spanking. Kneel and bend over and support your waist over the top."

Avril approached the bench with just a hint of hesitancy in her movements, grabbed either side, and knelt on the padded cushion. Having padding under her knees was a small blessing in itself. Avril hoped she would not come to hate this bench.

After adjusting herself, Avril leaned forward and rested her belly over the downward sloped platform. Wiggling a bit to find a comfortable posture, she tested the bench. The cushion was soft enough, and her knees sank into the soft pillow. Likewise, the shelf she rested on also had a cushion, though not as thick. The frame was just broad enough to support her waist and belly, but her breasts spilled over the edge, leaving them to hang freely, her bells playing music as they swung back and forth."

"Here, let your hands dangle down… good… that's perfect. Next, I am going to strap you down. Once done, you cannot move. You must trust me. I will not hurt you or cause you any pain today. Rather, I believe you will enjoy our session."

As he finished, he bent over and adjusted her knees to be about two feet apart from each other. She couldn't help wonder at how exposed she felt, her ass and pussy on full display while her pendent breasts played soft music. Tilting her head down, she looked between her legs and watched him strap her legs down, first at the top of her calves and then the top of her thighs. After he had finished, she experimented a bit.

"Yup, they won't be moving anytime soon," she acknowledged to herself.

He anchored both her legs in an 'L' shape, leaving them immobile. The most she could do was rock her feet at the ankles.

"Comfortable?"

"Yes, Sir."

Walking up towards her side, he bent over, pulled a strap over the small of her back, and buckled to his mate. Secured to the bench, he took each one of her arms and pulled them behind her back. Automatically, she clasped one hand inside the other. Gently, he strapped her arm to the belt across her back. He did the same to her other arm, securing both behind her back. She found the position of her arms curious, as he had never left her wrists unbound before.

Twisting her head around, she saw him pick up another strap, similar to one he used to beat her the last time. It looked ugly to her. Before she knew it, she was tensing up, fearing that he was going to break his promise.

"Please relax. I told you, I will not punish you or hurt you."

"Yes, Sir. It's just that… when I saw that strap, I couldn't help myself."

"I understand, but please relax." He said while gently stroking her back and derriere.

His touch on her tortured and bruised ass didn't hurt at all. Instead, it soothed her, and soon, she felt herself unclenching and her body relaxing. After settling herself down, unable to see what he was doing, she sensed him thread the strap under her arms, just below the elbows. He pulled the ends over the top and buckled them together, forcing her elbows to touch each other behind her back. The sensation wasn't exactly painful, but it was uncomfortable. She didn't know whether she was flexible enough to accomplish this feat.

"Before long," he told her, "you'll be able to do this easily and even more tightly. Almost done," he finished the thought, "and we'll move on to fun parts of the play session. Though being honest, strapping you down like this is fun for me. Seeing you like this gives me great pleasure and enormous satisfaction."

Tilting her head up to look at him, she said. "You're welcome, Sir. I don't know why I am about to say this, but I will. It pleases me that I could do this for you."

As soon as she finished, she wondered why she said that.

He smiled in acknowledgment, and for some unknown reason, warmth flooded her body. Then he stepped up to her, softly pressing her head down so that it dangled just as her breasts did. He then did the most unexpected thing. He took ahold of her hair and began fashioning it into a braid. As he worked, he wove in a bit of long cording. By the time he finished, the cord had become a part of her hair. The cording firmly held when he tugged on it. It felt like someone was pulling on her hair, though it didn't hurt at all.

Then he disappeared out of sight. A couple of minutes later, he returned and held an object in view.

"Do you know what this is?" he asked.

Studying it, it looked like a hook. It was shiny, but not chrome. Then it hit her. "Was it a high-quality polished surgical stainless-steel hook?" She thought to herself.

"Ah, no, Sir. It looks like a hook, but what is that ball on its end?"

"It is a hook, alright, and it's for your ass. The ball will act as an anal bead. The cording I just tied into your hair will feed through this hoop on the other end to support your head. It won't damage or hurt you. If you relax, it will slip in easily. You have already accommodated my cock, so this should be natural for you."

She nodded, agreeing to what he was about to do. He was right. She had his cock buried deep into her ass many times. She had learned that she could find pleasure having it stuffed up there, thrusting away. Besides, the thickness of the steel of the hook was thinner than his cock.

In thinking about his cock up her ass, she began feeling as if she missed it being there. The last time he took her that way was just before he beat her ass for breaking the rule about asking permission to cum. That was a while ago. As she thought about his cock, she realized that he had already placed the hook against her sphincter and pushed. It slipped in smoothly. She hadn't felt its transition until she felt the coolness of the metal inside her rectum.

Sensing him move to her side, he picked up the end of the cord and threaded it through the loop on the exposed portion of the anal hook. Gently lifting her head, he pulled back on her hair until her head faced forward and outward and tied the cord off. Releasing his hold on her, she felt the weight of her head pull downwards, tugging on the hook inside her. Testing her predicament, she figured out that she could relieve the tugging pressure in her ass as she lifted her head. Allowing her head to fall forward, increasing the pressure, and impaled the hook deeper into her ass. Simultaneously, it pressed against her G-spot. She discovered that she could easily stimulate her G-spot to a rising climax by moving her head around.

"Nice, eh?" He said as she studied this peculiar behavior.

"It is interesting, Sir, but I will have to be careful to ask permission. I can already tell that I can climax in this position with the hook in my ass."

Grinning with a mild evil grin, he replied. "Just remember the rules, and you'll be fine."

"Yes, Sir."

Squatting down in front of her, he took a long look at her, studying her, appreciating the view. As he watched her, every little, minuscule movement she made, the bells hanging from her nipples rang, filling the area with a soft melody of music. She studied him back, and for the first time since she had come here, she looked at him, staring into his eyes and seeing his soul. He had deep gray eyes. She hadn't noticed that before. Perhaps that was why he seemed to wear gray and black a lot.

As she studied his face, she appreciated the concern in his eyes. She also noticed the hunger he seemed to have for her. Yes, that was right. He was hungry for her. She had never seen that look on anyone before, including guys who she thought were hot to trot. The hunger she observed was different somehow. Sure, she knew that he wanted her sexually. He took her body any time he wanted, which was frequently. Both of them enjoyed the romp. But there was more in there, hidden behind those gray eyes of his. Was it need? She didn't know. She only knew that he desired her. He hungered for her more than any man had ever wanted her in all her life. The revelation shook her a moment. She didn't know what to make of it, nor how she should react.

Lost in thought, studying those hungry gray eyes of his, she followed his face when he finally stood up and walked over to a nearby wingback chair. Sitting down, he removed his shoes and socks, shirt, and slacks before standing again in just his silk boxers. His erection, visible in the opening of his boxers, communicated the hunger he had for her. Before her eyes, the erection grew and poked out his fly to come to its full, upright stance. She licked her lips in anticipation as she watched it grow just for her.

"Do you want this?" he asked her.

"Sir, yes, please."

"Ask me," he told her directly.

It took a moment by what he meant, and then she realized. "Please, Sir. May I have your cock?"

"Be more specific," he replied.

"Sir, please, would you please put your cock in my mouth so that I may suck on it and please you?"

"Yes, you may," he replied as he removed his boxer shorts and stepped up to her face. Teasing her, he let the head of his cock dance before her mouth and eyes, almost with a glancing touch, but never touching. She opened her mouth, fully extending her jaw to accept him. Sticking out her tongue, he was just out of reach. She strained, pushing her head forward, working hard to get to touch him, as the hook dug deeper inside her rectum.

Oh, it was ever so close. Avril could smell his musk and feel the heat radiating off its head. To have it so close and yet so far was maddening.

Finally, he came close enough that she could reach him with her tongue. Caressing the underside of his cockhead, that sensitive part she knew he liked, she massaged him. He let out an involuntary sigh of pleasure, enjoying the touch, feeling his heat transfer to her tongue.

It was maddening. Avril wanted him inside her mouth, and he continued to hold back. Her efforts pulled the hook in her ass, softening her frustration of not having all of him inside her. Then she figured out that by rocking her head back and forth and extending her jaw, she could establish a rhythm of stroking him with her tongue while stimulating her G-spot with the ball on the hook. It turned out to be a pleasing combination. She could make him feel pleasure while her excitement steadily grew.

As she worked, and yes, it was work; she felt her body build to a climax. Before she knew it, she was in trouble. She needed to stop pleasing him and allow her pre-climax to fade, or beg permission, hoping Sir would grant it. She had no choice. She needed to decide.

"But what if he says no?" she thought. With little to lose, she decided.

"Sir, may I cum?"

"Are you asking my permission to cum?" he affirmed.

"Yes, Sir. May I please cum?" she responded, clearly struggling to contain herself.

"Wait for it."

Frustrated, her excitement growing, she waited but continued the rocking motion, pleasing him as she pleasured herself.

"Sir... may I please...?" she begged.

"Wait for it," he commanded.

"Shit!" She cursed in her head, but she didn't stop rocking either.

She was close to being in trouble, suffering punishment for breaking one of his rules. She started not to care. She was that close to cumming. She would suffer his discipline, as excruciating as it would be, to satisfy her immediate need for a climactic release. Struggling to reach out and slide more of her tongue on his shaft, she garbled.

"Sir, may I please cum! Please?" Avril begged, frustrated by his denials.

"Cum now," he commanded. Receiving permission, her body fell over the chasm and into the world of ecstasy.

Wrapping her tongue as hard as she could around his cock head, she forced that hook with the evil ball on its end to smash up firmly against her G-spot. The resulting explosion of sexual release flowed right through her body. As she came, he shoved his cock in one smooth motion to the back of her mouth and down her throat. A feral growl flowed past her vocal cords as she clamped down on his shaft and held him firmly in place. Determined not to let him pull it out, she sucked on it with everything she had, her climax racing throughout her body, drenching her in sheer pleasure.

The surrounding room disappeared. In fact, except for his invasion into her mouth, Sir vanished from her world. Avril no longer heard the music from her bells swinging wildly beneath her. She could see nothing past the base of his cock, nor could she feel her body strapped to the bench. Avril felt the soft hair on his loins as they tickled her nose. All she felt was the pleasure of the moment.

Even though Sir had vanished from her world, she felt his surges, his cock building rapidly to a release of its own. She heard his urgent breathing, demanding more and more oxygen, preparing for the time when he would hold his breath amid his climax. She could smell and taste his pre-cum, tracing lines across her tongue, as his cockhead skewered her throat. She felt her throat respond and expand to accommodate his growing girth.

Expecting her airways to close off, she discovered that she could still breathe. Apparently, in this position, with his manhood clogging her throat, her airways remained open. Air continued to flow easily to her lungs. The discovery drove her to an even higher level of excitement, allowing a robust, deep growl to rumble past her vocal cords and vibrate his cock.

At the exact moment of her latest and primal growl, his cock seemed to clamp down on itself before expanding once more, shooting his cum down her throat. Her tongue, still wrapped around him, caressed him, feeling his contractions as he expelled his seed again and again. She felt the volume of his release shoot directly down her throat. She milked him, draining his balls while wallowing in her orgasm. She did not know how long their combined climaxes carried the two of them on their roller coaster ride of pleasure, and she didn't care. He had given his permission to cum. She was no longer afraid to ask.

She experienced her first major orgasmic release in countless years, and she rewarded him as a result.

Chapter Fifteen

When she found herself back in her room hours later, she reviewed their time together. It had to be late in the day. She wondered just how long it would be until the overhead light went out, denoting night time. While she usually went to bed soon after that light went out, she was under no orders to do so.

Determined, "Let's work on this pose," Avril thought as she pondered the events of the day.

Stepping up to her full-length mirror, she realized that it faced an empty wall behind her, perfect to practice her posture. Picking up her rulebook, she stood against the wall and fitted the thick book behind her back's small. With her butt pressed firmly against the wall, she pushed her shoulders back and let go of the book. It sat there, perfectly happy as a bug snug in a rug, resting on her hips. However, he said that it should easily slip sideways. After a couple of adjustments, she could hold it in place while being able to slide it easily from behind her.

"Would wonder never cease?" she considered. "Now, for the hard part, putting her hands behind her head."

Looking at her reflection, she adjusted her arms until she thought she had achieved the position he wanted. With her arms square to the floor, she pressed her elbows back until they touched the wall. Though she thought she was pretty loose and flexible, there was a noticeable strain on her shoulders. It took a lot of effort to keep them pressed against the wall. The thing was, she didn't think it required this much effort when she was with him down the hall. It was certainly odd.

Returning to the day's events, she found that as she pleased him and focused on him rather than on herself, she found simple pleasures in giving to him. Fucking each other, their sole purpose to delight each other, rather than trying to take pleasure from their partner, turned out to be remarkable. To date, he just took his pleasure from her. Today, he seemed to do just the opposite. He seemed to focus on her, giving her exactly what she needed, without making it all about him.

"Yes, that was it. He made it all about me." Avril realized.

"He made me the center of the session. It was not about him. It was all about me." She muttered, surprising her.

"And that is what I wanted for him. I made our time together all about him. Imagine that!"

Reflecting upon the day, she first recalled their adventures in the Playspace. After their first shared orgasms, orchestrated by Sir teasing her with his cock just out of reach of her greedy mouth, they moved on to more traditional fucking, where he'd thrust into her pussy a thousand times over. While she relished having him being inside her, all she wanted now was to please him. Unable to move about, all she could do was clamp down on him, caress him with her vaginal canal, and pull him into her. He responded similarly, driving his cock in and angling it so that it stimulated both her cervix and her G-spot.

Other times, he pulled on the hook, forcing the ball to slide around inside her. She presumed he could feel it sliding along the top of his cock. He would reach down and finger her clitoris, giving her the best of both worlds. Sometimes, he withheld his permission to come, but this seemed to add to her orgasm when he finally did give her the go-ahead to climax. It was strange. Waiting for his permission, she never seemed to lose the drive ask built. It was as if she banked her pleasure, withdrawing it from the bank when she finally needed it, augmenting what she had already stored.

"Hm, it's hard to believe that he could make me climax like that." Avril reflected as she stood against the wall, trying to practice her new pose.

"They were the finest orgasms I've ever experienced. I wonder, though, was it because Sir forced me to hold back over all these many weeks, or was it because of being strapped to the bench and totally out of control? I can't figure it. We've fucked daily for hours on end, week after week, and while I had a grand time most of the time, I can't say for sure what did it for me this time. Was it the permission to cum finally, or was it his total control over me? One thing is for sure. I'm looking forward to finding out."

Pausing her thoughts for a moment to readjust her position, seeing in the mirror that she was slipping, Avril continued her reflections.

"I'm glad I'm not sore from all that sex. Notwithstanding the peculiar circumstances, I feel a warm satisfaction all over. I can't wait until we resume my training and do it all over again."

"Hey, hold on a minute! Do I want to discover this new side of me? The one he wants me to discover? I still need to escape my imprisonment. But how? As long as he keeps me locked up in this room, there's no escape. So, should I continue to go along with his tender care mixed with his abuse? Notwithstanding the beatings, everything else is fun and exciting. Should I go along with it and enjoy it? I have no choice, and if this is what I can expect to continue in my training, then I'm all for it. I have to admit it is fun. I hope that I don't regret it."

"Oops, you're slipping, girl. Square up those elbows and press them against the wall." She admonished herself. "Damn, consistently holding this pose is harder than I thought. I hope it is worth it," she added, unsure of herself.

Resigned, she kept at it as best as she could for the rest of the day, taking only bathroom and meal breaks until bedtime.

Sleep came slowly to Avril. Her mind raced with thoughts and images that she could not settle down. She tossed in bed for hours, more and more frustrated with each passing moment. She tried to force herself to sleep, but it was to no avail. For the first time since being locked in this room, she was grateful that she didn't have a clock.

Mostly, it was the lessons of the day that weighed heavily on her. Her body was still feeling the aftereffects of the sex. She felt satiated and yet felt eager for more.

"How strange, I can't remember ever a time when I felt this way. Always, once the guy closed the door behind him, I felt satisfied, and sleep quickly consumed me. Now, my desire is overwhelming. But there has to be more to it. Doesn't it? Besides, it's not just sex. Oh, the sex was grand and all. That wasn't the issue. I enjoyed sex before they took me, but now I know. I LOVE sex. What is it about this bastard that makes me feel this way?"

"Every time we couple, it's as if every cell and atom in my body rejoices in the pleasure it feels. In the old days, sex was more convenient and a simple act to relieve certain stresses. Now, sex is different. It is a part of me, enveloping and consuming me. It's more than a way of releasing stress. It was now a significant portion of who I am. It was refreshing in many ways. The more and more he shared his body with me, the more feminine I feel, and the more of a woman I am."

"Wait, the old days? What? The old days?" Shaking her head slightly, she put that thought aside.

Thinking about sex was not what was bothering her. It was this assignment to learn how to stand in this new pose. As an athlete, she never worried about not preparing for a run, lift weights, or exercise using gym equipment. This new assignment seemed easy at first. Just stand there against the wall, hold your hands behind your head, and touch your elbows to the wall. She regularly failed throughout the day. She found the strain on her shoulders, clavicle, and her collarbones hard to manage. She had always figured that she exercised every muscle in her body. Now, though, she found ones she never knew she had. It was, frankly, frigging hard to do.

Further, standing still seemed foreign to her. While she understood the concept of isometric exercises, such as yoga, the one he assigned her appeared to be without purpose. Standing still and unmoving, in what she felt was an unnatural position, failed to give her insight into what he was trying to accomplish.

Just what the hell was his end game? Why did he target her and bring her here in the first place? There were days when she thought that those women hanged at the auction, and the one at the training center got off lucky. They were now at peace with the world, their souls communing with the maker.

"The way Sir keeps at it, and if I am lucky (or was it unlucky?), it would be many decades before I will meet my maker. In all that time, how will I handle his absurd cruelty?"

"What does he want from me? Does he want me to submit to him? Well, right now, yes, that is just what he wants from me. What about a year from now, two years, five or ten years from now? Will I be around that long, or will they roast me alive for someone's dining pleasure. I had better figure this out and quick."

"Yeah, just what the fuck does he want?" she yelled at nothing in particular. Frustrated and irritated, she finally fell into a restless sleep.

As the first days and nights, so went the days and nights for the following weeks. Sometimes, Sir would share breakfast with her and, after eating, watch her do her homework. As she practiced standing in her new pose, frequently falling out of it, she had hoped he would give her some encouragement. She waited in vain. He just sat there, in his wingback chair, and appeared to see her not at all. On these occasions, he worked on his tablet. She ached to use it, but he never offered it to her. Instead, he sat there reading it and occasionally typing on it in apparent oblivion to her struggles.

Try as she might, she didn't seem to be able to hold the pose. Keeping her elbows touching the wall at all times was proving impossible. It was maddening, and at times, she wanted to give up. Only the rule book forced her to keep on trying. Rule sixty-three stated something to the effect that failure to do the assignments would incur the severest of punishments. Rule sixty-two, at least, allowed her to keep trying despite failing time after time.

After the mandated six hours of practice, she stopped to eat. Usually, he left her alone, affording her a respite from his ever-watchful eyes. Now that she thought about it, he rarely sat in his chair and watched her. Most times, after having breakfast together, he would leave her to her assignments. It was late in the afternoon or evening when he collected her to escort her to the play space.

She smiled at the memory of their time in the play space. True to his word, Sir never punished her while inside the play space. Instead, at each session, he introduced her to the furniture and equipment placed around the room. He even had a bed in there, which they used frequently. However, it wasn't an ordinary bed. It didn't exist for sleeping. Instead, it was for what he called 'play.' It didn't have much of a mattress. The mattress reminded her of those she used during summer camp when she was a girl, though this one was bigger. When they used it, he tied her down to it.

The first time using the bed, he tied each of her limbs to the corner posts. Having her hands restrained behind her head, and her legs pulled wide apart, fully exposing her groin, left her feeling on display and very vulnerable. Sometimes, he added a pillow under her ass and other times not. Once, in the spread-eagle formation, he had wrapped a rope around her hips and upper thighs and hoisted her into the air, leaving her hands and feet tied to corner posts. With her back bent backward and her hips suspended several feet off the bed, he climbed up on the mattress and fucked both her holes for hours on end. It was fun, in a way, but not as much fun as other positions.

So far, while they experimented incessantly, he had never once hurt her. Sometimes, though, the equipment strained her muscle and joints, but running often felt much worse.

After two weeks, instead of going right to the equipment, he had her stand in the pose. Her posture was still not great, but maybe it was getting there. He offered suggestions on her progression to help her succeed. Once she settled in, wearing nothing by skin and heels, he started talking.

"Today, I want to talk about two things, first about your efforts in mastering this pose and then moving into the next phase of your training. For this session and while standing in this pose, you may ask questions, add comments, or share your thoughts about our discussion. Please limit your comments to the topic at hand. Alright?"

"Yes, Sir. Thank you."

"Would you like to start?" He asked her.

"Ummm, well, Sir, it's like this. I… um… don't know where to start?"

"Can I guess? You're frustrated at your progress with the pose, and you're angry at yourself, me, and the world? I could go on with a litany of what's bothering you."

"Well, I guess that's it, Sir. My immediate frustration is my inability to excel in this pose. Logically, it should be easy. I just stand here and don't move. Even now, my bells are ringing, playing their music, while my elbows falter. The rest, well, that's probably for another time."

"You almost had a mental breakdown the other day. Didn't you?"

"Sir, Yes, I did. How did you know?"

"Let's just accept that I knew, and I wanted to see if you could work your way through it."

"I did, in a way, Sir. Though at the moment, it felt good to get it all out."

"It was more of a tantrum, wasn't it?"

"Ah… I suppose so, Sir, though I didn't think of it that way."

"Did you not scream at the air, stomp around the room, throwing pillows, and the like?"

"I guess I did, Sir. I do remember some of it. I also remember, as much as I wanted to break something, I didn't. At the time, I thought you would punish me if I did."

"Is there something in the rulebook about breaking items in your room?"

"Ah… no, Sir, I guess there isn't."

"Then, if you had broken something in your tantrum, would I have punished you?"

With a lot of hesitancy, not wanting to answer him, she finally timidly said, "No, Sir, I suppose not."

"That's right. You would not have earned a punishment. The items in your room are yours. I don't care whether or not you break them. You will just have to do without in the event you take out your frustrations on inanimate objects."

Thinking about that, she dropped her head and nodded.

"Head up, shoulders and elbows back," he scolded her. She immediately complied.

"Sir, this pose, this posture with the elbows, I didn't think it would be so hard to maintain. I was wrong. I am finding it impossible to do. I… well, I don't like failing, and yet, here I am, failing to do such a simple task. I don't get it. Why do you wish me to master this pose?"

"The simple answer, I wish you to master it. You need no other reason. Besides, you look beautiful, standing there for me. I like seeing you in that pose. Trust me that I have my reasons, which I may or may not share with you. As for your feelings of failure, you're not used to failing. I get it. You're an athlete and an accomplished runner. I get that you believe that this should be a simple task to master, and yet, you know that it isn't. Let me ask you, did you learn to run a marathon in just two weeks?"

"Ah, no, Sir. It took months to get good enough to do that. However, this is not the same thing. I'm just standing still. Running the marathon required me to train, to teach my body how to run over just a long-distance over many hours."

"And how is that different from this task? I am asking you to train your body to hold that pose for many hours. Don't you think you need to teach your body how to do that?"

"Yes, Sir. I suppose you're right, but this is just standing still. I'm not running or jogging. I'm just standing still. Standing still does not exert much energy."

"Doesn't it? Think of it as an isometric exercise. You are trying to maintain your balance by standing on the balls of your feet and keeping your shoulders and elbows back beyond where you normally keep them. I'll bet you're discovering muscles you never knew you had before."

Laughing, "That's putting it mildly, Sir," she nodded and then had to fix her posture yet again. Those damn bells were giving her away.

"Good, you adjusted all on your own. Would you like to know what I see in your progress?"

Nodding again, she quickly adjusted her pose once more. "There go those bells again," she chuckled softly, loud enough for Sir to hear.

"I see a woman giving it a concerted effort to master the skill. I see a woman who is doing it because I require it and knows if she doesn't, I will punish her. More importantly, I see a woman learning to master the pose and her body for personal reasons. This woman has taken ownership of the challenge and is embracing it. She saw the test as easy, and it surprised her to find out otherwise. It has become an obsession to master it, just as it is an obsession to run."

Sir stopped for a time as she thought about what he said. After an appropriate time, he continued.

"You are making progress. You may not see it, but I do. You're very hard on yourself, demanding more from your body than I am. I would not tell you this before, as you had to get to this point in your lessons, but I did not expect you to master it quickly. Very few of my women master it at all, and most fail. If you had started when you were a child, then maybe it would come easily to you. It takes time, practice, and effort to achieve this skill. Any skill learnable by putting time and effort into it, and you are doing that. That is all I ask."

"Sir, it doesn't feel like I'm making progress. However, what you just said makes a kind of sense. Do you honestly believe I am making progress?"

"Whether or not I do is not the issue. It's whether you believe you are making progress. So, I ask you, do you?"

"Sir… I don't know. Some days I think I have, and other days, I don't. Other times, I feel I've regressed from any progress I made. So, Sir, to answer your question, I suppose the answer is no."

"Well, I disagree. I'll leave it to you to figure out why. I can't do this for you. Only you can. Whether you continue and master the skill or give up and fail is up to you. If you continue, I know you will master it."

"Sir, then I'll do it. As you said earlier, I have taken ownership of mastering the skill. It is less important to me to show you I have done it and more important to me that I do it."

"That's my girl. See, that's progress, mind over matter. You can do anything you put your mind to."

Avril smiled at this, redoubling her efforts to maintain her posture.

"Do you have anything else to discuss before we move on to the next phase of your training?"

"Many, Sir, but none pertinent to the topics on hand."

"Fair enough. Rest assured, I will allow you to ask further questions, perhaps at breakfast one day. We'll see. Right now, I want to introduce you to another component of BDSM."

Nodding, Avril waited for him to continue.

"Tell me what you know about pain," he asked her.

"Well, Sir, it's the body's way of warning of danger. You pull your hand away from a hot pot on the stove because you feel pain in your hand. The pain is to help you minimize the damage the heat may cause."

"But what explains a headache then? You feel pain, but what triggers it, and how do you stop it? If you sprain your ankle, you feel pain, but by then, it's too late. You feel the pain of the injury, but you can't minimize it as it has already happened."

"I don't know, Sir. Possibly, you feel the pain to warn you the next time. Maybe then, you can avoid whatever caused the pain."

"That explains the sprained ankle, but not the headache. People get headaches all the time. What then?"

"Honestly, I don't know, Sir. In acute cases, it could warn you about an aneurysm or something else going on inside your brain, but in most cases, headaches just are not that severe. I don't know why. Pain is just something that we humans learn to deal with."

"So, you're saying; it's something we can learn from?"

"Well, yes, Sir. That's true."

"Do you feel pain when you run or jog?"

"Sometimes, Sir. Usually, I just ignore it, and it goes away."

"What happens when it goes away?"

"Sir? I don't get your meaning. What are you asking me?"

"I want to know how you feel after the pain goes away."

"I don't rightly know. Sir, I know I feel better, sometimes better than before."

"Do you get a second wind? Do you feel that you could run all day and all night and then all the next day?"

"Sometimes, Sir, though I rather doubt anyone could."

"Do you know that before the Europeans invaded the Americas, many of the natives found it second nature to run, in the barest of footwear, through the forests, for days on end, stopping only for a quick water break before continuing? Often, they ate and drank while running. Besides, they did it all night long in a time where there were no electric lights to illuminate the way. At most, they had moonlight or carried a flaming torch. But they ran and ran, hour after hour, often for days on end."

"No, Sir, I did not know that."

"Well, they did, and do you know why they could run that long?"

"No, Sir."

"Primarily, no one told them that they couldn't do it. Their family and tribe taught them from birth to run like that to achieve adulthood. As adults, they used their skills to communicate important messages or deliver a needed supply to a tribe or family member. The thing to remember is that no one ever told them that it was impossible to do such a feat. Therefore, they could."

"Sir, but didn't their bodies breakdown as a result?"

"Sometimes they did, but rarely. They trained from birth to run long distances at a decent clip. Their bodies gave them the energy to handle it. Food and water were all they needed to keep up what most people think of as a grueling pace. To them, it wasn't. They just did it."

"Sir, this is fascinating, but what does that have to do with pain? How does that figure in?"

"Let me ask you, have you ever experienced a 'runner's high'?"

"Yes, Sir, of course."

"And what causes that?"

"Ah, I don't rightly know, Sir. I do know that it takes time to feel the high, and it's different for everyone. For me, I have to run about five miles before it kicks in. Until then, it's only through sheer grit that I get past the pain and fatigue until it kicks in."

"But, it does kick in eventually?"

"Oh, yes, Sir, at least most of the time."

"And when it does, what happens then?"

"I feel euphoric. I can see inside myself, almost as if I am another person behind my eyes, directing my body to run while concentrating on other things. As I run, the miles seem to go by effortlessly. I can usually run another ten or fifteen miles before the effect dissipates. Then, I have to work through more pain and exhaustion to keep running."

"And can you regain that high?"

"Sometimes, Sir, but not always."

"Can you feel that 'runner's high' without running?"

"Ah, I don't know, Sir. I rather doubt it."

"What if I said you were wrong? Would you believe me?"

"Ah… I don't know, Sir." Avril hesitated, sensing a trap.

"Have I ever lied to you before? Haven't I promised you that I would never lie to you, under any circumstances?"

"Ah, yes… Sir," Avril answered cautiously.

"Oops, you're losing your pose. Fix it, please. That's better. What I am telling you is the truth. I suppose you need to understand what a 'runner's high' is, so you can believe that you can achieve the high without actually running. However, teaching you the scientific reasons behind this phenomenon would take months, so I will try to simplify it for you."

Avril nodded, a sign that she was listening and waiting for the explanation.

"Simply put, a 'runner's high' is the body's state when it releases several chemicals into the bloodstream. These chemicals send energy to the body's cells, allowing them to process stored sugar into energy, allowing the body to continue its activity for the duration. These chemicals are called endorphins. Oh, sure, other chemicals, such as dopamine, are involved in this exchange, but most people call them endorphins. Have you heard of endorphins?"

"Yes, Sir, though I did not associate the term with 'runner's high' before."

"Not to worry. Anyway, the body releases endorphins to deal with stress, exercise, and a host of other reasons. The body also releases endorphins to deal with pain. Unlike taking a pill, it is the body's natural way of alleviating fatigue and pain. The result is that you feel better, even better than better. You feel euphoric, to use your words."

"I see where you are going with this, Sir. As I run, fatigue sets in, and I feel sore. It's sometimes painful, but I know that my body will help me deal with the pain when I work through the pain. After that, I feel better. From what you said, it's my body releasing endorphins that helps me deal with the pain."

"See, you're making progress. That is exactly right, though there is much more to it than what I just described. What I said is a simple description of a much larger process."

"So, do I gather that you are about to inflict pain on me?"

"Yes, that is right."

"Sir, I don't mean to be forward, but I recall you promising you would never hurt me in this room."

"That is not quite correct. I promised that I would never punish you in this room. That is not the same as not hurting you. I may not hurt you either, but I will cause you to feel pain. Pain does not have to be harmful, but it is possible. I will do everything I can to prevent harming you, but I cannot guarantee that. During the next stages of your training, you will feel pain, just as you feel pain when you run. Does the pain you feel when you run hurt you?"

"Ah, no, I guess not, unless I push too hard or there is an accident."

"The same will be true here. Together, we will explore a series of new experiences, which will free you from decades of misinformation and false teachings. I will do things to you, and you will feel pain, but I will not hurt you as a result. Do you know the difference between 'Good Pain' and 'Bad Pain'?"

"Sir, I confess, I've never heard of the concept before."

"No, I suppose you haven't. From what we've talked about so far, can you make an educated guess? I assure you, there is such a thing."

Taking her time to process their conversation, Avril took a very long time to consider the concept of 'Good Pain' versus 'Bad Pain.' Fearful of what she was about to experience, she had to admit that the painful episodes she encountered in the past while running weren't all that bad. It was nothing like a fall from a sprained ankle. Instead, it was more of a general ache that seemed to get her to stop running. When she didn't and forced herself to run on, the pain morphed into something else—something she didn't understand but subconsciously accepted. Sir did not interrupt her and just waited for her to resolve the issue.

Finally, she offered. "Sir, while I don't understand the difference yet, I am forced to admit that there is something to your argument. Sometimes I do not shy away from pain because I know that there is something good on the other side."

"That's as good an answer as any I could come up with, given your knowledge on the subject. Do you feel ready to explore this?"

"I suppose so, Sir. I admit it's scary."

"Fear is just a component of our experiences. Think about that. In the meantime, for this section of your training, you must give me everything and hold nothing back. I want you to take and accept everything I do to you, no matter how much it hurts, holding nothing in reserve. In return, I will give you everything I have to make your gift worthwhile."

"Gift, Sir?"

"Yes, I said gift, and I meant it. To progress, I ask that you freely give me your trust, that I will do what is best for you. In effect, I want you to give me your mind and your body freely. I've taken power over you, but there is still something held in reserve that I cannot take. I am asking you to give what little remains freely to me, at least for the short duration of our play scene together. You may take it back after the lesson."

"You want me to give everything of myself and turn it over to you? Did I understand you correctly, Sir?"

"Yes, you did. I want everything and without reservation. For you to progress, the quicker you give me power over all of you, the quicker we can move on to other stages of your training. It will be harder for you if you don't, and it will feel more like a punishment than pleasure. So, you see, I am offering you a chance to experience greater pleasures, a deeper intimacy in the workings of your body, interacting with the world around you. This newfound intimacy is something that will stay with you for the rest of your life, whether or not I am in your life. You will grow in endless ways and love yourself more in the process. You don't have to tell me what your decision is. I will feel it in your responses to our play. We will begin shortly."

"Sir, thank you for that. I still don't know what to make of all this, and I am still nervous and scared. However, I am open to trying, and I will do the best I can to give you what you ask."

"Good. Stay in your pose while I prepare. Like you, I need to prepare for this next stage. I won't be long."

Standing in front of her, she felt his warm, appreciative eyes looking at her. She felt his acceptance and even his stated feelings about how beautiful she looked. Then he turned and walked out of the room. He didn't return for a long time. Nervous and scared, she waited for him with a bit of excitement for what was about to happen.

Chapter Sixteen

Avril watched him turn and leave the play space. Nervous, she wondered just what she had agreed to allow him to do to her. To be sure, it frightened her. It took all her willpower to remain standing in pose and not bolt for the open door.

"Oh, shit! He left the door open!" She realized before coming to the obvious conclusion. "Oh, my God, can I escape? Should I?"

Indecision tore Avril into frozen inactivity. "He has held me captive for so long, and yet, here I can get away and escape, or do I? Was this an opportunity, or is it a test?"

Looking down at her feet, even though the posture did not allow it, she considered willing her feet to move. No, not move, but run. Staring at her feet, adorned with her cobalt blue heels and single crystal on her heel, she willed them to inch forward.

Her feet refused to move. "Come on, feet. Move, damn it! Just take a step," she commanded her feet.

She tried; oh, she wanted to get them to move. They declined to budge even an inch.

"Why are they not moving? Why are they balking at the simplest thing, their reason for existence? Why? I'm in control of my feet. Aren't I? Did he have that much power over me? How was that possible?"

As Avril considered the issues at hand, an escape route was suddenly presenting itself, yet her feet failed to move towards it.

"Why? Oh, wait, there's that collar around my neck. I had become so used to it that I had forgotten all about it. Now, what was it that he said regarding the collar? He had put it on me so long ago. I can't remember. Unless I'm with him, I'm always locked in my room. Till now, testing the capabilities of the collar was beyond my ability."

"Oh, that's right. He told me that if I went where I'm not supposed to go, the collar would shock me into unconsciousness. But wasn't there more to it? What was it?"

Studying the problem for several minutes, she remembered that if she tried to remove or cut the collar, it would—what was that, oh, yes, it would separate her head from her body.

"Well, that's a bit permanent. Escape, yes, followed by a quick and painful death. No, that's not the answer, at least right now. I might take that route one day, but not now. If I stay and play his game, I might get to live. If I try to escape and get caught… well, I need to figure a way to prevent that. I need to plan my escape very carefully, and that takes information. Just as he is studying me, I need to study him and learn as much as I can about him and his intentions for me. There's no doubt about it. He is perplexing, but until I get more data, I need to focus on staying alive."

"In the meantime, what kind of life would I have to accept? Do I live as a subjugated servant? The sex is fine, great in fact, but satisfying his sadistic appetites does not appeal to me. What should I do? Should I choose life as someone's owned property or suffer excruciating pain followed by death?"

With no other alternatives, Avril pondered the question, searching for a sliver of a plan.

Then the answer came to her. With every breath, it brought her closer to a solution. If she jumped now, then those possibilities were closed to her forever. Therefore, she was going to stay right where she was. Reaffirming her posture in the pose, she allowed her mind to go blank while she waited for him to return.

With an empty head, minutes stopped ticking inside her head. When he came back, she had no idea how long she had stood there. Just before he returned, she made a startling revelation. Maybe it was the sound of his footsteps approaching that broke her out of her reverie. Perhaps it was something else. However, it happened, with her mind walking the road to awareness, she realized that holding her pose had been easy, very comfortable with her mind free of all thoughts and concerns. Could that mean that she could master this pose while keeping it for hours? She decided she was going to try it the next time she was alone in her room.

"Ah, very good, very good. You're still holding the pose, and it's near-perfect as well. I wasn't sure you could do it. Well done." Sir said to Avril as he walked into the room.

She smiled a tight, brief smile, barely acknowledging her appreciation of her effort.

"Are you ready to get started?" he asked her.

"Yes, Sir. Nervous, but I'm ready."

"Good, you may relax and stand at ease."

"Ah, Sir, if you don't mind, I would like to continue holding the pose. I've just realized that I am making progress, and I would like to continue to practice."

"I appreciate your dedication to practice, but you can pick that up back in your room. Right now, I need you relaxed and pliable."

"Yes, Sir," she said, lowering her arms and clasping her hands behind her back. "I, ah, well, you know, Sir."

"Yes, I believe I do. So, I have an important question for you. You must answer honestly. Just as I will tell you the truth, you must tell me the truth. Why didn't you try to run?"

"Run, Sir?" she started, pretending that she hadn't considered an attempt to escape. Before she knew it, she realized what she was doing and recovered, but continuing her answer. "Well… I will admit that I considered it. This was the first time you've ever left me alone in a room with an open door."

"And what conclusion did you come to?"

"Sir, to be fair. At first, I tried to get my feet to move and bolt for the door. However, they wouldn't move. They refused even to inch forward. If they had done at least that, I probably would have made a break for it. When they didn't move, despite my best effort to force them, I stopped trying and tried to figure out why?"

"And what did you conclude?"

"Sir, I still don't rightly understand it, but I figured that if my feet refused my command to run, there had to be a reason. I suppose something in my subconscious held me back."

"But to stay put had to be a conscious decision. What was it?"

"That it wasn't the right time, Sir."

"Will there ever be a right time?"

"I don't know, Sir. Frankly, I don't know what to make of it. Logically, as someone kept without my permission, I should look for every opportunity to escape. Yet, I figured that now was not the time. The probabilities of successfully escaping were low. If I had tried and failed, I would incur a severe, even fatal punishment. My chances of a successful escape increase with each passing day."

"So, you thought it out. Good. I am glad you decided, as I hoped you would. You are correct. You would have earned a severe punishment. I don't want to discuss what that punishment would have been, but I would have lost all trust and faith in you, and I would have responded in kind. I'm glad you stayed."

Avril didn't have a response she felt was appropriate, so she said nothing.

However, Sir continued, "I will say this, I hope that one day, you will decide for yourself to stay with me and accept a permanent place in my household, on your personal choice."

"Sir, in the spirit of being honest with each other, I rather doubt it."

"We'll see, we'll see. As you near the end of your training, you may feel differently."

"I don't see how Sir. I'm just saying."

"Think about what you want. I told you when I put that collar around your neck; your fate was entirely in your hands. What you do with it is up to you."

"Sir, aren't those words without meaning? I mean, I have no control. You have all the control. My fate is in your hands, not mine. Therefore, I am powerless to do anything to direct my life."

"Really? Don't you think the decision you made not to run proves that you are in control of your fate? Run or not, you reached that decision. I had nothing to do with it."

"Except Sir, I would earn a formidable and terrifying punishment if you or the Consortium recaptured me."

"When not if, we recaptured you."

Avril did not respond. She suspected he was right in saying, 'when' and not 'if.'

"Oh, pooh, that's an excuse for the masses. You are an intelligent individual who can evaluate a situation and make your own decisions. That proves that you can direct your fate."

"Possibly, Sir, I must reflect upon that."

"You do that. Still, I'm pleased that you chose not to run. I am looking forward to many weeks of play as you learn to experience a new existence plane. Oh, that reminds me, not only will you be experiencing this new plane of existence. You'll experience it with me and me with you. I'm looking forward to sharing the journey with you.'

"Sir, if you're ready, so am I."

"Good. I'll escort you to your room. Get a good night's rest. Eat and stay hydrated. I will come to you right after dinner tomorrow. We'll play together well into the wee hours of the night."

"Sir?" Avril asked, confused that he would not start their play right off.

"Are you questioning my decision?"

"Ah, no, Sir. I'm just confused."

"Good. Better to keep you off-balance. Practice clearing your mind as you work on your pose. That skill will come in handy and make it easier on you during our play." He told her as he opened her door and held it open for her. She walked in and turned to face him.

"Till tomorrow then," he said as he closed the door behind him and locked it.

Staring at the locked door in disbelief, Avril tried to figure out just what happened. Shaking her head, she turned away and made her way to the en-suite. First things first, take care of business and then practice the pose until bedtime. Tomorrow, she vowed to incorporate clearing her mind while in pose and see what happens. To be sure, it was going to be an exciting day.

Chapter Seventeen

Over the next several weeks, he kept her busy. She had long ago lost count of the days, so she presumed it had been weeks. Most days, he came for her towards the end of the day, usually after dinner. Occasionally, he collected her before dinner, and so she missed her evening meal. Whether or not she had eaten, she was ravenous after every session. She often had to wait until breakfast to refuel.

Mornings found her anxiously waiting for breakfast. When she was alone, she wolfed it down, wishing for more. When they shared breakfast, she forced herself to eat slower, despite her hunger. Perhaps it was his presence or something else, but she was grateful for the extra food that came with his attendance.

Before this latest stage in her training, she felt rubbery from the exhaustive fucking. Now, although they fucked, the sessions in the play space had left her exhausted for other reasons. Satiated but not ready to stop their play, she craved for more. It was a strange experience.

That, perhaps, was the issue. This alternate state of reality he was trying to get her to experience eluded her. She didn't know how to help. Seeing her miss out on the adventure frustrated him. She could see his frustration growing. She wished she could experience what he wanted her to feel. He kept reinforcing that once she slipped over the edge and entered this alternate consciousness, she would feel pleasure as she never felt before. She would exist in an alternate reality, for lack of a better word, where only the two of them lived. Everything else would disappear and become insignificant. Even if she entered it alone, she would find a kind of fulfillment that would leave her completely relaxed and comfortable with the actual world. He made everything sound so enticing.

Throughout the sessions, he kept reminding her that she needed to relax completely, wipe her mind of all concerns, and give him everything. He used the word 'power,' but she didn't honestly understand what he wanted. He wanted her to give him power over her, which confused her to no end. He already had power over her. He was in complete control of her life and her body. What more did he want? She had no idea. As far as she knew, he already had it.

Waking up this morning, she followed her usual routine. First, she took care of business in the en-suite. Then she made the bed and cleaned up the room. After her shower, she ate breakfast, savoring the coffee Sir allowed her. After taking the time to enjoy the coffee for an hour or so, she practiced her poses. While she had mastered his number-one mandated posture, including keeping her hands behind her head and her elbows held back, she needed to practice every day to ensure consistent compliance.

When she didn't practice, Sir always commented during their session, adjusting her and chastising her inferior position. Besides, he added a couple of new poses for her to master. The most challenging one was kneeling upright with her knees spread far apart and her ankles crossed over themselves. Keeping her balance, and remaining upright, taxed her back and shoulders as she, once again, discovered muscles she didn't know she had. Her concerns about mastering postures behind her, she felt confident that she would learn this pose. It amazed her that such simple postures would tax her body so much until she mastered them.

Usually, when lunch arrived, she immediately broke to eat. Occasionally, she would postpone it to continue working on her assignments. Once, she missed lunch entirely after it disappeared from the alcove before she stopped to eat. Fortunately, that day, he collected her after dinner. Today, she paused on time and fueled up. After eating and cleaning up, she sat down at the desk and began drawing.

After all this time, she composed a significant number of sketches. She filled the desk with filled sketchbooks, most denoting her feelings and experiences of her enforced captivity. Some were works of art, while others were mere doodles. Sometimes she flipped through them to see how far she progressed. Some days her artwork helped cheer her up, while other days only reinforced her feelings of helpless despair.

Once, last week, she noticed an interesting pattern. The tone and tenor of the drawings changed throughout her captivity. Her earlier work reflected her dark, angry moods, filled with resentment and anguish. However, her recent sketches, those done since her introduction to the Playspace, captured an entirely fresh perspective. The tenor of the drawings perplexed her. They appeared softer, calmer, and even erotic, reflecting contentment she never expected to feel. She had rendered her sessions with Sir on paper shortly after he gave her the drawing materials. After he began taking her to the Playspace, despite how challenging and painful the sessions often were, the renderings showed an entirely different viewpoint than before he brought her here. They revealed a serenity that she never expected.

Take, for example, one of her first sessions with him. He bound her to a post, her hands held high above her head, and attached a long bar at each end to her ankles. The bar forced her to stand with her feet uncomfortably apart. Exposed, it kept her off-balance and feeling completely vulnerable. He used various instruments throughout the session, mostly floggers, slowly warming her skin with soft, flexible fronds before progressing to harder, stinging ones. He flogged every part of her body from above the knees to below her neck throughout the evening. He mostly focused his attentions on her thighs, belly, and breasts, but nothing like his focus on her vagina. He targeted her sensitive pussy more than any other part of her body. The funny thing was, none of the strikes hurt. Sure, most strikes stung, but she didn't feel pain. Even now, she didn't understand how he could strike her with stinging or thudding floggers and still not feel pain.

When he finally took her down from the post, she was hungry for his cock and practically raped him. Though stamina kept him ready for action, for the first time, she thoroughly depleted him, and still, she needed more than what he could handle. Sensing her need, he startled her by going down on her. He had never done that before. He surprised her. Sir climbed between her legs, bent over, and ate her out with the expertise of a cunnilingus master. He knew precisely how to address her clit with the tip of his tongue, lightly caressing it on the upstroke and relaxing it with the downstroke, dragging the underside of his tongue on her sensitive nub. Most guys she had ever been with pressed too hard with the full width of their tongues, which was pleasurable but rarely satisfying. His tender technique was more than satisfactory. She had almost squeezed him to the death between her legs when he allowed her to cum.

Since that first night, Sir tried her out on every piece of furniture and equipment in the room. Some were easy to relax and enjoy herself. With others, she spent more time trying to get off the equipment than she did to focus on what he was doing to her body.

Then, there was the time he had her strapped to a large freestanding frame in the shape of an 'X.' He had a name for it, but she couldn't remember what it was. When he told her its name, she was already well into the session and only heard his voice but not the words he used. That night, upright and spread-eagle, he warmed up with his various floggers before he brought out a new toy. She did not know why he called his instruments toys. This toy was a whip. About four feet long or so, the sight and sound of it brought out her fears in full force.

Wide-eyed in fear and whimpering, expecting the worst, he calmly spoke to her in a soothing tone while swinging the whip back and forth. At first, the noise it made as it cut through the air in a back-and-forth motion paralyzed her. Raw memories of the whippings at the auction house filled her with dread, bordering on terror.

All she could hear was the swishing sound of the whip cutting through the air. When he snapped it, the sound it made as the tip cracked screamed at her, reminding her just how painful the whip could be. Struggling and strapped to the 'X' frame and focusing her sole attention on the lash, she cringed, fearing what he was about to do to her. The memory of the girl at the training center as he severely whipped, leaving deep, bloody cuts all about her delicate skin before they hung her, consumed her. Visions of matching angry red welts crisscrossing her body filled her mind. She whimpered at the thought of the severe strokes painfully landing about her body. Her fear taking took control of the innermost recesses of her mind. She never noticed the whip kissing her belly.

Even after her mind detected the kiss of the whip, it took several additional gentle lashes before her fear settled down and finally, gratefully disappeared. To Avril, the strokes felt tender, in a tingly sort of way. Almost as if an insect briefly landed on her body before flittering away. The strokes didn't hurt; they didn't even sting. Her skin tingled, raising goosebumps along the way. Even the strokes that landed right on her nipples and clitoris felt good. It didn't take long before those strokes got her sexually excited. As he progressed with his whipping, more and more, he focused his attention on these spots until he brought her right to the edge of her exploding orgasm.

Putting aside the whip left her wanting. She begged permission to cum. The first time she asked, he permitted her, and she came right there, hanging on the cross, shaking it as she rattled her chains. Unable to touch herself in the process, the climax raged through her body. As her orgasm progressed, enthralled and overwhelming pleasure consumed her, even as stroke after stroke of the whip landed on her clitoris. Eventually, her climax resolved, and she gave up control of her body, hanging from her chains, her little death taking all that she had, leaving nothing behind. Wallowing in the aftermath, it wasn't until she regained some control of her body that he released her from her chains and took her down. She fell into his arms and allowed him to carry her to the sofa to recover. Later, she decided that he enjoyed watching her writhe on the cross before collapsing and hanging there as if she were a piece of meat.

However, in every subsequent session, she begged him to allow her to cum only to be told no, denying his permission. Sure, he eventually allowed her to cum but not until after he had taunted her many times over, bringing her right to the edge of climax before backing off again. It was maddening and yet narcotic in a strange sort of way. As much as she begged him, she came to accept his denial, knowing full well that the refusal only led to a more incredible explosion down the road. Oh, but did she ever want to cum when she wanted it.

The flogger and the whip weren't the only toys in his bag of tricks. He also tied her, using intricate patterns of rope across her body. The ties constrained her but left her free to experience the building immobility as he added length after length to the growing harness he tied around her body. He used all sorts of clamps on her, especially on her nipples and her vaginal lips. The first time he applied them to her nipples, she had to grit her teeth until she acclimated to the painful pinching. Still sensitive from the brutal piercings, when he attached the clamps, the stabbing pain forced her to take several deep, cleansing breaths. She wondered if the discomfort bordered on the threshold of hurting her or not. She decided not to press the issue.

A few weeks after getting pierced, the sensitivity decreased a bit as they healed. Now, all these months later, their sensitivity only heightened her pleasure whenever he played with them. After a while, Avril almost forgot she still wore the clamps. That is until he removed them. When he did, she screamed as blood flooded back into her nipples, reminding her that her nipples didn't like getting clamped. Every time he used them on her, she wanted to cuddle them, soothing them of the duress they suffered.

Bound as she was, she could only grin and bear it. She didn't know which bothered her more, putting on the clamps or taking them off. Never mind, she knew. Removing them hurt more, much more. She glared at him. The first time he did this, a blood-thirst glared in her eyes. He just smiled, enjoying her discomfort, and went on with his play. Well, she still glared at him every time he put them on, but he seemed to benefit from the look as the grimace passed across her facial expression. Now that she was used to them and knew what to expect, she didn't give them much thought. Of course, the memory of the clamps caused her nipples to harden and stand at attention, a welcome reminder of experiences. Regardless of how she felt about the use of clamps, her nipples grew to welcome their use.

"I'll never understand that," Avril replayed again and again in her thoughts.

He played with electricity by attaching various leads to different places on her body and shocking her. None of the shocks was powerful enough to harm her, but their vibrating stinging caused her to laugh at times or cringe and cry out on other occasions.

He also poured hot wax on her body, the wax's burning heat quickly dissipating to a soothing warmth. After being coated with layer after layer of wax, she enjoyed him peeling it from her body, touching her everywhere to make sure he got every bit off her body. He oiled her; he spanked her, not in punishment but sensually. He teased her, and he played mind fucks with her.

Like the time he strapped her to a chair and showed her pot after pot of boiling water, resting on red-hot hotplates distributed all around her. He threatened to pour the boiling water on her, burning her skin to angry white blisters. She stared at the bubbling water in disbelief, believing he meant every word as he threatened her. Then, picking up a pot of boiling water, he had walked up behind her and poured it over her head. She shrieked a bloodcurdling scream, suitable for a horror film.

Convinced that burn blisters were popping out all over her body from the boiling water washing over her, she screamed and screamed. It was only later when she realized that he had substituted a bucket of ice water. That was one of the worst mindfucks he did to her. He hadn't hurt her, but for the longest time, she believed he did. It wasn't until he proved it by showing her the ice cubes drifting lazily on the floor that forced her to accept the truth.

"I swear, I'm going to get him back for that one," Avril vowed afterward.

She lost count of how many times he played these games, trying in vain to entice her into this alternate reality of his.

"Just what did he call this alternate reality?" She couldn't remember. "It had something to do with a term used in those science fiction stories; stories of ships traveling faster than light by leaving the known universe and dropping into someplace else."

"Space, something to do with space, that's right! Space – space – something space. Warping space? No, that wasn't it. What was that term anyway? He equated it to a submarine diving under the ocean. 'Submarine?' No. That wasn't it. Oh, I remember. 'Subspace' he called it."

She had yet to experience it, but she felt that it would come in time.

"Subspace... subspace, sub, was that a reference to a submissive?" she wondered.

If it was and he was right that she was more of a dominant than a submissive, she might never experience the phenomenon. Perhaps, but he also felt it likely that she could share this state of 'subspace' with him.

Hearing a key unlock the door, she jumped from her desk and took her usual kneeling pose in the designated spot before he could enter.

"Good evening," he greeted her. "How are you today?"

"Well, Sir. Thank you for asking."

"I have a surprise for you, but to have it, you must be on your best behavior. Can you be?"

"Yes, Sir, though I am at a loss why you asked that question."

"Yes, yes, I know. However, tonight, more than ever, I want your reassurance that no matter what happens, you will behave and make me proud. Can you do that?"

"Yes, Sir. I will."

"Good, I expected that to be your answer. Tonight, you are coming to dinner with me as my guest and my submissive. I will entertain guests, and I would like you beside me at the table. What do you think about that?"

"Oh, Sir, I'm honored. I promise. I'll be on my best behavior." Avril answered with an uplifted tone.

"Fair enough. However, you need to know some of the rules for this dinner. You will be at the table as one of my guests. You are also my submissive. As my submissive, you will not speak unless spoken to. You will not volunteer information, nor will you ask questions. You will stand at my side, one-half step behind me. You will have a place setting beside me at the table. Should I sit down elsewhere, you will kneel in your standard pose beside me."

"My guests will know you are my submissive. They will also bring their submissives, who will behave the same as I have instructed you. If you question how to act, look to these other submissives to guide you, but always look to me for confirmation. At all times, you will make sure my glass is full. Further, you will not eat a single morsel of food or taste a single drop of any liquid without my explicit permission. Is that understood?"

"Yes, Sir. No food or drink unless you permit me, and I am to keep your glass full at all times."

"Excellent. You will only answer to me. The rules remain in effect at all times. If my guests request anything of you, including the use of your body for sex, your only answer will be. 'If my Master permits it.' Is that understood?"

"Yes, Sir, though, if it pleases you, I do have a question."

"Go ahead, you may ask."

"Sir, is it your intention that your guests will fuck me?"

"Perhaps and maybe more, but only if everyone is on their best behavior. I want to see if you can please them, as well as you please me. I have every confidence that you will."

"Thank you, Sir. That answers my question. I look forward to pleasing them just as I please you."

"One last thing, some of my guests like to get rough. You will permit this. I will watch closely, and if I feel they are going too far or abusing you, I will stop it. Under no circumstance will you attempt to interfere and prevent them from satisfying their pleasures. That is my responsibility. Further, if you believe a guest is pushing beyond your limits, even if you think I should intervene but don't, it's a clear sign that they have not. Remember, it is for me to decide, not you. Is that understood?"

"Yes, Sir."

"Good. Now clean up and dress. You will find a pale-yellow gown in your closet that will go very well with your cobalt heels. Wear a pair of sheer white thigh-high stockings with a matching white garter belt, trimmed in yellow. You may select subtle, appropriate accessories from your jewelry box. Use your discretion. A little will go a long way. Put on too much, and I will not look favorably upon your selections. You have about two hours to get ready. Do you have any questions?"

"No, Sir. I'll be ready, and thank you, Sir."

"Thank me after the night is over. If I am pleased with your behavior, you will earn a reward, just as you earn punishment for the most minor of infractions."

"Yes, Sir. I understand completely. I will be ready."

"Good. I'll leave you to get ready." With that, he turned and locked her door behind him.

Jumping up and down in glee, she quickly jumped into the shower.

Spinning in front of the full-length mirror, she admired her reflection. The dress she found in the closet was fabulous if revealing. Weren't they all, for that matter? The dress, fabricated from soft, metallic yellow fabric, sparkled in the light. The dress's color was unlike the bright sunny lemony color, but more like that of a lily. It had a wide fabric belt sewn into the dress and cinched tight to her frame right under her breasts. A sheer, flimsy material made of a shimmery translucent metallic yellow flowed from the top of the belt, over her breasts, and up to her shoulders. It gave the effect of water spilling down from her shoulders and over her breasts.

The fabric over her chest was sheer to the extreme. Her erect nipples stood out visibly through the material, calling attention to where to focus one's eyes. The nipple piercings forced her nipples to stand upright, leaving tiny little shadows beneath them. She tucked her bells into a small recess built into the sheer fabric under her breasts.

Below the wide fabric belt, a skirt fell tight to her waist before spilling over her hips. As her hips widened, so did the skirt, which seemed to flare out and up as she spun around. Should she turn on her heels a bit too fast, the dress would do little to hide her pubic region.

"Perhaps that is what Sir wanted from her, to give his guest a show?" she wondered.

Coupled with the white thigh-high stockings and garter belt, she looked incredible. It felt terrific to wear clothing again. While she had been naked for months on end, her nudity was now second nature to her. On most days, she didn't notice it anymore. However, now that she was wearing an outfit, she realized that clothing could emphasize her nakedness while creating an air of beauty. She was beautiful, and she knew it. Knowing it allowed her to feel it, and in return, others would see and appreciate her as a beautiful, confident, and desirable woman. That was something she had never felt once in her old life.

"Perhaps there is an advantage to this life as a kept woman?" she reluctantly considered.

Sir had given her free rein to choose her accessories. She selected a single pair of drop crystal earrings that matched the crystals on her heels. Besides the earrings, she added a surprise. She draped a string of pearls front to the back of her garter belt and threaded them between her ass cheeks and the lips of her labia. It made for an exciting feeling as she walked, teasing her excitement.

Anyone looking at her would imagine the pearls flowing out of the cleft between her legs. They would draw the attention of anyone looking at her. She expected that someone would rip them aside when they fucked her.

"Wouldn't it be grand if they stayed in place as a cock slid back and forth against them?" she wondered. "I wonder how that would feel to the owner of the cock?"

The final subtle touch would reveal itself when they bent her over to fuck her ass, finding a silver butt plug with a cobalt blue crystal matching her shoes. It would be interesting sitting down for dinner while she was wearing it.

"I hope he likes my added touches," smiling at the thought.

Satisfied with her outfit, she moved to her designated spot and stood in her standard pose to await his arrival. Later, when she heard the lock on her door turn, she knelt, perfected her posture, and watched him enter.

"Good evening. Are you ready?"

"Yes, Sir."

"Then let's go. You look beautiful. Stand up and turn around for me."

Smiling at what she was about to reveal, she spun around quickly. As expected, the skirt rose and displayed the pearls peeking out between her lips.

"I like it. You look fantastic. I especially like the pearls. Nice touch. I'm sure my guests will be pleased."

"Thank you, Sir."

"Okay, let's go."

Chapter Eighteen

Following him up the stairs, she walked a half step behind him, as instructed. When they reached the house's main level, noting none of his guests had arrived surprised her. As they walked into the great room, she noticed that the bartender had a drink ready and waiting for him.

Without asking to be excused, she retrieved the glass and presented it to him. He took it from her and put it to his lips. As he did so, she returned to his side and stood slightly behind him.

Clasping her hands behind the small of her back, she looked at the room. It looked much the same as when she saw it for the first time all those many weeks ago. Missing were the two women standing on either side of the doorway. However, she realized that other women were standing about the room, wearing lampshades on their heads, and holding light fixtures in their hands. As she expected, they were nude, wearing high-heels and a collar similar to hers. Looking around the room, she counted six of them in various locations. The lamps they held were the only illumination in the room, and the light's mild intensity made for an intimate environment.

As she looked at them, she suddenly realized that she could have been one of those women, their brief lives forever tasked with the menial jobs serving him. He could just have assigned her to do laundry, and she'd never see the house's primary levels, eventually dying in one of his torment rooms.

"Well, that was something to be grateful for," she supposed.

Startled, she realized that he had walked off towards the main foyer. She quickly fell in step with him, cautious to stick close to him at all times. As they approached the great room's entrance, she heard the sounds of the first of his guests arriving. Turning the corner, Sir welcomed the guests as they passed the house greeter who had opened the door for them. As expected, the greeter wore outfits similar to the lamp women, minus the lampshade. Instead, she wore a top hat, tilted to one side of her head.

"Hello," he greeted the guests. "It is so good to see you."

"Thanks for the invitation. It's been a while, hasn't it?"

"How are things?" A guest, a tall blonde woman, asked.

Avril stopped listening to their conversation and studied the submissives who attended their mistress. There were two of them, a young woman and a young man. Both appeared to be barely twenty years old, if at all. Both were naked.

"A common theme around here," Avril thought.

The woman was wearing black high-heels, which sported two crystals similar to hers. The boyish man was wearing sandals, with no indication of status. Presumably, he was a recent addition to the woman's harem. More memorably, he sported a shiny massive cock ring strangling his cock and balls. The cock ring made his cock and balls appear bluish and stand fully erect, almost as if a balloon was on the cusp of exploding. Avril sympathized but glad that she didn't have to share his ordeal.

Not wanting to stare too much, she forced her eyes away from the pair and returned to check on Sir. Seeing his drink was nearly empty, she briefly left him with his glass, replacing it with a fresh one. One of the guest's submissives, the girl, accompanied her to the bar for her mistress's cocktail. The other submissive, the boyish man, bent over on his hands and knees behind his mistress. Still holding her drink, the guest sat down on his back and crossed one knee over the other, using him as a chair. Startled, Avril realized that she used him as furniture, just as Sir was using his women around the room as floor lamps and such. Keeping her opinions to herself, she tried to empty her mind of the ramifications that she saw.

Soon, other guests arrived. Six guests attended along with their entourage of submissives taking care of their various needs. The visitors totaled three women and three men, not including Sir. As she surmised, they considered the submissives servants and not guests. Like Sir, his guests dressed elegantly. The men in their tuxedos, while the women wore exquisite gowns and stunning, expensive jewelry.

Without being outlandish or carnal, everyone wore beautiful outfits that did little to hide their sexuality. None of them would have looked out of place at an awards function in Hollywood.

The group mingled together for about an hour and chatted about all sorts of things. Avril tried hard to distance herself from their conversations, which she found a challenging exercise. Never once did anyone refer to Sir by a proper name. In return, he never once referred to any of his guests by name. It seemed to Avril to be an odd way of conversing. However, she recognized they had known each other for a very long time.

After about an hour or so, one of the house attendants announced dinner, and they gathered in the dining room. As she entered, Avril noted a significant change in the room's decorum from the last time she was in here. This time, the table did not include a nude woman covered in food all over her body. No, this time, the chandelier over the table turned out to be a naked woman suspended face down above the table with soft string lights draped over her body. The string lights hung from every edge and appendage of the girl. Between her widespread legs, a dildo lamp combo protruded from her vagina, casting a warm glow along her outstretched legs and onto the table. Two other light fixtures hung low from her nipple rings like lanterns, and a final lamp hung from a ring threaded through the septum of her nose. Last, she noticed her hair tied to an anal hook inserted in her rectum—similar to one she had experienced on her first visit to the Playspace. Amazed, Avril realized that it must have taken Sir hours to decorate the rooms with living furniture.

"Oh, my! How many girls does he have in his cells?" Avril wondered to herself, suppressing the urge to reveal the query on her face.

Following Sir, he stopped in front of a chair at the table's head and waited for his guests to find their seats and sit down. As he did so, Avril noticed something else that was a bit of a shock to her.

Flanking either side of the double doors leading into the dining room were two women wearing gags and blindfolds. The women were hanging by their wrists against the wall, their feet well above the floor. Other than hanging from their wrists, the women had no other visible means of support on which to stand. Their heeled ankles lashed together and tied to the baseboards near the floor. A short, thick shelf behind the small of their backs forced their hips farther out away from the wall. Sitting on the shelf behind their backs sat small lamps casting a warm glow on either side of the girl's buttocks. They reminded her of a pair of sconces flanking the entrance to a high-end dining room.

With their hands and feet secured to the wall, the women's bodies bent backward, their hips and genitals thrust out into the room. It was almost as if Sir presented their vaginas to the guests to view and touch as they desired. Staring at them, Avril realized Sir and his guests would enjoy hearing their muffled moaning throughout the proceedings, ignoring their suffering.

In the meantime, each guest's submissives held the chair of their Masters and Mistresses as they sat down. Once seated, they retreated and took station against the walls behind their Masters and Mistresses. Avril hurried to position herself behind Sir, prepared to do the same.

After the last of the guests had sat down, Avril held Sir's chair as he sat down. Avril looked to his side, noticing a place setting for her, but did not find a chair for her. Uncertain what to do, she stood behind him and took her standard pose.

Pointing to her place setting, Sir commanded, "Kneel there."

"Thank you, Sir," Avril replied and knelt on a thickly upholstered cushioned ottoman she had not previously noticed. Kneeling brought her to the height of the table as if she had been sitting. Avril remained quiet as the diners drank a toast to the evening and their host.

The group's conversation renewed; Avril stood ready to refill Sir's glass as necessary. A couple of new servers entered the dining room, carrying the first course in the meal. Delivering a plate to each of the diners, they retreated from the dining room. Sir and his guests began eating while continuing their conversation. As previously instructed, Avril waited for permission to pick up her fork and eat.

On her plate rested a seafood cocktail, comprising three shelled prawns arranged around a dollop of cocktail sauce sitting on a bed of lettuce. It looked scrumptious, and they smelled wonderful. Her mouth watered in response. Without Sir's permission, all she could do was kneel and wait, hoping he would allow her to eat.

Sir finished his first prawn and started on his second when he indicated that it was okay for her to eat. Nodding her appreciation, Avril said, "Thank you, Sir," and picked up her fork and knife, slicing off a portion of the prawn dipped in cocktail sauce and popped it in her mouth.

Avril still had a full prawn and a half left on her plate as the others finished their appetizers. Before she finished, Sir signaled to remove their servings. Avril did not stop them from taking her unfinished plate, not wanting to question him. As the meal continued, so did Sir's behavior towards Avril and her ability to eat her dinner. He delayed his permission to eat with each course and had the plate removed before she finished eating. His behavior confused her. She didn't know what to do. In the absence of any direction from him, she kept her mouth shut.

Sir denied her dessert, and the servers removed her plate untouched. In time, during their after-dinner conversation, she noticed that they were talking about her. "This is the new one, the one you are so fascinated about?"

"Yes, this is the one. She shows promise, but she's still early in her training. I have high expectations for this one."

"I'd like to take her out for a spin before you confirm her."

"Oh, I assumed that would be the case. I intend to make her available to you tonight. Between the six of you, I expect that you will break her in properly."

"All six? At once?" Avril silently realized, doubting herself. "Can I handle that?"

"Shall we all go into the Great Room then?" Sir asked.

"Yes, shall we?" Several of the guests answered.

No sooner had they entered the room then she noticed a large upholstered ottoman sitting in the middle of the room that wasn't there before dinner. Stopping in the center of the room, Sir turned to her.

"Do you remember what we talked about earlier?"

"Yes, Sir. You expect me to please your guests to whatever extent they require."

"That's correct. Please stand and take off the dress."

Reaching up, Avril slipped the shoulder strap off, and her dress fell to the floor, piled up around her ankles. Stepping out, she took her usual pose, her hands clasped behind her back, and waited.

"Pretty, isn't she?" someone said. "She looks good enough to eat."

A look of concern flashed across Avril's face, only now figuring out that this must be the woman that bid against Sir at the auction. This woman bought humans, spitted them on a skewer, and roasted them alive over an open fire. A shudder rippled uncontrollably through her body. Taking control of her emotions, she hoped Sir had not noticed the slight indiscretion.

"Ah, careful, remember, she's my property. She's not available for that," Sir reminded the group.

"Oh, pooh, I meant eating her pussy. What did you think?" She teased; while staring at the area between Avril's legs, she added. "It must taste delicious."

"Well, you are welcome to find out for yourself."

"Oh, I intend to."

Then Sir turned towards Avril and said. "Lay down on your back and put your feet up on the cushion and spread your knees wide."

Avril sat down, slid down a bit, and pulled her feet up onto the ottoman. Spreading her legs wide, she waited for them to take her. As the pack circled, they kept commenting on her looks and her body's apparent readiness for a good fucking. They seemed to like the pearls, especially. She felt Sir's smiling gaze upon her body. Then, someone noticed the bright, cobalt blue jewel poking out of her rectum.

"Oh, look. She's wearing a butt plug, a pretty one at that." Someone said. She didn't dare look up to find out who. A brief streak of paranoia flooded her body. Was Sir going to like the accessory she chose? He said she could select her accessories.

"Oh, very nice, and look at that, it matches her heels. Nice touch."

"Thank you," Sir told the rest of them. You're welcome to find out what other surprises are in store for you."

"Gladly," the tall, statuesque blonde said as she squatted down between her legs and kissed the inside of her knees. Her lips felt soft and warm against Avril's skin, and she could feel thousands of goosebumps pop out all over her body. The blonde continued kissing the inside of her thighs, working her way down towards her pussy. Taking her time about it, she eventually planted her lips on her pussy, her tongue lightly caressing the core of her femininity. Never had she felt the tongue of a woman on her clit, probing the folds of her pussy. She felt grand as the soft texture gently stroked her sensitive regions. Slowly, her goosebumps faded, and she felt warm all over. It differed from anything she had ever felt before, and she surprised herself by thrusting her hips towards the face of the woman between her legs.

"Ah, she's an eager one, for sure." The blonde woman said.

As she relished the touch of lips and tongue on her pussy, someone suddenly grabbed her by the hair and pulled her head down over the edge of the ottoman. Startled, she gasped in surprise, only to have someone stuff a hard-erect cock into her mouth. Coughing and gasping for air, the cock's owner fucked her face continually, rarely stopping to give her a chance to breathe. She felt him build to a climax when he withdrew, and a new cock replaced the first one. This one was bigger all around, only not quite so long. The added girth stretched her jaw further than ever, and she started feeling sore just in trying to accommodate him.

Then, once again, a new and yet untasted cock replaced the one in her mouth. This one was about as thick as the last one; only it was unquestionably longer. It reached into the deepest depths of her mouth and found its way down her throat. Although she had learned to swallow Sir's cock, this one stretched her throat beyond her comfort level, and she gagged. The contents of her stomach threatened to come up, and it was only with an extreme effort that she held it down. It didn't stop the slime that erupted into her mouth, coating the insides of her mouth, throat, and the cock with the slippery substance. The slime was okay with the pack as they cheered when it spilled into her nostrils, further restricting her airway.

As the men face-fucked her and a woman ate her pussy, another woman straddled her chest, planting her pussy onto her chin. With the woman's clit against her nose, she smelled delightful, leaving Avril eager to taste this woman. As the various cocks fucked her mouth and against the woman's clit, she rode their cocks, while grinding her pussy against Avril's mouth and nose. Frankly, she was finding it hard to breathe. It was then when she realized that someone was pushing aside her pearls and teasing her pussy lips with the head of a cock. A moment later, he plunged inside her. Hands stroked her belly as fingers found her clit and started playing with it, even though a pair of lips continued to kiss her. Another set of hands began massaging her tits.

The variety of sensations threatened to overwhelm her. Strangely, she found all the attention on her body exciting. She was having a grand time, even though a memory in the back of her mind told her she shouldn't. As she enjoyed the many sensations attacking her pleasure centers, she felt a part of her recall that she would never have considered sexually entertaining multiple partners before they stole her off the street. Still, here she was, being fucked by several people, men and women alike. She was having fun, and she liked what they were doing to her.

Then suddenly, everyone climbed off her, and a man picked her up. Lying face-up on the ottoman, he dropped her on top of him, her back lying on his chest. Someone removed her butt plug, replaced it with a cockhead, and jammed it into her anus. It took all of her training to relax enough to ease the entry into her ass. After a few building strokes, he buried it deep into her rectum.

"Oh God, was he ever big! Was that the third guy to invade her mouth, the one with the enormous cock that made her gag?" Avril wondered.

She found out a moment later when that third guy positioned himself between her legs and pushed his enormous cock into her pussy.

Together, the two men established a rhythm of alternately thrusting in and out. It seemed strange and yet fulfilling, feeling the two cocks rubbing against each other, sliding past each other, separated only by a thin wall of flesh between her pussy and her rectum. They fucked for some time while the others stroked her and played with her mouth.

Eager to taste the cock brought within reach of her lips, she surprised herself by attacking it, voraciously sucking it as deep as she could and swallow it. Between the women kissing her and stroking her breasts and men stuffing her every orifice, her body sang songs of pleasure and growing excitement. Every so often, the cocks in her pussy and mouth would switch, though the cock in her ass never let up on pile driving deep into her.

She felt grand.

After a time, they picked her up and flipped her over again. Finding herself face down on top of the guy who recently occupied her ass, she felt him enter her pussy, followed by another cock forcing its way into her pussy while a third cock thrust into her ass.

"Huh, two cocks in my pussy? How was that possible? Was there enough room for all of them to attack my lower region at the same time? Where did they find room to squeeze in there? What are they going to do next, put two of them in my ass?" Avril wondered in the back of her mind. At the forefront of her mind, she didn't care. She was enjoying herself.

She focused on the pleasure they were giving her, surprised by the thrill. The sensation of being wholly stuffed back there nearly overwhelmed her as their combined pounding hit all her right spots. Her mouth wide-open and moaning with deep pleasure; she accepted their attentions with great satisfaction. As she processed these new joyous feelings, a fourth hard, hot cock pushed past her open lips.

"She now had four cocks in her? Did Sir join in the fun?" she speculated. She tried to look behind her to see if she could figure it out. However, the cock in her mouth limited her ability to see. For sure, the cock in her mouth wasn't his. Yet, the ones behind her didn't feel like his.

"If it wasn't Sir joining in the fun, then who was fucking my ass?"

She knew that she was straddling a guest. However, she knew the fourth cock wasn't Sirs. She was sure of that. She knew intimately everything about Sir's cock, and none of these were his. She could feel a man's chest squashing against her tits as his cock pounded her pussy. The other cock in her pussy felt like a guy, hot and hard, thrusting into her to its tune. She could feel his legs firmly against her thighs, and his rhythms were all wrong. She was pretty sure he wasn't Sir. Three male guests accounted for the three cocks in her mouth and pussy.

"So, who then was buried in my ass? I have no idea? Was it one of the submissives, perhaps? That can't be, can it? Surely, they would not invite the submissives of Sir's guests to join in, would they?"

It took a while, but eventually, she figured out that one woman had put on a harness with a realistic dildo. She must be the one fucking her ass while the other two women were playing with her nipples, swinging on the ends of her dangling tits. Never had she felt so full, realizing that, for the first time, she was genuinely airtight, with every one of her holes stuffed with something.

Throughout the evening, the six guests took her in every conceivable way. At another point in the fuckfest, straddling a guy face down while he fucked her, another guy fucked her ass. Her body slick with sweat and cum, she was sliding up and down the length of the guy's body, pushing herself onto their cocks buried inside her. The cock in her ass kept getting swapped out with another one, and the double fucking continued.

Then, the guy who buried himself in her ass wrapped his arm around her waist and picked her up, while she remained impaled on his cock when he stood upright. He shifted his support from underneath her thighs and spread her legs wide as if to show off his catch. Her skin slick with sweat, and her slick pussy exposed and dripping, a woman came up to her and buckled a ball gag into her mouth. With her back resting against the guy's chest, he paraded her around the room, showing off and bouncing her up and down on his cock. As he strode her around, her bells swinging from her nipple rings filled the room with music, enticing the others to clap and applaud her performance.

After the parade, another guy stepped up and stuffed his cock into pussy. As they sandwiched her between them, she wrapped her legs around the newcomer to aid him in driving into her. The two men fucked her while the others poked, caressed, and fondled her body. They even teased her by clipping all sorts of toys on to her body. The toys were a fine addition to her bells, but Avril preferred the warm flesh inside and against her body.

Being the center of attention, as they cheered and enjoying themselves, was fun. Sir's guests were having a great time, and she was happy that she was an integral part of their good cheer. Having all those cocks in her at the same time wasn't bad either.

The guys shot cum everywhere. They coated her entire body and, of course, her face. The women massaged it into her skin, the same way one would use a body lotion, or they licked it off her, relishing its flavor. Wash and repeat.

As cocks left her mouth, a pussy replaced it, their owners grinding their clits against her lips and tongue. Avril liked this portion of the night. It allowed her to find out how different other pussies tasted. None of them tasted the same, and all tasted delicious. Avril relished sucking them into her mouth and teasing their clits to orgasm.

On one occasion, one woman climaxed as Avril ate her, nearly drowning her as she squirted her ejaculate. It flooded her mouth and nose, causing her to breathe in the salty liquid. Unable to stem the tide, she coughed and choked, trying desperately not to drown. Fortunately, Sir stepped in and helped her recover, though he did nothing to stop the fucking still going on at the other end of her body. Despite nearly drowning on the woman's ejaculate, to know that she could bring another woman to such a climax made Avril deliriously happy. She looked forward to a repeat performance.

Hours later and spent, Avril felt the jelly-like feeling she experienced when Sir first fucked her. She couldn't move and only realized later that Sir had left her lying there, spent as he said goodbye to his guests. When he returned, he delicately carried her from her altar of sex to her room and gently laid her down in her bed.

Kissing her, he whispered into her ear. "Well done, my dear. I am very pleased. Now, get some sleep. Training resumes tomorrow."

"Yes, Sir. Thank you… Sir," she purred as she drifted off to sleep, drawing her covers up under her chin. She never heard him leave or lock the door behind him.

Chapter Nineteen

When she woke up, her hand immediately moved to that special spot between her legs and gently stroked herself. She wasn't masturbating in the genuine sense of the word. She was feeling the after-effects of the previous evening, and her body wanted to reminisce. She tried to ignore her bladder, which was making itself known. She got up anyway and dealt with her need before returning to bed. Cupping her hand between her legs, she softly caressed herself to sleep. For the first time in a long time, she dreamed sweet, happy dreams, filling her contented soul with warm visions of her newfound sexuality.

When she next woke up, she felt refreshed and well-rested. Gone was the rubbery feeling in her legs, and she bounced out of bed. After taking care of business in the en-suite, showering, and firmly situating the heels on her feet, she couldn't resist standing in front of the full-length mirror, twisting her body about and getting a good look at herself. She didn't know about anyone else, but the woman she saw in the reflection was radiant with a healthy, rosy glow. The mirror accurately reflected how she felt inside.

Enjoying her good mood, she went about making the sheets to the bed and prepared herself for the coming day. After eating breakfast, she sat down at her desk, took out the drawing pad, and drew a beautiful rendering of her legs upended and apart, adorned by her heels and set off by the crystal. She added the string of pearls as if casually dropped over the spiked heels, and a drop of cum stretching to the floor.

For the first time, in a very long time, she felt euphoric. The thing was, she didn't know why, and she didn't especially care. When it came time for lunch, instead of finding it in the food alcove, she heard a knock on the door.

Surprised, she responded, "Come in."

Sir walked in, followed by a food cart pushed by one of his other women. Another pair of women followed, ready to serve a tasty lunch for two.

"Set them up right there," he told the servers before turning to Avril. "Well, how's my girl today? You look radiant if I say so myself."

"Thank you, Sir. I feel radiant. Last night was phenomenal. I had a great time."

"I'm pleased you had a great time, and I'm pleased with your behavior. It was perfect, just as I hoped it would be."

"Sir, I look forward to pleasing you again in this way. I've never felt like this before. I had lots of fun." Avril said as Sir held the chair for her while she sat down."

"It's alright," he said, "you may speak freely and ask questions if you like," before taking his seat.

"Thank you, Sir." Avril continued as the three servants laid out the food. After they had finished, Sir motioned, with his open palm, that it was all right to eat.

"As I said, I had a great time. I've never taken part in an orgy before. Never in all my adult life had I ever thought I would welcome and enjoy entertaining so many cocks at once. I've never eaten a woman's pussy and sucked on her tits before. To enjoy three sets of each in one session, well, it was just incredible. Thank you, Sir, for the opportunity. I had a grand time."

"You're welcome. There will be plenty of opportunities. I assure you."

"I felt great, and I feel even better now. Sir, if it is all right with you, will you give me some time to recover before going again? As much as I enjoyed myself and feel good right now, I know that I am not at my best right now. If I am to take care of your guests, I need to recover my strength."

Laughing aloud at the thought, he replied. "Don't worry. Those kinds of sessions won't happen every night. After all, I must have my alone time with you. Let me ask you, would you like a night off from your lessons and pick it up again tomorrow?"

"Sir, if it pleases you, I don't need a night off from our lessons. However, whatever you feel is best, I will accept."

"Good, then tonight it is. Since I did not take part in last night's festivities, I'm feeling a bit randy to take what is due me."

"Oh Sir, I am honored to give you what is due you, now even."

"No, that's alright. I'll stop by tonight."

"I look forward to it, Sir."

Taking a pregnant pause, he continued. "Tell me about last night. I want to know how you felt from your point of view."

"Sir?"

"Express yourself, just as if you were retelling the events of the evening to your best friend."

For the next few minutes, Avril related to him her wonderment of the night. She started with walking up the stairs from her room, noticing the human furniture and how she might have been one of them, through dinner, and onto the after-dinner show, in which she was front and center. She tried to summarize the orgy as best as she could, but frankly, she could only remember her feelings as the night progressed. The exact details were missing, and only the highlights remained. The contentment her body felt was all that she could communicate. He seemed satisfied with her answer.

After that, they ate quietly, a companionable silence between them. Neither felt the need to talk, and both were comfortable in another's presence. Throughout the meal, Sir kept looking at her. To Avril, it was a bit as if he was tossing a decision around in his head. Avril had little idea of what was bouncing around in there, but she knew enough of him to see that he would tell her when he decided.

"I would like to ask you an important question. As always, I expect an honest and truthful answer."

"Sir, I will give you one as best as I can."

"How do you feel about staying here with me?"

Taken aback at the question, Avril knew he would never show the slightest interest in how she felt about her captivity until now. His Consortium had stolen her from the streets, and he had bought her at auction. She was his property to do with as he pleased. That was all he cared about. She had to accept it or deal with the consequences of fighting him at every turn.

"Sir, honestly, I don't like being a prisoner. I wouldn't say I like being locked in this room all day and all night long. I fear what would happen if the place burned down and whether you would come and rescue me. I have visions that a demolition crew would find my body burned to a crisp, with nobody knowing who I was. I also don't like anyone buying and selling people, turning them into playthings, or, worse, roasts for someone's dinner. There's a lot I don't like about staying here with you."

"But I sense there is more."

"Yes, Sir. There is. Despite being a prisoner in your home, I somehow like living here. I don't have to worry about paying rent, where my next meal is coming from, or satisfying some prick of a boss. I surprise myself in enjoying the lessons you are teaching me, despite the punishments I earned along the way. I love sex, and I enjoyed being the center of attention at last night's dinner party. When I first came here, you scared me. No, better to say that I was frightened, not knowing what you would do to me. I was anxious about my future. Now, I know what you expect of me, and even if I fail and earn a punishment, I learn something in the experience. In so many ways, I think I love this life, except for the prisoner thing."

"Let me ask you, which do you hold dearer to you, your hate of being a prisoner or your love of the lessons and your life?"

Thinking about his question for a moment, Avril answered, "Sir, if I could combine the two, remove my status as a prisoner kept against my will, stop locking me in this room, and remove this collar from my neck, I might welcome the life you offer me. Honestly, I haven't thought of escaping for some time now, which surprises me as I say it. I used to think about escaping all the time. Now, I don't know what I would do if given the opportunity. Wow? I can't believe I just said that."

Smiling over his drinking glass, Sir looked at her, drilling his eyes into hers as if he was trying to strike oil. He kept quiet for the longest time, and Avril was getting a bit nervous about her answer.

"Avril, are you finished with lunch?"

Startled at the sudden turn in the conversation, she picked up her napkin and wiped her mouth before dropping the napkin on her plate. "Yes, Sir."

Sir snapped his fingers, and the serving women collected the food trays and left.

"Sir, did you just call me by my name?"

"Yes, Avril, I did."

"Sir, in all my time here, you have never once called me by my name or even a nickname." He just smiled. "Is there something significant to your use of my name?"

"Yes, Avril. I am promoting you."

"Sir, I don't know what to say?"

"Well, you've earned it. Please lie down on the bed, on your stomach, and fold your legs up. I'm installing a second crystal on your heels." Avril practically jumped up and laid down on the bed as he directed. After caressing the inside and backs of her legs, he attached the crystals to her heels.

"Turn over," he asked her before giving her a playful smack on her ass. Avril gleefully flipped over onto her back, planted her heels on the edge of the bed, and spread her legs.

"Oh, you are the eager one," he teased. "Before I take what is mine, I am going to give you one additional token of your promotion. I am going to give you a new piercing, one that is commensurate with your new status."

"Then, by all means, go right ahead, Sir."

"Avril," he began as he pulled an object from his pocket. Whatever it was, it remained hidden within a sealed plastic envelope. "This is a piercing for your clitoral hood," he told her, opening the envelope and holding it in front of her so she could see it.

"Sir, I see it has two deep blue crystals on it. Is that to denote my new status?"

"Yes, Avril, it is."

"Sir, will it hurt? I ask because when they gave me my nipple rings, the guards weren't particularly gentle with me. My nipples were sore and extremely tender for weeks afterward. It hurt to touch them, and worse, to keep them clean. Even now, they are still sensitive."

"Avril, I don't know whether it will hurt. For some people, it can. It is a sensitive area of your body, and I will respect that."

"Sir, will it be as sensitive as my nipples are?"

"It's possible, Avril. It's different for everyone, so I cannot give you a definitive answer."

"Sir, if you will, would you please fuck me first? I will gladly wear your gift, but I want to be at my best for you. Will you please take me now?"

"Avril, you couldn't have asked me a more delightful question."

"And afterward. when I'm spent, please, Sir, pierce me again."

"Certainly, Avril, you can count on it." With that last comment, Sir took her, piercing her repeatedly. As usual, and as his stamina allowed, he pierced her everywhere and even reinserted the blue crystal butt plug she wore the previous night before fucking her again.

For his last act, he pierced her hood and fucked her once more, solidifying that she was his and that she belonged to him.

Later that evening, Avril carefully examined her new status symbol. It looked pretty, and as it dangled from her hood, it made her feel pretty. After thoroughly washing it, she walked to the full-length mirror and scrutinized her new achievement symbols. Twisting her body around, she scanned the dual crystals living on the backs of her heels. They sparkled as they captured and refracted the light. Then, posing in front of the mirror, she scanned her genital area and saw the blue crystals, glistening from her hood, proudly showing off her womanhood. She never thought she would wear this kind of jewelry. Still, she admired them. Frankly, she loved the jewelry and what it represented.

She imagined she was a supermodel, showing off a set of designer jewelry. Walking back and forth, she imagined walking a runway, hundreds of eyes looking at her, as camera flashes took photographs of her from every angle. She was beautiful, and she felt it. Yelping for joy, she jumped up and exclaimed her delight. Then, sitting down, she drew another sketch of her legs, wearing the heels and sporting the dual set of crystals. This time, she included her pubic area highlighting her new piercing. As she drew, she couldn't help but play with her clitoral jewelry, fingering the piercing while whisking her clitoris with the pads of her fingers. When she finished the drawing, she sat back, satisfied with a job well done.

Tonight, he would continue her training, and she looked forward to it. Then it hit her. Her lessons were practice for a performance, and she was the star. She enjoyed being the center of his attention and not just his guests. She was performing for him, and she liked it.

She was his, and she belonged to him. They belonged together.

Chapter Twenty

That night, he came for her. Arm in arm, he escorted her to the Playspace. After crossing the threshold, he released her, and she took her customary place in the center of the space and knelt in her Playspace pose. Unconcerned, she kept her eyes downcast and waited for him.

Avril could hear him wander around the space, touching items and moving them around. After a time, he came up to her and stood in front, just staring at her.

"Give me your right hand," he finally told her.

Avril extended her hand towards him. Taking her wrist in his hands, he slipped a broad leather strap around her wrist. Ensuring that it sat correctly on her wrist, he firmly buckled it, ensuring that it could not slip off past her hands. The wrist strap had a protrusion of leather that ended in a one-inch steel ring lying in her palm. Once satisfied with the straps fit, he dropped her right hand and held out his hand, silently asking for her left one. Returning her right hand behind her back, she extended her left hand to him. After stroking her palm with his thumb, he buckled on a matching wrist strap. Satisfied with the fit, Avril returned it to clasp the other hand behind her back.

"Come with me," he said to her.

Rising, she followed him to an area where he indicated that she should stand. Above her head, she noted a heavy metal bar with two rings on either side. To her, it reminded her of a lat-pull-down bar one might find at a gym.

Sir walked over and pressed a button on a control attached to a nearby column as she stood there. She heard a whirring sound and, looking up, noticed the bar slowly descending. He released the button when the bar was just above her head.

When he walked towards her, he held out his hand. Avril gave him her right hand. He raised her hand above her head and attached it to one end of the bar. He repeated, fastening her other hand to the far end of the bar. Relaxing her arms, she stood there and waited, her arms resting comfortably at shoulder height.

"You okay?" He asked her.

"Yes, Sir."

"Avril, we've never done this before, so I want you to tell me instantly if you are having any issues."

"I can do that, Sir."

"Good. We're going to experiment with suspension. It's one of the easiest and simplest of suspensions. Soon, I'm going to raise that bar and, in turn, lift you off the floor. The straps buckled around your wrists will carry your weight. We design them for this and should keep you secure. Do you understand?"

"Yes, Sir. You're going to suspend me off the floor by my wrists. It's not so different from hanging from a chin-up bar."

"True, only when you are working out, you can let go at any time. This way, you will depend on me to let you down. I may not be ready to do so if you ask me."

"Oh, yes, Sir. I understood that. However, you said that if I was experiencing any problems, to let you know immediately."

"I said that, but I will still determine whether or not to let you down. I will evaluate your request and act accordingly. If I determine that you are in no danger, I am likely to leave you up there. If you are in distress, I'll have you down in moments, and I will make sure you get any treatment you might need."

"I understand, Sir. I trust you."

"While suspended, I'm going to flog and whip you. The difference is that you'll be able to spin around, bounce up and down, and anything else you want to do while suspended."

"Oooh, that sounds wonderful, Sir. Can we get started? I'm ready."

"Don't be too sure, Avril. I've suspended many women, and some can't take it, and others panic as soon as I get them off the floor. While I understand panicking, I have little use for women who can't handle suspension. Think of this as a test in your training. If you honestly can't deal with it, I want to assure you. I won't hold it against you. However, you will need to find other ways to replace suspension by means that I'll appreciate and enjoy."

After a moment's brief hesitation, Avril composed herself and said. "Sir, I will do my best to do as you ask. But honestly, I have hung by my hands before, and I don't anticipate an issue."

"Yes, but have you hung twenty feet or more in the air?"

"Ah, no, Sir," she answered before continuing. "However, I will do my best. That's all I can say at the moment."

"Fair enough. Assuming you can manage this suspension, expect many more suspensions, in more challenging positions and orientations."

"I thought as much, Sir."

"Okay then, let's get started," he said and walked over to the controls to the suspension bar. Pressing a button, Avril heard that whirring sound once again, and the bar began rising. He stopped the lift when she was standing on the balls of her feet. Coming over, Sir checked the straps, making sure they supported her correctly. After making a minor adjustment with her left hand, he returned to the controls and said. "Ready?"

"Yes, Sir."

"Then let's fly," he said, lifting her into the air before stopping a few inches above the floor.

"Okay, so far?"

"Yes, Sir."

"Okay. I'm going to leave you there for a couple of minutes to get accustomed to it. If you're still okay, I'm going to take you higher."

Nodding, Avril waited, feeling the stretch in her arms and shoulders. It felt good. She even swung her legs about to get a feel for the suspension. She was in the middle of an arc when he resumed the lift.

Higher and higher, he took her. Looking down, she figured she was already more than two feet off the ground and still rising. At about three feet, he stopped and stood there, looking at her, watching her.

"Avril, you look delicious there. I could eat you right now."

"If it would please you, Sir, you're welcome to go at it."

"I believe I will," he said and approached her. Draping her legs over each of his shoulders, he dug right in, planting his mouth right on her sweet spot between her legs and began lapping up her wetness. Avril, feeling the pleasure of his snacking, let her head fall backward and stared at the ceiling. Her mouth hung open as she moaned in delight. He probed her inner reaches with his tongue, sealing his lips around her and sucking her clit delightfully into his mouth. As her pleasure grew, so did her wetness. It didn't take long before she detected the signs of a coming climax. Just as she was about to beg permission to cum, he let go and removed her legs from his shoulders.

"Sir, I was just about to ask permission to cum."

"I know. I want you to wait."

Disappointed, she added. "Alright... Sir."

"I will say. You taste fantastic tonight. Rest assured, I will indulge myself again before this night is over."

"Looking forward to it, Sir."

He just smiled and walked over to the lift controls. Avril found that he was lowering her. Assuming he was going to land her on her feet, she stretched out with her feet, searching for the floor. The whirling stopped. Looking down, she realized that she was still about a foot off the floor.

"Thought I was letting you down? You need to manage your expectations." He teased her.

"Yes, Sir," was the only response she could imagine.

"You hang there. I'll be back." He told her and then left the room.

"What the fuck?" she asked herself. "He's leaving me hanging like this?"

After what felt was a very long time, he returned and stopped at the doorway, looking at her. The image he saw was a relaxed person daydreaming. Walking to her, he stopped just in front of her and waited. Sure enough, she seemed to be in a meditative state, unaware that he was standing in front of her. She was breathing normally, so he wasn't too concerned. However, she had never done this to him before. Reaching up, he hovered his fingers over a nipple and waited for a reaction. He got none. Taking the initiative, he flicked it with his middle finger. Instantly, she opened her eyes and smiled at him.

"Oh, you're back, Sir. Are you ready to continue?"

"Oh, you witch. Were you playing with me, or were you genuinely meditating?"

"I don't know if I was meditating, but I can assure you, I was in a happy place."

"Oh, good to know, now, let's continue."

"I'm ready, Sir."

Over the next hour or more, he flogged and whipped her. Tormenting and teasing her, she twitched with every lash, flexing her back with every stroke; her skin warmed and turned a delightful pink. She moved about, helping him to strike every part of her body. She especially liked it when he whacked her tits, which in turn rang her bells hanging from her nipple rings. At some point, she relaxed and felt the renewed stirrings of orgasmic pleasure.

Relaxed and contented, Avril enjoyed the sensations all around her. At some point, she realized that Sir had clamped his mouth to her pussy and was eating her out. Moaning in pleasure, just the two of them, she wallowed in a sea of delight.

As her climax continued to build, she mumbled, "Sir... may I please come?" He granted her request.

Content in his permission, she stopped holding back, and a moment later, she slipped into a climatic trance—something she had never experienced. Usually, when she came, she would moan and scream in her orgasm. This time, she exploded silently, her soundless mouth wide open, and her body was shaking all over.

That was the last thing she remembered until she found herself back in her bed, alone.

When he came for her a few days later, he knocked once again. Jumping up, she took her pose at her designated spot, kneeling in her standard pose. "Come in," she said as she lowered herself to the proper position.

The door opened, and he stepped in. Somewhere in the back of Avril's mind, she noted that she hadn't heard the lock on the door turn. However, this thought didn't register right away. It was only later that it occurred to her.

"Good evening, Avril."

"Good evening, Sir."

"Avril, let me just say once again, just how beautiful you are. Your pose is perfect, and your new jewelry only accentuates your beauty."

"Thank you, Sir." Her eyes downcast, she could not see him smile, but she felt it.

Smiling, he responded, "Are you ready for your next lesson?"

"Yes, Sir. I am."

"Rise and take my arm," he told her.

She stood up, and after giving him a quick pose of a supermodel, one leg in front of the other and one hand on hip, she cocked her hips and showed him just what she thought of her appearance. In taking the pose, she heard him exhale that breath that could only mean appreciation. After the moment of mutual admiration, she walked over and took his arm he held out for her.

She expected that he would turn left out of her room, towards the Playspace. Instead, he turned right and escorted her up the stairs to the house's main level. She kept her emotions in check, but she was excited and nervous about finding out what was in store for her.

"Did he have guests in need of entertainment? Was it going to be another night filled with delight?" she wondered silently.

"Avril, other than minimal staff, there is no one up here. I locked everyone else in their cells," he told her. "Tonight, it's just you and me. You've earned the right to see more of the house. I intend to give you a tour of my home. From here on out, unless you earn a punishment, you now have free rein to roam most areas of the house."

"Sir, I don't know what to say. Thank you."

"See, you do know what to say. You're welcome. You earned it."

Avril had to keep closing her mouth as they toured the house, as it regularly gaped open at the luxury at every turn. He had elegant draperies and fabrics, oriental rugs, and comfortable furnishings everywhere. It had to have cost a fortune. She knew he had money, considering he paid over half a million Euros for her. In dollars, how much did he spend for her? She didn't know. U.S. Dollars she could fathom, but it took a lot of effort to convert between Euros and Dollars. Between the house and the furnishing, she couldn't fathom how much it all cost. It had to have cost hundreds of millions of dollars to build and furnish the home.

Then, he showed her the swimming pool, built right inside the house. It was big enough to swim laps. Next to the pool was a gym, with free weights and various weight machines and aerobic equipment. Among the equipment, she found the treadmill. She yearned to get on it and run.

"Avril, you are free to use the pool and any of the equipment in the workout room. I just want to caution you. It took a while to get you to stop exercising so much that you didn't look like a desirable sexual woman. That is how you appeared to me when you first came here. I saw the potential in you. I no longer see an emasculated female but a beautiful specimen of womanhood. If you exercise to excess, I will deny your privilege to use it."

"Yes, Sir. I understand. I am now a woman in the genuine sense of the word and in every way possible. Before coming here, I never felt that way. Now, I do. I don't want to lose that."

"Neither would I. Just remember, except for what we do together, everything in moderation. Tomorrow afternoon and every day hence, you can use anything you see here. I have a rule change for you. You may remove your heels to swim. However, you will continue to wear your heels elsewhere, including your use of the gym and around the pool. You will wear the heels even when you are lounging on a chaise. Violation of the rule will cause loss of the privilege. Clear?"

"Clear, Sir, crystal, and thank you. I do have a question, though."

"You are about to ask how you can use the gym equipment if you are wearing your heels. You would like a pair of shoes suitable for workouts, is that not correct?"

"Why, yes, Sir?"

"You will use the equipment carefully. You will manage in your heels. You will fail me if you sprain an ankle or break a bone."

"Oh," Avril murmured, surprised and discouraged by his response.

"Avril, I want you to be careful. The exercise will do you good. However, I still want you in your heels as much as possible. You still have a way to go with feeling completely at ease in them. Besides, I like seeing you in them. I am looking forward to watching you walk the treadmill while wearing them."

"Yes, Sir."

"You will continue to reserve mornings for your assignments, and in the evenings, you will keep to your training. Understood?"

"Sir, I am to break up my day to work on my assignments in the morning. In the afternoons, I may use the pool and gym to exercise or relax, maintaining the rules regarding my footwear, and then in the evenings, I will take the lessons you give me. By extrapolation, I also infer that I will continue to attend to your guests, whether sexual or otherwise, as you require. I may not work out in excess, preventing me from performing the duties you expect of me or losing any of the femininity you have worked so hard to instill within me."

"You understand correctly. Come now, let's finish the tour."

Avril retook his arm, and together they moved towards the central part of the house. As they turned to leave the pool area, Avril suddenly stopped and stared out of the glass wall representing the outside's windows. Her sudden halt caught him off guard, and he had to step back. She noticed he was looking at her, but she continued to stare out the windows at the grounds outside. Having not seen the outside in such a long time, she yearned to walk among the grass and flowers.

The only problem was, she noticed it was summer outside. If they took her in mid-July so, how could it be summer?

"Sir, forgive me. I have a question that I must ask."

"You may ask," he replied.

"Sir, how long have I been here?"

"Ah, I was wondering when you would ask me that. You've been here just over eleven months."

"Sir, I'm confused. I realized that I'd been here a while. I figured a few months, maybe even through the holidays, but that long?"

"Yes, Avril, you've been here about eleven months. Add to that the time you were in the auction house plus travel, maybe another few weeks."

"So, Sir, you're telling me it's late May?"

"More like early July."

"Forgive me, Sir. I need a moment," she told him, and then began processing that it was a full year since the Consortium took her. Where had the time gone? She tried to count in her head the days and weeks, but honestly, it's been such a long time since she saw the outside or seen a clock that it was unfathomable to comprehend how long he had held her captive. Had it been an entire year?

"Avril, are you alright?"

"Sir, I don't know. Have I been your captive for an entire year? I don't know what to make of it."

"Avril, you can either accept the facts as they are or not. It's up to you how you move forward. Either way, you decide, remember, you are still mine, prisoner or not. When you first came here, I told you that you were my property, to do with as I pleased and that you would be here for the rest of your life. I had thought you had come to terms with that. Was I wrong?"

"Ah, Sir, I don't know what to say. I thought I had, but now a new reality has set in. I just need time to process. That's all."

"Avril, please remember. I have your best interest at heart. That does not change the fact that you are mine, and I intend to keep you. You are my property, and you will always be my property. I will not apologize for that. Your old life is gone forever, and only you can embrace your new life."

"Sir, I get that. I do. It's just that… well, I don't know. It's a lot to take in. Please don't hold it against me. I just need some time."

"Alright, I'll give you the time you need. After all, you're not going anywhere."

"Sir, please take me inside. I don't want to see the outside right now."

"I understand, Avril. Come on; let me show you the rest of the house."

As they walked back into the house's central portion, Sir had to walk slower than usual, as Avril barely noticed her surroundings and her feet dragged along. Her thoughts were all in a jumble.

"A whole year!" she kept repeating in her mind. "A whole God damn year she had been missing. Was anyone even looking for her?"

Thoughts that had died down months ago suddenly roared back to life, filling her mind and blocking all comments that Sir said to her.

"Sir, I'm… I missed what you just said." Avril said to him, catching herself before she finished apologizing.

"I was just pointing out to you that the doorway to your right is my office. You may not enter it. You may roam around the house, but you are never to go in there. Please acknowledge."

"Yes, Sir. That is your office, and I may not go in there."

"Avril, I also want to remind you, I do not permit you to go outside. Your collar will warn you if you approach a forbidden door or window. Should you try to ignore it and go through it, your collar will incapacitate you most painfully. That includes my office. Please remember the rule."

"Yes, Sir. I'll remember."

"Now, let me show you this room. I hope you will eventually earn the right to move into it." Sir said as he turned from his office.

Walking up to a large double door, he pushed inward. On the other side presented one of the most fantastic rooms she had ever seen. In its center sat a sizeable king-size poster bed flanked by two bedside tables. On top of each bedpost was a framework that supported various gossamer fabrics draped between them. It was elegant and feminine without being girly. She loved it.

She noticed a seating area around the room comprising a sofa and two side chairs, and a wingback chair.

"Ah, that must be his chair," she realized.

Completing the sitting area was a coffee table and a pair of side tables. The coffee and side tables looked substantial, definitely not delicate, just as the poster bed looked to her. On another wall were a desk and bookshelf filled with a library's worth of books. Her desire to pick one up and start reading almost overwhelmed her. A large oriental rug sat on the floor in front of the bed, and another smaller oriental rug lay underneath the coffee table. She also noticed a massage table and a few other pieces that she knew Sir would be interested in getting her to experience.

"There's an en-suite as well, which includes a walk-in curbless shower with multiple showerheads and a couple of rain heads, a large soaking tub for two, and all the amenities found in an upscale spa. You'll like it, but you will have to earn your place here. For it to become yours, you will need to earn your third crystal. In the meantime, you can look at the room all you like. You may touch nothing in here, including the books."

"Alright, Sir, I understand. Earn my third crystal, and this room will become mine."

"That's right, Avril. Now, I have one more room to show you."

He said as he closed the doors and directed her to a similar set of doors on the other side of the landing. Opening them, she realized that this was his room, decorated in a Spartan and masculine manner. Centered in the room was another king-sized bed with substantial posts on each corner. Flanked on either side of the bed was a pair of bedside tables. A wingback chair and a small round side table sat next to the full-length windows. Other than that, there was no other furniture in the space. Fabric draperies framed the windows, and a few rugs rested on the floor, but otherwise, the bedroom was empty. It looked like him, not a single thing out of place, nor an item that complicated the room.

"Sir, I like it. It suits you."

"I think so. Come in. I want to share it with you."

"Yes, Sir. I would like that as well. May I have a moment in the en-suite first? I would like to clean up and prepare for you."

"Go ahead. Ten minutes."

"Yes, Sir."

After he directed her towards his en-suite, she took every second of the ten minutes to prepare. Dozens of thoughts were bouncing around inside her skull. Sometimes, it was overwhelming, but she knew she would process them tomorrow. Tonight, it looked like he was inviting her to his bed, and she didn't want to disappoint him.

Exiting the en-suite on the stroke of ten minutes, she walked to the foot of the bed, knelt, and assumed her standard pose. With her hands behind her back, she knelt and cast her eyes downwards.

She waited. Sir was sitting in his chair, appraising her response to everything he had revealed to her. She was a bit nervous, wondering just what he thought of her reactions since they were in the natatorium where the swimming pool begged for use. However, she could not still her thoughts focused on the discovery she made earlier.

Her newfound knowledge consumed her. "A whole year, a whole fucking year, a whole goddamn fucking year!" repeatedly echoed in her mind.

Kneeling, with a resounding silence between them, she waited. Several minutes went by before he spoke.

"You're thinking about escape."

Silent in her thoughts, not anticipating that he would guess the turmoil that was going on in her mind, she waited.

"Answer me!" He commanded rather sharply.

"Yes, Sir." she meekly responded.

"Talk to me. Tell me what is going on in that head of yours."

After several moments to compose herself, she started. "I... I don't quite know what to say, Sir. I mean, it's been an entire year. I had no idea it was that long. I've missed an entire year. I'm... overwhelmed; that's all."

"Avril, you knew that you would never leave here, right from the start."

"Yes, I know, Sir. I remember you telling me. I suppose that I had always hoped that one day I would find a way out."

"That is not possible. Even if you escaped the boundaries of my home, with your head intact, I would track you down, bring you back, and likely kill you. Surely, you know that?"

Dropping her head down, Avril nodded, acknowledging the inevitability of his words.

"Avril, you've told me yourself that all things considered, you prefer your new life to your old one. You are the center of my attention. You have learned how to be a desirable woman. You have discovered your femininity, and you embrace your new life. So, what's changed?"

"I don't know, Sir. I just don't understand it. It's just… it's just when I realized it was next summer; I feel like a truck hit me. I just didn't know how long I had been here. I missed celebrating all the holidays, Halloween, Thanksgiving, Christmas, and the New Year. I missed my birthday, and I missed my girlfriend's birthday. They must all think I'm dead, and no one is looking for me."

"Avril, they overrate holidays. Most are corrupted to market products to a stupid population. All the ones you mentioned are the worst of them. As for people you used to know, I suppose you are right. However, I don't care what they think. You are mine, and you will remain mine until I say otherwise. No one will find you. No one is looking for you, and no one will rescue you. You're not even in the country of your birth anymore. You probably guessed that during your transportation to the auction house and then onto here. The Consortium takes great pains to hide their tracks and ease the way for its members to partake in their activities."

"But Sir, an entire year, how is it possible? I don't understand."

"Avril, think about it. Before today, when was the last time you saw outside, or for that matter, a clock, or a calendar?"

"Ah, before the Consortium took me, Sir."

"Exactly, since then, you have had no way of measuring the passing of the days. How do you know whether a night of sleep was just eight hours or eighty hours? How would you know whether the time between breakfast and lunch was four hours or six hours? How would you find out when it was noon or midnight? You had no frame of reference to measure the passing of time."

"Sir, I see what your point." Avril started and then, upon reflection, added. "Did you manipulate my perception of time, Sir? Did you play with my circadian rhythm to make me think that day and night differed from it was?"

"Avril, see! You proved your intelligence once again. The answer to your question is yes. For the first six months, I played with your sense of time. At one point, having breakfast with you was closer to midnight than daybreak."

"But why, Sir?"

"I wanted to adjust your biological clock so that you were at your best, well-rested, in the evening, so that our sessions together would benefit me. I am at my best after dark."

Avril nodded, realizing yet again, she was powerless to do anything but accept his control.

"Avril, I had thought you were ready to come to my bed, but I see that you are not. I am going to return you to your room, and you will continue where you left off. I see no reason to revoke my permission to allow you to roam the house and use the gym and pool, as we discussed earlier. However, besides my office, you may not enter my bedroom unless I say otherwise. All other rules are still in effect. Now, stand up and follow me."

"Yes, Sir." Avril acknowledged and followed him out of the room. He led her directly to her room, using the shortest of routes possible, and followed her in.

"Put your hands behind your back," he commanded.

A moment later, she found her wrists tied together with a length of rope. Following his prodding, she approached her bed, where he roughly bent her over the edge and planted her face on the bedspread. Her thoughts were in a whirlwind. He grasped her bound wrists and entered her roughly in one smooth thrust. Her mind disconnected as he fucked her, and she found herself unable to control the thoughts of her captivity raging between her ears.

He pounded away at her, gripping her bound wrists for leverage and thrusting into her recklessly. Without first registering his withdrawal, he removed her butt-plug, pressed himself against her anus, and shoved. For the first time in a very long time, his entry hurt. She wasn't ready for him. She hadn't lubed, and she wasn't naturally wet enough to accept him. That was it. Unprepared to be fucked anally, she knew it didn't matter to him. She was his property, and he would do with her as he wished.

What was better? Was it better kept as his concubine or tortured and killed for his pleasure? She honestly didn't know the answer to that one.

As was typical, his need took a long time to resolve, and he came several times over before he finished. Finally, standing up and putting his trousers back on, he stepped away and looked at his cum leaking from her. After giving her a quick slap on her ass, he turned and left, closing the door behind him, leaving her wrists bound behind her.

Avril laid there for a long time. Slipping to her knees and overwhelmed by the emotional torrent flooding her, tears soaked the bedspread. Her body heaving; she allowed her emotions to go unchecked. It had taken an entire year to release them, and they continued their outpouring well into the night.

Somehow, an indeterminate time later, she pulled back the covers and climb into bed. She cried herself to an uneasy sleep, her wrists still bound behind her back, uncovered and cold. She didn't care. She fucking didn't care about anything anymore.

Chapter Twenty-One

Waking up the following morning, she laid on her side and stared at the wall. Her fingers were tingling. Flexing them, she tried to get the blood circulating past the ligatures that slowed the process.

"Was it really the next morning or days later?" She had no idea.

Sir was right in that respect. Without a clock or a window, she had no idea what time it was. He regulated night and day by turning the ceiling light on and off. She had no control over that one light. After all this time, she came to associate the light with the time-of-day. When it came on, it was morning. When it went off, it was night. Now she couldn't even trust that. Had she slept the entire day away? She had no way of knowing.

When her bladder demanded relief, she made her way to her en-suite and emptied it. With her hands tied behind her back, wiping was impossible. Therefore, she used a towel hanging on the rack and rubbed up against it.

Somehow, she unbuckled her heels, started the shower, and climbed in. Unable to wash well, she let the hot shower clean the stains of her tears away. Dropping to the floor, she positioned herself so that the falling water directed itself onto her pubic area, washing away the residue of his discharges. As the water cleansed her, she resumed crying, further cleansing her soul. She sat there for a long time, letting the water and her emotions drain away.

Toweling off, an arduous task, she let the residual moisture evaporate from her body. Stuffing her feet into her heels, it took a very long time to buckle them to her feet. Using the toilet and then the vanity for support, she stood up. Determined, she walked back into her room and somehow made the bed, changing the sheets as per the rules.

Her morning routine finished, she took her place, kneeling on the designated spot, and waited.

He didn't come to her all day. She ignored her dinner when it arrived in the food alcove. When the ceiling light went out, she stood up and went to bed. After staring forever at the wall, she fell into a restless sleep, tossing and turning until the ceiling light turned on. Groaning, the pattern of the day resumed.

Kneeling in her designated spot, she let her mind go blank. The raging thoughts consuming her fell by the wayside. Her food alcove opened and closed several times that day. She ignored it.

Well into the day, the sound of a knock rapped on the door. At first, she hadn't heard the knock, nor the second one. The emptiness of her thoughts consumed her. Unresponsive, the door opened, and Sir stood waiting at the threshold.

"May I come in?" He asked.

Barely acknowledging his presence, she said. "Whatever, Sir…"

"Avril, are you alright?"

"Alright? No, Sir, I'm not alright, though it doesn't matter. You have all the control, and I have none."

"Stand up."

Avril stood up, barely keeping her balance without falling over. Not being able to use her arms, she found it hard to keep her balance. She stood dispassionately, not looking in his direction. He stood there, watching her for a time, and then moved around to her back and untied her wrists. Despite a need to rub them, she maintained her posture, leaving her hands clasped behind her. After pocketing the rope, he walked around her and stood in front, facing her.

His hands behind his back, he said. "What am I to do with you?"

She stood mute.

Snapping his fingers, a couple of women pushed a food tray into the room. After placing the food on the small table, they left, closing the door behind them.

"Sit," he commanded.

Autonomously, she stepped up to the chair and waited.

"Sit," he ordered her again.

"Must I pull out my chair, Sir? After all, you already granted me this privilege. Do I take it that you revoked it?"

"Oh, very well," Sir answered her, exasperated by her audacity. However, he held the chair for her, and she sat, laying her hands in her lap. Undercover of the tablecloth, she rubbed her wrists as if to heal them.

Sir sat down across from her, tented his hands under his chin, and studied her.

"Please eat," he asked her, "or do I have to make it an order?"

"Maybe, Sir, however, to follow your orders, I'll eat. Thank you, Sir, for the food I am about to eat."

"Avril, this impertinence is not becoming of you. I suggest that you reconsider your options and your behavior."

"Yes, Sir," she answered and picked up her fork, took a dainty morsel, and placed it in her mouth. Sir did not eat from his plate but continued to scrutinize Avril, his hands tented under his chin, allowing his elbows to rest on the table.

"What's going on with you?"

"Sir, surely, I don't know what you mean. I am here, as I have and always will be."

The dishes bounced when he slammed his fist on the table.

Yelling, "Damn it, Avril, what has come over you? Nothing has changed from last week, except that you excelled in your training, and I promoted you. I give you more freedom of movement, and this is how you treat me? I will not have it, do you understand?"

"What you say is true, Sir, except that I changed. I am different."

"How are you different?"

"Sir, the revelation that you have held me captive for a year is what is different. I almost wished you left me ignorant you have held me locked up and imprisoned in this room for a year. For an entire year, I must remain naked at all times, wear your stupid heels, even to bed, do your bidding, and used as your concubine property for your pleasure, submitting my body to whoever you serve me to, is what has changed."

"I've changed. I should have rebelled a year ago, and I didn't. I still don't understand why I did not. I should have, I ought to have. You take men and women off the streets and subjugate them for your amusement and those of people like you. I don't care what you or the Consortium believes. It's immoral, not to mention illegal. I hate you and what you and the Consortium did to me, to women, to everyone."

Sir, let her go on like this without interruption. He let her get it all out before responding. He almost spoke when she resumed her tirade. When she slowed and stopped, he continued, waiting to be sure she didn't start up again. When she held her tongue for several minutes, he broke the silence.

"Avril, whether you hate what the Consortium or I did to you is irrelevant. Either you accept it or not. If not, you will die. You have no other choice. As for the rest, I agree with you. It would be best if you had rebelled a long time ago. I am surprised it took you this long to do so. That said, I should hope you have gotten it out of your system. I will give you time to process this, and then we will resume your training. Unless your behavior improves, you will force me to rescind your privileges, maybe even take back your promotions, to when you first arrived."

After a moment, Sir continued.

"I assure you, you will not like that. You will likely become like one of those pieces of furniture you noticed at the dinner party. What would it be like to become a floor lamp, a chandelier, a wall sconce, or how about a footstool? Maybe I'll lay you out on my dining table and allow my guests to carve meat from your living body and eat it. The choice is up to you."

After a pregnant pause to allow her to consider his comments, Sir continued. "Now, you will follow the rules precisely. You will not waste the meals I provide. You will eat them. Do I make myself clear?"

"Yes, Sir."

"I will give you some time to get over this funk, but I'm telling you right now, do not test my patience. There are still many lessons I would like to go over with you. If you don't come around, I will have no choice but to rescind everything you have achieved and treat you accordingly."

Nodding, Avril looked at him. "I understand, Sir." What else was she going to say?

"Good, now, finish eating and take care of yourself. I'll see you later. As I told you the other day, you have my permission to wander about the house, swim in the pool, and workout in the gym. I will be back this evening, where I expect you to be ready to receive me."

Stomping out, he closed the door behind him and left her alone.

Sitting back in her chair, she exhaled a deep breath and stared at the plate, moving the food around with her fork but not eating it. Her thoughts were racing once more. Finally, she picked up a morsel and ate it and then repeated. Before she knew it, her plate was empty, and she cleared the table, putting everything in the food alcove. Minutes later, she heard the food alcove open and close. The dirty dishes had disappeared.

"Shit, a whole year, a whole fucking year. It's so hard to believe. A whole goddamn year, without a stitch of clothing to wear, a cocktail or a glass of wine, or running a single mile. An entire year has gone without seeing the sun and the change of the seasons. A goddamn fucking year…"

Pulling into his private hanger at the regional airport, the Chairman parked the car and sat there for several minutes. Staring straight ahead at his private Gulfstream G650 luxury jet, his flight crew went through their last checks before takeoff. It was a comfortable aircraft, suitable to fly him anywhere in the world. There were days when he wished he could upgrade it to a more luxurious model. After all, he could easily afford it, but that would increase his exposure, and that would not do. He wanted to keep a low global profile.

His current jet was just one of tens of thousands of these planes flying around the world. An upgrade could stand out. Still, it was sufficient for his needs, as not only had he outfitted the passenger compartment for his long-distance travel, including a big comfortable bed. He pressurized its cargo hold to carry human cargo when necessary. It wasn't often when he loaded this kind of freight onto his plane, but it was ready if needed. On those occasions, he would not fly with the cargo. He needed to separate himself from the freight and maintain reasonable deniability.

When the crew spun up the plane's engines, he turned off the car, got out of his Town Car, and climbed the stairs to the jet's cabin.

"We're ready to go, Sir. Anytime you're ready."

"Then, let's go."

"Yes, Sir. Please take your seat. I'll clear our takeoff with the tower. Traffic is light this morning, so we should be in the air in a few moments."

"That's fine, Captain. Do I have a moment to pour a drink?"

"Yes, Sir. Your flight attendant should already have one ready for you."

"Thank you, Captain. Do you expect any issues during the flight?"

"No, Sir. Today, the air seems calm with light trade winds from the south. We will have a tailwind most of the way. We should be on the ground in just under two hours."

"Good. Let me know when we descend."

"Yes, Sir. I will. If you'll excuse me, I'll get us underway."

The Chairman nodded as he watched the Captain return to the

cockpit. Turning towards the main cabin, he walked down the center aisle and took his customary seat. He preferred the sofa installed just in front of the leading edge of the plane's wings. As he was buckling his seat belt, his attendant handed him his single malt scotch with two clear ice cubes in it.

"Thank you," he told her.

"Will there be anything else, Sir?"

"As soon as you finish your take off duties, I would like you to sit here next to me."

"Certainly, Sir, I'll be back shortly."

"No rush. Finish what you need to do."

"Yes, Sir. It'll be just a few minutes," she replied and turned towards the back of the plane after he nodded his acknowledgment of her comment.

After sipping his drink, he rested his head on the seat back and closed his eyes. Avril's recent despondency and rebellion was on the front of his mind. He had done everything for her. He didn't understand her behavior change. He thought that she had her breakdown months ago. Since then, she was progressing quite nicely. He hadn't expected her to react as she did when she found out how long she had been there with him. He honestly didn't understand what was going on with her.

Feeling the plane leave the ground behind and climb into the sky, he continued sipping his scotch, pondering just what to do with the girl. Should he cut his losses and dispose of her? If she didn't turn it around, he was going to have to abandon his objective. He had to come with something to shake her up and turn her around.

"Fuck, she had so much going for her, and she was about to throw it all away," he complained out loud.

"Sir, did you say something?" the attendant leaned in and asked.

"Ah, no, sorry, I was thinking about something. Are you finished with your duties?"

"For now, Sir, may I?" The attendant said, pointing towards the sofa.

"Please," he said, patting the seat beside him.

Sans uniform, having removed it after takeoff, the attendant sat down and buckled her seatbelt around her waist. She was now wearing just a pair of high-heel shoes, thigh-high stockings with a garter belt, and a lacy shelf bra allowing her erect nipples to poke out over the edge. She also handed him a fresh drink, taking his empty glass and putting it in a compartment off to one side.

"You are magnificent!" he complimented her.

"Thank you, Sir. I am happy you are pleased," she replied, placing her hand on his thigh. "Whatever you need, I'll be glad to give you."

"Thank you. I appreciate it. Just having you sit next to me, looking as you do, is all I need."

"As you wish, Sir," the attendant remarked, crossing one leg over the other, showing off her long lines ending in those tall stiletto heels he loved so much.

The Chairman continued to reflect upon the problem of Avril. He had no answers and hoped one would present itself in short order. He tossed his thoughts around for half an hour before he spoke to the attendant sitting next to him.

"May I ask you a personal question?" He directed towards his attendant.

"Ah, yes, Sir. I suppose," she remarked, taken aback by his sudden and unexpected question.

"How long have you been in my service?"

"Three, maybe four years, Sir."

"And how do you feel about how you came to be in my service?"

"Sir?"

"Tell me, how do you feel being owned property? My property?"

"Sir, okay, I guess. I haven't thought about it for a very long time. You care for me, feed me, and a place to live. I have all the sex I ever wanted, and I want for nothing. Is that what you mean?"

"Well, yes. That is part of it. Tell me, have you ever wished to go back to your old life, the life you had before being taken?"

"No, Sir, at least not in many years. As I said, you take care of me, and I want for nothing. As I see it, my life now is far better than the life I used to have."

"Why is that?"

"Uh, you mean, about my life before I came to you?"

"Yes, that's right."

"Sir, in my old life, I lived in a tiny single room apartment. I struggled to pay the rent, buy food, and have a life. Even with two jobs, I had to sell myself frequently for food or rent to make ends meet. I never wanted children, yet I risked becoming a single mother from unwanted pregnancies implanted by several ghosts of a man, or worse. I worried all the time about what tomorrow would bring. Now I don't. The life I have now, well, it's just better. That's all."

"And you don't wish to leave my service and go back to your old life, knowing that by staying here, I am your owner and Master, I will do whatever I want with you, even kill you one day?"

"Oh, no, Sir, I don't. I wouldn't even consider it," she answered with a look of horror on her face at the thought of leaving his service.

"Hm," the Chairman muttered, processing her comments.

"Sir, may I ask you a personal question?"

"Uh? Ah, yes."

"Sir, is everything alright? Is there something I can do to ease your mind?" she asked, sliding her hand up his thigh before resting it on the bulge between his legs.

"Possibly later, my dear."

"Yes, Sir," she answered, quickly withdrawing her hand.

"Oh, please, don't let me interrupt. Leave your hand there." He smiled at her.

Replacing her hand, she gently cupped him before turning her body towards him and presenting a knee for him.

"Can you tell me what changed your mind from wanting to leave and wanting to stay? What made you willingly agree to stay as my property?"

"Sir, excuse me? You want to know why I willingly was your property."

"Yes, that's it exactly."

"Sir, please forgive me. I haven't thought about this in years. However, if I recall correctly, there were two things. In the beginning, I knew you would not allow me to live if I attempted to escape. When you recaptured me, my death would not be easy and quick. Every one of us knows what you do to those who go against you."

"And yet, many do and suffer the consequences."

"Yes, Sir. They do."

"Even though I enjoy taking my pleasure from you, even if it is often cruel and excruciating?"

"Sir, I will admit, I don't look forward to those sessions. You're right. You do hurt us, or rather me. I hurt to where I can hardly bear it, and I want to die. However, after it's over, I don't remember the pain. I only remember something pleasant that I don't know how to describe. If I may be so bold, Sir, you are a sadist and enjoy torturing us so you can hear us scream in anguish as well as writhe in pleasure. I now believe that one cannot exist without the other. Besides, you give me a good life. Outside of taking care of your needs, you give me the freedom to enjoy life in better ways than I would have otherwise."

"Is that your second reason?"

"Well, kind of Sir. The other reason has to do with you giving me something I needed but never had. It's something I was missing from my previous life. I suppose it's different for everyone, but knowing that someone would care for me was something I always wanted in my life. Now I have it. I am a kept woman, and I like it. In the old days, I thought I would have to win the lottery, or if not, marry a wealthy man who I hated. I just wanted to be taken care of, and you have given me that."

"Even knowing that I will certainly kill you one day?"

"Yes, Sir. I am aware of that, and as your property, that is your prerogative. Until that day, I will serve you to the best of my ability. It's a fair exchange to being cared for, having a roof over my head, food in my belly, all the sex I could ever want, and without the need of anything. It's a small price to pay, and I plan to make the best of it. As I said, you give me the ability to enjoy life in ways that I could never have done in my previous life."

"And do you hate me?"

"No, Sir, not at all, at least not anymore."

"Why is that?"

"I guess I used to, Sir, but not any longer. I'm not even sure why I don't hate you. I should. However, I like being your property and belonging to you. I learned that deep down; you are a good person."

"Would you say you love me?"

"Honestly, Sir?"

"Always, the rules have never changed. I will never lie to you, and you, in turn, will never lie to me."

"Sir, I suspect you want me to say that I love you. That would not be the truth. I respect you, I care for you, and I even like you. However, I don't love you, at least like a wife or a lover. In some ways, I love you like a father, but since we have sex together, that is not entirely accurate. I don't know how to describe it. I know you don't love me either, and that's okay too. I love my life as it is."

"You're right, I don't love you in that way, but you would be wrong in thinking that I don't love you at all. A part of me loves you and my brood, even when I torture and kill you."

"Sir, are you planning on torturing and killing me?"

"Oh, no, sorry," he said, chuckling. "No, not today, and not anytime soon. Who else would help me maintain my membership in the mile-high club?" He scolded her with a smile.

"Now, Sir?"

"Sure, why not?"

The attendant unbuckled her seat belt and unzipped him. His erection free at last, she bent over and kissed it, briefly taking him into her mouth, ensuring she gave him the proper kiss that she knew he appreciated.

Straddling his lap, she lowered herself and eased him inside her. A few minutes of air turbulence increased their pleasure as every bounce forcefully drove him into her, eliciting deep moans of pleasure emanating from her throat. One particularly forceful bit of turbulence dropped the plane and the attendant with it, driving her hard right onto his shaft. As the jet bottomed out, he shot his load while gripping the attendant by her shoulders, forcefully keeping him deep inside her.

By the time the pilot announced that they were descending to prepare for landing, they had each enjoyed their encounter. Slowly standing up, the attendant bent over and kissed the Chairman on the lips, whispering, "Thank you, Sir. That was great."

"And thank you for your thoughts. You just may have helped me with my problem."

"My pleasure, Sir."

Chapter Twenty-Two

Kneeling in her designated spot, Avril waited for Sir to come for her. She continued to consider her situation. A few afternoons ago, after he had untied her and forced her to eat, she had a troublesome time dealing with her new reality.

When dinner arrived, she ate the meal, but more because he commanded her to eat, rather than because she was hungry. After dinner, he came to her room, tied her wrists once again behind her back, and fucked her until it satisfied him. As usual, his stamina was insatiable, and he wasn't gentle with her, as he usually was before all this shit happened. Before he left, he untied her and took the time to study her lying on the bed. After he left, she got up and showered, washing his stink off her body so that it wouldn't invade her dreams.

When she woke the next morning, she went about her routine. A casual observer would think she was an automaton, emotionless, a programmed mannequin. Thinking about her behavior, she realized that he had programmed her. He had programmed her with all those fucking rules in the rulebook and his training. She couldn't figure out why she had even bothered learning those lessons and follow his stupid rules. If she hadn't, by now, she might have escaped this imprisonment, even if it meant her death.

As the day progressed, Avril evaluated her position, considering when and how she could run or whether she should try to escape. Uncertain of what she wanted, her indecision froze her in place. Even when she picked up her sketchbook, she found her drawings were discordant and fraught with desperate slashes of the pencil. Flipping page after page, none of the new renderings looked anything like her earlier works. Those were fine works of art. Now, her drawings weren't anything like them. She hated them but could not bring herself to destroy them. They accurately communicated her dark mood.

Tossing the sketchbook aside, she got up, went to the en-suite, and took yet another shower for the day. Scrubbing as much as she had done over the past many hours, trying hard, she couldn't wash him entirely from her body, though the hot water certainly helped her feel better. After her shower, she put the heels back on and took her place at the designated spot, waiting for him to collect her.

That is how the days went by, day after day. On the fourth or fifth morning since her breakdown, Avril again waited for him to collect her, not caring if he came for her or not.

When he finally came in, she didn't acknowledge his presence, preferring to stare into space. Studying her, he finally opened his mouth.

"Why haven't you used the gym or pool? It would do you good to get some exercise."

"Sir, it's kind of hard to go to the pool or gym when I'm locked in this room."

With an air of exasperation tinged with compassion, he replied. "Avril, I did not lock your door. It hasn't been ever since you received your second crystal. Didn't you even try to open it?"

"Ah… no, Sir, I did not know you hadn't locked it. Locked for so long, I gave up testing it ages ago. I can't handle any more disappointments or failed expectations."

"And you never thought to ask?"

"No, Sir. As I said, I can't handle any more disappointments."

"Let's talk about expectations since you brought up the subject. What expectations do you feel were broken?"

"I don't know, Sir. I only feel that way." Avril replied after considering his question for a long time.

"Have I said anything to you that wasn't the truth or what I expected from you?"

"No, Sir. Not to my knowledge."

"Did I promise you something that I never delivered on?"

"No, Sir, again, not to my knowledge."

"No, that's correct. From the start, I have been clear about my expectations, and while I know I have always told you the truth, only you can determine whether or not you believe me."

"That's true, Sir."

"Then what are you going to do about pulling yourself out of this mental state of yours. From my perspective, your behavior is becoming questionable. If this continues, you will earn a severe punishment. A punishment more severe than you have earned in the past."

"I understand, Sir."

"Can you elaborate on your last answer?"

"Sir, all I can tell you is that I don't know how to resolve my tumultuous emotions."

"Stand up and follow me."

"Yes, Sir," she answered him and followed him out of the door and up the stairs.

He led her to the swimming pool and said.

"I require you to swim forty laps, one for each down and back. Someone with your abilities should find that easy to do. Take your heels off but put them back on as soon as you finish your laps. Use whatever stroke you care to use; I don't care. Just swim the forty laps. When finished, go to the gym and do five miles on the treadmill. I'd order you to do more, but it's been a while since you were on a treadmill. And since you will wear your heels, I prefer you slowly work your way back to marathon levels. Don't cheat on the laps in the pool. The pool wall has a touchpad that will count your laps and your times. I don't care about the times right now; that will come later. Just swim the laps and walk the treadmill. Both will record your time and distance. Take as much time as you need to complete the five miles. You may run a longer distance, but the five miles is what I require."

"Now, Sir?"

"Yes, now. Get your ass moving."

"Yes, Sir," Avril said and walked over to the chairs alongside the pool. After sitting down and taking her heels off, she slid into the end of the pool and began her laps. The pool was a long one. The markings on the sidewall indicated that it was a fifty meters pool. Forty laps meant she would swim two kilometers. It's been a long time since she had swum that distance. Competing athletes should be able to swim that in about thirty-five minutes. But as Sir said, she hadn't swum or run in a long time. She figured that if she could do it within an hour, she'd be happy with the time.

As she started her second lap, she realized the pool had one of those lap clocks. It didn't tell the time of the day, but just the minutes within an hour. As she swam, she calculated that she would finish in an hour and maybe a little sooner. Halfway through, her pace slowed as her muscles burned. By the time she finished, she was breathing heavily and barely able to stand. Her arms draped over the side of the pool, supporting her body from slipping under the surface, she sucked wind. Her chest heaved with each big breath, working hard to catch her breath.

As her breathing returned to normal, she slid out of the pool, dried off, and put on her heels. Approaching the treadmill, she took a moment to study the machine before stepping up on the unit. Looking down at the control panel, she noticed that she was looking down past her naked breasts and nipples. She had never run naked before, and it mildly concerned her. She wondered how her breasts would react with all the bouncing.

'Say la vie,' time to get to it.

Programming the machine, she noted a full water bottle resting in the cup holder built into the treadmill. After drinking water, she pressed the start button and began walking.

From her previous experience, doing five miles should be easy. However, she had never done it before in high-heels. She wanted to start slow and edge her way up to faster speeds. After finishing her first mile, she had wondered whether she had been too aggressive with the pace programmed into the machine.

While she programmed the treadmill to present a relatively flat course, she struggled to keep up the pace she set. Her body was fighting her, and she was tiring. Playing it safe, she slowed her pace and immediately felt better with her decision.

Pushing through the caution, fatigue, and burn, she managed the program and finished the five miles. Walking around the room, she cooled off. Inventorying her body, she realized that, despite the fatigue and sore muscles, she felt good. The swim and run just reaffirmed that she missed the exercise.

"Tomorrow," she vowed, "I'll be back."

Toweling off the sweat, she made her way back to her room and took a long, hot shower. After she finished, she found Sir sitting in his wingback chair.

"How do you feel?" He asked as she stepped into the room.

"Better, Sir. The exercise felt good."

"And tomorrow…?"

"I'll be back. It felt good, and exactly what I need right now."

"Good, I'm happy to hear that. Now, unless I tell you differently, you will swim the forty laps and run only five miles every other day. No more and no less. I want you fit and healthy, but I don't want you to lose the perfect figure that took so long to turn you into a desirable, feminine woman."

"Yes, Sir. I don't want to lose my femininity either. I love how I look. So, I will promise you I will find the right balance between swimming and running while maintaining my femininity."

"That is what I wanted to hear. You are to use the weight machines to work on your upper body one day, your lower body on another, and your midsection another on alternate days. Keep track of your progress with the weights. I am interested in how you do. You may use the free weights for arm curls, bench presses, and such, where you are sitting down. Do not use weights while standing on your heels. Squats and standing lat-pull-downs are good examples of that."

"I can do that, Sir. Thank you."

"Now, let's go to the Playspace. Since you have already done much of the work to prepare your body for our play, it shouldn't be long before I get you to experience subspace finally."

"Yes, Sir," Avril said, stopping herself from rolling her eyes, lest he saw her and punish her for the tease.

Hours later, she lay on a sofa with her head on his lap. A light blanket rested on top of her, keeping her warm. Her body tingled with the experience while her mind continued to float above her body. The last thing she remembered was lying on her back as Sir methodically teased her body with various toys, clamps, and sharp pointy things. He had started with a light flogging all over her body, warming her skin and giving it a rosy sheen. Then, using a piece of soft animal skin, possibly rabbit or mink, he rubbed her body with the smooth, sensuous fur. The fur felt incredible, as it seemed to float across her warm, reddish skin. She remembered the last thing Sir used was a device with lots of sharp pin-like protrusions around a rotating wheel. It looked nasty, and he worried her that it would cut her. As he rolled the spiked wheel across her nipples, she experienced a moment of wonder, and then the world disappeared.

A fog seemed to consume her. She felt what he did to her body, but she thought she was no longer a resident in it. She seemed to float above it; her body completely relaxed. Her head felt too heavy to support itself, intriguing her somewhere in the back of her mind. As she floated nearby, she could see Sir next to her. He had put down the toy and was caressing her body with oily hands. A part of her could feel him stroking her, but that was a small part of what she was experiencing.

What she sensed was the world outside of herself. There was fog all around her, and she felt as if she could touch the night sky, cradling the stars in her hands. Turning her incorporeal head, she thought she could sense more than what she could see or feel. She felt her heart pumping blood throughout her blood vessels, carrying oxygen and glucose to the cells. She felt his fingers caressing her body, even pinching her nipples. She could see deep into the pores of his skin, drilling deep into his soul. Realizing what she was sensing, she studied him, trying to know the truth of his heart buried beneath that shell of a sadistic man.

Then she felt him join her, floating alongside her above their respective bodies. Watching him alongside her, she felt him reach out and touch her, not with his fingers still caressing her body but with his mind. It suddenly occurred to her that he was experiencing his form of subspace. She didn't understand it or how he had achieved it, but it didn't matter. It as if their souls had touched and merged. She finally saw him for what he indeed was. He truly was a good man. His methods and desires may be suspect, but deep down, he was a good guy. Suddenly, she sensed a love broadcasting from him to her.

"He loves me!" she realized. "Oh, my... he loves me! He doesn't know it, but he loves me. Oh, my God. I never imagined he could love me, or anyone."

At some point, his soul disconnected from hers. Watching him caress her body, he gently picked her up and carried her over to the sofa. After joining her, he rested her head on his lap and covered her with a blanket. She felt warm and comfortable in his arms and more than ready to remain there forever.

Nature seemed to have other ideas because she felt a powerful force pulling her towards her body. Merging with her body, she began feeling her head on his lap and her body lying on the sofa. Little by little, her soul reconnected to her body, and her eyes fluttered open.

"Welcome back," he greeted her.

Avril was still too out of it to respond, but she could tell that he felt her appreciation at his words. She felt him stroke her body through the blanket, soothing her as she recovered from her experience.

"Sir, was that what you wanted me to experience?" she whispered, her eyes closed.

"Yes, Avril. It was. What did you think?"

"Sir, it was... I don't know how to explain it, but I liked it."

"I glad you did."

"Sir, you call that subspace, am I correct? And did you experience it as well?"

"Avril, it is called 'subspace,' but that term is reserved for the submissive experiencing it. I was dominant, so for me, it's called 'Domspace.' It's all called 'Headspace' when referring to them both. To answer your question, I did."

"Did we enjoy that together?"

"Well, I don't know about you, but I certainly touched you during our trip. Did you notice me?"

Sighing in that cooing sort of way, Avril merely said, "Yes, Sir."

She was still out of it, so things weren't logical and straightforward. She just felt mellow and relaxed, warmed by the blanket and his arm stroking her body.

"Better than sex?" he asked her.

"It could be, Sir, although, if we did the sex right, it could be a tie."

"I agree. In the meantime, lie there and take it all in. Now that you've experienced subspace together, we'll make sure you experience it a few more times before I introduce you to the other side, Domspace."

"Sir, do you honestly think I am a dominate?"

"Yes, I do, but that is a discussion for another day."

"Alright, Sir," she responded wistfully.

"Rest now. You earned it. Later, I'll take you to your room."

"Yes... Sir..." she responded as she drifted off to sleep.

Chapter Twenty-Three

Waking up, Avril discovered she was back in her bed. Rubbing her eyes, she brought the room into focus.

"Yup, her room…"

Lying in bed, she took several minutes to review the night before. Focusing on that feeling when she seemed to separate from her body and float outside it, well, it was intoxicating. She didn't know how she had achieved it. The two of them had worked hard over many weeks trying to get her there. The only difference was the exercise.

"But was it just the exercise?" Avril asked herself. Her muscle fatigue must have had something to do with it, but that could not have been everything, could it? What else was different? Could it have been her emotional state leading up to the session?

Except for her despondency, in the days before, she didn't rightly know. Could her depression have been a part of it? During those couple of days, her thoughts had been running wild in all directions. Her emotions ran unchecked as she experienced the emotional pain and suffering from her extended captivity.

Staring at the ceiling, she considered that Sir might be right. Her extended captivity wasn't the problem. She had lived every one of those hours. So, what if he oddly divided them. The hours were the same, and she lived every one of them.

"What was it he wanted her to do all those times she failed to go into subspace? What was different, and what did he want her to do that she never did? She experienced subspace last night, but she was at a loss as to know what she did do that made all the difference?"

Her eyes focused on nothing in particular. She decided to keep reflecting upon the question. In the meantime, she had to get up. The promise of the pool and the gym excited her. She was eager to get started.

After taking care of business in the en-suite, making up the room, and doing her morning assignments, she approached the door. Standing in front of it, she cautiously reached for the doorknob. After a brief retraction of her hand, nervous about being disappointed, she tentatively grasped the knob. Uncertain what would happen, she took a deep breath and turned the knob.

To her surprise, the door swung open for her. Joy filled her core as she stepped out into the corridor. Looking around, she looked first towards the Playspace. Smiling at the memory of last night, Avril turned right, headed towards the stairwell, and climbed. Slowly at first, she took them one step at a time. Halfway up, she quickened her pace. On the landing at the top of the stairs, she stared at another closed door. She reached for the doorknob, almost afraid that it too would not turn. She hesitated, her hand trembling, and then turned it. The door opened, and she stepped out onto the main level. A cheer resounded within her as she peeked her head out into the hallway. Taking one tentative step after another, she walked into the central part of the house.

She had been here before, so she knew what to expect. This time she was alone and unescorted. She felt free, even though she was a prisoner. She roamed, looking into all the nearby rooms. Even though he had toured the house with her, this exploration felt different. She observed things that she hadn't noticed during the official tour. For example, in all the rooms, she found the walls covered with fine artwork from all ages of man. Predominantly nudes, he arranged them to blend into the room's theme rather than control the space. The art included statues, paintings, and tapestries. The floors had beautiful, tightly woven rugs complementing elegant, silky floor-to-ceiling drapes flanking the windows. He had excellent taste.

Avril realized she was wasting time. She wanted to get to her workout, and her body was aching to get started. Walking directly to the pool, she quickly shed her heels and jumped in. Halfway through her laps, she stopped a moment, hung on the side of the pool, and looked around. Her chest heaving as she gathered the air she needed for the swim, she discovered that in the far corner was a large hot tub spa, big enough to seat eight or more people. On three sides of the natatorium, windows stretched from the floor to the ceiling, curving over to the far wall. They reminded her of a solarium.

Around the pool deck sat various tables, chairs, and chaise lounges. The chaise lounges sat to take advantage of the sun shining through the windows.

"I guess I need to take the time to soak up some sun." Avril resolved before finishing her laps and moving onto the treadmill. After completing her five miles, she studied the sweaty sheen on her body. Frankly, it felt good to work out and get that shiny sheen all over her body. Even that small droplet hanging from one of her nipples made her smile.

Making her way back to her room, she wondered what was behind the many doors she passed along the hallway. Part of her did not want to know. More than likely, they held other captive women like herself. Shedding her heels and jumping into the shower, she washed the sweat away, shampooed, and conditioned her hair.

After lunch, she sat down with her sketchbook and drew several rough sketches. They turned out very different from the ones of the previous week and reflected her better mood. Selecting one composition from the rough sketches, she began drawing it in earnest, wanting it to be the finest she had done so far.

Engrossed in her work, she did not hear the knock on her door. Additional knocking broke her concentration. Startled, she jumped up and knelt in her designated spot.

"Come in," she said loud and clear, responding to the knock.

"Good evening, Avril. How are you?"

"Very well, Sir."

"Did I disturb you?"

"No, Sir. That is, I was sitting at my desk drawing."

"May I?" He asked her, implying that he wished to review her work.

Nodding, she replied. "Yes, Sir. Please go right ahead."

Reviewing her work, he flipped through the rough sketches drawn earlier in the day along with her latest piece, still in development.

"These are excellent. May I see more?"

"Ah, yes, Sir," she said hesitantly, "though my last few drawings aren't all that good."

Sitting at her desk, he picked up the sketchbooks and studied her previous work. He flipped page after page without saying a word, examining each drawing before moving on to the next. He worked his way backward in time, moving from sketchbook to sketchbook. After a year, she had several filled sketchbooks stored within the desk.

"Avril, I like your work. You have a way of capturing emotion in the subtle lines in the eyes and face that few artists can do. I especially like the ones of your legs wearing your heels with the crystals, including the one showing off your clitoral piercing. They show me how proud you were to achieve your new rank."

"Thank you, Sir. I appreciate your comments."

"You may not believe this, but I also like your drawings from the past couple of days. The ones you drew while you were angry, depressed, and in that funk. They reflect the raw emotional distress you felt. They may never make it to an art museum, but they are good."

"Sir, I'm not particularly proud of those drawings."

"Nonsense, they are a perfect representation of your state of mind. Drawing them helped you resolve some of your issues related to your captivity. Never discount that."

"Alright, Sir, I'll try not to. I was nervous to show them to you, and I almost destroyed them."

"I'm glad you didn't. Please don't on my account. You're free to do with them whatever you want, but I will tell you that these are from your heart, just as the drawings of your heels are from your heart. I love them, and I would mount and hang any of them were they mine."

"Sir?"

"What?"

"Sir, you like them that much, even though you have art from various masters displayed throughout your house?"

"Yes, Avril. I've told you many times that there is something special about you. Your drawings reflect that particular uniqueness that I find very attractive. You would please me to let me hang your work in my home."

"I don't know what to say, Sir. You honor me."

"I do, and proud to do so," he said to her after closing the sketchbooks and sat down in his chair. Without either of them speaking, they shared a sort of companionable silence. Avril remained kneeling, facing the door, her backside towards him. She felt him lean back, cross his legs, and drape his arms on the armrests of the wingback chair. She sensed him scanning up and down her spine, wondering what he had in store for her tonight.

"Tell me what you're feeling and thinking right this moment."

"Sir, I… ah… I'm just wondering what you have in store for me tonight. I'm not feeling nervous or anxious or anything like that. I'm feeling, oh, I don't know what I'm feeling. I'm just waiting to find out what we're going to do this evening."

"Avril, tell me, how do you feel about the time you've been here with me?"

"Sir, I don't mean to be offensive, but do you want to know how I feel about being your captive?"

"Yes, Avril, I do. Please don't question my motives. I always have a reason behind what I do or ask."

"Sorr... ah, yes, Sir. I don't know how to express my feelings about my captivity. I think I have moved past the depression. My despondency overwhelmed me, and I struggled with how to deal with that. I'm past that now, at least I think so, but I can't promise that it won't rear its ugly head again."

"Avril, I don't believe you are stupid enough to make that kind of promise. I would take it as a lie, earning you punishment."

"Glad to know that, Sir."

"Getting back to your feelings regarding your presence here, what are you feeling right at this moment?"

"Sir, a gilded cage, no matter how beautiful it is or how much it offers, is still a cage. I don't know if I can ever accept my captivity, nor do I like being anyone's property."

"Fair enough, just as long as you understand that this is the only life you will ever know from now on, and you are my property."

"Yes, Sir, I know that."

"And are you still thinking of escape?"

"No, Sir, not now. I can't promise it won't cross my mind from time to time, but right now, no, I'm not."

"Let's move onto another topic. Tell me your thoughts and feelings about last night's session in the Playspace."

"Sir, I'm still trying to figure that out."

"Avril, let me stop you right there. There is nothing to figure out. There is no logic involved with transitioning from normal space to subspace. It is not a matter of physics or any of the physical sciences. You cannot evaluate it, theorize, and develop a proof. It just is, and it exists on a non-physical level."

"Sir, I think I understand. I was trying to figure out why I transitioned, use your words, into subspace last night when all of our previous attempts failed. I want to know what was different that allowed me to transition to subspace. That's all."

"Avril, it is okay to think along those lines, but just don't put too much logic into your review. It's better to accept it and move on. Now that you achieved your first transition, you know that you can do it again since you've done it once. That is all that is necessary. Being open to the experience and accepting it into your soul is all you require."

"I'll try, Sir. However, you're right about one thing. I know I've done it, so I know I can do it again. I'll let it go at that."

"Good girl. That's the right attitude. Are you eager to try again?"

"I am, Sir. Right now, if it pleases you."

"Avril, we can try again tonight, but I would like to hold off for another night or two. Sometimes, attempts too close together may be detrimental to the result we're trying to achieve. I think it would be better to continue the feeling and look forward to the next time. You can't plan it. You cannot just wake up one morning and say, 'I'm going to enter subspace today.' It doesn't work that way."

"Hm, yes, I see the validity in that, Sir."

"Alright, we'll play in the Playspace and see how it goes. Just don't expect it to happen every time we play. I guarantee you that it won't happen that way."

"Yes, Sir. I get it."

"Alright, how was your workout?"

"Fine, Sir. I swam the forty laps and ran the five miles you asked me to do. Afterward, I felt grand. My body misses the exercise, and it's eager for more."

"Just keep it in check and only do what I allow you to do. Tomorrow, you'll forego the swim and run, working on weight training instead. Is that correct?"

"Yes, Sir. I thought I would work on my lower body tomorrow. I miss doing leg presses and curls."

"Good, but don't overdo it. I don't want you to pull a muscle, tear a ligament, or sprain an ankle. Besides, I want the weight training to tone your body, not buff it up. Clear?"

"Yes, Sir. Tone it only. Works for me."

"Do you understand why I want you to tone only?"

"Yes, Sir, to keep my body looking firm and feminine at the same time."

"That and it makes for better sex and playtime."

"Oh, Sir, I understood that, but I thought you wanted the other answer."

"Avril, answer honestly. Include all relevant information in your replies as they occur to you."

"Yes, Sir, got it."

"Sir..." Avril said, wanting to ask permission to pose a question.

"Yes, go ahead, ask."

"Sir, I thought that after I work out tomorrow, I would lie down on one of the chaise lounges around the pool and soak in some sun. Would that be alright?"

"Yes, it is, Avril. Just be careful you don't burn. We've spent a lot of time getting your body just the way I like it, and I don't want to see it damaged."

"Yes, Sir. I got it. Don't get a sunburn."

"You got it, Avril. If anyone is going to burn your body, that would be me. I reserve that prerogative."

"Yes, Sir, got it."

"Now follow me to the Playspace. I want to tie you up on the bed and fuck you. Are you game?"

"Yes, SIR!"

Sir was true to his word. After arriving in the Playspace, he tied her up, using what must have been a thousand feet of rope, though that could be an exaggeration. After tying her tits until they turned blue, he tied what he called a pussy harness on her, including side-by-side lengths of rope cutting either side into her pussy and up her ass crack. He tied her arms behind her back and folded her legs over before tying them tight, crunching her ankles up firmly against her thighs.

He gagged her with a ball gag, and later, he used a piece of silk stuffed into her mouth and used a wide-stretch sticky tape wrapped around her head and mouth to hold it in place. Trussed up like a suckling pig, he fucked her repeatedly, causing her to beg permission to cum, despite the gag in her mouth.

Fortunately, he allowed her this courtesy, and she practically soaked the bed with her ejaculate. She had never been a squirter before. She never knew she could do that, but tonight, she found out she could. At first, she feared it was her bladder kicking loose, soaking the bed with urine. It turned out it was not the case. It didn't look like or smell like urine. When he swapped one gag for another during one of those free minutes, she smelled and tasted the fluid she had expelled. It tasted salty and most definitely not acidic. It tasted a lot like her vaginal secretions that naturally lubricated her during sex.

Satiated and exhausted, Sir carried her, still tied and gagged, to the sofa where he laid her down and rested her head on his lap again. There, he stroked her naked body, caressing her and occasionally probing her lower regions with his fingers. Opening herself up as best as she could, she felt him pry her pussy lips apart and insert two fingers into her and two more in her ass. She felt comfortable and at ease as he gently probed her, playing with her. Somehow, he knew all the right places and techniques because she had to beg permission to cum again. She climaxed again, not caring if she soaked the sofa.

Relaxed, she drifted off to sleep, her head resting on his lap. When she awoke, she realized that he, too, had drifted off to sleep.

"What a pair we make?" She thought.

Still bound and gagged, she waited for him to wake up. Wanting to take his cock into her mouth to wake him properly, she wished she wasn't wearing the gag. In the meantime, she thought about her life, pondering whether or not she could accept her situation.

She was still considering the question when he stirred. Gently removing her head from his lap, he stood up and faced her. Avril could see him smiling in the dim light. It was almost as if he was deciding whether or not to leave her like this. Deciding, Sir bent over and picked her up off the sofa. He carried her back to her room, still bound and gagged, and gently laid her on her bed.

"Shhh..." he started. "I considered leaving you like this. After all, you are breathtakingly beautiful, bound like this. I could get used to seeing you like this more often."

After a moment of gazing, he reached down and began untying her. "Unfortunately, the human body was not built to allow being bound indefinitely. Leaving you like this would inevitably hurt you. I can't have that. Besides, untying you now will allow me the pleasure of tying you up again."

Avril closed her eyes, and sleep took her.

The following morning, Avril stirring from a restful slumber. Opening her eyes, she scanned the room. She hoped to see him sitting in his chair. Alas, he wasn't. Rolling over, she threw her legs over the side of the bed and sat there for a time. Reviewing the day and night before, she wondered just what he had in store for her tonight. As much as she didn't understand his perversions, she was getting into them. She welcomed his control over her during their play in the Playspace. It was the rest of his power over her that continued to bother her.

"Just what did he want from me?" she asked herself. "Oh, sure, he wanted to possess me. He even believes he owns me. Does he suspect that he loves me?"

"Yet, there has to be more than that. What was his end game? I have no idea. Perhaps, one day, he would allow me to ask. I must look for an opportunity."

Getting up, she went over to the en-suite and started her morning routine. As she moved about, she couldn't help but wonder just what he had in store for her. She hoped that she wouldn't suffer too much as she found out.

Chapter Twenty-Four

Many weeks later, after finishing her workout in the gym and pool, she laid out a towel on one of the chaise lounges and took in a bit of sun. She figured it was towards the end of October, as the days were getting noticeably shorter.

Lying on the chaise, she inspected her body, now dry after her post-workout shower. She could tell that her body had toned up once again. The exercise had taken its time, but little by little, swimming the forty laps and five miles on the treadmill became natural. Part of her wanted to do more, but, fearing his wrath, she kept to precisely what he had prescribed. Besides, she liked the femininity her body had developed. The soft layer under her skin that smoothed out the muscular definitions appealed to her. Her body regained that tone she liked, and it allowed her to take part in the various positions he subjected her.

Her flexibility allowed her to enjoy their sex and play more thoroughly. Looking at her hips, she realized that they were showing some angular lines that weren't there a couple of months ago. She lightened up her aerobic workouts to restore her body to the softer shape they wanted.

With nothing to read and occupy her mind, her thoughts returned to wondering what Sir's end game was. These last few weeks had been fun, but she sensed something was up. His mood towards her was growing darker. There wasn't anything specific she could put her finger on, but as the days crept by, it was apparent that he was getting anxious.

"Did I upset him?" she wondered. "If I did, I have no idea what that might have been."

Avril continued contemplating what might be on his mind. She reflected upon their interactions since getting over her crisis and depression. She didn't think it had anything to do with the sex. It was incredible as ever, and he continued to amaze her with his stamina.

"So, was it their sessions in the Playspace or her behavior at one of the dinner parties? I don't know."

His behavior, she figured, must have stemmed from the dinner parties. Sir continued to offer her to his guests, and she thoroughly enjoyed those hours as they had their way sexually and more with her. She was often starving for more moments after the party broke up.

"I have to admit they are fun. He's never punished me afterward, so I presume that I behaved acceptably. Besides, as the center of their attention, I had fun. I can't figure out what's bothering him."

At one of the dinner parties he hosted, he shackled her ankle to a long chain attached to an eyebolt in the center of the great room. She dragged the chain around as she served refreshments, ate dinner, and enjoyed their attention at the sex-fest afterward. At times, the chain would snag upon something or someone, nearly tripping his guests.

"Was that it? Had I accidentally tripped up one of his guests with the chain? I don't think so since he hadn't mentioned it or punished me after the party."

One time, he locked a chrome steel belt high around her waist at another party, handcuffing her to hoops hanging from its front. The steel belt was very tight, squeezing her diaphragm and barely allowing her to breathe. It had this annoying bit of rectangular steel reaching down from the belt where a sharp edge dug sharply into her pubis mons. It was extremely uncomfortable, but his guests seemed to enjoy seeing her struggle with it.

"Could that be it?" She mused but discounted it as he would have said something after the guests left. Besides, they had taken her many times and seemed to have fun doing so.

One thing about Sir, if she showed the slightest disrespect or misbehavior, no matter how inadvertent the transgression was, he harshly punished her forthright. None of the punishments were as severe as in the early days when he beat her bottom bruised and purple, making it impossible to sit for days on end.

"No, if I messed up, he would punish me quickly, taking me over his lap, barehanded spanking me in front of everyone. The spanking wasn't so bad. I'll take barehanded spanking any day before getting the belt. I felt humiliated, getting spanked in front of others. That was the real punishment."

So, if it wasn't the dinner parties and it couldn't be the sex, did it have something to do with their Playspace time? What was she doing that wasn't living up to his expectations? She didn't transition into subspace every time they played, but he kept telling her that it was normal.

"So, what then?" Avril asked herself. "What?"

Besides, he kept telling her that he would introduce her to her dominant side and have her take control.

"When was that going to happen?"

He told her that he would introduce her to the whip's other side when she was ready.

"But that can't be it either. He was following a curriculum in her training, but to what end?"

"What was bothering him?" After going over various scenarios in her mind, she gave up, hoping that maybe it had nothing to do with her at all.

Lying back, Avril closed her eyes and allowed the sun to embrace her body and warm her skin. Feeling the warmth, she settled in to enjoy a few minutes of sun before she had to get up and return to her room. Trying to blank her mind, she was about to give up and leave the pool area when a shadow blocked the sun. Opening her eyes, she discovered Sir was standing over her.

"Sir?" she said, as she tried getting up off the chaise lounge gracefully when he stopped her. Thankfully, she settled back in. After all, it's just not possible to get up gracefully from a poolside chaise lounge. Everyone knows that.

"Stay there, Avril. I just thought I would join you for a few minutes." He told her as he removed his clothes. "I'm just going to take a quick dip, enjoy the water for a few minutes, and then I'll come and join you."

"Sir, I have a question."

"Go ahead."

"Would you like me to join you in the pool?"

"Yes, thank you. That'd be great."

"Then, Sir, I'll join you in the water. Just give me a moment to take my heels off."

"No rush, Avril. Take your time."

"Yes, Sir," she said as she sat up to unbuckle the heels.

In the meantime, Sir walked over to the deep end, in one polished motion, and without hesitation, he dived in, straight as an arrow. He sliced through the water, surfacing after about twenty-five meters halfway across the length of the pool.

Without losing his momentum, he swam freestyle to the end, turn and swim back to the other side. Using smooth, powerful strokes, he covered the distance end to end faster than she could do. Watching him swim, the rippling of his muscles and the smoothness of his strokes enthralled her. She had never studied his body in this much detail. Usually, he was always right on top of her or behind her. From a distance, she felt the familiar stirrings of a woman attracted to a fine physical specimen of a man.

Realizing that she was staring and not removing her heels, she quickly finished and dived in just as he was about to start a new lap. Though he could easily outdistance her, he slowed his pace so that they could swim together.

As they swam together, she watched him underwater during the portions of the stroke when she was face down in the water. His muscular body ripped the water as he quickly slipped between the water molecules. It was almost as if he oiled his body, allowing him to slide, no glide was the better word, through the water.

As her breasts heaved in time with her strokes, she realized that his cock was fluttering back and forth in time with his strokes. On the power stroke, it seemed to disappear between his legs. Then, on the resting stroke, it poked its head out and dangled from his body. Watching him, she almost thought that his cock was growing erect. She was sure of it when she realized that he was looking at her while she watched him.

Reaching the pool's shallow end, he stopped and went towards her, scooping her into his arms. A moment later, he was inside her, her legs wrapped around his waist and her arms around his neck. The water churning around them, the pace of his thrusts picked up speed. Her mouth open, her excitement growing, she felt his warmth coat her insides. His demanding thrusts drove deep inside her. More than once, she sensed him breach the entrance to her inner sanctum, invading her uterus as if her cervix grabbed ahold of his cockhead and not let go. Waves of pleasure exploded, stiffening her body and wrapping him even more tightly between her legs. She frantically tried to keep him buried inside her.

With her knees throttling his legs while she wrapped her arms around his neck, Avril felt him surge, his body preparing to pump her full with his milk. His body's rise to release seemed to urge her to even greater heights of pleasure, almost as if it responded to his excitement more than her own.

Approaching her limit, she wasn't sure she could regulate her body anymore.

"Sir, may I?" she begged in a low, throaty voice.

"Yes, cum for me," he told her.

That was all it took. Avril's eyes rolled up inside her head as she tightly gripped him with her legs, driving him inside her as far as she could get him. She felt him press her against the side of the pool and help her force his spurting manhood deep into her. Avril couldn't help it, but when she heard him loudly grunt as he came, she added her scream of joy and joined him in ecstasy.

"Oh, Sir," she murmured as she returned to her senses and began kissing him.

Shocked, since they hadn't kissed this way since her depression, she immediately unlocked her lips and was about to apologize when she suddenly recalled rule three from the book.

Catching herself, instead, she said, "Sir, that was wonderful. I don't know what came over me."

"Don't worry about it. I know from where it came. We'll talk about it later." He reassured her.

Then, pulling free of her, he grasped the side of the pool and pulled himself out of the water. As he walked over to grab a towel, Avril followed him and snagged a fresh towel for herself. Observing him, expecting a punishment at any moment for her indiscretion, she coyly teased him as she caressed her body with the towel as he sat down.

She started with her toes, bending over at the waist. She twisted her folded body around, showing it off. Moving on to her legs, she slowly and carefully stroked every portion of her skin, removing the droplets of water clinging to them. Feeling his enthrallment with her performance, she made a show of moving up her lithe legs, slowly parting them as she worked her way up. Reaching the end where her limbs joined at her hips, she carefully avoided cleaning off the pearly-white ooze seeping from her primal bloom. After making a show of drying off her chest, Avril finished by toweling off her hair and then wrapping it in the towel.

Finished, she retrieved her heels, and as she did with the towel, gave him a show as she put them on. Standing on one foot, she slowly slipped her other foot into the shoe. Bending over to strap it on, she carefully flashed him her bottom and bejeweled vulva as she buckled the shoe in place. Turning, she repeated the performance, only this time flirtatiously hiding her flower petals set off by the blue crystals.

Satisfied, she stood in front of him, one foot slightly in front of the other, and the knee bent. With her hands lightly clasped behind her back, she lowered her eyes and smiled. She welcomed Sir's appreciation and admiration; her smile was telegraphing her contentment. He leaned in and touched her pussy, caressing it with his warm lips and tongue.

Avril's knees failing, she let out a moan and surrendered to his kiss.

Chapter Twenty-Five

"Avril, go sit down on the chaise. I want to talk to you."

"Yes, Sir... and Sir, I just want to reiterate, I don't know what came over me. If I could take it back, I would."

"Avril, I'm not concerned with the kiss. I enjoyed it. Is there a rule in the book prohibiting kissing?"

"Ah, no, Sir, there's not."

"Are you sure?"

"Yes, Sir. I am," she answered him quickly. "There is no rule against kissing."

"Good, then let's move on, shall we? I want to talk to you about something else. I thought that we could enjoy each other's company in the pool area, which you may feel as neutral space."

"Neutral space? Sir, I have questions about this conversation."

"Avril, it is okay for this discussion to ask questions. I want to encourage questions as I have something important to discuss with you."

"Yes, Sir. Thank you, Sir. What do you mean by neutral space?"

"Let's say when in your room, we are in your comfortable space, and when we are in the Playspace, we are in mine. We can think the pool area of as neutral territory, so to speak."

"Okay, Sir. I understand."

"Avril, for many weeks, a nagging question is bothering you. I sense it, yet you've never brought it up. What is bothering you?"

"Sir? If anything, I was going to ask you that question. Something is bothering you and appears to grow each day."

"Avril, you are right about that, but I'm more interested in what is on your mind. I am asking you to tell me what is on your mind, and not about what you perceive in me."

"Well, Sir. Since you ask, I must tell you. I am nervous about asking you something that you may not like me asking."

"Nevertheless, I want you to ask. How I deal with what you tell me is my problem and not yours. I can't say I won't react if you are impertinent to me. However, I do expect that you carefully phrase your comments to respect my feelings as well as yours."

"Yes, Sir. I will try." Avril answered as she considered how to phrase what was bothering her. Eventually, she decided that come what may, just saying it untempered and with no softening techniques was the way to go.

"Sir, I know why I am here. It's because you want me here and here, I'll stay. I just can't help wonder, what is your endgame? What is the goal you wish to achieve in keeping me here forever, as you have told me?"

"My end game, eh? Is that it? What is it that wants me to keep you here? Is that what you want to know?" he asked her.

Nodding, Avril just looked at him, acknowledging her comment. "I'm not sure you will believe me, should I tell you."

"Sir, forgive me. I have no choice but to believe you. In all this time, as best as I can determine, you have always told me the truth, or you've withheld the answer. However, you have never lied to me, at least as best as I can tell. I don't expect you will do so now."

"Avril, you're right. I promised you I would always tell you the truth, and I will do so now. But before I do, why is it important for you to know the answer to this question?"

Staying silent for a time, Avril considered his query. In all her reflections on this topic, she had never thought about why it was important to her, only that it was.

"Sir, I don't know the answer to that. I just feel it is important to know."

"Well, perhaps that is what my end game is. Perhaps it is just important for me to possess you, to have you, to own you. However, that would only be a half-truth, and I will not do that to you. Are you sure you want to hear the answer?"

"Sir, rule one hundred thirty-nine states that I may never ask a question that I don't want to know the answer to."

"True, Avril. It makes me happy to know that you know the rulebook so well. Well then, in response to what is bothering you, I have been thinking about that very question myself. Oh, sure, when I first brought you here, I had clear expectations of what to do with you. However, as I have said frequently, there is something special about you. You may not realize it, but you force me to reevaluate my expectations and my desires with you."

"Sir, if I may, perhaps if you would share with me what your early expectations were about me. That may help."

"Avril, do you really want to work through this topic? I assure you, you may not like what you will hear."

"Sir, does rule one hundred thirty-nine apply to you?"

"What? Don't ask a question that I may not want to hear the answer to? I guess it does. Fair enough, I'll give this one to you. As I recall, you asked what my original expectations were regarding you. Is that correct?"

"Yes, Sir."

"Avril, I've told you that my family line goes back a thousand years. In all those years, my family took what we wanted. That is how they raised me. I take what I want. That is the person who I am. You have also learned that I can be a cruel person, as well. And by cruel, I mean that I enjoy inflicting pain and suffering on others. I watch it, and I inflict it. To me, there is no greater pleasure than to enjoy another's suffering."

Nodding, Avril acknowledged that she had known this but didn't interrupt his conversation. Listening intently, he continued.

"Until you came along, I would hunt my prey, bring them here, and evaluate the best ways that they could satisfy me. Yes, they indulge my yearnings with their suffering. You felt some of that when you earned your first punishments. I loved watching you scream and cry as I spanked your ass with my belt. I enjoyed watching each stroke raise ugly welts on your backside and turn black and blue over the following days. I enjoyed watching you avoid sitting as you healed, knowing that it was painful. I made you sit just so that I could see you squirm."

Avril watched him intently, her memory renewing the pain and suffering she experienced in the opening weeks of arriving here. As vivid were her memories, she involuntarily squirmed sitting on the chaise lounge. She saw him smile at her sudden discomfort.

"It is in my nature to derive pleasure from the suffering of others."

"But I changed all that, Sir?"

"Well, partially. With every woman I bring here, I intend to inflict pain and suffering. I don't bring men, just women. I don't consider myself misogynistic. I don't like fucking men. When I tire of fucking them, I pass them around to my guests. It's during this phase that I tend to start their torture. Eventually, they all live out their brief lives to my pleasure in their pain, in ever increasingly difficult and unpleasant ways."

"Sir, if I may, by brief lives, I presume that at some point, you kill them?"

"Yes, Avril. I do, though sometimes, I pass them off or sell them, just as I did last year to satisfy my honor of the woman who wanted to buy you for herself."

"Sir, would that be the woman who roasts women alive and then eats them?"

"Yes, that's the one. Only she roasts both men and women alike. She has no sexual preferences but buys whatever suits her fancy at the time. I might tell you more about that if you like at a later time."

"That's alright, Sir. I'll pass on that."

"As I assumed…"

He paused several seconds, almost as if he was considering roasting her, which led to an involuntary shudder, before continuing.

"Whenever I get a new acquisition, I evaluate them for several weeks, seeing how they respond to their newfound situation. Usually, I start by roughly fucking them, often ruthlessly and without regard to their pleas for relief. After that, I bring them to another room, and no, not to our Playspace. I bring them to another room where I torture them for days and weeks until I kill them. It depends on how well they stand up to my torments."

"In the last stages of their anguish, I set about killing them using various agonizingly creative means. The stronger willed ones tend to last a long time. The crybabies die early, but not quickly. The whiners tend to go down the most painfully, while the tenacious ones I tend to grant them an honorable, respectful death. Of the ones I deem worthy, they may be around for years, serving my house and serving me. Some attend me in various duties that support my lifestyle."

"But they all die, Sir, and they usually die in extreme pain."

"Yes, Avril. They all do."

"So, Sir, as I understand. Every woman I've seen in the house will eventually die by your hands?"

"Yes."

"The bartender, the women who were acting as furniture, floor lamps, all of them, after you torture them, you will kill them all?"

"Yes. You should also know that each of the women knows what their ultimate fate is. They all know that any day may be their last. They know that one day I will call them upon to feed my lust to torment and kill them."

"They do, Sir? They all know that they will suffer excruciating agony before you kill them?"

"Yes, Avril"

"Wow," she said. Then, probing further, Avril added, "and that is what you originally intended for me, Sir?"

"Yes, I meant for you to die that way as well. But then I saw something in you, which gave me pause. When I first read your stats, I figured you would provide me months or perhaps years of pleasure and service."

"Through sex and torture before ultimately killing me."

"Yes. That is until I learned more about you."

"And you changed your mind, no longer wanting to kill me. You even struggle to torture me. Is that right, Sir?"

"Yes, Avril. When I first bought you, I knew you were one of the strong-willed ones, and it thrilled me at trying to break you and watch you die ever so slowly. I even had a plan worked out for your death."

"But something changed, Sir."

"You could say so. For one, you never broke. Oh sure, six months ago, you crashed and told me that you hated me. Then you had the meltdown that led you into a depression. In both cases, you didn't break, at least in the genuine sense of the word. I work hard to break all my women, you included. All the women before you broke spectacularly. You? No, you didn't break as they did. Despite the circumstances, you maintained your self-esteem and your wits. You never gave up looking for an opportunity to escape. That's one reason why you could never leave your room unescorted by me."

Pausing for a moment for Avril to collect her thoughts, he went on.

"In those early days, I looked forward to breaking you down. I wanted to hear you beg for your life and to stop hurting you. I had everything set to move you into a new phase of painful interactions, and then the strangest thing happened. You memorized the rulebook inside and out. No one has ever done that before, and you did it very quickly. Once you knew the rules, you followed them exactly."

"Except for the pettiest infractions, you never earned a punishment after the first couple of months. I kept putting challenges in front of you, opportunities to violate a rule and draw yourself a punishment. Even when I punished you for no reason, you accepted them and continued to follow the rules. You never truly broke. Instead, you threaded your way through the minefield I established and came out virtually unscathed. No one has ever done that before."

Leaning forward, Avril continued to listen intently.

"You confused me, so I decided to take a closer look at you. That was when I gave you the drawing tablet and pencil set. I felt you would take out your frustrations in your sketches and, along the way, break a rule. You didn't. I carefully studied you from then on. I learned your mannerisms, your subtle body language, and I learned something."

"Dare I ask, Sir?"

"No need, I'm going to tell you. Despite protesting your captivity, you accepted your fate and enjoyed yourself. Oh, I don't mean being locked up, left alone without external stimulation. You welcomed my visits. You may not have realized it, but you looked forward to me taking your body and sexually satisfying myself. I know I astound you with my ability to fuck you continually, maintain an erection, and cum several times before I finish with you. I could do that because I believed you would reject me and beg me to stop, in turn, driving me on. You never did. No one ever did that before. Avril, to me, you seem to like being ravished for hours on end. You even seem to crave it. Am I wrong?"

"Sir, before I came here, I would have answered differently, but now, yes, you are correct. I love getting ravished by you and your guests. I enjoy being the center of everyone's sexual fulfillment."

"Yes, I figured that out. Which perplexed me and pleased me."

"Yes, Sir, but if I am not mistaken, there is still something else you want from me, something that you wish to take from me rather than give to you? Am I correct?"

"That is one part, yes. Right now, I also want your willing acceptance and agreement. In the Playspace, I've been training you that our play is a form of power exchange. You give yourself, in every way, to me, and in return, I give you pleasure and satisfaction as you have never felt before."

"And Sir, you have done so very well, I might add. Thank you for those lessons. I have learned much how to accept your power over me."

"And that is where I am having difficulty."

"How, Sir?"

"Avril, I promised you that in our Playspace, I would never punish you."

Gulping ever so slightly, Avril nodded.

"You have to know just how much effort it has taken me to abide by my promise. Yet, I will continue to do so. When you earn a punishment, I will exact my satisfaction somewhere else. However, there is a fine line between hurting you and punishing you. To you, they may feel the same. It's just that our play sessions are no longer enough for me. I told you then that while you would feel pain, and you have. However, that pain is not permanent nor agonizing. You may feel that it is but in the bigger picture, it is not. The agony you feel in the Playspace is an end to a pleasure enjoyed by both of us. The torment you feel in there is nothing like what I lust from you. Frankly, it's mild compared to what I do to the others."

"Mild, Sir? I shudder to think about how much worse your torments could be." Avril interrupted.

"Let me remind you, I won't intentionally hurt you. From here on out, that will not be the case. With any other woman, I would have been doing some remarkably nasty stuff on them, painfully hurting them, and relishing in their screams."

"Sir, if that is what you need, I'll scream for you."

"Avril, I know that you would, and thank you for your offer. However, it's not that simple. The screams have to be real. I would know you were faking them. You cannot fake a fitting scream; no one can. The screams I need do not come from pretending, like in some horror film. They come from genuine terror, fearing for your life. That is what the others give me. If you were in that position, you would scream in sheer terror before I finally ended your life. I assure you. You would die in the most horrible, painful way I could devise."

"And this is what you want from me, Sir?"

"Yes, in many ways, I do. I always have wanted that for you. However, I don't because there's something special about you that I want to preserve. It takes effort not to take my screams from you. I am honest with you. I may never lose that desire. All I can say is I will do my absolute best not to take them from you. However, should we ever cross that boundary, there would be no way to stop, and you survive."

"Sir, I must say I am getting nervous about what you are telling me."

"As I expected, which is why I wanted to have this conversation on the pool deck, in neutral space, and both of us naked."

"Sir, I get everything you are telling me. I even accept your need to pleasure yourself by making others suffer and die for your pleasure. I have a hard time understanding it. I doubt I will ever understand it, but I accept it."

"Intelligent statements like that are why you make things so difficult for me. Part of me wants to treat you like I do with every other woman, and another part of me hates the idea."

"Sir, can't you continue satisfying your fundamental needs without involving me?"

"Avril, believe me, I tried. I have exacted my desires on several women in the last few months, and I still want. My bloodlust is no longer satisfied, despite my growing number of kills. I'm accelerating my sessions, trying to extract my screams at an ever-increasing rate. You are becoming an obsession for me, and that is never good."

"I agree, Sir. Still, if there is something you need to preserve in me, wouldn't that outweigh your need to hurt me?"

"Possibly, but I have yet to find it."

"There's something about me that is holding you back, is that right, Sir?"

"I don't know if it so much about holding me back, but yes, with you, I want something different. There is no shortage of women to satisfy my rudimentary needs. Unknown to you, I have had many women come to this house and exit in just the manner I've described for you during your tenure here. Until recently, they helped me maintain my sanity and needs. As I mentioned a moment ago, they are no longer meeting my needs, and I am going through them at a faster rate than ever. This concerns me, and that is why I am coming to you. I've kept them hidden from you on purpose, but I can no longer do that. I have given your free rein of this house, and you would eventually stumble across them."

"Sir, are they held locked in the same hallway where my room is?"

"Some of them are, yes. The ones in those rooms are usually my new acquisitions and don't stay there very long. There is another underground level where they habitually end up suffering my torment before they succumb and die."

"I'm not sure I want to know about those areas, Sir."

"Ah, but you will, one day. I hope that you won't end there like the rest of them."

"So, Sir, despite my unique status, I may one day end up like the others?"

"Yes, that is correct. I hope that it doesn't come to that. As I have said before, how you live out the rest of your life is in your hands. I will guide you, but you may choose that ending, and I will accommodate you. I have never given that assurance to any of my other acquisitions."

"Sir, even if I said no?"

"That is correct. Your life is mine to do with as I please, just as the others' lives are mine. That will never change. Under ordinary circumstances, we would not be having this conversation. I would have just taken you to that subterranean level we spoke about and tortured you, possibly to death, just to hear you scream."

"Yet, Sir, if I understand you correctly, you are offering me a way of avoiding that fate, one that I must choose."

"Yes, there is, Avril. I'm sorry to say. I did not wish to put you in this position, but here we are. I'm fast approaching a crossroads, and I have to decide which path to take. To be fair, I decide this kind of thing often, and I will do so again. I tell you this to assure you that I don't take your feelings lightly, and I will try to forestall these crossroads as long as possible. Being a study of human nature, I must make these decisions from time to time. When I can, I would like you to share in the decision. I know that by putting you in this position, I am unfair to you."

"Sir, I have to be honest. You're scaring me."

"You know I like that."

"Yes, Sir. I do. That doesn't stop me from being scared."

"No, I suppose not."

"Sir, I think I know what one of the decision points is. That is, I reject you and consequently painfully suffer as you take my screams and my life."

"Correct."

"What is my other option, Sir?"

"You will not like it?"

"Sir, I don't like it already. Just tell me."

"Avril, I want you to give of yourself willingly to me, to stop being my prisoner and willingly stay with me. You agree to suffer my torments and my pleasures. I will torture and injure you, but in return, I will give you joy beyond your comprehension. You've already experienced some of what I offer. All I can tell you is that those pleasures and delights will match or exceed anything you've experienced to date."

"But Sir, I also have to suffer your torments, suffering in painful anguish to give you honest screams that I cannot fake."

"Yes, Avril. That is correct. Before you answer, I will promise you this. Should you take this second option, I promise I will not kill you. I have never broken a promise to you, and I will not do so in this case."

"Either way, Sir, I am going to scream. In one instance, I will scream for a time and die with them erupting from my throat, without experiencing pleasures along the way. In the other case, I will experience agonizing torment, screaming throughout, and experience an offsetting intense pleasure for the rest of my life. Which, according to you, will last for a long time. You wish me to make this choice, to choose one over the other. Sir, this is not much of a choice."

"No, I suppose not. Should you take the first option, I will have my fill, end your life at some point, and miss you terribly. In the other choice, you will receive more than you can ever imagine, including an elevated status within this house. All you have to do is suffer at times to appease me, and in return, I will give you pleasures beyond compare. Also, please keep in mind that I will not need this from you all the time, just now and then. I will always have the others to torment and appease my basic instincts. With you, I hope to elevate both of us into newer levels of passion that have so far have eluded me. I would like to take you with me, and together, explore these new heights."

"But Sir, I will need to feel pain and anguish to experience these heights of pleasure?"

"Yes, that is correct. You will feel pain as you've never experienced before. I want to say that it will be a good kind of pain, but I cannot promise that. I will most definitely hurt you. The pain you feel will be excruciating. I cannot dodge that."

"Sir, I need to know something, something important. Besides experiencing this ultimate pleasure, you promised me, what do I get out of this decision?"

"Avril, that's an excellent question. First off, you get to live."

"Suffering along the way, Sir, let's not forget that."

"True, but only occasionally, and likely, not all that often. You will also experience delight and ecstasy to levels never achieved in your life."

"Sir, to be perfectly honest, that is not enough. You could one day change the agreement and torture me to death, breaking your promise not to kill me. After I'm dead, the broken promise is immaterial."

"No, you're probably right. There is that chance. Yet, I have never broken a promise to you, and I don't intend to do so. You will have to trust me."

"Which brings me back to my original question, Sir. What's in it for me?"

"What else would there be. Getting to live a long life is big. I've never offered that to anyone before. Add to that the delights and pleasures you will feel far exceeding what you have experienced to date. That should be enough."

"Sir, with respect, I don't think so. I need more."

"Negotiating with me, aren't you?"

"I guess so, Sir. I suppose I am. I feel that suffering the way you describe suggests that I should take the straightforward way out and just let you kill me. That way, it's finished, over and done. I'll let God judge me and my decision. I don't expect that he will have a problem, given the circumstances."

"Yes, I can see your point. I don't know what else I can offer you, but I will ponder the question."

"Sir, punish me if you want, but I'm sorry, that's not good enough. You've thought about this for a very long time, and you have a goal you wish to achieve. You are springing this on me, and I presume you are giving me very little time to decide. Either I'm a part of it, or I'm not. I need to know what your end game is."

"All right, Avril. For what it's worth, I am searching for a lifetime companion. Someone I can share my life with for the rest of my life. I want to bind myself to this person, as she also binds herself to me. I think that person could be you. It's too early to tell right now. Much has to happen before I can say that I have found her. Before you get too excited, know this. Whoever this person is, she will always be my submissive and my property. She will accept her place behind me and support me and be my equal in all other ways. If that is you and you willingly give your body, mind, and soul to me, then maybe you are the one I have been seeking. If you can't or aren't willing, I will move on and continue my search."

"Oh, wow! I had no idea, Sir."

"Yet, that is where we stand."

"Sir, you're not talking about marriage, are you?"

"Oh no, I shudder at the thought. No, what I am searching for is something that transcends marriage. I am searching for a binding of souls at the very core. A binding will outlast the relationship or even our time on Earth. You may not believe it, but I believe it is possible to have two or more people bind themselves together in a manner as I describe that will last an eternity. There is evidence to support my assertion."

"Sir, I don't know what to say?"

"You need not say anything. I want to make sure you understand. My end goal is not up for discussion, nor should it factor into your decision. Only the choice you must make is at hand. Do not take credence in the rest, as even if you stay, you may not be the companion I seek. There is still much you have to learn, and much more I want to teach you."

"I see, Sir. Do I need to answer you now?"

"No, Avril, but soon. I know that this is an important and hard decision. I will give you time to decide. Study the problem, work out the ramifications for yourself. I permit you to ask me anything related to this decision. You have a week to decide. In the meantime, we will continue your training, play in the Playspace, and you will work on your assignments as directed."

"Not much of a choice, Sir."

"Yet, you will need to make one. One week, Avril. I give you one week from today. We'll share a private dinner for two, and I'll expect your answer afterward. If you don't decide, I'll assume you choose the former, and I'll escort you to your new quarters, where I will start extracting my screams from your useless body. I'll leave you now. I'll see you after dinner."

"Yes, Sir."

Chapter Twenty-Six

As Sir walked away, carrying his clothes with him, Avril fell back in her chaise in a state of shock. The issues plaguing her these past several weeks vaporized as if the sun burned away a fog. Only this time, she felt like she was in the midst of a fire tornado, sucked from the ground, swirling around as debris pummeled her beaten body as it burned to a crisp.

"Breathe," Avril told herself, letting out a deep exhale after he finished telling her what he wanted from her.

"His endgame, wow! I imagined nothing so terrifying. He really fancies hurting me in horrific ways. SHIT!"

That was it. The prospects of the future terrified her.

"How the fuck can I get out of this?" She thought to herself, absentmindedly stroking the training collar around her neck.

She needed to figure out a way to escape, now more than ever. Experiencing the kind of pain he described appalled her.

"God, please help me. If ever I needed your help, it is now. Oh, God, what should I do?" She pleaded with the man above who had given her life and comforted her.

"Damn, either way," she thought as she considered her options, "either way, I am so screwed. He's going to hurt me in unimaginable ways. He admitted it, and I believe him. His sadism consumes him, and he needs a release. But why me? If he had all of those other women to hurt, torture, and kill, why focus his sadistic feelings on me?"

"Fuck!"

Avril finally returned to her room, where she threw herself down on her bed, tears pouring out by the bucket full. Later, her tears dry, and her mind still in a state of shock; she curled herself up in a tiny little ball. Skipping dinner, Avril continued to lie there, forgetting, perhaps intentionally, that he was coming for her soon. When she boiled it all down, he had delivered an earthquake in her world, and he was sucking her into his perverted world. She didn't care about what he wanted.

"To hell with him," she repeated as she drifted off to horrifying dreams.

The sound of insistent knocking at her door roused her. It took a moment to recognize that he was at her door, collecting her for her next session.

"Fuck it," she thought to herself. "He can just go screw himself."

Still curled up on her bed, her back facing the door, she heard him throw open the door.

"Get up!" he commanded her.

"Fuck off," she screamed back. "I don't want to take part in your stupid games. Leave me alone."

"You will get your ass up right now, clean yourself up, and prepare for your next lesson."

"Go to hell!"

"You're earning a shit load of punishment."

"What do I care? You're going to punish and hurt me regardless of what I do. If not tonight, you surely will next week."

Storming over to her bed, he grabbed her by an ankle and dragged her onto the floor. "Get up, now," he commanded again.

"No!" Avril snapped back, obstinate that she had had enough.

"I will not ask you again. Now, get up and clean yourself up. Enough of this wallowing in self-pity. This 'woe is me' attitude is not helping."

"I don't care. You're going to do whatever the fuck you want to me, anyway. I don't have a choice. So, do what you're going to do, anyway. You can go to hell for all that I care."

At that, he reached down, grabbed her by the ankle, and dragged her into the shower. She kicked and screamed the entire way, trying desperately to get away from him. Unrelenting, Sir ignored her stabbing him with her stilettos, and dumped her into the shower enclosure. After turning on the water tap, ice water instantly drenched her, shocking her as she screamed indignantly. Goosebumps immediately erupted all over her skin. Avril ignored them, and a minute later, she shivered from the cold.

Sitting up, she pulled her knees to her chest, not caring in the least that she was still wearing the heels that were getting soaking wet. Wrapping her arms around her legs, she rested her head on her knees. Her screams and indignation subsided and transformed into hysterical crying. It didn't take long before her body rocked back and forth as her rib cage heaved in despair.

Then he surprised her. He sat down beside her, fully clothed, and wrapped an arm around her shoulders. Unable to stop herself, she rested her head on him and let it all go. Unable to move, every muscle in her body capitulated. She felt she could no longer support her frame. It wouldn't have surprised her if she melted and washed down the drain.

Later, much later, and she had no idea how long that was, she felt him slowly stroking the back of her head. Part of her wanted to revolt and pull away, and a part of her welcomed the soothing, comforting stroking of her head.

"What was wrong with him?" She considered. "One minute, he was warm and compassionate, and the next, a cruel sadist who took pleasure in hurting others, in hurting her."

On and on, the icy cold water fell on the two of them. As the water fell, she stared at the swirling water making its way to the drain. She imagined her body melting, carried away by the water, slowly circling the drain before finally taking her away from this evil nightmare. On and on, together, they sat on the floor, and he held her, trying hard to comfort her while she was numb from cold, grief, and fear.

"When would it all go away?" she bemoaned to herself. The water continued to fall.

After a very long time, Avril mumbled a question between her sobbing. "Sir, why must I choose at all? It's not fair."

"No, Avril, it's not fair. Life is not fair. It is my hope you will choose the one that includes incredible pleasure. I want you in my life. I want you to be a willing participant and to be at my side for years to come. I want to spend the rest of my life with you at my side."

Listening to his answer, a sense of calm settled over her mind and body. Avril didn't understand the calm she felt but decided it was likely more from exhaustion than from relaxation.

"Is this supposed to be some sort of proposal?" She asked.

"No, Avril, not in the sense of what you mean. To me, what I am asking you transcend that. Forget about everything society taught you about marriage and such. I am offering you an intimacy that exceeds anything you have ever experienced. It's a binding that is greater than love and more profound than what wedded couples share in their times together."

Shocking him, Avril asked, "Do you love me?"

"Avril, I consider that what I feel for you is more than love. It is something that one cannot express in words, only in feelings and actions."

"Yet, these actions include hurting me in unimaginable and horrific ways."

"Yes."

Trying to process his words, she felt numb. "But in my suffering, I will experience unimaginable pleasure commensurate with my pain?"

"Yes."

"And I will feel contentment far above anything that I can imagine?"

"Yes, assuming you give yourself completely to me, without reservation, doubt, or hesitation."

"Sir, I don't know what to tell you. What you are asking of me, what you will do to me, terrifies me."

"I know. That is what will make everything alright for both of us."

"Sir, I don't understand."

"No, I don't suppose you do. Nevertheless, I require you to decide. Believe me. You are not choosing between the lesser of two evils. What I offer you, if you accept and embrace it, will afford you a new level of consciousness and existence that few people will ever know. You just need to commit to your decision completely."

"I still need time, Sir."

"Agreed, you still have several days to mull it over and ask questions. I expect you to use them wisely. At dinner on the seventh day, I will expect an answer from you. One way or another, your life will change once again. Whether it is for the better or worse, it is up to you."

"Sir, I don't know whether I can. Is there another choice?"

Chuckling, he responded. "No, Avril. There isn't. All I can offer you is that one option ends in death, and the other ends in life. A life that, I believe, you will embrace and enjoy."

"I don't see how, Sir."

"No, of course, you can't. You have to experience it to understand and accept it. Until then, all you can do is take it on faith."

"You're asking a lot of me, Sir."

"Yes, I am, and I understand the gravity of what I am asking. What I can tell you is that I've searched for years, looking for someone who I feel can accept the life I offer and would like to share it for the rest of my life."

"For the rest of your life, but not mine?"

"Yes, Avril, my life, a life I offer to share with you, starting a week from now. I tell you repeatedly that you are unique. I believe that to the deepest part of my soul. I want to explore your special uniqueness. I suspect that I will never discover all that is special about you, but I want to try. So, you see, to learn all that this is about you, you need to be by my side, suffer my torments, and relish the joy I offer you. In short, I want you to be a part of me."

"Sir, I don't love you."

"Avril, I am not asking you to love me. I am asking for something more, much more. I believe you have it in you to offer me what I hope you will freely give me. As I said on the pool deck, it is a level of intimacy that few experiences and, once shared, are forever embraced and cherished. It is this intimacy that will give you the supreme pleasure greater than you could ever imagine."

"But that pleasure requires an equal level of pain."

"Yes, Avril. There can be no light without the darkness."

"Hold me, Sir," she asked, dropping her head once again on his shoulder as she reflected upon their conversation. The icy water continued to fall.

The week didn't drag on. It seemed to fly. After breaking down in the shower, the two of them sat under the cold water long after their conversation ended. It was one of those 'companionable-silences' they had both come to enjoy. Shivering from the cold, she was eventually ready to get out. He helped her up and carried her back to her bed. A minute later, he returned with a towel and dried her off. Stripped of his wet clothes, he warmed her with dry towels, rubbing heat back into her shivering body.

Removing her heels, Sir made sure that she was warm and comfortable before disappearing. He returned with a fresh pair of heels, thankfully dry, and strapped them to her feet. Sliding into her bed alongside her, he took her in his arms. There was no raging desire to screw her, tease her, or play with her body. For the first time, he just held her.

She started crying again, not the body racking, hard crying that tired her out, but the soft sobbing of dealing with emotions beyond her control. Sir was a perfect gentleman. He held her as she sobbed, comforting her, before finally drifting off to sleep.

The following morning, he was still with her. She woke up with her head on his chest. He was sleeping on his back with an arm wrapped around her, holding her. Strangely, she felt comforted to have him in her bed after waking. He had never spent the night with her. Usually, they played and fucked, and left her to the isolation of her bed with only memories of their recent encounter to keep her warm. She was somewhat comforted to find him sleeping next to her.

She listened to his heart beating slowly under her ear. His chest was gently rising and falling with each breath. Not wanting to disturb him, she laid there, trying to get a sense of the man.

Over the days that followed, she considered what he wanted from her. It had to be more than just torturing her. He had many opportunities to do that to her as he did to any of the women he possessed. No, there had to be something else, of that she was sure. After he had woken, he had made love to her. He didn't just take her body in an animalistic and brutal way he usually did. Instead, he made love to her, as a compassionate lover might do. She relished that moment in that she felt cherished for the first time since she had come to this house. Their lovemaking had been something different, and she had to admit, she welcomed it. She wanted more of that kind of attention.

Later, they shared breakfast, each of them sitting naked around the small table in her room. Neither appeared to be aware of their nudity as they ate, sharing meaningless conversation. She thought their nakedness was natural.

After breakfast, he left her to her thoughts, and she went about her routine. That night, he claimed her and brought her to the Playspace. They played as they had done so many times before. This time, there was no painful whipping, flogging, or caning. Instead, he had lightly restrained her and then used several sensual toys, everything from the comforting fur to a feather toy one might use to play with a kitten. Together, they seemed to soothe her and delight her. She had come close to slipping off into subspace, but her mind's turmoil held her back.

Over the following days, they had played, made love, and savored challenging, exhausting sex. She kept up with her assignments, going to the pool, and working out in the gym. Not because she took joy in the exercise, but more out of maintaining a routine that allowed her to consider her options. Throughout the days, she contemplated escaping. She had even tested the collar by approaching several exit doors and windows. As soon as she got within ten feet of an exit, her neck started tingling with pins and needles sensations. The first time she felt it, she touched the collar, and her fingers immediately felt an electrical shock jump to the pads of her fingers. When she got within a couple of feet of uncertain escape, she knew without a doubt that any closer, she would regret it.

Two nights before she had to give him her decision, he had taken her to a previously unexplored area of the house. This area was where he took out his cruel, sadistic special interests with his other women. The room was empty, except for the body of a dead woman, naked, her back leaning against a post. Her arms hung limply at her side. Notwithstanding the horrific scene, Avril could not shake her eyes from the body.

Avril saw that the young woman sat on the edge of what looked like a construction board sandwiched between her legs and tight into her groin. The wood shaved into a narrow wedge. Imbedded into the thin edge along the top were tall, sharp, metal teeth, similar to that of a tree saw blade. Her full weight rested on the board while her feet barely touched the floor. The bloody saw teeth dug deep into the clefts between her legs, slicing her partly in half. Fresh blood still dripped from the deep wounds to her delicate flesh, adding to the large red pool on the floor below her body.

The young woman had evidently died only a short time ago. Her head and face were a dark bluish color, while the rest of her body remained a pale ghostly pink. A length of rope cut deeply into her neck, almost invisible from the folds of skin and flesh wrapping around it. A large wheel attached to the back of the post appeared to be the instrument of her death, strangling her as the wheel turned. Bloody fingernail marks were all around her throat, provided clear evidence that she had tried to claw the rope from her neck during her dying minutes.

Except for the rope around her neck and the saw-toothed board between her legs, there were no other visible means of support to hold the dead woman upright against the post. Her feet barely touched the floor, providing no help to the woman's frame. The razor-sharp teeth of the saw blade sliced deep into her groin, allowing the body to slide down the post ever so close to the floor. In struggling with her strangulation, the woman assisted her gruesome death by sawing herself partially in half.

The woman's legs rested at relaxed but awkward angles, the apparent aftereffects of her thrashing about to fight for her life. It was clear to Avril that her struggles contributed to her death. The saw teeth had cut deep into her lower abdomen, ripping her organs to shreds. Had she lived, Avril doubted that the woman could ever bear children, not to mention taking part in the simple act of copulation or moving her bowels. It was probably better that she had not lived. No doubt that either way, her final moments had to have been excruciating.

In the scene, Avril was unsure of just how the woman died, be it from strangulation or exsanguination. Which one of the horrific tortures finally finished her off? Avril only knew that Sir performed the ritual to the very end.

Avril tried to back out of the room. He stopped her and made her take in the entire scene. Closing her eyes to the horror, she tried to wipe the image from her thoughts.

"Open your eyes. I want you to see this. It's important."

"Why, Sir? Why would I want to see this?"

"Because you are better than this."

"But Sir, she's not even twenty."

"She didn't work out. Like most women her age, she was too into herself, too selfish to bring me much pleasure. She fought me from the beginning, which was my only joy with her. Ripping her life from her was the only pleasure I could wring from her."

"Well, Sir, I can see you certainly wrung it from her. That contraption with the rope around her neck, I presume turning the wheel would tighten the rope around her neck."

"Yes, Avril. It's an ancient form of execution, going back thousands of years."

"It's cruel, Sir."

"Yes, it is."

"And that thing between her legs?"

"An invention of mine, though undoubtedly, I'm not the first to think of it."

"And this is what you have in store for me?"

"No, it's not, especially if you choose the second option. However, I assure you. If you choose the first one, you will not die like this. This death was not an angry one. I did not expect much satisfaction from this one, and she didn't deliver. With you, I don't know what I will do should you not accept my proposition. I can tell you this. I will be angry and extremely disappointed. I suspect your death will be long, drawn-out, and painful. This one was over in a short time and fulfilling me in only a superficial sense."

"And mine will be worse, Sir?"

"I cannot say so with certainty, but I know myself well enough that it is highly likely."

"I still have a couple of days to decide, Sir?"

"You do, two nights hence."

"Can we leave now, Sir?"

"Do you have any other questions?"

"Sir, I... I don't know. I may, but right now, I'm still too stunned to think of anything."

"Then, let's play."

"As you wish, Sir..."

Chapter Twenty-Seven

The following morning, a full day before deciding between two evils, Avril awoke in her bed, her mind flashing unrelenting thoughts and images in the wee hours of the early morning. In her old life, she might have thought that it was four-thirty in the morning.

She had gotten little rest. As usual, the night before, Sir took her to the dungeon and played with her for several hours. During that time, she had felt both pain and pleasure, each building upon the other. When he finally took her, entering her body and thrusting into her very core, she begged and finally got his permission to climax. He made her wait, though, which she quickly forgot when he finally said yes. By the time he finished with her, she was a quivering mass of gelatin, barely able to walk without help.

She recalled that after carefully unstrapping her, he carried her to the sofa. After draping her with a soft, cuddly blanket, he sat down and settled her heavy head on his lap. She curled up, enjoying his soothing caresses, and fell asleep listening to just how much she had pleased him. She had no idea how or when she got back to her room and her bed.

Lying on her back while staring into the surrounding darkness, sleep failed her. As full consciousness returned, an idea sparked from the thrashing thoughts raging chaotically through her head. Staring at nothing and reluctantly accepting that she would never go back to her old life, Avril began developing an idea.

Getting up, she made for the en-suite and prepared to face her owner and Master. By the time it took her to shower, make the bed, and be ready to face the day, Avril had formulated a plan. Nervous, afraid, but prepared, she knelt and took her standard pose in her expected everyday wear and awaited her fate.

An hour or so later, Avril heard a knock on her door, breaking her reverie.

"Come in," she answered.

"Good morning, Avril. I see you are up early today."

"Yes, Sir. Good morning. My mind was all a jumble, and I couldn't sleep."

"Ah, yes. I understand. I've had those nights as well. In my experience, there is nothing to do about it except get up and start the day."

"Yes, Sir."

"You look beautiful as usual. Would you care for breakfast?"

"Yes, Sir, I would. Thank you."

"Come then. We'll have it upstairs."

Rising from her kneeling position, Avril took his arm as he led her to his private, intimate dining room. Stepping into the hallway, Avril curiously glanced at all the doors lining each side of the hall. Curious what they were hiding, she honestly didn't want to know and hurried past them.

"I hope the thoughts that kept you awake weren't too disruptive?"

"Ah, no, Sir, well, maybe a bit. After all, you gave me an impossible choice. I still don't know what to do about it, and I'm scared." Avril answered as he held out a chair for her at the table. Sitting, she waited for him to sit before continuing.

"Sir, I'm struggling to understand why you insist I make this choice."

"Coffee?" he answered.

"Yes, please, Sir."

Pouring two cups of coffee and handing one to Avril, she continued.

"Sir, please forgive me, but I don't understand why you require me to make this decision. I mean, I know that I am your property, to do with as you please. That's the thing. You can do whatever you wish to me. You can torture me, make me scream at any time, and kill me to satisfy your desire and pleasure. I will live and die by your hand whenever you feel like it. Why then must I make this ungodly decision? And, please, Sir, don't just tell me that you wish it. I want to know what's behind your command."

"You ask good questions, fair questions. Let's just say; I have a plan. One that I hope you will help bring to fruition."

"And this requires me to decide between two horrific choices, Sir?" Avril asked as she drank from her coffee cup.

"Eggs?"

"Thank you, Sir. Yes, please."

As Sir dished up a couple of poached eggs and a slice of toast and handed the plate to her, he continued. "Yes, Avril. It does. As you said, I could just force my screams from you. They would be eminently satisfying. However, I want more, and I am hoping you give me that."

"And to give you that, Sir, I must decide between a quick and excruciating death, or be by your side and occasionally give you the screams your need?"

"Ah, don't forget the unfathomable pleasures I will give you in return."

"Yes, there is that, as you said, Sir," Avril said, staring deep into his eyes. "I just can't imagine pleasures beyond what you have already given me. I can only envision more of the same."

"Avril…" he started, staring right back at her, first by scanning her naked breasts proudly standing just above the table edge before sliding his attention up to her eyes, returning the deep gaze into the depths of the windows to her soul. "I can assure you what I offer you, should you live by my side, those intense pleasures will outweigh any begrudging unpleasantness."

"Sir, you say that, but how do I know? How can I decide if I don't know what you are offering me?"

"Avril, you will have to take it on faith. Have I ever lied to you before?"

"No, Sir. Not to my knowledge."

"Then, there is your answer. You either believe that I will deliver what I am offering you or not. If not, then your decision should be easy, though I will miss you after you are gone."

"Sir, can you offer me any reassurance beyond what you have already said?"

"No, Avril. I can't. You'll just have to take it on faith."

"To be honest, I'd rather not have to decide anything, on faith or not. Quite literally, I'm scared to death, which I know you are enjoying. Sitting here, I may look composed, but my insides are a wreck, and my belly is doing somersaults. It is taking all my effort to control my growing panic."

"Then, just breathe. You're doing fine."

"Thank you, Sir. I appreciate that. However, I have a proposal for you, one that will help me decide. As my choices stand now, I just can't see the benefit either way. Part of me wishes you would just end my misery and take your last screams as you kill me. Part of me is trying to figure out a way to survive and, hopefully, remain unscathed. I just can't see the upside for either choice, ultimate pleasures notwithstanding."

"Hm, I'm not sure I want to hear your proposal."

Pushing aside her breakfast dish, Avril continued.

"Sir, as I understand your proposal, should I choose the second option, you are expecting me to be at your side, a compliant and consenting companion to share your life. Is that not correct?"

"How very astute, Avril. You are correct, though ultimately, I want more from you. As I recall, I mentioned something to that effect when I first sat you down in the natatorium and presented you with your decision. Ultimately, I want you to stay with me of your own free will."

"Yes, Sir, you said that. You've also been telling me for some time now that you see a dominant within me. A dominant that can take screams from my very own submissives."

"Yes, that's true," Sir interrupted.

"Yes, well, that's the thing. How can I work on that? I don't suppose you'll allow me to dominate you."

Chuckling, he said. "No, you won't. You will never have that pleasure."

"Yes, Sir, as I supposed. Then, how am I to bring out the dominance within me if I cannot dominate you?"

"Avril, that's easy, with any of the others within my house. I'll introduce you to a few that should satisfy you. Using them, I will teach and guide you into exploring your ability to top another."

"Yes, Sir. I had thought about that. However, they would still be beholden to you, not me. They will not respect my power over them. They will always look to you for guidance."

"Yes, I see where this is going. Initially, though, I think in your dominance training, the stock I supply will be sufficient."

"Yes, Sir. I agree. However, I anticipate that with the excellence of your training, I will quickly outgrow them and need additional subjects to practice my dominance."

"Yes, that's true, and I will supply them."

"Sir, with all respect, that will not allow me to progress very far in my training. I believe that I must be free to choose my subjects, learn from my mistakes as well as my successes."

"Avril, when you are ready, I will allow you to select your subjects from within my household and turn them over to you."

"Sir, please forgive me, but you chose your property to please and satisfy your needs, which may differ from mine. I may not be there yet, but I can foresee a time when none of your stock will satisfy my needs."

"Yes, that is possible. I will admit. But that is a long time from now."

"Sir, I beg to differ. I believe that within three to six months, I will outgrow the available submissives within your stock. God, I can't believe that I'm saying this. If I am right, you intend to teach me how to inflict pain and suffering on my submissives so that both of us may achieve higher levels of pleasure."

"Yes, Avril, that is correct. I am astounded by your reasoning and by your conclusions. I knew you were intelligent when I first bought you, but you continue to amaze me with your insights regarding me as well as your situation."

"Thank you, Sir. You give me plenty of time to examine my thoughts."

"So, what do you have in mind? You said you had a proposal. Spill it."

"Yes, Sir. You want something from me, a decision that I have to make tomorrow night. Neither choice is alluring. Yet you require me to select one over the other. Frankly, I'm inclined to select the first option and end it all. God will understand. I'm sure of it. Since I cannot foresee an attractive selection, either way, I want something from you to help me choose."

"What do you want?" he asked, a bit impatiently.

"Sir, I want a full individual membership into this Consortium of yours. I want to stand beside you at meetings and auctions as a member, not as owned property."

"You will always be my property..." he interrupted.

"Yes, Sir. I understand that. However, within the Consortium, I want to stand beside you as a peer, with rights equal to any member. With this membership, I am free to choose my stock and submissives. I will train them as I see fit and learn the depths of dominance that you wish to bring out within me. I will make mistakes, of course, and you will allow me the freedom to make them. You will also be there to mentor me and guide me throughout my training and help me get beyond my mistakes. You proposed that should I choose the second option, it would be a long-term choice that forever bars you from killing me. Torture me, yes; yank screams from my anguished body, yes; but killing me, no. That means we will be together for years and perhaps decades. I need to share a common understanding of you if you are to keep your promise."

"Avril, how would you pay for your submissives?"

"With your money, Sir, you can afford it. It will make little difference to the funds you already budget for your purchases. I can foresee cases where I can make a profit on my selections. As you suggested a while back, I can run my very own company while making a hefty profit. Whether the product is soap, marketing, or people, there is no difference. Only the products are. If I should turn a profit, I will use a portion to reimburse you."

"Avril, you make a sound argument. I can see where this may be helpful to both of us. However, there is a flaw in your argument. There is a substantial membership fee, which I suppose you expect me to pay. You should know that the Consortium is very stingy with their memberships. They grant them only after extensive background checks and only with the approval of the three-quarters majority of the membership. Besides, I don't recall in the Consortium's history, one of the hunted becoming a hunter and member."

"Sir, I dare say, most of those hunted by the Consortium die in short order. They don't live long enough to apply for membership. What you are asking me to do is to decide whether I should die now or live for decades in your world."

"Avril, so far, your logic is spot on."

"Thank you, Sir. As I understand it, you are a senior member of the Consortium and exert a lot of influence. I find it hard to imagine that you couldn't gather enough support to grant me my membership. As for the membership fee, yes, I expect you will pay that without debt to me. I am, after all, your property and your responsibility."

"You will always and forever remain my property, even if you get your membership."

"Granted, Sir."

"Avril, against my judgment, I feel it necessary to repeat myself. To my knowledge, the Consortium has never granted membership to prey and property."

"Then, Sir, you will set precedence where they will remember you for centuries to come. You will have the potential to become the most revered member ever, just as in my country; we revere George Washington and Abraham Lincoln centuries after their deaths."

"Interesting..." Sir commented thoughtfully before continuing. "That is possible; however, it is also possible that the future will remember me as the moron who became a bondsman to his personal property. Which way the Consortium remembers me is all up to you and your behavior?"

"Yes, Sir. That seems right."

"Are you going to do something that I will regret?"

"Sir, I will promise you this. If I do so, it will not be from something I intentionally conceive and orchestrate. Should I choose the second option, I will willingly stay with you, harbor no thoughts of escape, and become your devoted companion and consort for the rest of our lives. That is how I see your requirement for my decision."

"You see correctly and maybe even a bit further than I had envisioned. What you propose is not impossible, but is certainly improbable to accomplish."

"Sir, I have every confidence in you that you can do it."

"It will take time to get the membership application up for a vote."

"Sir, by that time, I will have passed your intermediate level dominance training, and I will be ready to apply my new skills to those individuals I acquire."

"Most of the prey you purchase will not willingly submit to you."

"Sir, I have every confidence that you will teach me how to get them to submit."

"Or die if not?"

"If it comes to that, yes," Avril said confidently. "Eventually, according to your standards, they will die, and I will have to do the honors. Is that not true?"

Inside, though, she abhorred the thought of killing another person, or for that matter, any living animal. However, if she was to survive, Avril knew she had better learn how to get them to bend to her will. Hopefully, she could sell them off before it came to having to end their lives.

"True, you will have to kill them. Avril, I can't promise you a membership. The best that I can do is submit your application along with my recommendation for acceptance. Anything beyond that is out of my control."

"Sir, are you accepting my proposition?"

"I'm thinking about it, Avril. I haven't decided, that's all."

"Oh, one more thing, Sir…"

"Yes?"

"I want to sleep in your bed, Sir. Give me my own room if you like, but at night, I sleep with you, in your room, and your bed."

"I may come in very late in the night."

"Sir, when you come to bed, is none of my concern. Besides, we are just as likely to go to bed together."

"There may be more than just the two of us, and not for sleeping."

"Yes, Sir. I anticipated that. I might even enjoy it."

"Anything else?"

"Well, now that you mention it when you travel, I want to go with you."

"With no aspirations of escaping?"

"No, Sir; none whatsoever."

"You will abide by all the rules in the rule book. Regardless of your decision, they will always be in effect."

"Yes, Sir."

"You will still wear my collar."

"Happily, Sir…"

"And as a member of the Consortium…"

"Sir, as your property and devoted companion first, and as a full member of the Consortium second."

"You will still have to submit to me as I pull screams from your tormented body."

"As you said, Sir, the pleasures you give me will offset many times over any pain I suffer."

"True. What I have given you so far pales compared to the ecstasy you will experience as my property and my companion."

"Permanent companion, isn't that correct, Sir?"

"Yes, Avril. We can assume permanently."

"Sir, forgive me. Assumptions with you are dangerous to my health."

Laughing, he added. "Yes, they are. All right then. I accept your proposal with the stipulation that I cannot guarantee your membership. However, I will submit your application, pay the non-refundable application fee, file a letter of recommendation, and fight for your acceptance. You must agree that you may not get it, despite my recommendation. I cannot force the Consortium to accept you as a member. They will know everything about you before they vote on your application. That means they will know we once hunted you, sold you at auction, and ultimately sold you to me. We may even have to change our charter to allow your membership. I don't know how they will take it, and I cannot promise you your membership."

"Sir, I know the Consortium's mission. I still don't agree with it, but I understand and accept it. If you and I are to be long-term companions, I must become a part of your life and everything that goes with it. That means being an active member of the Consortium, sharing the experience with you, just not as your owned property standing behind you, but as a peer standing alongside you. Outside of Consortium activities, I will remain your property to do with whatever you wish within the boundaries of our agreement. I do not doubt that you will get my membership approved."

Taking a deep breath, she concluded, surprising even herself in even suggesting the proposal, never mind getting him to agree. "Sir, I agree with your stipulation."

"With the stipulation I added, I too agree to your proposal," he confirmed.

After a pause, Avril added. "Sir, just to be clear, I still have until tomorrow night to make my final decision."

"Yes, Avril. Tomorrow night, after dinner, I expect an answer from you, one way or the other."

"Your mandate is still daunting. Sir, I'm still frightened and panicky. I still don't know what I will say tomorrow. I may toss in the towel and choose the first option and finish it."

"I understand. I gave you an impossible choice, and somehow, you got me to agree to an amendment. Don't make me regret it."

"No, Sir. I won't."

"Alright, I'll escort you back to your room where you can do whatever you need to do to decide. Take a long hot bath in the jet tub, draw, walk on the treadmill or anything within the rules' boundaries. You can also do nothing but lie on your bed and rest if you want. I grant you leave from your lessons and assignments for today and tomorrow."

"Sir, thank you for last night. I had fun."

"You're welcome, Avril. I look forward to future engagements."

"I wish I can do the same, but right now, your demand consumes me."

Chapter Twenty-Eight

On the final, fateful day, the one she dreaded, Avril awoke in her bed, alone after a restless night of nightmares. As much as Sir had tried to soothe and comfort her, she still didn't know what she wanted to do. For her, it boiled down to a quick and agonizing death or a lifetime of anguish interspersed with periods of ultimate bliss. She found it hard to decide. She knew how bad the agony could be, but how good would be the pleasure? Was it worth it? Without a frame of reference to draw upon, it was impossible to decide. Fortunately, she had gotten him to add in the amendment. Despite the alternation, she knew that ultimately, it might not matter. He could change his mind at any time and kill her, and she was powerless to prevent it.

Did she have it within her to choose death? She didn't honestly know. It went against everything she believed. That decision was akin to committing suicide. To her, it was a stain upon her soul, and God may never forgive her, despite the circumstances. Yes, Sir would be responsible for her death. However, did one more murder staining his soul make a difference? Not likely.

Yet, if she chose life, she would suffer painful, agonizing sessions where he would torture her mercilessly. While he promised unimaginable pleasures as compensation, how would she know whether what he offered would be worth the suffering that went with it? She would live, leaving her soul unstained by the experience, but at what cost?

Then there was the membership in this despicable organization called the 'Consortium.' Would she be able to purchase her very own property, torture them, and probably kill them? How would God look at her stained soul? Would he forgive her, knowing the circumstances? Would he give her a pass and accept her into his care at her death? She had no idea. She only knew that she wanted to survive and that she could only do that one day at a time. This small win she had secured was a fleeting one and could quickly burn away like an early morning fog. He could still break his promise and kill her. She knew that was the more likely scenario for her future. Should she choose the second option, she would have to find opportunities to avoid that fate.

Following her routine, mostly because it kept her sane, she went through the motions of the day; eating, making the bed, cleaning the room, working out, and showering afterward. At one point, she stood at her desk, staring at her sketchbook. Disgusted at what awaited her at dinner, she tossed it into the desk drawer and walked out to the pool area.

As she sat down on one of the chaise lounges, she realized that he gave her his ultimatum one week ago in this very spot. Soon, she had to choose between two terrible evils. She was at a loss as to how to decide. Putting aside the decision, she laid back, closed her eyes, and soaked in the sun for the time being. Soon enough, she was fast asleep, her mind quiet for once.

Hours later, she felt a gentle hand on her shoulder. Opening her eyes, she saw Sir standing over her and the sun drifting towards the horizon. "Have a good sleep?"

Rubbing her eyes, she sleepily replied, "Yes, Sir."

"Come on then. We will have a quiet dinner in the private dining room. I've laid out an outfit for you in your room to wear. Please come up to dinner in an hour."

"Yes, Sir, as you wish."

As she stood up to comply, he stopped and stared at her. She watched his eyes roam up and down her body, appreciating the view.

"Come here a moment, please." When she stepped up to him, he reached out and removed the bells hanging from her nipple rings. "These need to go. You do not need them any longer."

"Yes, Sir," she responded as she crept from the pool area.

He gave her a soft slap on her ass as she passed. She almost smiled in response, recalling an earlier, more pleasant time. Her mind in turmoil; she didn't want to go to dinner. Going to dinner meant that she had to give him her decision. She ached to stall as long as possible. Knowing he wouldn't let her, she almost ran for the front door, not caring whether or not the collar shocked her to death.

Giving in instead, she turned towards the door that led to the stairs and down to her room. Closing the door behind her, she fell back against the door, trying to compose herself. She was trembling in fear. She hadn't found a way out. Taking a deep breath, she ignored the outfit draped across the bed. Instead, she went straight to her en-suite and turned on the shower.

Forty minutes later, she was back out in the central part of her room and scared out of her wits. Looking over at the bed, she saw the evening ensemble laid out for her. It was beautiful, suitable for the red carpet at a famed awards ceremony. An off-white gown left her arms and shoulders bare; it had a built-in corset bodice trimmed with intricate embroidery.

Interspersed within the stitching, hundreds of small pearls and crystals shimmered and sparkled in the light. The bodice's top supported and drew attention to her chest, severely curving over the top of each nipple before diving low between her breasts, showing off deep cleavage. The bodice rode up her hips while flaring down in front, implying the magical triangle hidden beneath. Below the bodice, a long, pleated shimmery skirt surrounded her legs and trailed behind her as she walked, her heels peeking out as she moved.

He had also left her a beautiful diamond necklace and matching earrings. Draping the jewelry between her fingers, she realized that the set must have cost well over a million dollars. It was beautiful. Also laid out for her was a diamond tiara in the same style as the necklace.

Was he trying to buy her decision to become his companion? She doubted he would ever tell her, although the set was stunning. Any woman would welcome wearing it, even if it were for a single night.

Looking at the tiara, she realized she probably should have looked at the outfit earlier, as she had not done her hair in such a way as to accommodate the tiara.

Hopping back to the en-suite, she rearranged her hair, and five minutes later, the tiara sat comfortably on her head. Putting on the dark thigh-high stockings he had laid out, she slid into her heels and slipped the gown on. Taking in a breath, she stood a moment in front of the full-length mirror and studied her reflection.

For the first time since she had arrived, she was fully dressed, without a hint of a nipple showing. The gown complimented her tan with a dramatic flair she could not help but like. She knew she looked stunning, but now, the only thought on her mind was the decision she had to make, a decision she had not yet decided. It was a judgment she did not want to make.

"Let's get this over with," she finally muttered and made for the door.

Slowly and with as much grace as she could muster, she stepped out onto the main level of the house to meet her fate. Sir was standing in the main foyer waiting for her. He wore a white tailored tuxedo jacket, a starched white fitted shirt, and a white bow tie. His black patent leather shoes peeked out underneath a pair of black slacks with a black satin stripe running down the outside legs of his trousers. He cut a fine figure of a man. If only she cared.

"Hello, Avril. You look gorgeous. May I have the honor of escorting you to dinner?" He said, reaching out to take her hands.

"You are breathtaking," he complimented her after kissing her on the cheek.

Holding out his arm for her, she slipped her arm around his.

"Thank you, Sir."

He led Avril to the small private dining room and held out a chair for her. The table was set for an intimate dinner for two. A single candle and a bud rose sat in the center. Soft music played in the background. After pushing in the chair for her, he placed a cocktail in front of her. After taking his seat, he raised his glass and offered a toast.

"To Avril, the first woman ever to tempt me to change."

Taken aback by the toast, Avril thought about it a moment and then tilted her glass towards his.

"Thank you, Sir," and took a hesitant sip of the fine liquor. Delicious, she thought before returning for a second longer drink from her glass, quickly draining half in little time. She needed to boost her resolve.

"Delicious, Sir, vodka-based, I presume. However, there are other liquors I can't quite make out."

"You're correct. I make it with vodka along with some other liqueurs. It is my invention, and I thought you would like it."

"You're drinking single malt Scotch, I presume, Sir."

"Yes, my favorite. For tonight, this dinner is all about you. There are no servers, no cooks, no guests, no one but the two of us. I locked everyone in their rooms so that they will not disturb us. I am your host, cook, server, bartender, and maître d'."

Not knowing quite what to say, Avril just sat there for a moment, still feeling a bit numb.

Finally, she said. "Thank you, Sir. Once again, you hold me speechless. I don't know quite what to say."

"You need not say anything. Let's have a quiet dinner together, enjoy each other's company, and see where it goes. We'll discuss the decision later. Until then, can we forget all the other concerns? Can we do that?"

"I'll try, Sir. That's the best I can offer you."

"The dress looks fabulous on you."

Looking down at her lap, she could only agree. "It is, Sir. Thank you for allowing me to wear it. It's beautiful, and I feel like I don't deserve it."

"Oh, I couldn't disagree more. You have more than deserved it, and I'm glad to see you wearing it. I've never seen you more beautiful."

"Thank you, Sir."

"Would you like a refill?" indicating her empty cocktail glass.

"Please, Sir. Also, a glass of ice water with lemon if that would be alright."

"Certainly," he said, standing up and refilling her cocktail from a shaker that was sitting on the buffet. He also filled both of their water glasses, putting a slice of lemon in hers. Afterward, he topped off his scotch and sat back down. For the next half hour or so, they conversed in strained conversation. Avril didn't know quite what to say, and Sir did his best to dance around the issue. After their third cocktail, he served her the salad course, already dressed with a dressing of his own concoction. When they had finished, he collected the plates and disappeared into the kitchen, leaving her alone for a couple of minutes.

He returned with a pair of filet mignons sizzling on a small bed of steak sauce, grilled asparagus lightly drizzled with balsamic vinegar, and a scoop of garlic mashed potato with chives sprinkled on it. He also delivered butter, sour cream, and other accouterments that go with a steak dinner.

After pouring two glasses of red wine, he sat down and lifted his wineglass. Avril raised hers, and with neither of them saying anything, she nodded towards each other and drank her wine. Cutting a dainty slice of the filet, she let it melt on her tongue, the delicate succulence indicative of an excellent steak cooked to absolute perfection, just the way she liked it. As the dinner progressed, they barely spoke, each unsure what to say to each other. Avril knew that time was short. She wasn't enjoying herself, and they both knew it.

After cleaning away the plates, he sat down once again. Looking past the candle and the rose, he studied her. Uncomfortable with his gaze, Avril dropped her eyes and stared at her lap.

"It's time, Sir?"

"Yes, Avril. It's time."

"You know I hate this, Sir, don't you? You are putting me in an impossible position."

"And yet, this is where we are."

"Yes, Sir."

"What have you decided?"

"Sir, please? Don't make me."

"Avril, if you force me to choose for you, I promise you, you will not like what happens next. At least this way, you are in control of your destiny."

"Sir, I don't know. Please?" She begged, on the verge of tears.

"Avril…"

"Sir, I'm scared."

"Avril…"

Paralyzed with fear and with the decisive moment at hand, Avril stumbled over her thoughts, and her soundless mouth hung open. Unable to breathe, she sat there, staring at her lap.

"Avril, it's time. What is your answer?"

"I… I…" Avril could barely talk under her breath. "I… guess… so."

"Avril, speak up. I couldn't hear you."

"I said, 'YES,' you son of a bitch. Yes, I choose to live." She screamed at him before dropping her head and crying profusely again into her hands.

Sir got up, walked around, and squatted next to her. Draping an arm around her, he gently said. "I promise you. It will be all right. I am very pleased with your decision. We are going to have a very long and happy life together. I assure you."

"Yes… Sir," she barely got out between her sobbing. "Whatever…" she finished, her comment drifting off to the silence between her tears.

He let her cry for a bit more before encouraging her to stand up. Wrapping her in his arms, he cradled her as her tears ran their course. Soothing her, she eventually stopped crying into his tuxedo and just stood there, giving herself over to him and his care. She hadn't finished with her tears; she knew that.

Now that she had made her decision, she didn't have to fret over her future. She now knew what was going to be her fate and what she needed to do. Sir was right about one thing. The decision gave her a bit of control over her destiny. It also gave her a bit of power over him. The beginnings of a plan that included membership in the Consortium sparked into existence. One thing she knew, they were all going to underestimate her.

As she collapsed in his arms, he continued to soothe her by continually whispering, "It's going to be alright."

With her future decided, she turned everything over to him. She was his, and every cell in her body knew it.

When she seemed capable of letting go of him, he held her out at arm's length.

"I'm glad you chose as you did. You have made me very happy. Now that you have decided, I will admit that I care and cherish you. In your vernacular, I may even love you. Though with you, I feel much more than love, and I only see it growing day by day, even if I don't know what the word means."

"Sir, I don't know what to say. If you want me to say I love you, I can't. Not now. The memory of this impossible choice you gave me is still fresh in my mind. I don't know if I can ever love you, but my decision also comes with my commitment to give us a chance."

"I expected no less, and I thank you for your commitment. I promise you will find your life to be fulfilling and enjoyable. I know it seems strange to hear that, knowing what I want to do to you, but I assure you, with an open mind and a commitment to give it a chance, I know that your life will be fulfilling."

"If you say so, Sir, I'll have to take it under advisement."

"Give it time, Avril. We'll work through it together."

"Honestly, Sir, that's what scares me."

"And to be just as honest, that's what excites me. I promise you. You made the right choice."

With a gentle nod, he led her out of the room and up the stairs. "Sir, where are you taking me?"

"To bed, my dear. We are going to consummate our new commitment to each other."

"Yes, Sir, as you wish," Avril replied as he led her to his bedroom.

Stepping inside, he held her and unzipped the dress. As it fell to the floor, she stepped out and embraced him. He returned the embrace by passionately kissing her. If anything, the best thing about him turned out to be his kisses. Until that day at the pool, they had never kissed like this even once over her entire stay here. What kisses there were, paled when compared to the men she kissed before coming here. Over the past week, he had kissed her many times over, and she had kissed him back. With the decision made, she poured her entire self into this kiss as he held her close, his arm around her waist.

Breaking free of the kiss, he cradled her face in his hands and looked deeply into her eyes.

"It'll be alright," he reassured her.

"Yes, Sir. I hope so. Perhaps one day, I will believe you. I'm putting my trust in you. I hope and pray that I chose wisely."

"I will do my best to live up to your expectations. See, now I'm not the only one to have expectations. You now have something to look forward to, and I promise. I will do my best to give that to you. Your acceptance and putting your care into my hands is the first step. Thank you for putting your heart and your body into my hands."

"What I have is all yours, Sir."

"Avril, that is the best answer you could have said to me. I am pleased to accept it. Now, kiss me again," he said, as he lowered his mouth towards hers and received her lips to his.

Before long, he scooped her up and gently laid her on his bed. Within minutes, he was beside her, holding and comforting her, before sliding inside her. Over the next several hours, he was the lover she had come to know over the past week. He was gentle and rough. He was demanding and attentive. He used her and allowed her to use him. Hungry, she gave him her body as she took his. He allowed her to climax, several times over, before they both fell asleep, Sir cradling her in his arms.

For the first time in a very long time, she slept a restful, dreamless sleep, free of terrors and the unknown. The trouble was, tomorrow was a scant few hours from now.

Connect with the Author

website – RichardVerry.com

Facebook – richardverrywriter

twitter – @richverry

blog – RichardVerry.com/blog

Author's Notes

Thank you for reading Avril's story. If you enjoyed it, won't you please take a moment to leave me a review?

Telling her story preoccupied me for months, demanding to be let out of my consciousness and written down. An idea that consumed me, scratching to get out of my head the way a pet begs at the door. Anyone who has a dog or cat knows what I mean. Thank you, Janet, for putting up with me during all those weeks.

I wrote 'The Trafficking Consortium' from a bit of inspiration that hit me one day out of the blue. After I suffered a severe concussion several months earlier, my stream of creative consciousness left me devoid of any ideas or insights into a new story. Frankly, I was scared, worrying that it was gone forever. I struggled with headaches, short-term memory loss, and cognitive thinking issues. Several months after suffering my injury, an idea for this story sparked to life.

One day, while sitting in the waiting room of my doctor, I asked myself this question.

"What could happen to a person, by going to a doctor's appointment, gets noticed by the receptionist and a member of a human trafficking ring? What would happen if the traffickers determined that he or she was a worthy addition to their inventory for sale to the highest bidder?"

Avril Gillios became that person. From that question, this book became a reality, and the rest is history.

I appreciate your sharing this book with your friends and acquaintances and posting a review.

Also, by the Author

Consortium
The Trafficking Consortium (Book #1)
Perfect Prey (Book #2)
UnderCurrents (Book #3)
Infiltration (Book #4)

Mona Bendarova Adventures
The Taste of Honey (Book #1)
Broken Steele (Book #2)
Lucky Bitch (Book #3)
Angry Bitch (Book #4)

Her Client Trilogy
Her Client (Book #1)
Her Overseer (Book #2)
Her Essentia (Book #3)
Her Client Trilogy (Books 1, 2, & 3)

Novellas and Short Stories
The Breakup
A Mermaid's Irresistible Curiosity

About the Author

Richard Verry is an Information Technologies Engineer who has coded and supported computer systems for decades.

He wrote many stories in his youth; all lost to history. He wrote his first short story as an adult in 2007 and dabbled in writing stories over the next few years, not expecting to publish any of them.

He created a vast gallery of artwork of oil and watercolor paintings, sketches, and drawings along the way. In 2012, he began writing full-length novels and novellas, where he is finally able to capture some of the ideas and story concepts steadily invading his mind.

Richard grew up and lives on the North-East Coast of America, where he lives with his life partner, Janet. He enjoys skinny, sugar-free vanilla lattes, Kamikaze cocktails, red wine, single malt scotch, and a good steak, grilled rare, of course.

Richard ponders, sometimes to the point of excess, the myriad of images and scenarios, mostly including the captivating nude female form, streaming through his consciousness. A rare few eventually come to life in his artwork and writings.

richardverry.com

Made in United States
North Haven, CT
10 April 2024